Born and raised on the Wirral Peninsula in England, **Charlotte Hawkes** is mum to two intrepid boys who love her to play building block games with them, and who object loudly to the amount of time she spends on the computer. When she isn't writing—or building with blocks—she is company director for a small Anglo/French construction firm. Charlotte loves to hear from readers, and you can contact her at her website: charlotte-hawkes.com.

Award-winning author **Louisa George** has been an avid reader her whole life. In between chapters she's managed to train as a nurse, marry her doctor hero and have two sons. Now she writes chapters of her own in the medical romance, contemporary romance and women's fiction genres. Louisa's books have variously been nominated for the coveted RITA® Award and the New Zealand Koru Award, and have been translated into twelve languages. She lives in Auckland, New Zealand.

THE BODYGUARD'S CHRISTMAS PROPOSAL

CHARLOTTE HAWKES

THE PRINCESS'S CHRISTMAS BABY

LOUISA GEORGE

MILLS & BOON

First Published in Great Britain 2020
by Mills & Boon, an imprint of HarperCollins*Publishers*
1 London Bridge Street, London, SE1 9GF

The Bodyguard's Christmas Proposal © 2020 by Harlequin Books S.A.

The Princess's Christmas Baby © 2020 by Harlequin Books S.A.

Special thanks and acknowledgement are given
to Charlotte Hawkes and Louisa George for their contribution
to the Royal Christmas at Seattle General collection.

ISBN: 978-0-263-27989-4

THE BODYGUARD'S CHRISTMAS PROPOSAL

CHARLOTTE HAWKES

MILLS & BOON

CHAPTER ONE

IF TWELVE YEARS as an ER nurse had taught Kat Steel anything, it was that there were two things that travelled ridiculously fast around a hospital. One was a winter flu bug. The other was gossip. Right now, the latter was rife.

Even as Kat silently navigated her way around the small cluster of colleagues at the nurses' station, all typing up notes or getting their next shout, the air was positively buzzing. The downtime was one of the pitfalls of cases coming into the ER in fits and starts on some days.

'I mean, seriously, did you see the guy?'

'Of course I saw him. How could anyone miss him?'

'I missed it. I was with the woman in bay two. What happened?'

'He was like some kind of superhero.'

'Yeah, I'm calling him Comic Book God.'

'For pity's sake, Gemma, you're such a nerd.'

But there was no malice in the last comment, and Kat couldn't help but smile.

She might have only been at Seattle General for the past eight months, but she'd quickly discovered that Gemma was funny and kind, and a self-proclaimed comic nerd. She was also the closest thing Kat would describe as a real friend.

As if reading her thoughts, Gemma looked up and caught her eye.

'Did you see him, Kat?'

There was no question who they were talking about. After all, it wasn't every day that a gurney raced through the ER with one patient astride it, their knee rammed into the femoral artery of an older man who'd lain, unconscious, beneath him. Evidently the man—or indeed, superhero—had been doing all he could to plug the bleed and save the older man's life.

At least until Dom di Rossi, their Head of ER, and the rest of his team could stabilise him enough to get him into Theatre.

'Yeah, I saw him. But I was dealing with the female passenger who came in with them.'

'Oh,' Gemma moved slightly away from the group so that no one else could hear. 'I saw her, she looked very... autocratic.'

'Yeah, nice, though. Clearly more concerned about her fellow passengers than herself. She refused an X-ray. Insisted on seeing Lucas.'

'Lucas Beaufort?' Gemma named another ER doctor.

'The same.' Kat shrugged. 'But don't tell the hyenas. They'll only read something into it.'

'You know I won't.'

Picking her way around the group to collect the notes for her next patient, Kat ignored the rumourmongers and pretended that she wasn't interested. That the whole incident hadn't looked like some incredible Hollywood action film.

It was irritating that she couldn't seem to shake the man out of her head. Like he'd somehow locked himself in there. The intense focus on his face. And...something else. Something she couldn't quite identify.

'Admit it, Kat, even *you* can't have failed to be impressed.' Another nurse dragged her back to reality, and back to the conversation about the *superhero* patient.

'It was certainly…unusual,' she conceded, after a moment.

Because, after Kirk, if anyone should be immune to men—even those who looked like comic book gods—then surely it should be her?

'Kat?' The low voice of one of the hospital managers snagged her attention and Kat turned gratefully as a tablet was pressed quietly into her hands. Anything that could spare her from thoughts of her perfidious ex was to be welcomed.

'Your next patient. I trust you'll be discreet.'

'Of course,' Kat confirmed, glancing down at the electronic notes before the hospital managers summoned her along.

Logan Connors.

She was about to locate the patient in the main ER when the manager shook her head.

'Not in there. This way…'

Making their way out of the general ER to the VIP patient area, they hurried along the wide corridors to the private rooms, right to the most restricted section.

Who were these people?

But there was no time to consider the question. The door to one of the rooms opened as someone went inside and, for the briefest moment, Kat glimpsed Emilia Featherstone, Seattle General's Head of Orthopaedics, who had collected the elderly man from the gurney earlier. Then, as Kat hurried along, the door closed again and her attention was snagged by another figure standing on the other side of the corridor with his back to her, almost as if on guard. As he turned his head to talk to her approaching manager, Kat startled, and then something rolled low in her belly.

The guy from the gurney—Comic Book God. Surely he couldn't possibly be her next patient?

She stood, rooted to the spot, as her manager bustled

back down the corridor to her, the man clearly reluctant to follow.

As they neared, she realised that the name Comic Book God wasn't nearly a lofty enough term to describe this hulk of a man, who was mouthwateringly tall, big and fit.

Very fit. In more than one sense of the word.

'This is Logan Connors,' the manager introduced Kat, the very nature of how this was happening warning her that he was also to be treated as a VIP.

Even his real name had a tinge of *superhero* about it. Or perhaps that was just her...projecting. There was no doubt about it, the man was attractive.

More than attractive. Even frowning at her, as he was.

'I don't need to be looked at.'

There ought to have been a law against any man having such a rich, seductive voice, especially when they looked like this one did. And especially when they were practically growling.

'I'll leave him in your capable hands, Kat,' her manager declared, turning to walk back down the corridor as she mouthed at Kat to convince him.

She had to be kidding.

'Thanks,' Kat muttered, instead. 'Mr Connors...'

'Logan.'

'Sorry?'

'I'm not being looked at. But if you're going to call me anything, just call me Logan.'

She swallowed.

'Okay,' she began, 'Logan... You're going to have to let me check you over.'

Heat zipped thought her. If that didn't sound like the most cringeworthy come-on, she didn't know what would.

But how could it not?

He was possibly the most beautiful, most masculine man she'd ever seen in her life, with a strong, square jaw that made her palms itch just to reach out and trace it, and teeth so white that it was impossible not to imagine them against her skin.

It had been impressive enough watching him sail in on that gurney but now, almost face to face, Kat felt a ripple of something else—something she didn't care to identify—cascade through her.

Fighting to regulate her suddenly erratic breathing, Kat wrested her gaze from him and glanced over his shoulder to the private room where Dr Featherstone and her colleagues were still with the other MVA victim. The man whose life this *Logan Connors*—Logan—had saved by compressing the older man's proximal right iliac artery.

Given the extent of the damage, he would have needed to apply upwards of one hundred and twenty pounds of pressure to stop exsanguination within seconds—something a first responder might have needed his entire upper body to manage—yet Logan had managed it simply by ramming his knee onto the critical point.

Ten minutes ago she hadn't thought it possible. Now, looking at the man standing in front of her, looking for all the world as though he was hewn from granite, she thought maybe she could believe anything of him.

He truly looked as though he could move mountains. Shape worlds.

Ridiculous, fanciful notion, she snorted inwardly.

He was probably just an ex-military guy. He certainly looked like one. And that compression technique was one she thought she remembered hearing military physicians were taught—to plug a main artery like that.

Not that it made any difference who he was, or what he'd done.

'Your…father…is in good hands,' she hazarded.

Instinct told her they weren't father and son, but Logan's protectiveness of the older man was unmistakable.

Even for a hospital accustomed to protecting VIP identities, the secrecy around these patients was unusually high.

And Comic Book God was looking particularly fierce.

She told herself it was the fact that he was standing there, so strong and upright, as though he had just arrived at some posh gala, the most well turned-out man there. As though he wasn't clearly injured or bloodied, or his clearly expensively tailored suit ripped and sullied with bloodstains.

And, somehow, that only made him look all the more... *sexy*.

You're being ridiculous again.

Shaking her head, Kat battled to focus. This wasn't like her. It wasn't what she did.

She prided herself on her reputation as an efficient, kind, approachable ER nurse, liked by patients and colleagues alike, just like all the nurses who had made her own childhood, spent in and out of hospitals, so much more bearable.

And above all—just like those nurses who had cared for her—Kat strived to be very, very good at her job.

She did *not* strive to feel *unsettled.*

Ever.

Which only made it all the more incomprehensible that, standing face to face with Comic Book God, she found herself...*rattled.*

Unexpectedly, that gaze slammed into hers, and this time she realised his eyes had to be the most incredible, piercing blue she'd ever seen. Pinning her to the spot. Making her feel as though he could peel back every layer of who she was, and leave her exposed and vulnerable, for the world to see.

And then they scanned her up and down. *Checking her out.* And everything...*compressed* inside her.

You're being ridiculous.

She pasted her best smile on her face and held her hand out to indicate a vacant consultation room.

'If you'd like to go into there, Mr... Logan.'

Not a single muscle twitched. He remained standing, feet shoulders width apart and arms folded over his chest—only making it seem all the broader, and stronger.

'I already told you,' he growled at last, 'I don't need to be checked over.'

The steely blue gaze swirled with emotion. For a moment she felt swept up in the maelstrom, her breath catching in her throat until, just as suddenly, they masked over and she tumbled to the ground—shut out. Relieved and bereft all at once.

He was acting like it was his duty to put the man in that room in front of his own health. But surely he could see that it benefited no one to stay outside a door when they had an entire team in that room?

'I understand that you're concerned for your friend—' Kat tried her usual tack of empathy, but right now it was all she could do not to melt under his laser glare '—but he is with our best team right now. And we *are* obliged to check you over. You could have internal injuries and not even be aware of them.'

'I don't have internal injuries. I'm fine.'

'You're covered in blood,' Kat pointed out as evenly as she could.

Right up until that startling gaze walloped back into hers, leaving her feeling oddly winded.

He glanced down in evident surprise.

'It isn't my blood,' he declared after a moment.

'If you don't mind, I think I'd like to ascertain that for myself.' Her voice sounded strange. Haughtier than she was used to.

Logan Connors was getting under her skin, and she wasn't sure she understood why, much less cared for it.

His eyes gleamed, as though he could read her thoughts. Slowly, he unfurled his arms and lifted them out to the sides in invitation.

Or in challenge.

'Fine. Be my guest.'

Either way, a tiny thrill threaded its way along her spine. *Wholly inappropriate*—not that she seemed to be listening, no matter how sternly she tried reprimanding herself.

'Not here, in the middle of the corridor,' she managed to bite out. 'Perhaps in the consultation room?'

He crossed his arms back over his chest, his stance seeming all the more rooted. If that were even possible.

'Like I said, I'm not going anywhere.' It was a voice that rumbled straight through her. *Again.*

Doing things to her. *Again.*

Something ached in Kat's chest. And lower, if she was going to be absolutely honest. My God, she had never, *never* responded to a patient this way.

She had never responded to *anyone* this way. Not even Kirk.

She cleared her throat, consulting the notes on her tablet and ignoring the odd tumbling, swooping sensation in her chest.

'And, like *I* said, I can't assess you in the middle of a corridor.'

He didn't answer. He barely even shifted. Yet this man—this stranger—somehow made the corridor seem brighter, and bigger and yet simultaneously he seemed to…fill it.

She pressed on.

'It's hospital policy.'

He didn't even blink. His eyes merely roamed her body, leaving her feeling as exposed as if she'd been naked.

And a helluva lot hotter.

She swallowed—hard—and struggled to refocus.

'I really ought to ensure there's no delayed injury that only becomes obvious once its already severe. Your own health is just as important as that of the man in that room.'

She didn't know what made her eyes slide over that chest and those folded arms to see a wedding band.

The feeling of disappointment that plummeted through her was illogical. Yet undeniable.

She thrust it aside.

'There must be people who care for you.' She glanced down at his hand, told herself that it was only professional interest that made her notice the lack of a wedding band. 'Someone to whom your welfare is more important than anything?'

It was like a switch flicked on again for a fraction of a second. Kat watched, mesmerised as a fierce kind of expression swam over his features, changing them for a moment. A love so intense—an emotion she suspected he usually kept well buried—swirled tumultuously in his eyes, buffeting her, and then it was gone.

A tight fist punched inside Kat's chest.

For a moment she wondered what it must feel like to be the woman who could elicit that kind of all-consuming re-action from a man like this one. Or indeed from any man. And then she shot down that line of thought because, for her, only grief lay down that particular road.

'Good,' she managed curtly. 'So now that's established, this way, please.'

He dipped his head curtly and, with a final checkof the door of the private room, he followed her down the corridor to another treatment room as Kat heaved a re-lieved sigh—at least it would keep her on the right side of Ayanna Franklin, the hospital's head of PR. But then, as the door closed behind them and Kat swung back only to find Logan watching her, she realised her relief was short-lived. Because she felt his gaze *everywhere*, heating her in places she had forgotten even existed.

Enough.

Hadn't she just established that he had someone in his life who he cared for? And who cared for him? So what was she playing at, imagining he was looking at *her?*

Furious with herself, Kat straightened up, as though the action could somehow shake off the alien sensations.

No matter what happened, she wasn't going to go off lusting after some unavailable male. It was time to stop talking, get her head down, and concentrate on the task she was *supposed* to be doing—tending to her patient.

'Can you tell me what happened?' she asked.

The information in her notes was quite good medically, if a little scant in parts which might have revealed unnecessary information pertaining to the identity of his group. But that was no surprise given that Seattle General was renowned for maintaining the privacy of its highest-profile celebrity clients. Even a B-lister with a sprained wrist from a minor vehicular incident could have the media splashing the story over the front pages on a slow news day.

'I'm not after any information relating to your…companions,' she said carefully. 'I just want to hear your recollection of events.'

Knowing how much Logan recalled would give her some idea of whether he might have sustained any unreported head injuries. Although there were no evident signs of anything on his skull. No bleeding from his ears. No indication of disorientation.

Except in herself.

'We were traveling at approximately seventy kilometres per hour on a relatively straight section of road when we entered a dip with unseen black ice, and the vehicle slid, hit the curb, left the ground and rolled twice before coming to a halt on its side.'

'All right.' Kat nodded.

'I exited the vehicle through the side window and, having assessed the likelihood of the gas tank leaking and the vehicle bursting into flames, I took my…companion with me. I assessed him for injuries, saw the laceration to the femoral artery. The driver, Giorgio, made sure our female companion got out safely, too.'

'Good…'

'I tended to the femoral laceration for approximately twenty minutes during which time the medics arrived and transported us to the hospital.'

'By using your knee over the proximal right iliac artery to slow flow velocity to the CFA.'

'Is that a question or a statement?'

She blinked at him.

'Both, I suppose. Okay, I need to check your pupils and then I'd ask you remove the top half of your clothing.'

For now there was no need to ask him to remove the trousers. Unlike the ripped, blood-soaked shirt, the only mark on the trousers was where his knee had been rammed into the older man's injury.

Worse, and more shamefully, she wasn't sure she had quite psyched herself up for the sight of him and his thunderbolt thighs. Still, as her eyes watched him shrug smoothly out of his jacket and shirt, Kat found her mouth going drier by the second until, finally, she was faced with the most chiselled, masculine chest she'd ever seen.

Muscles on muscles. Lean, hewn and flawless, leaving her heart in a dither over whether it could pound out the most energetic beat of its life or whether it should simply stop altogether.

He was surely too impossibly perfect to be real.

Her mouth felt parched, her skin tight and hot, and even her fingers were tingling with the ridiculous urge to reach out and touch those ridges and contours. And then he turned slightly and she caught the jagged edges of a scar; an old bullet wound by the looks of it.

A tiny imperfection, which somehow made him all the more beautiful, and rare.

Her guess would be that he was some kind of a bodyguard for whoever the VIP in that room was. And she couldn't shake the knowledge that she was going to need all her professional level-headedness to get through the next half-hour or so in one piece.

Logan didn't like it when the nurse—Kat, her manager had called her, hadn't she?—fell so quiet. It made him wonder what was going on behind those expressive eyes.

And then he didn't like it that he even wondered such a thing. She was pretty enough…more than pretty, *interesting,* he conceded grudgingly. But there was no reason for him to notice.

Look what had happened the last time he'd really noticed a woman. A trickle of bitterness threatened to weave through Logan, but moments before it did, it was instead washed out by a crashing wave of love. Love in the form of one four-year-old little boy.

Whatever hassle and grief Sophia had brought into his life, he wouldn't change a single moment of it if that meant losing the best thing he'd ever known—his son, Jamie.

'So…' The nurse cleared her throat. 'Let's get you sorted so you can get back to standing outside your…companion's door. I understand from the notes that you aren't from Seattle.'

'Actually, I am. Born and raised,' Logan surprised himself by saying.

'Oh.' She blinked. 'You're back, visiting?'

'Something like that.'

It was a stock response, so why was he having to clamp his mouth shut from saying anything more? What was it about this woman that almost had him opening up in a way that he *never* did? That had him about to tell her that he was home for good? *Finally.*

He was bringing Jamie from Isola Verde to the USA, to the very place where Logan himself had grown up, to try to give his son—or, if he was honest, both of them—a fresh start.

Ironic that today was supposed to have been his last day ever as royal bodyguard to Roberto Baresi—the King of Isola Verde. More than that, though, King Roberto was a good man, underneath it all. And he'd been more than just an employer to Logan. Over the years, the older man had been a kind friend, too. Now he was in that room along the hall. Possibly dying. The fallout was potentially cata-strophic—and not merely the political ramifications.

Logan hated that he was stuck here, in another room, not doing his job as bodyguard to the King.

Not that he could tell this nurse—Kat—why he'd been so reluctant to leave his employer's door, of course. The fact was that only a handful of people in this hospital were aware of exactly who their VIPs were, and even fewer of them were aware of the connections the Baresi family had to one of Seattle General's own consultants.

Not that he was about to be the one to spill that secret.

As the adrenaline rush that had carried him through the car crash, and the aftermath, was beginning to wear off, the sudden realisation that he'd been inches from los-ing his *employer*—and maybe even his own life—on the very last day of his assignment hit him.

And then what would have happened to Jamie?

The ugly question was there before he could snuff it out.

When the nurse had brought up the idea of someone out there who loved him, the rush of love and fear had been overwhelming. What would Jamie have done if that car crash had gone a different way?

In that one instant, his four-year-old son would have lost his father. Wasn't it enough that, for all intents and purposes, he'd never had a mother? What kind of start to life would that have been? His mother abandoning him and his father being killed because of a stupid area of black ice?

Jamie's grandparents would have looked after him, of course, as they had so often during the whole of his little life. But it was hardly the same.

Logan slammed his mind shut. But not fast enough to stop something dark, and ugly, from reaching out with its long, twisted fingers and scraping through him. He hadn't been the best father he could have been, away so much with work. But now he'd quit as a royal bodyguard. Now he was coming back to Seattle for a new life.

Not just back to where he'd been born and raised. But back to his medical career. Back to being a doctor.

As much as he'd known that being a bodyguard instead of a doctor had been the right call—his head hadn't been in the right space after that last, hellish tour of duty—a part of him had also missed the rush of the medical environment.

He just hadn't anticipated that his first tour of Seattle General's ER would be as a patient and not as a doctor.

Which was why it was professional curiosity, he told himself, and nothing else, that kept his eyes glued to Kat as she bustled crisply around the room. Selecting kit, arranging things, making certain she had everything *just so*, like she was on some kind of mission.

'Right, I'm going to run my hands over you to check for any areas of discomfort.'

'Be my guest,' he commented.

It was completely out of character, but the words had come out before he could bite his tongue. Then Kat wrinkled her nose and he couldn't have said how, but he knew that was her trying to conceal her embarrassment.

He found that oddly appealing.

And then she began to check him over and his mind emptied until all he could think of was the feel of her hands all over his body. Without warning, something rushed him and he realised that he had yet another reason to want to get out of this room—away from Kat, the ER nurse—as soon as he possibly could.

'Have you any pain?' she asked.

'None,' he lied.

He could tell she didn't buy it for a moment.

'Things will go a lot faster if you're honest.' She eyed him critically, a flash of that feistiness again, and he didn't know why but it made something kick deep inside him.

Focus.

'What makes you think I am?'

'Perhaps the fact that you have tiny shards of glass in your skin,' she retorted, and as his eyes moved to her lips again, he wondered what she'd do if he leaned forward and caught that tart mouth with his. 'But we can deal with those.'

What the hell was wrong with him?

Logan gritted his teeth.

'Just clean them up and I'll be out of here.'

He might have known she'd ignore that.

'Now the main pain,' she continued. 'Is it your back? Your shoulder? Your neck?'

It was all three, if he was going to be honest. The right side of his neck and shoulder were sore, and his head was beginning to pound, as though the pain was running from his back right up to the top of his skull.

Mainly because of the car crash, though he suspected it wasn't helped by the need to fight this sudden, wholly inappropriate attraction to a woman who was not only his nurse now but who would be his colleague in a matter of weeks.

Nonetheless, his right hand and arm were beginning to stiffen up, and even his right leg was aching. His professional assessment was that he'd torn his trapezius muscle. He imagined it was her assessment, too.

'Like I said,' he ground out, 'I'm fine.'

'You're clearly medically trained,' she said archly, 'so I think we both know what's likely happened. And that you aren't fine.'

'Fine, I have a bit of whiplash, but there's little that can be done but give it time to heal. Fortunately, I'm fit and healthy, so I should be okay.'

'There's downplaying it, and then there's *that*,' she commented. 'But if that's the way you want it, that's up to you. Either way, I'm going to be sending you to CT to ensure there are no internal injuries.'

But there was something in her tone that got under his skin. A compassion that he knew he didn't deserve.

What had happened to him had been luck rather than good judgement. He'd risked his life because that was his job. When, really, his main job these days should be his young son.

Because he got to go home to his son. How many of his former army buddies had lost that luxury when they'd lost their lives?

And what was it about today, the accident, *this* woman, that was all coming together to pry open a dark box inside him that needed to be kept locked? For ever.

'Agreed,' he ground out, standing up in a rush and taking some perverse pleasure at the shock on her face.

Let her wonder what had suddenly made him apparently take his health so seriously.

As far as he was concerned, he'd done so because she'd reminded him of the little boy who was at his grandparents' home, and even now was waiting for Logan to come home so that the two of them could start their new life together. Jamie had already lost enough with a mother like Sophia, but what the hell would his boy have done if anything really had happened in that car accident?

He was here to make sure that nothing happened to him for his son's sake. He was here because it was the responsible thing to do, to let this nurse check him over to ensure there were no internal injuries that the adrenaline was concealing. He was here because the quicker he let her assess him, the quicker he could get back to King Roberto's room, and make sure that he hadn't lost his employer—and friend—on the last day of his job.

He was most certainly *not* here because any part of him was intrigued by this *Kat* woman.

No part of him at all.

CHAPTER TWO

'ANY SIGN OF my bloodwork back for my lady in three?' Kat asked, as she finished handling a couple more IV bags for two of her other patients.

It was beginning to grate on her that, three hours after he'd left the hospital, she was still trying to get Logan Connors out of her head. Not listening to the medical advice to go home and rest, it had apparently taken someone from Logan's party to order him home, which only added to her suspicion that he was a bodyguard.

A very fit, very on-his-game bodyguard.

'No bloodwork back yet.' Her colleague shook her head. 'What's the preliminary assessment on that lady?'

Chagrined, Kat shoved thoughts of Logan to the back of her mind and conjured up her patient.

'She presented with lower quadrant abdominal pain, tender to palpation. She also complained of nausea, vomiting, fever, constipation and loss of appetite.'

'Yeah, appendicitis sounds like a good call.'

'Never mind the appendicitis.' Elsie, one of the other nurses, came scurrying over. 'I can't believe you got the hottie hero. What was he like?'

Kat flashed her brightest smile and tried not to bare her teeth. She didn't know Elsie all that well, but what she did know was that the woman loved a good gossip—the more scandalous the better.

Precisely the opposite of Kat.

'Like a patient who has been in an MVA.'

'Yes, but what was he *like*?' The nurse gave a staged wink and snorted.

Clearly, feigning misunderstanding wasn't going to work.

'He had some whiplash, but he was more concerned about his friend.' She smiled again but this time only enough to soften her words, and not enough to suggest that she was going to feed them the gossip Elsie so evidently wanted.

She didn't miss the scowl the nurse threw in her direction, but she didn't care. Logan Connors didn't deserve to be the source of today's rumour mill just because he looked…well, the way that he did.

And if she believed this uncharacteristic feeling inside her was a sort of *protectiveness*—of a complete stranger, no less—then she was more of an idiot that she'd realised. If only she could buy into her own cool, calm exterior, the way everybody else seemed to.

The truth was, Logan had left her feeling…*odd*. Not herself. There was a strange sort of ringing in her ears, or maybe her head, that was drowning out everything else and leaving her focussing internally instead. On images of his impossibly, deliciously honed chest, from its strong, broad shoulders to a six-pack you could bounce a quarter off.

'Seriously, Kat.' Elsie sniffed disdainfully. 'I don't know how you can be so blasé. The guy was an absolute sex bomb.'

And the rest.

She could picture it in all too vivid detail, even now. Those ridges that curved so temptingly over his chest, making her fingers itch to reach out and touch them. The smattering of dark hair over hard pectorals that dropped lower, down the centre of his body, and slipped—as though teasing the onlooker—below the waistband of those low-slung tailored trousers.

God, how her fingers had itched to trace that line, too.

She had never, in her entire career, lusted after a patient—*or anyone*—like this. Not even Kirk—the man who had been her rock for ten years. The man who had understood exactly how it had felt to be in and out of hospitals week after week, month after month, year after year. Ever since they'd been fifteen, they'd been each other's salvation. Each other's hope.

And maybe after a decade, and so much sadness, it had been inevitable that they would ultimately grow apart. But had he really needed to cleave her very soul, right at the end? Had he needed to hurl that one, single accusation that he'd known, whatever she tried to argue, she could never dispute? Had he needed to highlight the one deficiency in herself that she knew she could never—no matter what good she ever did—overcome?

Kirk hadn't merely *betrayed* her by those ugly, barbed, poisonous words that he'd sneered; he had *destroyed* her. He had poisoned every last, tiny, vaguely good thing she'd dared to think about herself, and he'd laid her out for the worthless, undesirable husk of a woman that she was.

And she'd let him do it.

Which only made it all the more preposterous that she was allowing herself to get caught up by another man. Even one who looked like Logan. Kat hated herself for such a weakness.

But that didn't mean she could stop.

'Actually, I have a bit of gossip,' another of their colleagues said as she appeared suddenly, sliding into a chair and beginning to quickly tap in some notes onto the computer as she spoke. 'Hottie hero is actually called Logan Connors.'

'Is he?' Elsie shot Kat a triumphant look.

'There's more,' the nurse continued. 'You know the new ER doc due to start next week? Well, apparently this Logan Connors is the guy.'

The revelation walloped into Kat. Surely that couldn't be true? She'd barely survived half an hour in a room with the guy. How could she be expected to work alongside him? How could *anyone* be expected to work alongside him?

She edged away, trying to clear her head as her colleagues crowded in closer, as if to try to contain their fervour.

'Mr Comic Book God?' Elsie clapped her hands in glee.

'Guess you'd better make it *Dr* Comic Book God.' Their colleague sniggered. 'I wouldn't mind being examined by him.'

As the conversation continued, Kat took her leave, going to check on each of her patients before returning to check on the lab results. All the while telling herself that the churning sensation in her belly had nothing whatsoever to do with the idea of having to work with Logan Connors.

With any luck, they would be on different shifts.

So why didn't she believe that was what she really hoped for?

Never, in over a decade of being an ER nurse, had Kat Steel ever felt quite so...*disquieted* by a patient.

In fact, the only other time she'd felt anything other than professional empathy for a patient had been almost five years ago, but under vastly different circumstances.

Back then, the patient had been Carrie, an eight-month-old baby who had fallen down a set of concrete stairs onto her head when her parents had been having yet another drunken brawl and failed to see her crawling to the steps.

As Kat had bustled about the resus bay with the rest of the team, trying to hook up the monitors to the little girl, who had been lying so still and silent on the enormous black gurney, Carrie had reached out with her chubby hand and had gripped Kat's hand tightly.

So tightly. Even now, if Kat closed her eyes, she could almost feel Carrie's tiny fingers clutching her thumb, as surely as if the little girl had reached into her chest and stolen Kat's very heart.

Love. The purest, most selfless, most beautiful thing. It made a person whole. It made them soar. It made them move heaven and earth for the thing they loved with all their heart.

Which was why, when she'd realised that social services were removing Carrie from the parental home, Kat had pulled in every favour she humanly could as an ER nurse, and as a foster parent with over four years' experience at that point, to make sure that Carrie would be going home with her.

For three glorious years she had been Carrie's foster mum, never daring to hope that one day she could be more than just the *foster* mum. She'd taught the little girl how to walk, talk, play and even just laugh. *Lord*, how she'd loved the sound of that little girl's laughter.

She doubted she'd ever hear it again.

Abruptly, Kat shook her head free of the memory before the waves of bittersweetness—swelling higher and higher above her right now—could crash over her and send her splintering into pieces where she stood. A wipe-out on the floor of the busy ER—just what all the rushing doctors and nurses needed.

Get a grip.

'Hey, I've got a minute before my trauma comes in.' Gemma appeared at her elbow as Kat was preparing to transport one of her patients up to CT. 'You okay? You look a bit…agitated.'

For a moment Kat considered telling her friend. But what would she say? That she had a crush on the hot new doc, just like everyone else? It sounded so banal. So, instead, she feigned a smile.

'Just a bit tired,' she fibbed. 'And I've got to wait for a porter for my lady. It's been a long week.'

'Tell me about it.' Gemma rolled her eyes dramatically, instantly believing her. Which only made Kat feel that much guiltier. 'I can't wait for Thanksgiving. Are you seeing family over the holidays?'

'Nope, I'm working.' Her cheeks were beginning to ache from smiling so much, and she pretended that she didn't feel a stab of pain at the question.

'What? All the holidays?'

'Yeah.' She couldn't let anyone see what it cost her to offer such a nonchalant shrug. Even Gemma. 'My family are scattered all over the place these days. We try to video message, but no one's able to make any trips this year.'

And there was no need to mention that she'd run away from them when they'd most wanted to be there for her because, in some perverse way, seeing them glowing with the happiness and love of each of their own families had only made her own pain all the more acute.

She'd turned down every offer to visit because she'd just wanted to be alone. Possibly even *needed* to be alone. This was going to be her first Christmas in years without Carrie.

The Christmas that she'd been planning in her head before she'd got the news that she wasn't destined to be Carrie's new mommy after all.

Even now, the memory left her chest feeling as though it was being gripped in a vice.

Better to let anyone who could spend time with their loved ones. She just wanted to get her head down, work and not have to surface again until the whole painful season was over and done with.

'What about that date you had with that lush doctor from…where was it… Ortho? It was a third date, wasn't it?'

'I cancelled,' Kat admitted reluctantly.

'What? No way? Why?'

'I just…wasn't feeling it.'

Not exactly a lie…just not the whole truth either.

'Oh. Pity. He was cute.' Gemma looked momentarily thrown, but regrouped quickly. 'Oh, well, plenty more fish and all that.'

'Right,' she agreed, as smoothly as she could.

It was easier to tell Gemma what she wanted to hear than try to explain a reluctance Kat wasn't sure she herself even understood. Still, by the way her friend was chuckling, Gemma had bought into it.

'You're incorrigible, Kat Steel. You must have more doctors running after you than any other nurse in this place, and you're the one who goes around "not feeling it" with anyone. What was it you told me when you first came to Seattle? *"Have a bit of fun? No strings, no hassle"?*'

'Yes, well.' Kat scrunched up her face. 'I've changed my mind.'

'You never even gave it a chance!' Gemma exclaimed.

'That's because, right now, my idea of a bit of *no-strings, no-hassle fun* would be curling up in a big comfy chair with a hot chocolate and a good book.'

Before she could stop it, another image of Logan flitted into her head. What were the odds that she would *'be feeling it'* if it was with *him*?

'Geez, Kat, how old are you?' berated Gemma good-naturedly. 'Thirty-two or seventy-two?'

'It isn't good, is it?' Kat admitted.

'It's a damned disgrace,' her friend teased.

But anything more they might have said was cut short by the sound of the emergency doors swishing open and EMTs racing in a gurney, and Gemma dashed off quickly, leaving Kat to wait for her porter.

* * *

She spent the last couple of hours of her shift busying herself with ferrying patients, booking in new arrivals, taking bloodwork, putting in IV lines and fluids, and administering medications. She cleaned up a knife wound from a kitchen accident, ready for suturing, and prepped a woman with shortness of breath and respiratory distress for a chest X-ray. And she restocked her assigned rooms.

All of it doing frustratingly little to shake thoughts of Logan from her brain. She couldn't erase that intensity of his gaze from her mind. And when she thought of the way he'd conducted that frank assessment of her—even if it had only lasted for a moment—her body felt as though it couldn't decide whether it was too hot or too cold.

He'd got to her in way no one else had in a long, long time.

Ever, a voice whispered, before she stamped it out quickly.

Which was why dating guys as decent as Chris from Orthopaedics ought to be the perfect antidote to the commitment of her past life, before she'd dropped her entire life to move to Seattle—a city where no one knew her. Or her story.

Casual dates and girls' nights out. All the things she'd never done—or wanted to do—as a foster mom.

So why wasn't it as easy and fun as it sounded like it should be?

Why was Logan Connors the first thing to make her feel something—*anything*—in almost a year?

It was nonsense.

Maybe she could go for a run when her shift ended here tonight? Clear her head and train for the charity Santa Run she'd entered last month—another activity she was pushing herself to do now that she was alone, with time on her hands.

Anything to stop her from going around in circles in her mind.

* * *

The little boy came out of nowhere near the end of Kat's training run in the park, the glint of the winter sun off the distant Seattle Space Needle almost blinding her so that when he raced out of the bushes, only to stop dead as he saw her hurtling down the path, she almost didn't spot him.

With a startled cry she leapt over him, like she'd somehow entered a steeplechase when she hadn't been paying attention, twisting around to ensure he wasn't hurt.

'Are you okay, sweetheart?'

Glancing around for a parent or guardian, Kat crouched down beside him. He couldn't have been much more than about four, with a shock of black, curly hair and rich, dark eyes that brimmed with tears as he cast his gaze around wildly.

'Where's your mommy?'

He shook his head, still searching past her.

'You don't know?' Kat interpreted, tilting her head to the side to try to get his attention. He strained to keep looking past her, but she tilted her head again. Reluctantly, his eyes alighted on her.

'Don't have a mommy,' he told her. 'Want Nana.'

The words walloped into her chest, landing a direct hit and winding her. How was fate so cruel? Kids like this who didn't have a mommy, and people like her who desperately wanted to be a mommy. For a long moment she couldn't reply. Then he turned his frantic gaze on her.

'Doc Twence?'

'Doc Twence?' she repeated carefully, her brain frantically trying to work out what the little boy was saying.

'Doc Tewence.' He nodded, sounding it out carefully, the way that Carrie used to do.

She stuffed down the bittersweet memory.

'Doc Terrence?' she tried cautiously.

The boy bobbed his head emphatically, making her feel as though she'd won the lottery.

'Doc Twence,' he confirmed. 'Doc Twence.'

'Your name is Terrence?'

His disdainful expression said it all and, despite everything, Kat had to swallow a gurgle of laughter. There was no artifice with kids, you always knew where you stood with them.

Which was more than could be said for plenty of adults.

Shaking the thought from her head, Kat dragged her mind back to the present.

'Doc Terrence is your daddy?' she tried again, though she was beginning to suspect who Doc Terrence might be.

'Doc Twence is a terrydac.'

'Doc Terrence is a terrydac?' she rolled it around on her tongue, her brain switching up a gear. But this time it didn't come. Still, she could go with her gut. 'Doc Terrence is a toy?'

'Not toy,' he scoffed, his eyebrows knitted together in a perfect little-boy frown that seemed to reach inside her chest, grab hold and pull. 'Din'saur.'

'Terrence is a dinosaur? Terrence the terrydac...hmm, he's a pterodactyl?'

'Yes, Doc Terrence is a pter'dactyl,' the little boy pronounced carefully, before practically jumping up and down.

'I see.' Well, at least that was cleared up. 'What about—?'

'Daddy!'

Kat was nearly bowled over as the little boy spotted someone over her shoulder, scrambled to his feet and ran past her.

Still, at least it was a happy outcome. She turned around, her mouth open in greeting. And felt her legs turn to lead.

Awareness leapt through her in an instant. That same

heady, slightly dizzying sensation that she'd experienced back at the hospital.

'Jamie, I've been looking for you everywhere.' He held the boy tightly to him in a hug. 'Why did you run off like that?' Turning to her, he said, 'Well, Nurse Kat, it seems we're destined to meet again.' He shot her look that she couldn't begin to interpret but which nevertheless set off goosebumps all over her skin.

She tried to answer but didn't know what to say. Was he mocking her? Or teasing her? It sounded ridiculously provocative, uttered in that velvety-rich voice of his that exuded sex appeal.

Or most probably that was her wishful thinking. The guy oozed sex appeal from every single pore. An afternoon around the nurses' station had revealed that much. And she—unfairly famed for her starchiness where members of the opposite sex were concerned—appeared to be lapping *this* man up.

How ignominious was that?

'He was looking for Doc Terrence,' she told him, fighting to keep her voice steady.

'That damned toy,' Logan muttered, but she noted there was no heat in his words. Just the undertone of relief that he'd found his son safe and sound.

'Bad word, Daddy,' the boy sniffled, lifting his head for a moment, then dropping it again as Logan apologised to his son. Then to her.

'It's the fright.' She dismissed his apology easily. 'I asked who he was with, but he didn't say.'

'Right.'

'I hope I didn't put my foot in it but I asked about his mommy.' She tried to sound discreet and jolly all at once. As though she wasn't prying. 'But he only said he didn't have a mommy, he had a nana.'

Logan didn't answer, but what did it say about her that she spotted a tiny tell-tale tightening of his jaw?

It says that you're paying way too much attention to the guy.

She fought to shut down the reproachful voice but it was apparently on a roll.

And to his private life.

'I'm sorry,' she managed, her eyes sliding away in embarrassment, trying to focus on the little boy instead of his father. 'It's really none of my business.'

Out of her peripheral vision she could see him do that curt nod thing of his and then, suddenly he said, 'Let's just say that she isn't around.'

Kat snapped her head up.

'Oh, I saw the ring, I just thought...'

'I keep it on because it deters interest.'

She wasn't sure who seemed more astonished at the admission, but then those shutters came back down, just as they had back at the hospital.

Kat opened her mouth to convey her condolences then closed it again. If the boy—Jamie's—mommy had died, wouldn't Logan have just said that? Instead, he'd been guarded, as though he'd been about to say where she was but had decided against it. Because it revealed too much about him? Or about his boss?

Was it just more secrets and closed doors—like when his party had been brought into the ER earlier? Not that she cared. Seattle General had its fair share of VIPs, but as far as she was concerned patients were patients.

Not that the head of PR would likely agree.

Nonetheless, now she knew that when Logan had reacted, back in that consultation room, to her comment about having someone to care for him, he'd meant his son. Not a woman. Not a wife. Not, apparently, even a girlfriend.

'Anyway...' he drew her back to the present '...thanks for looking after Jamie. We were lucky you were here.'

'It's fine.' She waved her hand dismissively, unable to shake the idea that she needed to walk away now. Before she found she couldn't. 'Anyway...bye.'

There was no reason for that to be so hard to say. She thought he paused for a fraction longer than was necessary and her stomach somersaulted. Then Logan dipped his head instead.

'Bye.' He turned around to walk away. 'Actually...'

She spun back around with shameless haste, not that Logan seemed to notice. He seemed to busy wrestling with his own thoughts.

'Jamie and I were going to get an ice cream—can I buy you one? To say thanks, I mean.'

Vaguely, she could hear the dim voice inside her head warning her that it was a bad idea. Then another voice drowned the first one out. An ice cream wasn't going to hurt, was it?

'They sell coffee, if you'd prefer,' Logan said, misinterpreting her hesitation.

She carefully ignored the first, logical voice. Instead, she wandered down the path towards them, and felt her mouth curve up into the most relaxed, genuine smile she'd managed all week.

'An ice cream would be perfectly lovely. Thank you.'

CHAPTER THREE

'So, DID YOU sleep with him?' Gemma asked a few days later.

Images of Logan whirled around Kat's head as she spun around to see Gemma grinning at her.

'Sorry?' She shook her head in shock. How did Gemma even know about Logan? 'Why would you even think that?'

'Because you look…different.' Her friend pulled a face. 'You've got a bit of a…glow going on. I thought you must have met someone. Maybe changed your mind about dating after all?'

'Changed my mind about dating?' Kat echoed numbly.

It had just been ice cream with Logan—hardly *dating*.

'Yeah. You started *feeling it* after all?' Gemma said encouragingly.

Feeling it. Well, Logan certainly made her tingle, from head to toe. She felt turned inside out just from the way his eyes swept over her.

She flushed guiltily and Gemma seized on it instantly. 'Aha!'

She'd certainly imagined it…that night. She'd spent an indecently good proportion of the night imagining how kissing Logan would feel.

Even now, her heart skipped a beat at the mere thought of it.

Totally inappropriately.

'It's none of your business. Also, I don't sleep with every guy who takes me out on a date,' she said primly instead, as Gemma gave a heavy sigh, her disappointment evident.

'You don't sleep with *any* of them,' she complained. 'And, okay, I'm not saying you should do the hokey-pokey with *all* of them, but you're supposed to be free and single, and having at least a little bit of what you fancy.'

'Yes, I know, but—'

'Nothing serious, you said,' Gemma reminded her. 'Just having some fun.'

'I *am* having fun,' Kat insisted.

Though she wasn't sure who she was trying to convince most. The truth was that the only thing she'd really wanted was to be Carrie's mommy. No amount of dating was going to make her forget that—although she was trying.

Much like the way she was trying to pretend that Logan's face wasn't flashing through her head every time her friend mentioned sex.

A call on the emergency phone interrupted their conversation, much to Kat's relief.

'Seattle General, ER.' Grabbing a pen, she began to make notes, twisting the paper around as one of the doctors quickly scanned it and mouthed that they would run the shout. Then Kat reached for the loudspeaker and announced the adult trauma call as the team came quickly together to get the rest of their equipment organised. Within ten minutes the team was all prepped and the patient was being hurried in.

One of the emergency responders was trying to hold down flailing fists in an attempt to prevent the man from being hurt as the gurney raced along and also avoid getting hit themselves.

As Kat's team stepped forward, the doctor leading the shout called timings for transferring the patient from the emergency responders' equipment to the hospital bed and then it was up to Kat and Gemma to keep him from sitting up.

'This is Adam, late thirties. He was discovered by his neighbour in the front garden of their apartment block. Posterior head injury. He has a blood coming out of his left ear, a pulse of seventy-one. There's evidence of alcohol intoxication and he's very combative. Because of the head injury we've had to tape his head securely to the blocks and the oxygen mask, but he keeps trying to rip them off and he keeps lifting his head to sit up.'

The atmosphere in the team instantly shifted. The blood from the ear was suggestive of a skull fracture, so now they were not only concerned about a significant head injury but also about any possible neck injury as well. If the patient wasn't going to be co-operative, then it was going to be that much harder to keep him safe. Experience told her that the best course of action now would be to get the man to CT.

'Okay, thanks.' Elizabeth—the doctor running the shout—stepped forward to her patient. 'Hello, Adam, I realise you've had a drink, but can you tell me what day of the week it is?'

For a moment the patient stopped flailing, pausing long enough to think.

'Friday. No…' He blinked, clearly confused. 'Saturday.'

'Okay, and—'

'No. It's Sunday.'

'All right, and can you tell me the month?'

'November…wait, December.' He tried to push himself upright as Kat and Gemma hastily pressed him back down and told him not to move his head. 'No. November.'

The confusion was evident, but it was impossible to tell whether it was injury related or as a result of the alcohol.

Kat could smell it on him from where she was standing, and she doubted it had just been the one drink.

'I want to go home,' he growled, lifting his hand suddenly and flailing his arm again.

Immediately, Kat twisted over, avoiding the fist, to hold his head down.

'All right Adam.' It was a necessary skill to be able to keep your voice amiable yet firm enough that the patient would listen, but not so firm that it provoked them. 'Try not to move, mate, we don't want you to injure your neck.'

'I think we might need to sedate him or we'll never get him into CT,' Elizabeth commented.

Not ideal, given the nature of the head injury, but without sedation it was likely that he would cause himself more damage if he kept trying to free himself and they weren't there to restrain him.

For the next twenty minutes they completed the rest of his obs, worked to temporarily remove the blocks and the collar to enable them to sedate him. Then Elizabeth took him to CT with a smaller contingent, freeing Kat up.

As Kat headed back to the nurses' station to pick up a new case, she certainly wasn't expecting to be greeted with a pterodactyl toy. It sat behind the counter, its toy bead eyes seeming to lock with hers.

Kat's heart pounded hard and fast.

'Where did that come from?'

Another nurse lifted her head from where she was making notes.

'Someone brought it in. They found it in the park and dropped it off here. Apparently it has "Doc Terens" scrawled on it so they thought it might belong here.'

'Doc Terrence,' Kat managed, the beat of her heart so loud now that it was almost deafening her.

It was hard to believe the rest of the ER couldn't hear it.

'You know who it belongs to?'

'Pretty sure,' Kat muttered, telling herself it was coincidence, plain and simple. Not some sign.

Not *fate*.

So why was she keeping the toy owner's identity to herself? And why was something suspiciously like *excitement* rolling through her like a train gathering speed down a hill?

'Do you mind if I take it and clean it up so that I can return it to its owner?'

Of course, she could just wait for Logan to start his first shift here and hand it over then. Better still, she could tell the ward manager, who would no doubt keep it safe and hand it over herself once Logan started work.

But surely she owed it to him to warn him that he was hot gossip around here. Not just because of the VIPs who were still in the hospital, but because everyone already knew Logan was going to be starting as the new ER doc.

Then she conjured up Jamie's distraught face, and told herself that taking the toy round to Logan's home as soon as her shift ended was being a good Samaritan. Returning Doc Terrence as quickly as possible was about sparing the child unnecessary additional distress. It wasn't about leaping at the first opportunity to go and see some man she barely knew.

Of course it wasn't.

'Sure, go ahead.' The nurse barely glanced up again. 'You've got a new admission in Room Four. A male in his sixties, presenting with chest tightness.'

'Right.' Kat nodded. 'I'll get to him now.'

She headed straight over to the room, pushing thoughts of Jamie—and ultimately of Logan—out of her head as she concentrated on her new patient.

Within minutes she had discovered that her patient had recently undergone ablation surgery for a cardiac arrythmia, but that he also had a history of asthma. That meant that his chest tightness and shortness of breath could be anything from atrial fibrillation to an asthma attack.

An echocardiogram and a chest X-ray would confirm which of those diagnoses were correct, but for now her first priority was to assess him, draw labs and carry out an EKG.

It was going to be a busy shift, and for that Kat was very grateful.

'Kat?' Logan opened the door and, for a second she thought she saw something flash though his eyes moments before he frowned. 'What are you doing here?'

Kat ignored that punch in her gut, the one that told her she wasn't here just for the one hundred per cent altruistic purpose of reuniting a sad four-year-old with his favourite dinosaur, no matter what she'd tried to tell herself a few hours earlier.

Still, she plastered a bright smile on her lips and held her trophy aloft.

'I found something.'

'My God, I can't believe it.' Logan swung the door open wider, inviting her straight in.

Whatever apprehension he'd had when he'd first seen her standing there had disappeared the instant he'd seen the toy. Clearly, he put his son's needs ahead of his own concerns, which told Kat a great deal about the man.

And then she pulled herself up quickly because she wasn't here to learn about the man. She was just here to return a toy.

And if she believed that...well, more fool her.

'Go through, first door on the right. He's barely slept since yesterday. I've tried to distract him all day, we've been to the park and the zoo, and now he's just settled down to watch half an hour of television.'

It shouldn't be that hard to get her legs moving. With a

slight lurch Kat moved forward, dutifully walking down the corridor and in through the door indicated. There on the sofa sat a glum Jamie, evidently fresh from a bath in pyjamas and race-car slippers.

His dark-ringed eyes testified to the lack of sleep and those eyes were glued to a kids' programme. Puppies on some kind of rescue mission. She recognised it only too well from Carrie, and her chest pulled a little tighter.

Still, this wasn't about her. This was about a little boy and his current best bud dinosaur.

Backing up a step until she was no longer in sight, Kat lifted the pterodactyl and poked its head past the door as she made a soft *roar* sound. There was a pause, and then a loud gasp.

'Doc Twence!'

Kat heard the distinct sound of Jamie bouncing off the couch and scurrying across the room, and she was only just able to kneel down as the four-year-old flung himself at both her and his pterodactyl.

An invisible hand reached between her ribs and clenched at her heart. Squeezing it. Making her wonder if she would ever breathe again.

'You find Doc Twence.'

'Found,' Logan corrected gently from behind Kat. 'Kat *found* Terrence.'

'Found,' Jamie choked out joyously, his arms squeezing her neck so tightly that it almost hurt.

Almost.

For a moment Kat couldn't stop herself from burying her head in his neck as she hugged him back. That little child scent was so wonderfully, painfully familiar.

So like Carrie.

And then she shut the painful memories out and forced herself back from the little boy.

'I think Terrence missed you,' she managed. And if her

voice sounded a little thicker than usual, well, who was to know? 'And he's all cleaned up, so I'm guessing you can probably have him tonight for bed.'

'You cleaned the toy?' Logan muttered above them.

'At the hospital.' She twisted her neck to try to look up but Jamie's grasp was too tight. And she wasn't really trying that hard. 'Who knows what adventures Terrence got up to?'

'I didn't even think about it.'

She didn't miss the note of self-censure in his voice, but now wasn't the time to delve into it. Instead, she spent the next ten minutes speculating with the blissfully happy four-year-old about where his dinosaur might have gone, and what wonders he might have seen, the television programme utterly forgotten in the little boy's joy.

By then it was Jamie's bedtime, and as Logan put his son to bed Kat found herself left alone in the living room. She shifted nervously on the sofa. Should she leave?

Logan had said something about not being too long as he'd ushered his son from the room, but somehow she felt like she was intruding. The sounds of a still happy, exhausted Jamie floated through the apartment to her ears. And Logan, with his hushed, soothing voice, reading a story to get his son to sleep.

Sounds that were as familiar as they were painful. Yet she couldn't bring herself to stand up and leave. Somehow it was comforting.

Certainly more comforting than returning to her own silent, empty apartment.

And then, suddenly, Logan's low voice went quiet and all she heard was a soft padding as he made his way back to the living room.

'I didn't think that would take long. He's shattered, poor kid. Now that his darned toy is home, I think he'll sleep for a week. I don't know what we would have done if you hadn't found it.'

'You'll have to buy another.' Kat smiled. 'If Carrie loved a particular toy, or jumper, or whatever, I used to buy another. Just in case one ever got lost.'

She didn't realise what she'd said until he frowned at her.

'Carrie?'

Horror unfurled within her. She stared at him blankly, her heart racing and her stomach flip-flopping.

'You have a daughter?' he pressed, his brows knitted tightly, as if trying to work it out.

It took everything she had to calm the slamming of her heart against her ribs and affect an easy smile. Good job she was so practised at it these days.

'Not mine. I just took care of her a few times.'

It was a million miles from the truth, but it was as close as she was prepared to get right now. Not that she thought Logan was buying it.

He fixed her with that intense gaze again and it was all she could do not to squirm away from the deep, unsettling sense that he was assessing her.

But then, without warning, he released her.

'I'll get us a drink.'

She was grateful for the reprieve, and it was insane just how badly she wanted to accept. Still, something about Logan got under her skin, and that made him altogether too dangerous to be around.

'It's okay.' She shook her head. 'I only meant to return Jamie's toy. I don't want to overstay my welcome.'

'You're not overstaying. Call it a thank you for coming out of your way for us.'

'Really, it isn't a big deal.' Heat bloomed through her, staining her cheeks pink. 'I only live five minutes away.'

Plus, if he could have read the not so altruistic reasons in her head for returning the dinosaur, he probably wouldn't be quite so grateful. Fortunately, he'd already headed into the next room and couldn't see the traitorous flush.

She really needed to relax.

'Red, or white?' he called through.

'Um...either.'

As long as it was with him.

There was the clinking of glasses and the pop of a cork, and then Logan was heading back through with two large wine glasses and a bottle of red. As if there was nothing more interesting he'd rather do than sit and share a glass of wine with her.

'I'm guessing that, by now, the ubiquitous hospital grapevine knows I'm coming to Seattle as a new ER doctor?'

She offered a sheepish grin.

'Actually, that was one of the other reasons I thought I'd return Terrence sooner rather than later.'

'So they know.'

'Yep. The place was buzzing with that particular gem that first day. Before you'd even left after the accident.'

'Of course it was.'

'I also heard that you've been in regularly to check on the older man. Speculation is rife, of course, but I haven't even told them that you were his bodyguard.'

'Who said I was his bodyguard?'

'You were literally guarding that door when I first met you, you look like a bodyguard and... I saw the exit wound on your shoulder.'

'Very astute.'

There was no need for that passing comment to make her feel quite so proud. But it did.

'Not that I've told anyone, of course,' she added quickly. 'It's nobody else's business.'

He eyed her for a moment.

'I think I believe you. Anyway, I thought maybe you could give me the low-down on the ER department from a colleague's point of view. Who makes the best ally, and who do I look out for?'

It was a deft conversation redirection, and one that had her stomach doing that strange jig thing it seemed to have taken up. He wasn't about to confide in her, understandably, but he wasn't exactly dismissing her either.

'As in female attention? Dating?'

He looked vaguely amused.

'More like, who is professionally territorial? I'm not afraid of stepping on people's toes if it's in the patient's best interests, but I like to avoid unnecessary conflict wherever possible.'

'Oh. Of course.'

Her cheeks flushed. Again.

'My life is centred around my son right now,' he added. 'I don't have time for dating.'

'Hence the wedding band. There hasn't been anyone?'

He didn't exactly shrug; his tone achieved that for him.

'A couple of hook-ups. But nothing serious. You're the first person who has even met Jamie.'

He didn't mean it that way, she knew that, but it didn't stop the heat from radiating in her chest. And then lower. Hotter.

'I guess they haven't had Doc Terrence to return,' she joked weakly, and pretended that a part of her didn't want him to say that it was more than that.

'Indeed,' he answered instead.

Which told her absolutely nothing. Or nothing that she foolishly wanted to hear, anyway.

'His grandparents will be pleased. I think they were beside themselves the first night.'

'Jamie stayed with them?' She didn't know why she was

surprised, it wasn't as though she knew anything about Logan, or Jamie, or their lives.

'He's spent most of his life practically living with them, I was away so much. And with the shifts I'll be working, they'll still be taking him a few times a week. It makes sense to keep him comfortable going between them and me.'

'Keeps some consistency for him.' Kat nodded, understanding it only too well.

Then, before she realised it, she found herself opening her mouth to tell him. To talk about her fostering.

What on earth was she thinking?

Snapping her mouth closed, Kat watched him pour the wine for them both, then took the proffered glass and reminded herself to take only one small sip.

She'd never felt so much like needing to down it in one.

But, then, she'd never met a man quite like Logan Connors before.

CHAPTER FOUR

WHAT THE HELL was he doing?

She was the nurse who had tended to him in the ER. The woman who had brought his son's toy around. In a matter of days she would be his colleague. And he never mixed business and pleasure.

And yet here he was, pouring wine and striking up a conversation with her because there was something about Kat Steel that drew him in. Even before that little revelation about the child she'd called Carrie. He hadn't believed her attempt to cover up for a moment.

With anyone else, he might have found it interesting. With Kat, he found he was intrigued. A score of questions tumbled around his brain, all vying to be asked first. Since when had anyone got under his skin quite like this?

Not even Sophia.

He wanted to know more about her. A lot more.

'Have you lived in Seattle long?'

He noticed how she dipped her head to take another sip of wine, her eyes sliding away momentarily.

'I moved here this year. I was in Philadelphia before that.'

'Long way to move.' He kept his tone casual, but filed away each nugget of information.

Something fairly significant must have happened to make her move practically across the country. Something that had affected her so badly that she didn't like to talk about it.

'How about you?' she asked. 'Where were you living before you chose to come to Seattle General?'

Clearly she still didn't know who he was. Or, at least, who Roberto was. Which meant she still didn't know that Dom di Rossi, her head of ER, was also Domenico Baresi, next in line to the throne of Isola Verde.

He needed to choose his words carefully.

So what did it mean that he already hated the idea of lying to a woman he barely knew?

'I originally grew up here, but in the last fifteen years I've travelled a lot,' Logan began slowly. 'I used to be an army doc, but since I left a few years ago I've been doing a slightly different role.'

'Ah, you're ex-military.' She eyed him curiously and he felt that awareness fizzle around them even as they both pretended it wasn't. 'That explains it.'

'Explains what?'

'The knee in the femoral artery. I thought I'd read somewhere that it was something military physicians were taught. Something about body armour, right?'

'Yeah.' An unexpected wave of nausea threatened to wash over him, but he pushed it back. 'Femoral artery wounds are more and more common as the guys are increasingly using body armour. In the event of an IED, the armour protects the body from the blast but the weak points are where the armour ends.'

'Ah, where the leg meets the trunk.' Kat considered. 'So the armour creates the need for more amputations, by virtue of the fact that it saves the soldier's life?'

'Pretty much.'

She eyed him again, and it was all he could not to shift uncomfortably. He got the oddest sense that she was reading him.

He wondered what she saw.

'So...' She lightened her tone. 'Now you've come home to Seattle?'

There was no reason at all for him to feel so...*disconcerted*.

'Now I'm in back Seattle, yes.' He tugged his mouth into some semblance of a smile.

'So Jamie has been here with his grandparents?'

'No. For the past few years I've been fortunate enough that my parents have travelled to me in order to help take care of Jamie. But they are getting older and they needed to come home.'

'So you followed with Jamie?'

'He'd have been devastated to lose them. They've been such a constant in his life, practically from birth, and, like I said, he's still going to need them when I'm at work. Besides, I was ready to come home.'

No need to mention Sophia again. He didn't want to sound bitter or vindictive. The simple truth was that she had her own life to live, and that life didn't include him or Jamie. Having his grandparents around had filled the void so that, for the moment, Jamie didn't feel the loss. But as he grew up and other kids talked about their own mothers, Logan knew that day was coming.

Jamie had lost enough, without losing his grandparents as well.

'I don't think I even have a home.' Kat broke the silence suddenly, and he thought it was telling that she didn't quite meet his eye. 'I have a big family, and we try to keep in touch, but everyone is scattered everywhere at the moment.'

'You don't see them at all?'

'We try to video message, but with my sister and my cousin in Australia with their respective families, one brother in Canada with his new wife, and my mother visiting my other brother in the UK with his wife and their new baby, no one's able to come together this year.'

'Is that why you're working so many of the holiday shifts?'

Her gaze collided with his, the wine sloshing danger-ously around her glass as a renewed sense of awareness crackled around them. It wasn't what he'd intended, yet neither could be bring himself to regret it. Still, he wasn't about to let her think he'd been stalking her.

'Like you said, I've been in a few times, visiting my... friend,' he acknowledged. It wasn't a complete lie. In many way King Roberto *had* been a friend to him, as well as an employer. 'I've seen you working there every time.'

'Ah. Right.' She wrinkled her nose. He couldn't ex-plain how such a simple gesture made him want her all the more. 'Then, yes, I suppose I have been trying to keep myself busy.'

There was clearly more to it, but he chose not to press her on it for the moment. It was as though he needed to take a moment to remind himself where his boundaries were. As if he wasn't entirely convinced he had full control over himself where this woman was concerned.

'I'm even doing a charity run in the park next month. I haven't been running for years.' She emitted a slightly nervous laugh, and he liked it that she seemed equally... *thrown*.

'Is that the Santa run I've seen advertised around the place?'

'That's the one.' Another laugh. 'I got caught up in the hype.'

'Are you entering as part of a hospital team?'

'No, just me.'

He was almost tempted to suggest joining her. He bit his tongue just in time.

This wasn't what he did. There hadn't been anyone else

for him in the three years since Sophia had left. His life was about Jamie, and about ensuring that little boy felt he had all the parents he needed between his father and his grandparents. Logan shouldn't need to have to keep reminding himself that he didn't have time for relationships. He didn't even have time for *dalliances*.

He'd never had to remind himself of it before Kat had turned up.

Yet this was nice. In his apartment, drinking wine, with a woman like her. He couldn't remember ever doing anything like this with Sophia. His ex-wife had been all about being in the best hot spots in town. Or, more accurately, being *seen* to be in the best hot spots. She'd been all about glamour, and social standing, and networking.

She'd called herself an influencer. He knew now what that word really meant.

Logan let his eyes roam over the woman opposite him. Kat was so different from Sophia. From *any* woman he'd ever met before. And though he couldn't have pinpointed exactly what it was about that that snuck under his skin, all he knew was that she made him...*yearn*. Though he couldn't have even explained for what.

And surely that, alone, was the most dangerous thing about her?

It was only when there was a noise down the hall, and Logan excused himself to check on his sleeping son, that Kat finally thought to check her watch.

She'd been here for hours.

Hastily, she reached over to place the wine—her third glass, already half-empty—on the coffee table and stand up. She'd lost all track of time.

Truth be told, she'd lost all track of herself. Long since ceasing to recognise the woman who was chatting about her life in Seattle, her globetrotting family.

She could even pretend that it didn't hurt to talk about her family. And, oddly, in a way it didn't.

And even though all the topics steered carefully away from anything *really* personal—like her childhood in hospitals, Kirk, or Carrie—it had nonetheless been the closest she'd come to removing the smiling, happy mask she was sure to always wear.

Their conversations had weaved together. Light and easy one moment, more personal and revealing the next. And all the while she watched his mouth, altogether too sensual as she told herself that it didn't do things to her. Observed his hands and pretended she wasn't imagining them all over her body. Roamed his body with her eyes and battled not to imagine it naked beneath hers. Or on top of hers.

Or any way he wanted it at all, actually.

It was definitely time to get out of here.

Softly, not wanting to disturb Jamie any more than he might already be stirring, she moved through to the hallway, plucking her scarf off the coat hook and winding it around her neck once, twice.

She was just swinging her coat on when she heard Logan coming around the corner.

'You're leaving?' his low voice rumbled down the hallway.

She painted a bright smile on her lips and was careful to be quiet.

'I had no idea of the time. I hope we didn't disturb Jamie.'

'He usually wakes up around now and needs to go to the toilet. If you can call that dreamlike state *waking.* But he's already back asleep now.'

'That's good.' She nodded, still with her coat half-on.

'You don't have to leave.'

You do, she told herself sternly. *This is your boss. And*

*you're already having inappropriate thoughts about him.
What is another hour going to do?*

'I really ought to,' she hedged.

'Sure,' he agreed, and she told herself she'd imagined
the fraction of a second of hesitation in his voice. 'Let me
help you.'

And then he was striding towards her, helping her with
her coat and lifting her bag off the hook to pass it to her.

The worst of it was the feeling of deflation. The realisation that she would have readily stayed, if only he'd insisted. That she'd hoped that was exactly what he'd do.

'Thanks,' she managed, her tone more clipped than she
might have preferred.

It was impossible to shake the impression that he was
trying to distance himself from her, and she had no idea
why. Inside, she sagged even further, though she kept
herself standing tall and upright, even as she lunged for
the door...at exactly the same time that he lifted his arm
around her and leaned across to turn the latch.

She backed up rapidly, but there was nowhere to go and
suddenly she was sprawled against the wall with Logan's
body pressed against hers.

Hotter, and harder, and so much more...*male* than even
her fervent imagination had fancied.

Kat froze. She felt edgy. Jittery. Like she was standing
on some precipice and the slightest thing—even a hint of
a breeze—could make her topple over.

All she could feel was those acres of muscle pressed
against her, and all she could hear was her breathing, growing more ragged, more telling by the second. She never
moved her hands and yet, without warning, her bag thud-
ded to the floor and there they were, splaying over his impossibly solid pectoral muscles.

'Logan...'

It was unmistakable, that needy note in her voice. So unlike her. And yet so real. Heat blazed between them, so hot that Kat feared she might be burned alive at any moment.

Then she felt it—the breeze that she'd feared—his head dipping so close to hers, his breath tickling her neck. She would never know whether he moved first or she did, but then his lips were brushing hers, tasting, wanting.

The effect of his kiss started in her toes, moving up through her body and leaving every single part of her tingling, even the tiny hairs that stood to attention on her arms.

It was like standing in the centre of a pyre and feeling the flames licking at her, before roaring inside her. Burning hotter, higher, brighter, with every drag of his lips and every sweep of his tongue. She didn't think she'd ever been kissed so thoroughly, so devastatingly before. Melting her.

If she hadn't been pinned so deliciously between Logan's too-perfect body and the hallway wall, she was sure her legs would have given way beneath her.

Her breasts felt swollen, achy and much too heavy. Her stomach somersaulted inside, vaulting off the walls of her abdomen, and lower than that…she throbbed. A violent, feverish pulsing that resonated through her entire body.

She felt entirely too tight in her own body, and too giddy in her head. When he muttered her name, the raw sound made her shiver. Desperately, she shifted against him, pressing her body closer to his, making him pin her even more firmly in place. As she moved her hips again, he slotted into place perfectly, his hard length nestled right where she ached for him most.

And Kat didn't just topple—she swan-dived.

You shouldn't be touching her. You certainly shouldn't be kissing her.

The words bellowed through his head, one after the other, but he muffled each of them. His mouth revelled in the taste of her vanilla cream lips, his hands in the feel of her silken skin beneath his palms, and something wild and untamed surged through him.

He couldn't even consider what his body revelled in right now, pressed as he was against her, for fear that she would drive him completely wild.

He kissed her like he'd never kissed any woman, though he couldn't have said what made it so different. And all the while his libido careened around like he was some kind of sex-crazed idiot.

What the hell was it about Kat Steel that made him forget every promise he'd made to himself?

Then he stopped thinking, because he feared that it might be enough to stop him from kissing her and right here and now he couldn't think of any punishment more unpalatable than stopping kissing this woman.

So he *did* kiss her. Over and over again, every slide, every lick, every graze devastating her and laying waste to them both. As though everything that had happened since she'd walked around the hospital corner, barely a week ago, had been leading up to this moment.

To her.

Slowly, delicately he unwound the scarf from her neck, even as his mouth continued to plunder hers, and then, after he'd let it fall to the floor, he lifted his hands to cup her face, his thumbs caressing her jawline as he angled his head for a better fit.

Vaguely, he was aware of her starting to shrug herself back out of her coat, and then her hands were raking over his chest, like she needed to touch him. Like she couldn't help herself. Logan found he liked that notion a great deal. Perhaps too much. Yet he couldn't even bring himself to care about stopping.

He hauled off her jacket, his mouth never leaving hers. He traced her jaw with his lips, her neck with the vaguest edge of his teeth, and the hollow of her neck with his tongue. Each exploration elicited more unrestrained moans, making her shiver that much harder against him.

He let his hands investigate over her top, tracing her, touching her. He took his time learning each curve and every swell. Committed them to memory, and then dipped his hands under her loose top to learn her all over again.

It should have set off alarm bells, realising how much he wanted *her*. As if he'd never wanted any other woman in his entire life. Certainly not with this hectic, frenzied urgency he felt inside.

He wanted to learn every inch of her. Taste her.

God, how he needed to taste her.

He was losing it, and he didn't even care. All that heat pouring out of her and into him was almost too much to bear.

If he slid his fingers under the waistband of her trousers right now, he could only imagine what he'd find. How wet she would be. The way she was rolling her hips against him, those greedy little moans escaping such plump, perfect lips, was making him ache so badly that it was almost painful.

'Kat.' He barely recognised the growl as his own voice. It sounded so coarse. So restless.

If he wasn't careful, they were going to end up doing it right here, against the wall. And the worrying part was that he wasn't even sure he cared. He wanted her so badly.

Suddenly there was a cry from down the hall and Logan crashed back to reality in an instant.

What the hell had he been thinking?

Had he really been kissing—no, *necking* like a teenage schoolboy—with a woman he'd only just met? About to have sex with her—because there was no denying that had been where they'd been headed—right there in the apartment? All this, when his son lay asleep just down the hall?

Not that Jamie could have stumbled on them, of course. For a start, he had installed a baby gate just by a short flight of five stairs, in case his son woke in the night and came looking for him, only to turn the wrong way in the unfamiliar apartment when he came out of his room.

Nonetheless, it was wholly, unequivocally unacceptable.

'This should never have happened,' he ground out, furious with himself.

'Logan—' she began, but he cut her off.

He couldn't listen. And the worst of it was that it was less about not wanting to hear what she had to say and more about the fact that he feared she would convince him to carry on.

He *wanted* her to say something to convince him to carry on. Instead, he tore himself away from her, hoping that the loss of contact might, somehow, break the spell.

It didn't. Which made it all the more imperative that he walk away. *Now.*

'I need to go and attend to my son. I suggest you let yourself out.'

CHAPTER FIVE

'UGH. YUCK.'

Logan stared at his son with something approaching amused despair as the little boy pulled a disgusted face at their latest baking attempt, setting it back on his brand new, glittery Christmas plate and sticking his tongue out. The evidence suggested that they were nothing like the cookies Logan's Nana had baked them all for Thanksgiving.

'I warned you that I had no idea how to bake cookies, champ.'

'Yuck, yuck, yuck,' repeated Jamie, taking a generous gulp of milk from his plastic cup.

'They aren't that bad.' Logan laughed, taking a bite of his own then pulling a face that he imagined to be pretty close to the one his son had made. 'Okay, they are. I'll ask Nana.'

'Kat,' Jamie said firmly.

'Sorry, Champ, I'm not asking Kat.' He gritted his teeth, determined not to let Jamie see.

It had been days since that night in the apartment and still, if he turned quickly, he could imagine he could catch a scent of her perfume, he could swear he could taste her on his tongue, and he wanted more. So much more.

It was crazy, but there it was. Which was why he'd spend the past couple of days putting such much-needed distance between himself and the too-enticing ER nurse.

She affected him too much. Made him forget who, and where, he was. If he was going to be honest, then she had been getting to him ever since that first time in the hospital when he'd felt her hands on his body, and he'd been turned on for the first time in a long time.

The last person to get under his skin like this had been Sophia—and look where that had led. Not that he could ever regret his beautiful, sweet son.

'Shall we put up the tree tonight, Jamie?' Logan lifted the tray and tipped the unappetising—all right, disgusting—cookies into the bin. 'It's the first of December tomorrow.'

'Yes.' Jamie clapped his hands in delight. 'Can Kat help?'

'No Kat,' he answered firmly.

God, his son was relentless.

Admittedly, it wasn't as though he'd been able to stop thinking about her either—or their kiss. It irked Logan that she'd even appeared in his dreams, although in those they hadn't stopped at merely kissing. In those she had been spread out in his bed, like his own personal feast, or clinging to him, moaning in abandon as he'd buried himself inside her.

Even now, he had to shake his head as if that could rid it of the unwanted thoughts.

But what really bothered him, above everything else, was the way Jamie seemed to have taken to her so fast.

The kid had met her twice, and yet Kat currently dominated his conversations. Even his grandparents had heard all about Angel Kat, and Logan didn't care much for the encouraging comments they'd tried not to make.

Like: 'It would be nice to have a steady, stable, more youthful female influence in Jamie's life', or, worse, that it was good to see him starting to 'come around' after everything that had happened on that operational tour, and then with Sophia.

But more than their comments, it was his own errant

mind that annoyed him the most, throwing up images of Kat whenever he was least prepared for them.

Making him take a detour past the ER department while he was making one of his visits to check on King Roberto, just in the hope of catching a glimpse of her. Like some besotted adolescent.

Which was why he was here now, talking to Jamie about all the decorations the four-year-old could imagine for their first real Christmas together, without work taking him away from him. And baking cookies that looked like cardboard and tasted even worse.

'How about your advent calendar?' Logan tried to distract his son. 'We need to go and buy one. I was thinking of a train one. You can open a carriage each day.'

'And we can get one for Kat.'

Logan gave up—he wasn't going to talk about Kat any more. It was only indulging Jamie. And with each of his son's attempts to wear him down it was getting harder and harder to refuse. Especially because a part of him wanted to agree for his own selfish reasons.

But this was his last day of R&R. His last chance to spend quality time with Jamie for a while. He was not going to think about the fact that tomorrow was his first day at work at Seattle General.

Nor was he going to think about how it was his first medical role back after losing his buddies in that last tour of duty.

And he was certainly not going to think about how good it would be to work alongside Kat.

The walk through the atrium to Seattle General was as arduous as Kat imagined it would be to trek across the Sahara.

It had been a difficult enough couple of days as it was, with that last evening at Logan's apartment replaying in her head on a never-ending loop. Reliving every last, glorious moment of that kiss—right up to the humiliating end.

She'd even gone running through the park—ostensibly training for her Santa run—every day, just in the foolish hope that she might bump into him and adorable Jamie again.

And it was perhaps that part that frightened her the most. Without the complication of Jamie, maybe she would have been tempted to do something more about the undeniable chemistry that arced between her and Logan every time they were together. Perhaps some of that *no-strings, no-hassle fun* that she and Gemma were always laughing about.

But not with Jamie around. Not when her presence could impact on a four-year-old boy. She knew that only too well from her fostering.

Who are you trying to protect? a voice whispered in her head. *Just Jamie? Or yourself as well?*

She tried to silence the voice, but failed. Her location probably wasn't helping.

It was the first of December and already a massive Christmas tree towered in the hospital's modern glass atrium. Stunningly decorated—and sweeping up into the glass roof of the atrium—it looked completely and utterly stunning.

And every last inch of it reminded Kat of last Christmas without Carrie.

All she wanted to do was get past the evergreen of memories, shrug off this shroud of grief—at least Carrie was happy, and well, and with her parents who hopefully were giving her all the love she deserved—and throw herself into her shift.

But as she stepped through the door and heard the buzz around the ER department, she just...*knew.*

Still, Kat found herself holding her breath as Gemma came hurrying over.

'Guess what?'

She didn't want to know. So why was her chest pulling so tight, as if it yearned to even hear Logan's name.

Insanity.

'What?' she managed instead, even forcing her mouth up into a friendly smile.

'You know the VIPs who came in? Especially the one on that gurney…?'

'Yes.' Kat nodded, pushing the image of Logan's poker face out of her mind.

'Well, rumour has it that Logan Connors—the guy who saved his life—was actually the man's bodyguard. And if that isn't enough, Comic Book God is starting today!'

How was it possible for her stomach to dip yet soar all at once? Her heart thumped wildly. And so loudly she imagined it could be heard on the other side of the hospital.

'Oh, that's good.' Kat had no idea how she sounded so calm and even. 'We can always do with more ER docs, especially at this time of year. So, who's my first patient?'

'No one, it's the usual lull before all hell breaks loose later tonight. But, Kat, did you hear me? Comic Book God. Apparently he's a former army trauma doctor.'

'He should be a good addition, then.' Even to her own ears her voice sounded tighter, squeakier than normal.

Gemma didn't appear to notice. Not that it mattered, because before either of them could say anything more there was another flurry and the doors behind her hissed open.

'He's here,' Gemma hissed, redundantly as it happened. Because—just like the other night—all the fine hairs stood up on Kat's arm.

Great, that was all she needed—her own personal *Logan Connors* radar.

And then she heard the unmistakably smoky tones of

his voice, greeting their colleagues and introducing himself. There was no choice but to turn around and look interested. Professional.

Right up to the moment when his gaze snagged hers. And held. She tried to look away, to move, but there was no breaking free. Kat found herself paralysed, and the worst of it was that some perverse part of her seemed to revel in that sensation.

It shouldn't have been possible for him to look any hotter than he had the other night. Yet here, now, in his scrubs, he had to be the most lethally gorgeous male doctor she'd ever met in her entire life. Judging by the reaction amongst much of the female contingent standing with her, she was evidently not the only one to think so.

Yet even that fact wasn't enough to set off the alarm bells in her head. Instead, deep inside, her stomach turned and twisted. One knot upon another, upon another.

Still, his gaze held hers.

She still could practically taste his kiss on her mouth and before she could stop herself she snaked her tongue out over the lower lip, as if to check. This time her stomach clenched at the way his eyes darkened. And she couldn't pretend his undisguised reaction didn't give her a bit of a thrill.

Right before a disgusted look flitted over his features, and he turned away from her.

At the kiss? Or at the prospect of them having to work together?

As she started her shift, something rolled and turned inside her, like a pit of baby snakes was in her belly. And it didn't stop.

For the next couple of hours Kat worked steadily to care for the patients in her allocated rooms. Her heart both leapt with relief and sank with disappointment every time she called for a consult and a doctor other than Logan stepped into the room.

She might have known that luck couldn't last. It was halfway through her shift when she was called to assist on a major incident only to find that Logan was the doctor running the shout. Her skin felt like it was tightening over her entire body.

All she could do, she decided as the EMTs rushed the patient towards them, was keep her head down, stay focussed, and work her way through it.

'This is Tom—he's twenty-nine,' the emergency responder began. 'He has a history of complex partial seizures and this seizure started approximately thirty-eight minutes ago. We were called by his girlfriend who said the seizure was different from any other she has seen before.'

Logan nodded his affirmation.

'We've put a line in, and we've given him two lots of ten milligrams of diazepam. The last ten milligrams were at eleven-oh-three. He had a previous seizure yesterday that lasted for fourteen minutes and was self-terminating. He has recently had a dosage change in medication and has been having repeated complex partial seizures over the last couple of weeks. We've got a bag of his medications here.'

'Great, thanks.' Logan took the bag and began reading out the medications before checking the clock on the wall. 'Let's push another ten milligrams of diazepam. Can we also get some phenytoin ready, just in case he still doesn't respond? Let's also get some bloods.'

As Kat and the rest of the team began to move around the patient, Logan turned back to the emergency responder.

'When you said the girlfriend said this seizure was different, do you know what she meant?'

'She said it was just more aggressive. The convulsions were more frequent and more violent than any other time.'

'Understood.' He swung back to the team, moving forward to the nurse who was about to draw blood and touching the patient lightly on the shoulder. 'Tom, we're just going to put a needle in your arm to draw blood, okay, mate? Kat, can you hold his head? Let's get him out of that soiled clothing.'

Kat liked it that Logan was caring for his patient, letting Tom know what was going on even though they didn't know whether the man could hear them.

'Can we keep talking to him, guys? Tell him whatever you're doing to him, yes? Do we know where the girlfriend is?'

'She's on her way in. They have a young toddler, so her father was driving to meet her to give her lift and look after the youngster.'

'Right, he has been fitting now for forty minutes. Let's push the phenytoin. If he doesn't respond, I think we need to get an anaesthetist in here to put him into a medically induced coma.'

The team nodded as they began to cut Tom's clothes away to clean him up and make him comfortable. They all knew that the longer the seizure continued, the longer Tom's body was being deprived of oxygen, and so the more likely it was that he could suffer brain damage.

A medically induced coma wasn't the most desirable option—the anaesthetic would stop the seizure, but Tom would need a tube inserted to enable him to breathe and would have a harder, longer recovery—but it would allow his body to get oxygen, ultimately keeping him alive.

The team worked quickly and smoothly—Logan was already proving a good doctor and leader—and they were soon rewarded by their patient's seizure finally beginning to slow and then stop. After checking the patient's obs, Logan moved to the head of the bed.

'Hello, Tom, mate. Good to have you back. You're at

Seattle General and you've been seizing for around fifty-five minutes.'

Kat watched Logan's interaction with the drained, exhausted patient, checking everything over again as the rest of the team began to disperse now that Tom had finally begun to settle. A whole room of patients was still out there, and it was no surprise when another nurse poked her head around to ask if Logan was free.

He stepped to one side and beckoned Kat.

'I want to send him for a CT to make sure there's nothing new going on in his brain that might have caused him to be fitting for so long.'

'Right.' She nodded.

'Can you keep a closer eye on him until he goes up?'

Logically, she knew it didn't mean anything that he'd chosen to ask her over any of the rest of the team. Yet a tiny part of her wondered if it was because he'd recognised her as a good ER nurse.

She hoped it was.

He was clearly such a skilled, experienced doctor, she could tell that he'd already impressed her colleagues. Was it really such hubris, the idea of equally impressing him?

No, whispered a voice in her head, *but what is hubris is the fact that you're reading so much into everything.*

Irritated with herself, Kat straightened her shoulders and glowered.

'Of course, Doctor,' she replied professionally, before dropping her voice too low for anyone else but Logan to hear. 'It *is* my job after all.'

No one but her could possibly have seen that hint of a surprised flare in his expression. Thankfully her back was to everyone else so no one could see her expression—or the rising flush in her cheeks.

'I don't need to be micro-managed,' she muttered quietly.

It was so unlike her, yet she couldn't seem to stop it and, for a moment, Logan didn't respond.

If she wasn't careful, she was going to let Logan's reaction go to her head and start letting herself believe that he was bothered for personal, rather than professional, reasons. But that was just fanciful. Probably as a result of being unable to stop thinking about him for the past few days.

Then his eyes cleared and he acknowledged her brightly, efficiently. Professionally.

'Thank you, Kat.'

And as he began to walk away, she berated herself for acting like such an idiot. So much for her earlier self-congratulations on being able to work so seamlessly with the man. Didn't they always say that pride came before a fall?

'Okay Tom,' Kat announced in her cheeriest voice, even though Tom was drifting into a deep and much-needed sleep. 'Let's see how you're doing.'

With a sinking heart she knew she was going to have to find Logan later and apologise for acting so crazily. And then, just as she reached her patient's bed, she felt someone take hold of her elbow and steer her down the corridor and into a deserted one.

Even before she swivelled her head to look at him, she knew that it was Logan.

'What...what are you doing?'

'Relax,' he commanded. 'No one can see us. And I want to sort out this problem you have with me.'

'Around here, someone can pretty much *always* see you,' she snapped. 'And, for the record, I don't have a problem with you.'

'I'd like that to be true,' he continued, his tone measured. At least that was better than him sounding condescending or patronising. 'But you're clearly on edge.'

She didn't intend to bristle, but she felt herself doing it

all the same. Time for her to make that apology she knew was owing. Kat sucked in a breath.

'I'm sorry, I don't know what came over me. It's just that I always put the patient first.'

'I know,' Logan agreed. 'Even if I hadn't heard such good things about you from your colleagues, I can tell a good nurse from a bad one. And I don't believe anyone else noticed, but it was apparent to me that you...weren't entirely comfortable with my presence.'

She wanted to deny it. She even opened her mouth to do so. But what would be the point when they both knew it would be a lie? Surely it was better all round if she faced up to the truth? Maybe that way they could get over it quicker.

'Perhaps I am, a little,' she confessed. 'I don't make a habit of kissing my colleagues.'

'Is that so?'

He arched one eyebrow, and she instantly regretted such a candid confession. Especially since it only served to make more of what had happened between them rather than less.

'No, I mean, yes...' It was irksome that her attempt to remedy the situation wasn't entirely going to plan. 'I'm sure the longer we work together this shift, the easier it will become.'

'Kat—'

'Please don't.' She held her hand up, arguably too close to Logan's chest for comfort.

'I think we should talk about this.'

'I don't.' She shook her head.

'Then what do you propose we do?'

Quickly, she dropped her arm and gave him her most professional, yet cool, smile. 'We keep it strictly to innocuous subjects.'

'Like the weather perhaps?' She hated that his all-too-familiar crooked smile fired that heat up inside her all over again. 'The traffic?'

As ridiculous as it seemed, Kat found herself lifting her chin slightly, as though it would help her to convince herself that she was disdainful rather than charmed.

'How about the holidays?' she suggested, before a more pertinent question tugged at the edges of her mind. 'Is Jamie looking forward to Santa visiting?'

It was hardly the innocuous choice of subject matter that she'd intended. Far from it, in fact. Yet Kat couldn't help herself. She could pretend it was the emotion of walking through the atrium and seeing the enormous tree for the first time, but she wasn't certain she believed it.

Something gleamed in his eyes as he stared at her hard and then, just as she thought he wasn't going to answer, he spoke.

'Jamie can't wait. This will be the first year he's really understood the concept of Santa Claus and will be able to get into the excitement of it.'

'He's sleeping better again now that Doc Terrence is back?'

And, just like that, everything seemed to flip back from awkward to okay.

'Like a log,' Logan confirmed with a devilish flash of a grin.

'Is he with his grandparents now?'

'Actually, no. He's in the hospital crèche, and that damned dinosaur was the first thing he packed in his brand-new backpack. We're going to go shopping for more Christmas decorations as soon as I finish here today.'

'Didn't you mention your parents had already brought you some stuff over?'

'Yeah, but Jamie has seen some other decorations that he wants, and I thought, *Why not?*'

'*Why not?*' she echoed with a soft laugh. She would have done the same for Carrie. 'You didn't mention he'd be going to the hospital crèche.'

'Yeah, just some days to start to get him used to being around other kids, and for us to get a bit of a routine together. My parents are close by, though, so they'll be around for any night shifts, or if Jamie just wants them.'

'He really loves them, doesn't he?' A laugh slipped out as she thought about those few precious minutes with the little boy the other night.

That feeling of uncomplicated freedom that she'd experienced every time she'd spent time with Carrie. She knew it was pointless to torture herself with memories, but she couldn't help herself.

'Like I said, they've practically raised him for me,' he said fondly. 'But Seattle is a fresh start, and Jamie and I will get to be a proper family.'

'I think that's lovely.' Her throat felt thick, aching as it did with emotion.

And still she wondered what had happened to Jamie's mother. Logan had said she wasn't around any more, but what she found she really wanted to know was how Logan felt about that.

Was he relieved? Or did he want his wife back?

But before she could ask him—or even think about working up the guts to ask him—the loudspeaker sounded, another trauma code was announced, and Logan stepped past her, all business.

'We'll finish this conversation later,' he ground out over his shoulder, and she couldn't be sure if it had been a promise or a threat.

It didn't matter either way, because a second later he was gone.

CHAPTER SIX

MAYBE IT WOULDN'T be so difficult working with Logan after all, Kat decided as she strode back across the atrium after her shift was finally over. They'd worked together on another case after that encounter in the hallway and that time it had been as though nothing out of the ordinary had ever happened between them.

She wasn't sure she liked it. It unsettled her. And it wasn't helped by the fact that she was still trying to ignore the too-big, too-bright pull of the tree, only now she had the added complication of trying to avoid Logan.

Her body still threatened to melt when she saw him, of course. But if her head could just keep that bit ahead, they should be fine. No one appeared to have noticed the tension between them during that first shout, they certainly hadn't mentioned it. And Kat told herself that she felt intensely relieved and not at all piqued.

Eyeing the weather outside as she approached the glass doors, Kat pulled her coat more tightly around herself and had her hand on the metal framework when she heard her name being called.

The high-pitched, excited voice was unmistakable.

'Hello, Jamie.' She smiled, turning around and just about dropping to her knees as a little blur hurled itself into her arms.

'Jamie,' Logan censured him, 'you can't just jump on people, champ.'

But Kat simply shook her head to stop him, her arms going around the boy as she inhaled his little-kid scent and held on for as long as he let her, only making herself release him when he pushed himself back to talk to her.

'We're going to get new Christmas dorations.'

'Decorations,' Logan corrected.

'Dec-rations,' he repeated dutifully.

His little body practically shook with excitement, like an over-excited puppy, and his enthusiasm was so infectious it left Kat powerless to resist.

'Wow.' She laughed. 'That sounds super exciting.'

He nodded gleefully.

'It is. Daddy says I can choose one bubble all by myself.'

'Bubble?' she echoed cautiously, her mind whirring.

'He means—'

'Bauble!' she exclaimed, her brain ticking over after a moment.

'Bauble,' Jamie pronounced slowly.

Kat's heart swelled at the pride in his voice.

'That's amazing,' she told Jamie solemnly. 'Your daddy must trust you very, very much. You'll have to choose a really special bauble, okay?'

'Yes,' Jamie confirmed boldly. 'You help me.'

'Oh, no, sweetie, I…can't.'

But it shocked her just how much she wanted to say *yes*.

Only a couple of minutes ago she hadn't been able to look at the Christmas tree because of how painful a reminder it was of being without Carrie. Now her heart was aching because she wanted to accompany Jamie and his father on their Christmas-bauble shopping trip.

She ached to see that wide-eyed, unequivocal belief in the magic of the season that only a young child could show. The way she'd expected this Christmas to be for her with Carrie.

'Why?' Jamie's voice pierced her thoughts and, in a tiny sense, it was a little bit gratifying how crushed he looked. 'Pl-e-e-e-ease, Kat?'

She should say no. She opened her mouth then closed it again, but didn't dare look at Logan.

'I think this is a trip for you and your daddy,' she managed instead.

'I'm sure Kat has better things to do than come shopping for Christmas tree decorations,' Logan cut in, making her jump.

'Right.' She stumbled over the word, tugging her mouth into some semblance of a smile and pretending that her head wasn't screaming at her to disagree. 'Of course. Lots to do.'

She stood up, her eyes slamming straight into Logan's.

'Don't you?' he asked, a little more quietly this time.

She hesitated, unsure what to answer. The idea of returning to her empty place was no more palatable than it had been the other night.

'You're welcome to come if you want to,' he went on, just as quietly. 'I just didn't want you to feel obliged.'

'I don't.' She shook her head instantly. 'That is, I wouldn't. I'd love to join you both.'

There it was again, that infuriating unfathomable expression. And then it was gone, and he was addressing his son.

'Okay, champ, then that's settled. Kat can come after all.'

'Yay!' Jamie did a little dance in front of them before slipping his hand into Kat's. 'C'mon, Kat, help me find dinosaur bubbles.'

'Baubles,' she corrected happily, blushing when she chorused it in time with Logan.

'But,' Jamie announced imperiously, holding his hand up, 'first we're starting with a sleigh ride.'

And she told herself there was nothing in the least romantic about that at all.

'Well, that's the second colleague from the hospital to have seen us,' Logan observed a few hours later as they left yet another store with yet another Jamie-selected tree ornament.

The little boy's hand was still firmly lodged in Kat's—clearly his mother had been right about his son craving a younger female presence in his life.

'It's okay.' Kat turned around to answer him. 'We're just talking about innocuous topics like the traffic. And the weather.'

It took Logan a moment to realise that she was teasing him. He wanted to tease her back, but that was a skill slightly out of his wheelhouse.

'You might not be laughing when those two colleagues tell the hospital that they saw us together,' he pointed out instead.

Not that there was anything they could do about it now. He waited for the stab of regret to hit him. But it didn't come.

'You're very much about being ordered and correct, I think.' She tilted her head at him. 'About protocol.'

He hadn't really considered it like that before, Logan realised. But it made sense. First in the military, then as a bodyguard, his life had been about keeping things neat and squared away, whether it was his kit or the separation of his personal and private lives.

'I suppose I am,' he conceded eventually.

Except he'd been breaking his own rules ever since Kat had come into his life. And he could pretend it was about the way she had clicked with Jamie, but that would be pretending there hadn't been that…frisson between them that first day when she had examined him.

'At least, that's the way I usually prefer it,' he amended.

'So it bugs you that colleagues have seen us together?'

He knew it ought to. But he found he felt remarkably, uncharacteristically, carefree.

'Actually, no.' Logan leaned on the doorframe and folded his arms over his chest as Jamie and Kat stopped to admire a Christmas-themed model train set in a window. 'People love a good gossip, whether it's those two or someone else.'

'Those *three*, actually.' She wrinkled her nose as though in apology. 'There was someone you probably didn't recognise in the last shop we went into. I just didn't like to say anything.'

'I guess that's a new supply chain for the rumour mill, then.'

And even then he didn't care, he was having so good an evening with Kat. Plus, it had turned out that her presence was helping him to connect a little better with his son.

He'd always thought he and Jamie had a good bond, but Kat had a knack of being able to interact with him on topics he'd never before considered but which seemed so obviously perfect for a four-year-old once she'd highlighted them.

'You're really good with him.' The words tumbled out as the stood at the crossing and Kat entertained Jamie by singing funny kids' Christmas tunes.

It had been intended as a throwaway remark, but something flitted across her features, too fast for him to read, reminding him of that night at his house when she'd mentioned the child she used to mind. *Carrie* or something.

Now, like then, she made a point of deflecting, putting it down to her nursing skills, and Logan nodded, as though he agreed.

But he filed it away for another time.

If he wanted to get to know Kat Steel a little better, then he had a hunch that the key lay somewhere in that.

For now he just watched her, and how happy Jamie was to have her around, and he felt more relaxed that he had in a long time.

Clearly Jamie was crying out for a younger female in his life, and he'd fallen for Kat's charms—he couldn't fault his son's choice. And, all right, Kat might not be a long-term solution, but it was working for Jamie, and bringing him out of the shell he'd started to retreat into. When he weighed everything up, Logan calculated it could be good for his son—just as long as he kept some distance from Kat and kept reminding Jamie that she was just a temporary person in their lives,

And if that was also his own take-home message, then so what?

'Daddy, Kat, look at all the trees,' Jamie enthused a few moments later as they turned the corner to see the square full of Christmas trees—at least one hundred of them—all decorated differently.

Logan grinned as Kat allowed herself to be dragged along by the little boy as he—carrying the bags—merely lengthened his stride to keep up. They had enjoyed the sleigh ride, been to Santa's grotto, and wandered through a snow village with little wooden sheds decorated to look like life-size gingerbread houses. Jamie had been thrilled and awestruck in equal measure.

But even Logan had to admit that the waves of trees, all decorated in their own unique way—some quirky, some traditional, and some absolutely breathtaking—looked pretty damned spectacular.

'It's the Christmas tree parade,' Kat realised. 'The public can judge them. Gemma told me about it—her niece entered a tree this year. You can buy tickets and there are several categories you can judge, like Most Beautiful, Most Fun, Most Original, et cetera, and you get to choose your favourites.'

'Can we choose, Daddy? Please?'

'It's good fun,' Kat encouraged, not even attempting to hide her bias.

'Oh, it's like that, is it?' Logan laughed, and she nodded so preposterously that all he wanted to do was cup her face and kiss her.

'It's like that,' she told him blithely, completely oblivious to his less than platonic thoughts.

'All right,' he agreed, setting the bags down to pull his wallet from his pocket.

'No, these are on me.' Kat put her hand on his, a bolt of electricity shooting through him at the mere contact. She snatched her hand back, tellingly, which let him know she'd felt it too. 'You've paid for everything else tonight.'

Then she was darting away with Jamie holding one hand before he could say anything, and he was glad because he wasn't sure what he would have said.

It was strange, the things that made an impact of different people. For him, that simple gesture unlocked a slew of emotions from him. In three years with Sophia, she had never—not once—offered to pay for anything. She'd expected people to indulge *her*. Always. And they had, because she was pretty, and flirty, and exceptionally practised at being manipulative.

How had he fallen for it for so long?

Except that he already knew the answer. *Mild PTSD*, the army doctors had called it when they'd…*encouraged* him to leave after that final tour. Grief at the loss of his buddies.

He'd thought Sophia had been his saviour. An outgoing, breezy, fun-loving girl to breathe air back into his dying life.

He'd realised too late that she was demanding, volatile and avaricious. Well, perhaps not too late, or else he wouldn't have his incredible Jamie now. But certainly she hadn't helped to pull him up from that dark pit he'd been in.

King Roberto had done that. Though the old man would say Logan had done it for himself in the end.

'Right, here we go.' Kat bounced back into sight with a deliriously happy Jamie, his little hand still firmly lodged in hers.

'Okay, you get five tickets each and the categories are written on each of them. Come on, sweetheart, let's read them together and then we'll go and look at the trees. I'm sure I saw one with wellies all over it.'

'Wellies?' Jamie chortled into his hand in typical four-year-old fashion. 'Not real wellies.'

'Oh, yes. Real, bright red wellies,' Kat assured him. 'I think it was probably the coastguard's Christmas tree. What do you think?'

'I think that's getting my...' checking his tickets, Logan was determined to join in the fun '...*quirkiest* ticket.'

Kat beamed at him, and he couldn't stop his chest from tightening at her approval.

'Well, now, wait just a moment, we should see what else is out there first, don't you agree, Jamie?'

'No. Quirky wellies.' Jamie grinned up at him, and his heart swelled with happiness.

Even as she waggled her finger, Kat laughed.

'Oh, siding with your daddy, huh? I see how it is.'

For the next half-hour or so they wandered up and down, admiring the trees and choosing their winners, although the latter part became ultimately a matter of choosing one of any of the nearest trees as Jamie's attention began to wane.

And once again Logan marvelled at how instinctively Kat picked up on Jamie's mood changes a fraction ahead of him, and he was supposed to the parent.

'Time to go home, champ?' Logan asked, as Jamie wrapped his arms around his leg and nodded.

'Do you want me to take the bags so that you can carry him?'

Another touching gesture that Sophia would never have made. Not that she'd have even stooped to come to somewhere like this in the first place. Not even for Jamie.

Not unless some VIPs were attending and it was an opportunity for her to *network*. Or, in simpler terms, *social climb*.

'Thanks, but they're pretty heavy,' he declined, dragging himself back to the present. 'But if you can lift him onto my shoulders I can carry him too.'

'Yay! Shoulder ride.' Jamie applauded, but for the first time all night it was slightly muted, his tiredness showing through.

Logan bent his knees and dipped his head as Kat lifted Jamie up.

'I guess that's me, then.' She smiled as he stood up again with his son. 'I'd better be heading home.'

And Logan realised he didn't want her to go. He wondered if it was just his imagination—or wishful thinking—that her smile looked slightly fixed.

He scanned his brain for something, anything, to say, but it came up with nothing. Probably for the best. There were a million reasons why her coming back to his apartment was a bad idea. Not least to avoid a repeat of what had happened last time she'd been.

'Okay, well, thanks for joining us tonight.' The words felt thick in his mouth.

'I had fun.'

Another over-bright smile that Logan abruptly decided he hated on sight. His mind whirred for excuses even as he pretended it didn't.

'Didn't you say you lived close to me?'

She blinked, then looked sheepish.

'Yeah. I do. I pretty much walk past your door to get to my apartment.'

There was no reason whatsoever for him to feel quite so elated.

'Come to mine. I'll get Jamie down for the night and we'll call a cab for you.'

She hesitated, and he knew he had her. Victory coursed through him, though he couldn't have said why.

And he ignored the voice that said he just didn't want to *admit* it.

'The place looks like amazing,' she marvelled, as Logan handed her the key to open the front door and he carried a sleeping Jamie inside.

He'd fallen asleep mid-shoulder ride and Logan had been forced to give Kat a couple of the bags after all so that he could carry his son in his arms.

'It's like a grotto,' she continued, stepping a little further inside.

'Yeah, I know, I might have gone a little overboard, but in a way it's our first real Christmas together. I was always travelling such a lot.'

'As a bodyguard?' she asked wryly.

'Fine, as a bodyguard, yes.'

'For who?'

'You know I can't divulge that,' he replied. 'Feel free to head to the lounge. Or grab some wine from the kitchen. I'm just going to put this little man to bed.'

'Okay.' She kept her back firmly to Logan as she headed through to his lounge.

It felt as though she was walking on the softest, fluffiest clouds. He might not have confirmed who his VIP was, but he'd admitted that he'd been working as a bodyguard, which was more than he'd told anyone all day. And she knew that because she'd heard them.

She tried to caution herself that it probably meant nothing. But it didn't work. She felt special. Trusted by Logan Connors. It was an inexplicably heady sensation.

Wandering through to the kitchen, she stopped and surveyed the scene. A half-mutilated gingerbread man lay next to a knife on a kid's plate. Like a culinary crime scene. A pile of washed baking equipment sat, clean and dry, on a draining tray.

'That's one exceptionally tired little boy,' Logan announced, stepping into the kitchen through the far door and making Kat jump. 'Ah. I meant to clear up that horror story before I went out but everything was such a rush, and, well, time got away from me.'

'No need to explain, I understand,' she assured him, before realising that she'd almost begun talking about Carrie. Again. 'And it isn't too bad. It's just that poor gingerbread blob. What happened?'

'No idea.' Logan grinned. 'I've never baked in my life. I now realise it's an essential skill that I need to know.'

'Well, at least learn how to make gingerbread men look like they aren't gingerbread cacti.'

'Their undefined forms are the least of their problems. You didn't have to taste one.' He hung his head in feigned shame. 'Jamie was wholly unimpressed.'

'At least you tried.'

'It was for the hospital baking competition. He really wanted us to enter.'

'Is there a booby prize?' she deadpanned.

'Funny.' His lips twitched, and she had to fight to urge to step over to taste them again.

Just like the other night.

Taking a bottle of the festive drink she'd dared him into

buying, Logan collected two glasses and led the way back through to the living room, leaving her to follow.

'I could probably give you a few pointers,' she announced, out of the blue.

'Sorry?'

She lifted her shoulders.

'For your baking.'

'You bake gingerbread men?'

'Gingerbread folk, cookies, fairy cakes, you name it. I also make a mean frosting.' She laughed.

'For Carrie?'

And, for a moment, Kat could only stare at him. She felt physically winded. Then, just as quickly, she slipped her mask back into place and made herself answer.

'I was a foster mom.'

'*You* were?'

'Before I moved to Seattle,' she confirmed. 'I fostered quite a few kids.'

'Did something happen?'

'No, I just…changed.'

He eyed her intently and she tried not to squirm. Could he tell she was lying? He wasn't stupid. He would know that whatever had happened, it had to be significant. She'd not only moved across the country, she'd also given up a lifestyle she'd loved.

And then Logan surprised her with his soft tone.

'No wonder Jamie took to you so easily. You clearly find it easy and natural to relate to him, knowing just what to say to sweep away his…potential issues.'

'You're worried about abandonment,' she realised. 'You think that his mother's…lack of presence will leave Jamie feeling he was somehow at fault? Not good enough?'

She knew she'd hit the proverbial nail on the head by his taut features and locked jaw. But to his credit he dipped his head once in acknowledgement.

'So she *is* still alive. She just isn't in your lives any more?'

The silence stretched between them for an eternity, before Logan finally spoke. Biting out each word.

'She left when Jamie was sixteen months old. But do you want to know the worst of it? I sometimes feel it would be better if Sophia *had* died. At least that way I could lie to Jamie and tell him that she'd loved him very much, and she would never have left him if she'd had a choice. But then I feel guilty...'

He tailed off but she knew what he'd been saying and her chest constricted.

'You wish you could spare your son the pain and the *what ifs*. That's understandable.'

It was a dilemma all too easily understood. But another question clamoured for her attention, demanding to be answered. She would just have to be subtle about asking it.

'But what about you? Would that have been easier for you, too?'

Logan eyed her shrewdly.

'You're asking if I miss her? If I still love her?'

So much for subtlety.

'No. I don't still love my ex-wife,' he stated simply, and it was ridiculous how much her heart soared. 'In truth, I'm not sure that I ever really did. I think I loved the idea of her, but never really her.'

'Oh.' Whatever she'd been expecting, it wasn't that.

Logan shrugged, as though it wasn't that big a deal that he was talking to her, opening up to her, but she knew that it was. She could tell.

'I'd just left the army, not entirely by choice. I was angry, and lost, and in a bit of a grim place. I met Sophia and at first I fell for her bright, vivacious charms. Her partying lifestyle was so far removed from the world I'd inhabited that I could pretend to be someone else entirely.'

She wasn't sure it sounded like a solution. More like

trying to cover an amputation with a sticky plaster. She'd met enough former soldiers in her nursing career to know that the army had often been their lives. When they'd lost it, they'd lost their identities. And a few superficial parties weren't going to solve that.

Not that she felt she was in any position to voice that to Logan. But then it didn't matter, because he was continuing by himself.

'It took me twelve months to realise that I didn't like the person I was pretending to be. And that Sophia was avaricious, egotistical and self-centred. She used people until she'd exhausted what they could do for her, and then she cast them aside.'

'She married you because you were a bodyguard?' Kat guessed.

He pulled a wry face, his gorgeous eyes colouring to a hue she hadn't seen in them before.

'She thought it meant a glamourous lifestyle and access to lots of highly connected people. As soon as she realised my—our—life wasn't going to be like that, she left to move on to the next guy who could give her what she wanted.'

'But not before she'd had Jamie?'

'I'll never regret him,' Logan said fiercely. 'He's the best thing in my life. He makes everything worth it. But the truth is that I'd told Sophia that I wasn't ready for marriage or a family. She told me she was on the Pill, and then eight months after we started dating she got pregnant.'

Shock wound its way through Kat. Though she didn't know why, she'd seen it enough on the wards.

'She knew you would marry her.'

He pulled a grim face.

'Yeah. We lived on a small island. Everyone knew everyone else, and scandalous news travelled fast. She knew I'd *do the right thing*.'

'It must have hurt, though.' Kat frowned. 'When she left.'

'Not for a moment. If anything, the only thing I felt was relief for myself.'

'You don't sound too sure.'

He paused, and something she couldn't identify swirled around them.

'You think I'm bitter.' He offered a twisted smile. 'I'm not. I didn't love her. For pretty much two of our almost three years together, I didn't even like her, so I don't entirely blame her for walking out on me. But I can never understand, never forgive, how she could walk out on our son.'

Kat shook her head.

'No, I don't think you're bitter. I just think you're more like me that I realised.'

'Indeed?' his brow drew tight.

But she didn't want to explain herself. Not yet. But maybe someday soon. So she did the only other she could think of. She put down her drink, dropped to her knees on the rug between them and looked him straight in the eye.

'Are we done talking?'

CHAPTER SEVEN

THE QUESTION RUSHED at him, then pooled low and heavy in his sex.

The friction had been arcing between them all night, he'd lost count of the number to times he'd almost gone to her.

The last thing he had remotely expected had been that Kat Steel would take the lead. He found he rather liked it.

Perhaps too much.

'Be very careful, Kat,' he muttered.

'Or…?' she prompted gently.

'Or you may find that agreement we made to keep things platonic goes up in flames,' he growled.

She eyed him for a moment longer then simply shrugged her shoulders at him.

'Maybe I rather like the idea of setting fire to something for once.'

If he'd expected her to have second thoughts, he would clearly need to think again. And now he was restless, edgy. He'd wanted her since that first moment he'd seen her, and just now he'd ended up telling her a raft of private details he had never told anyone else before. *Ever.*

Maybe Kat was right. The time for talking was over.

Unable to hold himself back any longer, Logan sank onto the rug in front of her, moved his mouth over hers and finally, *finally* kissed her for the second time.

Thoroughly and completely, the way he had in every fantasy he'd had about her since he'd met her that first day in the hospital.

The way he'd been telling himself all night he didn't want to.

Kat didn't stop him. She didn't want to even try to. He claimed her again and again as her hands inched their way up solid biceps, greed and hunger pumping through her.

He tasted of cinnamon, with that kick of the festive wine they'd been sharing, and the memory of their afternoon together only made her feel that much closer to him. Then he slid his hand to into her hair and angled her head until he was kissing her deeper. More carnally, if that were possible.

She couldn't breathe. She was sure she'd stopped. And yet she could feel the slow, heavy thumping of her heart against her ribcage. Like the timpani drums she'd heard earlier, playing that medley of Christmas carols.

She had never felt so untethered and adrift. But she simply couldn't bring herself to care. All she wanted was Logan. Right here, right now. He was so very strong, was it any wonder that she trembled so deliciously from head to foot at the feel of his sublimely chiselled body covering hers?

He made her feel wanton, needy, and she couldn't get enough of him. She pressed herself closer, shamelessly rubbing herself against him, and the rough growl he made shook right through her.

Pure lust shimmered between them. It danced. It teased. She lost herself in it, letting her palms graze over his arms, then his shoulders, indulging herself and revelling in the pure physical strength of the man.

Kat hardly noticed when he slid his own hands down her body, hooking then under the hem of her jumper and pulling it up. But when he broke the kiss long enough to tug it over her head in a slick movement, she heard a low sound of protest that was so needy it couldn't possibly be her.

And then he was back, fusing his mouth to hers, and pouring so much into that kiss that she felt as though she might spill over from the sheer, dizzying thrill of it. He moved his hands to cup her backside and shifted them both in one efficient move that had him sitting on the couch and her sitting astride him.

She gasped and then, unable to help herself, she rocked herself into him. Her softness against his unequivocal hardness. And heat. *So much heat.* Her heart clattered louder at the dark flare in his eyes. So black it was almost feral.

Reaching down, she pulled her T-shirt up over her head and dropped it to the floor. Then she did the same for him.

Her insides lurched.

The man really was Comic Book God. Or, at least, the latter part. He had abs that even the fictional heroes would have coveted. Almost reverently, she reached out and traced every perfectly hewn contour. It should be illegal for any man to look so mouthwateringly irresistible.

And then, as if compelled by some unheard voice, she dipped her head and pressed her lips to the muscles instead. As if they were there purely for her pleasure. Her body was on fire. Her breasts felt heavy, her nipples too tight, and between her legs she felt molten.

Backwards and forwards, Kat explored. Right up until he lifted his hand and traced a soft line down the centre of her spine, and she lifted her head in question.

'I think,' he drawled, the thickness in his voice moving through her like slick oil, 'it may be my turn.'

Before she could answer, he dipped his head to her breast and drew one of the hard peaks into his mouth—lacy bra included—and she couldn't tell whether it was the frustrating barrier of the material or the graze of the lace against her already sensitive skin that sent her wild.

'More,' she muttered, arching her back—the action making her press down on him all the more urgently, that hard ridge of sheer masculinity flexing where she ached for him the most.

And then his hand was grazing her belly, sneaking lower and lower until he was toying with the waistband of her trousers and she thought she might go up in flames from the liquid heat that pooled between her legs.

The sound of the zip being tugged down, slowly, deliberately. And Kat thought she'd never heard it sound quite so deliciously rude before. But then the back of his hand was sliding over the front of her briefs and she stopped thinking anything at all.

There was nothing but the feel of one large hand cupping her backside, and the other hooking under the material to graze over her and then cup her, wet and hot, in the palm of his hand.

She feared she might break, humiliatingly, apart from just that single action.

Then his fingers began to move, tracing her, learning her, making her grow slicker and heavier with every stroke. But still making her wait. Torturing her with the tantalising promise of exquisite pleasure, which he kept Just. Out. Of. Reach.

'Logan...'

Kat bit her lower lip, helpless to keep the desperate longing from her voice.

'Tell me,' he commanded hoarsely, as if it was taking just as much for him to resist.

'You already know...' She tried to drop her forehead to rest on his shoulder but he wouldn't let her.

He shifted back until he could see her, until they were gazing at each other, and then finally—*finally*—he slid his fingers inside her, driving her to dizzier heights. And she, to what should have been her shame, simply threw her head back and rode his hand as long and as far as he wanted to take her.

Propelling her closer and closer to that magical edge. Making her entire body fizzle and ignite. And then he did something incredible with his hand, some twist and flick, and suddenly she was soaring. Shattering into a thousand pieces and raining down in a shower of colour and light.

Like nothing she'd ever known before. And Kat thought she might stay up there for ever.

Logan didn't think he'd ever been turned on so much in his life, watching Kat Steel come apart at that moment.

It had to be the most beautiful sight in the world, from her shocked, bright face to the white-hot heat on his fingers. And those naughty, ragged sounds were making him so incredibly hard that it was almost painful.

All he wanted was to be able to do it to her all over again. A part of him feared he would never be able to get enough of it.

But that was a concern for another day. Another night. Right now, he just wanted to be inside her.

Flipping them both around so that she was on her back on the couch with him between her legs, Logan slid his hands to grip the waistband of her trousers, wanting to lower his head and taste for himself what he'd just done to her.

And then, when he'd made her come part all over again, he would slide inside her and topple them both off the edge.

He was just about to slide her trousers down when she struggled upright and stilled his hand.

'What about Jamie?' she croaked hoarsely.

It was like a blast of cold air, and he had no idea how managed to stop himself. But he didn't trust himself to speak.

'He might come down the hall,' she continued after a moment.

But he thought that reminder was more for herself than for him, and he liked the fact that she was nowhere near to being in control. Certainly no more than he was.

'There's a baby gate,' Logan ground out, as he pulled her up into a more seated position and then proceeded to sort his clothing out. 'And we'd hear him.'

'Oh, I didn't...' She paused, stilling in her actions. 'I wasn't saying...you know, stop. I just—'

'We have to stop,' he cut in before she could say anything more. 'This is entirely inappropriate.'

Her eyes clouded over, a sort of shame flitting through them, and he hated that he made her feel that way, but he couldn't do a thing about it. If he started to explain it to her, he feared he might give in to temptation. Give in to *her*.

He didn't want to take her on the floor of his living room like they were a pair of sexed-up adolescents. And he certainly wasn't about to take her to his bedroom and have her stay the night when his four-year-old son was in the apartment.

Or at all, a voice rang out belatedly.

But either way it was a loss of control.

He was a father, not a single man. His only responsibility was to his son, and not bringing back random women to their home.

Except that Kat wasn't random. And Jamie adored her. But none of that was reason enough to let her stay the night and confuse Jamie when he woke up in the morning to find her there.

So, if he couldn't seem to control himself around this woman, there seemed to be only one other solution.

As if she could read his expression, Kat licked her lips nervously.

'You want me to go home?'

'I think that would be for the best.'

He sounded like a jerk, but that was just too bad. He could still taste her, *smell her*. And she was driving him crazy with need.

If he softened towards here, even for a moment, he feared he might be too tempted to finish what he'd started.

'I'll call a cab for you.'

Kat could feel the hot prickling behind her eyes, and it was a battle to hold her head up. To square her shoulders.

She could not let Logan see how humiliated she felt, or how much his rejection stung.

How it played on insecurities she wished she could stuff down.

After all, how could Logan's rejection compare to when Kirk had called off their engagement, throwing the one argument at her against which she could offer absolutely no possible recourse? Kirk had wanted kids of his own—*real* kids of his own, he'd said. He'd meant biological, and that had only driven his barbed little knife home all the deeper.

Of all people, she'd thought Kirk was the one person she could always rely on. They'd met as kids. Two fifteen-year-olds sitting on a ward, staring out of the window to the parkland beyond, watching normal kids do normal things whilst they were attached to a gamut of drips and needles.

They'd endured it all together. A team. Understanding things no normal, healthy kid could ever have appreciated.

He was the one person she had thought would always stand by her. Or, if he'd had to leave her, it would have been because they'd grown apart.

She would never have expected him, of all people, to have been so cold-hearted.

So cruel.

He'd made her feel worthless. Undesirable. Valueless. And she had let him, because he had been the one person who'd known exactly which buttons to press to hit every single one of her crippling insecurities. Every single fear they had ever talked about on those wards when life and death had been such everyday topics. When you walked into a room, scanned it, and worked out who wasn't there any more.

Clenching her fists, Kat indulged a little in the sense of anger. Because it was either that or fall back into the sea of self-loathing that had almost drowned her for years, until she'd found a way to pull herself out by her fingernails.

She wasn't about to let this man—a relative stranger, for goodness' sake—see how his words sliced through her. She was stronger than that.

Even if she wasn't, coming to Seattle was supposed to be her chance to reinvent herself.

Fake it until you make it—wasn't that what she'd told herself?

Straightening her shoulders, she made herself look Logan in the eye.

'I don't need a cab, I'm perfectly capable of walking.'

'Not at this hour,' he scoffed, but something flashed across his expression.

If she hadn't known better, she might have thought it was care. Then again, the guy was a decent human being. Just because he didn't want to…be intimate with her, it didn't mean he wanted to see her walk the streets alone at night.

'I only live a short walk away.' She tried to smooth her tone into something less prickly. 'The other side of the park.'

'Far enough for a cab,' he repeated, and Kat didn't know if it was the way he moved, or the tone he took, or a combination of the two with something else entirely, but she suddenly discovered that she didn't much care to argue with him.

There was something utterly focussed about him. Just like when he'd come into the ER on top of the VIP patient, saving his life.

When Logan Connors made a decision, she didn't imagine he was used to backing down.

She pitied anyone who tried to counter him on that hospital floor.

Kat forced a smile.

'Fine, a cab sounds like a good idea. Thanks.'

And it gave her a tiny victory that she now knew more about Logan Connors than she suspected he knew about her.

CHAPTER EIGHT

'WHAT HAVE WE GOT?'

As Logan stepped around the curtain to the consult bay, Kat snapped her head around for a split second, her eyes widening before resuming a professional demeanour in front of her patient.

But he didn't miss the tell-tale staining of her cheeks, or the way her hands shook, and he hated it that he was the one who'd caused it. He hadn't meant to hurt her, thought he knew that had been the result.

So, after his loss of control the other night, he had determined to stay away from the temptation that was Kat.

But he hadn't taken account of them having to work together. The least he could do was keep things strictly professional.

Dragging his eyes from her, he made himself focus on their patient. The guy was clearly in pain, but trying to stay tough. Kat edged a little further around the bed, enabling Logan to see for himself.

'Dean is twenty-four. He was out in the woods with his mates when stepped on a small animal trap.'

'It's bad, man,' the young man groaned.

'Yeah, I can see that.' Logan nodded, moving to assess the guy. 'I don't think you're going to need a surgical consult, but we're going to need to get it off now. The longer it cuts off circulation, the worse it can be.'

'Right,' Kat agreed uncertainly.

'Keep your hands clear for now, but you're going to move his foot as soon as it's free.' He indicated a part of the trap. 'I'm going to prise the jaws apart on three. You ready, Dean?'

Dean grunted in some semblance of agreement.

'Okay, here we go. One. Two. Three.' He pulled the jaws back and as the patient bellowed in pain, Kat quickly lifted his foot out of the way.

'Good. Nice,' Logan announced brightly, after examining the wound. 'All right, let's you get you cleaned up, stitched up and out of here, Dean.'

'What were you doing in the woods anyway?' Kat asked, keeping his mind distracted as Logan prepped the area.

'We were going to cut down a Christmas tree, you know? We share a house and money's tight and, well...'

'It seemed a good idea at the time?' Kat asked.

'Yeah, man.' He winced at the pain, but tried to smile at her. 'You think we're idiots, right? I bet your tree is all up and nice.'

'I don't think that at all,' she told him gently. 'And, no, I haven't got around to putting a tree up this year.'

'Yeah, but you will?'

'Sure. On my next day off.'

She sounded so offhand, so casual. Was it only him who could read that undertone of sadness? He wanted to understand. To know Kat better. And that realisation should worry him a hell of a lot more than it did.

He listened to their easy conversation as he finished up, then sorted out the paperwork for Dean before finally finding himself alone again with Kat.

'You're not intending to put up a Christmas tree at all, are you?' he asked without preamble.

So much for sticking to the strictly professional.

'Sorry?' She stared at him in shock.

'You told that young man you'd put up the tree on your next day off.'

'Ah, right.' She cast him a wary look but he liked it that she wasn't even trying to perpetuate that particular lie. 'I don't know. I thought I might not bother this year.'

'Nothing at all? Not even a mini fibre optic thing?'

He was teasing her, despite his cautions to keep his distance. She got under his skin far too easily. And he wanted her with a hunger that just seemed to keep growing.

'What's this about, Logan?' she demanded, her voice tight. 'One minute you're trying to throw me out of your apartment door in disgust. The next you're doing...*this*.'

'I wouldn't say *in disgust*.'

'I would,' she bit back, doing a good job of hiding the shake in her voice.

Just not quite good enough.

'If there was then it was disgust at myself. Not you.'

'For doing what you did *with me*,' she emphasised.

Everything screamed at Logan to walk away. To let her think that. Because if she did, then she wouldn't want anything more to do with him. And God knew he was doing a lousy job of keeping away from her.

He hadn't been this out of control with a woman since those first few months with Sophia. Had he really not learned his lesson from her?

Instead, he found himself grabbing Kat's shoulders and hauling her around so that she had no choice but to face him.

'Let's get one thing absolutely clear, shall we?' he ground out. 'Any disgust I felt was at losing my head with you on the floor of my blasted living room. With my four-year-old son in the apartment. It was *not* at you. Or at what we did.'

She blinked, and he could see the glistening in her eyes even as she tried desperately not to show it.

He wanted to say more. To reassure her further. He could have told her that he'd regretted his decision even before her taxi had left. That he hadn't been able to sleep all night, thinking about her. Imagining her. Fantasising about how things would have gone if they hadn't stopped.

But beyond that he wanted to tell her how she made him feel that he wasn't quite so alone. For the first time in a long time he'd felt carefree. Not weighed down by the task of trying to be both mother and father to his precious little boy. She had brought a renewed sense of fun into their lives.

He wasn't going to say any of it, though. He wasn't going to make things any more complicated.

'Jamie and I are going ice skating tonight.' The words were out before he could think about it. His mouth evidently choosing to ignore the commands the logical part of his brain was trying to issue. 'Join us?'

'Ice skating?' Kat echoed weakly.

'That's what I suggested.' He grinned, as though it was the most natural thing in the world to invite this woman to spend the evening with him. With Jamie.

Jamie like her, and as long as he managed his son's expectations, surely it couldn't hurt?

'Ice skating?' she repeated.

'Yes, in the park. For Christmas.'

'I...don't know.' She glanced away uncertainly, and he felt even more of a cad.

He needed to walk away.

'Call it my apology,' he pressed her.

'An apology.'

'I enjoy spending time with you, Kat. And Jamie certainly enjoys it.'

Her face softened.

'He's adorable,' she told him. 'No thanks to you.'

She was teasing him, or trying to. He fought to keep the grin off his face.

'Ice skating, then?

'Sounds lovely, but...'

She tailed off and as hard as he tried to stop his errant mind from wandering back down that path—from recalling just how perfectly mouthwatering she'd looked, *tasted*, half undressed, on his lap the previous night—it was impossible.

God, how he still wanted her.

Logan shifted. He felt edgy, waiting for her to agree. The air between them was beginning to take on that close, electric feel again, and he found he welcomed it.

It was far better than the distance between them.

'Unless you don't like ice skating, of course.' He suddenly decided to try a different approach. 'Maybe you don't like sporty activities.'

'I love sporty stuff,' she bristled, just as he'd known she would.

He ought to ask himself *how* he knew just what to say to push her buttons. Instead, he pretended to her—to himself—that this was news.

'Plus, I'm doing the Santa fun run.' She wrinkled her nose. 'So that's something sporty and something Christmassy.'

'Indeed it is.' He arched one eyebrow and was rewarded with a glare.

A flash of her old feisty self. And he found he welcomed that, too.

'You played me,' she accused.

Logan shook his head.

'I wouldn't say that exactly. But I think it could be fun tonight. And I know Jamie would love to see you again.'

She eyed him strangely. He squirmed a little under the

scrutiny. Another unusual response—since when did people make him feel...*unsettled*?

'Just Jamie?' she asked softly, at last.

The question caught him off guard. He knew the answer. Worse, he didn't like it. So he did the one thing he did best.

He took back control.

'It isn't a date, Kat.' He didn't know if he was reminding her or himself.

Still, he wasn't prepared for her to narrow her eyes at him and fold her arms over her chest.

Presumably she didn't know how it emphasised those perfect, soft breasts of hers.

'Rules, Logan,' she insisted.

He was irritated and intrigued all at once.

'What kind of rules?'

'It's an outing with your son. It's not a date. There will be nothing like what happened last night.'

'Suits me,' he agreed without a second thought.

And yet the moment the words were out, he hated the very sound of them. He shouldn't. It made sense.

'Listen, Kat, Jamie and I will be at the park rink from three p.m. Do you want to give me your address or will we just see you there?'

She bit her lip, clearly torn between wanting to join them and the same caution after the previous night. But then she lifted her eyes to his and he could have sworn something crackled through the space between them.

'Fine.' She nodded slowly, as if she couldn't help herself even though it went against all her instincts. 'I'll meet you there.'

Kat stared at the bustling ice rink and told herself that she didn't know why she'd agreed to come.

Only it wasn't true.

She knew *exactly* why she'd agreed to come. *Logan Connors*. He had such an effect on her that she was doing all the things she'd thought she wouldn't be doing this year. Not now that Carrie was no longer in her life.

She'd been dreading Christmas. Dreading the sight of the trees, which she'd imagined going to see with Carrie, dreading the festive songs that she'd envisioned teaching the little girl, and most of all dreading Christmas Day. Alone.

She'd come to Seattle to be as far away as possible from her old home and memories of the little girl she'd raised from a baby to four years old. She'd imagined retreating into herself for a while, and throwing herself into work whilst she took time to heal.

She hadn't imagined bauble shopping, Christmas tree judging, and ice skating in the park.

She certainly hadn't imaged riding Logan's hand, as she had done last night, until she'd splintered apart in a way she hadn't even realised was possible before. Or how, unless she was kept busy and distracted, she'd spent every moment of her shift today watching him move around the ward, fantasising about him playing with her like that again.

As though she was his to pick up and put down at will.

Then again, when he was the only man who had touched her like *that*—with such skill—was it any wonder?

The memory of it wrapped itself around her, dragging her back to the edge of madness. And she still couldn't bring herself to regret it. Or even to regret meeting him.

Logan—and Jamie—had bounced into her life when she'd needed them most. They lifted her, and made her feel part of something again. There was only one problem with that. What was she supposed to do when they were no longer there?

She didn't want to think about it.

'Kat!'

Spinning around, Kat laughed as Jamie darted up to her. She scooped him into her arms and hugged him tightly.

'Hello sweetheart, did you have a good day at the crèche?'

'It was great,' Jamie told her enthusiastically. 'I made a new friend. Tommy.'

'Super-cool.'

'We played dinosaurs.'

'Of course you did.' She grinned, lowering him down and straightening up again to look at Logan, almost shyly. 'Hi.'

He looked unreasonably fit and handsome as usual.

'Hi.' His blue eyes glittered and made everything inside her turn liquid. 'Are you ready for this?'

'If you mean can I ice skate? Then, yes, I can. At least, well enough.'

'Shame.' Those blue depths darkened. She would have said in anticipation. 'I had visions of having to hold you upright.'

She didn't want to shiver. She told herself not to. But the hint of promise in his words sneaked under her skin. Straightening her shoulders, Kat tried to act as though she couldn't think of anything duller.

'Well, it's a good job you don't, then, isn't it?'

He smirked as though he could read her thoughts and she felt a rattle of warning deep inside her. Something had changed with Logan, and she couldn't pinpoint what it was.

'This isn't a date, Logan.' She kept her voice low so that Jamie, who was mercifully absorbed with watching the skaters, didn't hear. 'You said it yourself the other day.'

'That was before I touched you. Tasted you,' he murmured, leaning in so close that she could feel his breath tickling her skin. Making her tremble.

'Logan...'

'I want you, Kat. And I want to get to know you.'

'I'm not... I can't... This isn't—'

'You want me to,' he cut in simply. 'You know my recently troubled past, and even thought I don't know what happened in your life to make you travel halfway across the country to take up a job here in Seattle, I know it must have been significant. Right now, we seem to be what each other needs. Why not just go with it?'

He made it sound so simple. So easy. When surely it should be anything but?

'Logan,' she whispered. 'You said it yourself, you like to compartmentalise your life. *Just going with it* isn't what you do.'

'And look how well that's worked out for me so far.' He pulled a self-deprecating face.

'So what is this? *Us?*'

Did that sound too presumptuous?

'We've both come to Seattle for a new start. I've returned home because I want to hit the reset button with Jamie, and you've left your old home because you want something different.'

'Last night I told you things I've never told anyone else—I've never wanted to.'

She told herself that his words didn't make her feel raw. Precious.

'I like the way you can relate to Jamie and understand what he's going through, and I like your company, Kat. I more than like it.'

'I more than like your company, too.' The words were out before she could bite them back.

His expression darkened.

'So why deny the sexual chemistry between us?' he demanded, making her mouth go dry. 'You once told me you wanted *"no-commitment fun"*. So if neither of us want a relationship, why can't we just enjoy time together for as long as it lasts, whether that's a week, a month? Two months?'

A *no-strings fling*? She wanted to agree, and yet something held her back. She didn't care to analyse it further.

'And Jamie?' she asked instead.

'You're helping me relate to him better, and I'm grateful for that. He's starting to spend time at the crèche now, making new friends, and soon he'll be starting school with plenty of female teachers to help be positive maternal-type figures in his life, additional to his Nana.'

It made sense. No need to balk at the idea of being so disposable.

'What about…if there's a repeat of what happened last night?' she hazarded.

Logan stepped closer but stopped just short of contact. The heat rolled off him, and she could feel the toes of his boots just pressing against hers, a kind of electricity crackling from him… Yet he didn't actually touch her. Like a kind of tantric foreplay. She could hear her breathing grow slightly ragged but was helpless to do anything about it.

'There will be no *if*, Kat,' he rasped. 'There *will* be a repeat of last night. It's inevitable.'

His words shook through her and all at once breathing became a complicated task. Last night had been a mere taster of what Logan could do to her, how he could turn her body inside out, and it had been incredible…right up until it hadn't been.

Right up until he'd thrown her out in all but words.

She didn't think her already broken sense of self-worth could take another battering like that.

'*Inevitable*, Kat,' he drawled, as though reading her mind. 'That chemistry has been there since the first day we met and, like all decadent things, denying it has only made it all the more of a temptation. So why deny it? It's just sex and we're both adults.'

There was a note in Logan's tone that licked its way deep within her. *Just sex*, he'd said. She doubted anything with this man would be *just* anything. Not if last night was anything to go by.

'Our only parameters will be that anything intimate happens when Jamie is at his grandparents'. Never when he is home.'

She needed to tell him that he was wrong. Nothing was ever going to happen between them again.

'Right.' She swallowed, nodding before she could stop herself. Unable to—or not wanting to—do anything else.

Kat felt herself swaying slightly towards him as he leaded in a fraction closer. It shouldn't have been possible to do so without touching her, and he didn't. He was so damned close she could smell him, woodsy, and lemony, and utterly male. It was driving her crazy.

'But for now we're skating.' He took a step back, as if realising they were in the danger zone. As if needing a buffer. 'All right, champ, shall we go and hire some skates?'

As the pair headed off hand in hand, she stood there for a moment, still trying to catch her breath and regulate her slamming heart.

'That was more fun than I remembered,' Kat told him a couple of hours later as they sat together on a bench, watching Jamie clamber up the baby climbing wall and onto the slide in the playground.

He had enjoyed the skating, taking it in turns to be guided around the rink by Logan, and then her, and then Logan again. But, inevitably, he'd grown tired and bored, so they'd taken him for hot chocolate and a play in the park.

It really was so easy between them. Both reading Jamie's mood, and adapting quickly without even a word. Logan was a better father than he realised. He just needed to stop trying to bear the load of his ex-wife abandoning them. He couldn't be both father and mother to the little boy, and he was doing a good job as he was.

Running her finger around the rim of her cup, Kat kept her eyes fixed on the kids, the unexpected urge to talk bubbling higher and higher inside her.

'Do you remember the little girl I mentioned I used to look after?'

She felt, rather than saw, Logan swivel his head to look at her.

'Carrie,' he replied instantly, and she was touched he recalled.

'She wasn't just anyone, but I figure you've already worked that out for yourself.' The words tumbled out one after the other. 'Carrie was actually my foster child. I had her from around ten months, after legalities had been dealt with, and when she was three I began the process of adopting her.'

Kat glanced at him briefly, unable to hold eye contact for long. It hurt too much to see the empathy in his gaze. Somehow it was easier to stare out into nothing.

'It was due to complete at the beginning of this year, just before her fourth birthday.'

'This would have been your first real Christmas together,' he noted softly, understanding immediately.

Her throat felt thick and clogged with emotion.

'It would have been,' she affirmed. 'Had her biological parents not cleaned themselves up and taken her back. That's why I came to Seattle.'

'You needed a fresh start in a new place where there were no memories of Carrie.'

'Right.' She lifted her shoulder, then let it drop. 'A move across the country seemed like a good start.'

'I can't imagine how much you must miss her.'

'Like you said, we're both here to press the reset button. And although I didn't plan on meeting you, you were right, we're both adults, and it's just sex.'

'Just sex,' he echoed. 'I did say that.'

'You did.' She couldn't name the odd lilt to his tone, but she couldn't afford to dwell on it. 'Transitory, no strings, no-commitment fun. Neither of us can offer the other any more than that. But, right now, that's all we need. Right?'

This was exactly what she'd told Gemma that she wanted, and this was what Logan was offering.

'That's what I'm saying,' he agreed, and again she couldn't shake the idea that there was an edge to his tone.

But then he straightened up and flashed her a megawatt smile that said he was wrapping up the conversation.

'I would kiss you,' he teased, 'but my son is over there and that would be breaking the rules.'

Kat laughed, in spite of everything. This was a framework she could understand. She could live with.

'Well,' she declared, standing up with a broad grin and lining up the perfect shot of her coffee cup into the bin. 'We wouldn't want to break the rules, would we?'

Before he could answer, she took the shot, turned around and jogged into the park to find Jamie.

CHAPTER NINE

'THIS IS LEO. He's seventeen, he was climbing trees when he slipped and fell, and he got crushed between a wall and a fence. His GCS was fifteen on arrival and he was complaining of reduced capability in his left arm and left leg. Tender at C2 and C3 with persisting sensory reduction in his left hand. We've seen no volume issues and he has been stable during transport.'

'Okay, thanks.' Logan stepped forward to take over from the EMTs. 'Hey, Leo, I'm Logan. I'm the ER doctor. My colleague here is going to draw some blood and I just want to listen to your chest.'

As Logan signalled to her, Kat stepped forward to greet the patient and get the syringe organised.

She felt strange. Not quite in her body, as if she was floating above the ER, watching everything unfold below her. Last night had been fun and revealing, in equal parts. She'd opened up to Logan in a way she'd never anticipated doing with anyone out here, even Gemma. Not that she'd told him everything, of course. Like they'd agreed, they weren't a couple, they were just two adults enjoying a mutual attraction for a while.

Questions slid into her head, but she shut them down quickly. They had their rules, and she'd thought she understood where she was with Logan.

This morning, however, he'd barely said two words to

her, unless it had been about patients. And maybe that was a good thing—they could concentrate on their work, and the patients gave them something safe to discuss. But she couldn't help feeling that he was regretting last night after all. Sex was one thing, but maybe opening up to each other was now against the rules.

It only made it all the more critical that she keep her eyes on her patient and her mind focussed on the task in hand. Working steadily, methodically. Letting the buzz around her wash over her. She was aware of Logan concentrating on the lad's leg and asking him to squeeze his hand harder.

None of the signs looked good, and Kat's heart sank on the kid's behalf.

It was a short while later when Logan called her out of the room, along with the rest of the team, whilst he carried out a preliminary bedside scan.

'Okay, I've called Neurology,' he advised them. 'Given that Leo can't feel anything when I palpate below a certain point, I want them to ensure he's stabilised before we risk moving him for a full CT.'

'Right,' one of the other nurses concurred. 'So we wait?'

'What other patients do you have?'

'I've got a possible mumps, a patient who has a cyst on her knee and needs it to be aspirated, and a probable asthma attack...' Kat's colleague listed them off.

Then Logan turned to her. 'Kat?'

'I have a dislocated finger, a young boy with lacerations that need suturing and a probable tetanus boost, and a patient with leg pain, possible DVT. I just need an ultrasound to check for a clot.'

'Fine, Kat, can you stay with Leo and let me know as soon as Neurology arrives?'

'Of course.' She slapped on a light, professional smile

as if that could somehow convince Logan that she wasn't thinking about anything she shouldn't be.

As if she didn't scorch from the inside out every time he looked at her.

It was driving her insane. Making her feel consumed. Leaving her itching too far beneath the surface to ever scratch.

And so she moved around her patient, carrying out a fresh set of obs and sitting down at the computer just outside the room to chart.

She was such an idiot. How had she let Logan—and Jamie—get so close to her? Lamenting something being *over* with Logan when common sense pointed out that nothing had ever really begun. Certainly a fumble on his couch couldn't be construed as anything of significance.

But it had been to her.

She'd already come to enjoy the time she spent with them. Both of them. So much for *no-strings, no-hassle fun.*

She was just finishing up her notes when she saw—or, more accurately, *sensed*—Logan coming back into the department and moving around the workstations towards her.

Kat began to swing round, jumping as she felt his hands, so electric, on her shoulders as he twisted her chair back, leaning over her as though he was reading something on her screen.

Only his breath was tickling her skin, and the blood was roaring in her ears, so it took her a couple of long, long moments to focus. And when she did, it wasn't at all the words she'd expected to hear.

'Don't turn around. Lots of flapping ears.'

Yes, there always were when the department was slightly quiet, as it was today.

'I thought I'd join you on your Santa run,' he told her unexpectedly.

'You want to do the charity run with me?'

It wasn't a big deal, so why did it feel like it was?

'I figured that if we started training together then it might give us a bit more of a legitimate reason to be seen around each other outside work.'

'You're worried what people will think?' she teased, more as a way of buying time to process how she felt about it than anything else.

'I figured we could do without having our relationship under scrutiny from the entire hospital.'

Taking a few surreptitious breaths, she fought to slow her racing heart.

He didn't mean *relationship*, she berated herself. And the training idea was a simple, effective solution to a legitimate concern. Nothing more. It definitely wasn't because Logan wanted an excuse to spend more time with her.

But she didn't care.

'We still haven't even kissed,' she pointed out as coolly as she could. 'Not since that night anyway.'

As though she didn't replay it, in startling clarity, every night in her head.

'Then maybe we can remedy that, too.' The corner of his mouth curved up until she could imagine that she could actually feel it against her skin.

'I think we should. You did promise me that at the start. *Just sex*, remember?'

'Oh, I remember,' Logan growled, and it sent a low rumble right through her.

'So, when do you want to start, coach?' She gave a bright laugh, proud that it didn't betray the gamut of emotions swirling within her. 'If I've got a former soldier training me, I should smash this thing.'

'Today,' he bit out. 'After our shift.'

She found she could hardly wait.

* * *

He'd never felt so damned horny out on a run before. Then again, he'd never run behind Kat before.

No matter how many times he dragged his eyes from that peachy backside of hers, they kept finding their way back. And the fact that she was wearing the tightest, sexiest one-piece running suit he'd ever seen certainly wasn't helping.

Part of it was the fact that they'd spent the past ten hours working together, and not being able to touch each other. The electricity between them had been building all day, like the most thrilling form of foreplay.

And now he was finding it exceedingly hard just to keep himself in check. And this was just the warm-up.

He felt like a randy teenager, and Logan had never been more grateful when she slowed to a walk…right up until she launched into her stretches. Starting with touching her toes.

'Jesus, Kat.' The breath whooshed out of him all at once.

Barely remembering to check no one was around them, he grabbed her hand and pulled her deeper into trees until they were out of sight of the main path. Then, practically throwing her against the oldest, thickest tree trunk, he pinned her there with his body, lacing his one hand through her hair and letting the other cradle her backside. He just about heard her muttering thickly about what had taken him so long, and then he dropped his mouth to hers and drank her in greedily.

It had been well worth the wait. She tasted of lust and desire, and he couldn't get enough. He kissed her for a long while—maybe years—feeling things roll through him, supercharging him.

Kat, for her part, clutched his arms tightly as though all she could do was hold on for the ride, and he found he liked that sensation rather too much.

He tasted her, and played with her, licking along her lower lip with his tongue, then plundering inside her mouth, revelling in every greedy, unrestrained sound that escaped her. And then he proceeded to explore her jawline, her neck and her throat as she tipped her head back and sighed with abandon.

He had no idea how much time had passed when they finally, reluctantly, came up for air.

'That's more what I wanted,' she whispered on a shaky little breath.

'You should have said earlier.' He might not be kissing her, but he still couldn't bring himself to release her. 'I could have accommodated it.'

'I'll bear that in mind,' managed Kat, moving one arm so that her hot palm was lying flat over his chest, travelling over the muscles beneath as though she was learning them.

'Anything else you wanted?' he rasped.

She looked up at him, her expression darkening, her eyes never leaving his. But suddenly her palm was moving lower, and lower again, until she was skimming past the waistband of his shorts and then cupping his length in her hand.

Need exploded within him and he drew in a sharp breath.

'Careful, Kat.' It was practically a growl. 'You don't know what you're doing to me.'

'Oh, I think I do.'

Then, with one slick movement, she slid her hand under his waistband, coiled her fingers around him and began to set a slow rhythm.

'Kat…' He breathed her name then muttered a curse, and she smiled softly in response.

'I've been wanting to do this ever since you touched me that night.'

'I've not been stopping you.'

'You haven't exactly been making it easy either.' He got the impression she was reprimanding him.

It wasn't an unpleasant experience.

He lifted his hands to caress her body, skimming his palms, his fingers, his thumbs over every delectable curve and hollow. Taking his time as his fingers danced down the length of her spine and his hands spanned her delicate waist.

And then he lowered his hands to her hips, taking the time to explore before tracing his way to the front, in between her legs. He revelled in her ragged breathing as he moved his hand back and forth, her wet heat so clearly evident.

But whilst the running suit clung so lovingly to every curve and allowed him to feel every inch of her through the material, he found there was actually no way in.

'This is a ridiculous garment,' he rasped, as Kat changed the pressure in her grip and made him feel as though he was spiralling out of control.

'It's meant for running,' she whispered, amused. 'Not for other…um…*activities.*'

She twisted her wrist and a low, guttural sound escaped him.

What she was doing felt so good, but if he didn't put a stop to this now, he feared he wasn't going to be able to, and he refused to embarrass himself right here.

'Not here.' Lowering his hand, he encircled her wrist, stopping her and freeing himself.

'Logan…'

He looked up. They were approximately in the middle of the park, part way between her apartment and his. But they only needed one apartment.

'Jamie isn't due home for a couple of hours,' Logan bit out, adjusting himself. 'We can go back to mine.'

'Then hurry up,' she urged. 'Because I was rather en-joying myself there.'

'You'll enjoy yourself more when I can touch you,' he promised. 'And taste you.'

He exulted when her eyes darkened with undisguised desire.

Then, interlocking his fingers with hers, he turned them both around and led them back to the main path.

Kat could barely believe she'd been so bold back there in the middle of the woods where no one could see them.

She wasn't sure she'd ever felt so wanton or daring in her life. But, then, she'd never felt as desired as she did when she was with Logan—when he wasn't throwing her out of his apartment, that was.

If it hadn't been for her clothing, she was sure she would have let him take her right there, against that tree. He made her feel like the most beautiful, craved woman in the world. And she liked how strong she felt she was becoming, the more time she spent in his company.

Hunger and need coursed through her every time she saw him. It was a heady experience, and one that she found she liked more and more.

Wordlessly, they ran through the park together. A thousand times better than the training run she'd expected. Nonetheless, her pulse thrummed frantically throughout her body as they reached his apartment building and he reached for her in the elevator. Her throat, her wrist, even her knees. And especially between her legs.

He crushed her into the corner of the elevator, and Kat reached around to hold his backside, nestling him right where she needed him most, driving them both wild as he devoured her with his mouth, leaving her panting and desperate.

She had never burned like this before. *Ever.*

They barely managed to tear themselves apart as the lift slowed and the doors pinged. They tumbled out and half ran, half walked down the corridor to his apartment. And then Logan was unlocking the door and pulling her inside, his T-shirt already off his body and on the hallway floor.

'Daddy?'

The sound of Jamie's voice from in the kitchen had them springing apart. Snatching up his T from the hallway floor, Logan had just about pulled it back on as his son came hurtling around the corner.

'Look who I found, champ,' he declared as Jamie came to an abrupt halt and gazed at Kat in delight.

Kat tried to smooth her hair and then, in vain, reduce the flush from her cheeks before a woman, who had to be Logan's mother, followed. Tall and slim, she wore her hair in a tight topknot, but there was no denying the elegant way in which she carried herself.

'Hello, Logan, dear. We got back early so... Oh, hello.'

Forcing a smile, Kat tried not to feel like a teenager caught heading up to her boyfriend's bedroom.

'Mrs Connors.' She extended her hand in greeting.

'Kat, this is my mother, Zula. Mom, this is Kat,' Logan instantly took control. 'Shall we go through to the living room rather than congregate in the hall?'

And as he ushered them through, Kat was shocked when she felt his hand on the small of her back, as though to lend her support.

She pretended that the gesture didn't mean as much as it did.

'She came to see me.' Jamie jumped up and down.

'Of course she did, pumpkin,' the older woman agreed, but Kat didn't miss the amused glint in her eye.

Kat didn't doubt for a moment that Zula had noted both Logan's hand on her back, as well as the fact that his T was inside out. And as nonsensical as it was, given the nature of their non-relationship, Kat found herself wanting to make a good impression on the older woman. So when he enveloped her in a huge Jamie hug and asked her if she wanted to play dinosaurs, she heard herself saying something altogether different.

'Actually, sweetheart, your daddy told me that you wanted to bake gingerbread cookies but they went wrong.'

'Yuck.' Jamie nodded instantly.

'Well, how about if you and I go and make a batch together now whilst your daddy and nana talk. Will you help me weigh out the flour?'

Just as she'd hoped, he could barely contain his happiness, and she let Jamie lead her through to the kitchen. She didn't dare to turn and look at Logan for a moment.

CHAPTER TEN

'I WON MEDAL!' Jamie cried, pride and jubilation bursting out of every flailing limb as he showed off his race medal.

'Careful, champ.' Logan laughed. 'But that looks amazing. You're a winner.'

Swinging his son into the air, Logan held the little boy aloft as Kat's gaze dropped from the delighted four-year-old to the man who was beginning to dominate her life. And not just because of the way he affected her body—although, as she tried to keep her eyes off Logan's rippling abs, a taut knot was already forming in the pit of her belly.

Her libido seemed to be in a permanently heightened state these days. No guesses as to why.

'We all got medals,' Jamie announced, wrenching her attention back up.

She told herself that was a good thing and lifted her hand up to Jamie's, to be rewarded with an enthusiastic high-five.

'Wow, that's super-amazing. Are you going to hang it on your bedroom wall?'

'Yes, yes, yes.' Jamie wriggled excitedly on his dad's shoulders, then his expression turned grave as he peered down at this father and Kat. 'Now, you have to win medals, too.'

'I can't promise anything, champ.' Logan laughed as Kat shook her head.

'I'll just be happy to finish, Jamie. I'm nowhere near as fast as your daddy. Maybe I should have done the kids' fun run with you.'

Besides, if Logan's parents didn't find them soon, to take Jamie, they wouldn't be running anywhere.

'You not twelve.' Jamie frowned, citing the upper age limit for the race.

A bubble of laughter rose through Kat. It happened more and more these days—always around Logan. Could it only be a year ago when she'd feared she might never laugh again?

'You're right,' she told the little boy. 'I'm not twelve, so I guess I would have been too old for the fun run.'

Jamie didn't look impressed.

'Not old,' he told her airily. 'Kind. Pretty.'

'Ah, thank you, Jamie.'

'Good recovery,' Logan added dryly, and as Kat looked at him, his eyes swam with a warmth that heated her very bones.

'We'll run together.' Logan shrugged, responding to Kat's earlier comment. 'What's the point of training together if we run separately?'

Her stomach flipped and rolled deliciously, but she tried to keep her grin light.

'The point,' she told him, 'is that you are competitive enough in training. You always push yourself that bit harder. I'm grateful for all the pacing and motivational speeches and all that, but I think I'd rather run at my own pace and enjoy the run.'

And not be distracted by him. Not that she was about to voice that one.

'It's a race.' He frowned before he could help himself, making her laugh again.

'Case in point.'

'Fine. We'll run separately. I didn't want to show you up with my costume anyway.'

'You have a costume?'

''Course!' he exclaimed, pulling items out of his rucksack. 'It's a Santa Dash after all. I have a red tutu and a green elf hat.'

Of course he did, because that was so typically military of him.

'It's a fairy dress.' Jamie eyed his father critically.

'It's a Christmas fairy. Good, huh?'

Jamie looked distinctly underwhelmed.

'Fairies are for girls. They're pink.'

'Who told you that?' Logan bent down to smile at his son. 'There are just as many boy fairies as girl fairies.'

Unexpectedly, he glanced over and winked at her, and her heart vaulted with all the energy of an Olympic gymnast. It was nice to be drawn in as though she was part of their little family.

'And they might be pink,' Logan was continuing, oblivious to her momentary distraction, 'but they don't have to be.'

Jamie still looked unconvinced, but now there was clear doubt in his mind. As he turned his focus back on his race medal, Logan turned to face her.

'I brought a set for you, too.'

'I like the way you handled that,' she told him quietly, before she could change her mind.

'I like the way you handle a lot of things.' He winked, and she tried not to flush, even though every inch of her body was tingling at the insinuation.

The past week they'd seen each other every day, not including the shifts they'd worked together. They'd been running together, taken Jamie out for festive treats, and had even decorated another room in Logan and Jamie's apartment.

They'd broken the rules and stolen a few kisses—heavy,

and passionate, and ultimately all the more frustrating—in every corner of his apartment, as well as empty consultation rooms at work.

But they still hadn't had a chance to be alone, and finish what they'd started that night.

It was driving Kat crazy. Her body felt like a messy melting pot of wicked desires and unfulfilled urges. She felt a permanent restlessness under her skin, like her body wasn't quite her own. Like she was ready to explode.

She craved him more and more, and not being able to have him was only making that hunger all the more intense.

'Don't tell me you're too afraid to put them on,' he baited her, holding up a second costume.

He was throwing down the gauntlet, and she was trying to think up a witty response. Then those wretched eyes of his twinkled mischievously at her, and they both knew she was lost.

'Fine.' She feigned a heavy sigh. 'Throw it over here.'

A green tutu and candy cane hat sailed through the air, and she shook her head she pulled them on.

But this was the side of Logan that she liked the most. The goofy side. Pulling the kind of stunts he'd pulled with his army buddies. She knew, because she'd seen the photos and she'd heard his stories.

And she'd tried not to read too much into it when he'd told her that she was the first—the only—person he'd told this stuff to since he'd been discharged from the army.

She was helping him. And that was okay because he was helping her, too. But when this...thing—whatever it was—between them ended, what then?

And it *would* end. That had been the agreement from the start.

Shoving the moment of apprehension to the back of

her mind, Kat tugged the tutu over her running shorts and rammed the hat on her head, just as she heard Jamie's shout.

'Nana! Gramps!'

Embarrassment burned through Kat even as she lifted her head to Zula, and Logan's father, smiling as widely as she could as the greetings were made.

Of course they would head over just as she looked a fool. Well, she could be embarrassed or she could own it, and the fact was that it shouldn't matter to her *what* they thought of her. It wasn't as though she and Logan were... anything. *Right?*

'There.' She bounced her head comically, making Jamie and even Logan's parents laugh. 'How's that?'

'Very festive.' The older couple smiled and Jamie clapped his hands in approval.

'Pretty Kat.'

And then Logan stepped forward between the three of them and her, making a show of adjusting the headband, the expression on his face making heat pool low, between her legs.

'Very pretty Kat,' he murmured, too quietly for anyone but her to hear.

The moment stretched out and, in that instant, Kat thought he was going to kiss her, right there in front of everyone.

Worse, she was standing there unable to move, unable even to breathe, waiting for him to. *Willing* him to.

And then he turned away sharply.

'Okay, the race will be starting soon so we'd better get going.' He stopped and dropped a kiss on his son's head. 'I want to hear you cheering, champ. The louder you shout, the faster I run—got it?'

'Got it,' Jamie parroted back happily.

'See you shortly.'

Then Logan was grabbing her hand and heading off. Almost as if they were a proper couple after all.

'What do you think, champ, will it do?'

Jamie eyed his father's first-place trophy with awe.

'It's 'mazing,' he breathed.

'Want to hold it?'

Jamie held out his hands reverently, sucking in air through his tongue and his teeth as he concentrated on not dropping it.

'Hardly fair competition, really, was it?' Kat chuckled quietly. 'You're a bodyguard and former soldier.'

'And Christmas fairy, let's not forget.'

He flicked his tutu and Kat wondered how on earth it was possible for it to make him look even *more* masculine, rather than less.

Possibly it was the all-too-broad, muscled shoulders and the chest that she kept dreaming about licking. Every hard ridge and every defined curve.

'So where's a fairy godmother when you need one?' she grumbled, only loud enough for him to hear, and certainly not expecting a response.

She almost leapt out of her skin when Zula appeared at her shoulder.

'Why, here, dear.' Logan's mother smiled impishly.

'Oh, I didn't... I wasn't...' Kat stumbled. She certainly hadn't been meaning Zula when she'd mentioned a fairy godmother.

'I'm teasing.' The older woman laughed, before turning to her beloved grandson. 'Gramps is just finding the car, but we'll be leaving soon. Shall we drop the trophy off at home for Daddy and you can get your overnight bag?'

'I'll walk you to the gates, Mom.' Logan put his arm around his mother, who batted his arm away good-humouredly.

'I can walk myself, I'm not decrepit yet. You just concentrate on saying your goodbyes to Jamie.'

Kat watched them wordlessly. Something about the way they interacted crept under her skin and wound through her, making her think of her own family. Had she done the wrong thing by pushing them away all this time?

She'd believed moving away had been for the best; that it would hurt too much watching them so happy with their own families. Now she was beginning to wonder if being part of them might actually have helped her to heal instead.

'Fine. Have a good weekend trip.' Logan offered his mother one final hug. 'I know Jamie has been really looking forward to it.'

'So have we.' Zula smiled. 'Hope you have a good shift at the hospital tomorrow. And you too, Kat, dear. Well done on the race.'

As the older woman strode elegantly ahead, ready to flag down her husband, Kat followed behind with Jamie and Logan.

It had been a nice day and Logan's parents were so welcoming, it had almost been like being back with her own loving family. Almost.

Ahead of them, a little girl was being swung between her mother and grandmother as they walked around, and Jamie stopped abruptly and spun around with excitement.

'Swing, Daddy?'

'I don't know, buddy...'

Logan glanced at Kat discreetly, not putting her on the spot but giving her the opportunity to decline.

'Swing?' the little boy pleaded.

'Sure.' She grinned, ignoring the unexpected pang in her chest as she thought of the times Carrie, too, had watched children being swung between two parents without ever being able to enjoy it for herself.

Did the little girl's biological parents do that now that they had her back?

Was Carrie's life better with them this time around? It had to be because no one had been in touch with her in the past year. And that was a bittersweet notion.

'Come on, little man.'

Shaking off the momentary melancholy, Kat held her hand out for an excited Jamie to grasp, then counted down with Logan as they swung the boy high into the air between them whilst he shrieked with delight. And as Logan turned to mouth a word of thanks to her, she told herself it didn't send a tremor of pleasure through her.

She told herself she was imagining this...*bond* that was budding between them. And, still, as they passed an older lady creeping slowly along the path towards them, Kat couldn't help returning the woman's indulgent smile with a wide grin of her own.

Right up until the old lady spoke.

'I have to tell you, dear, that you have a lovely family.'

'I... Oh...' A thousand answers chased through her head.

What was she supposed to say? That this wasn't her family at all?

'I—'

'Thank you,' Logan cut across her, flashing his trade-mark charming smile at the woman as they continued past.

It was all Kat could do not to drop Jamie's hand. Her face felt tight—rictus—with the effort of not crumbling. The effort of keeping Jamie swinging, as though her chest wasn't cracking, was almost unbearable.

As though she didn't want to curl up in a ball right there on the pathway.

But, somehow, she kept going. The silence a deafening howl between them.

'Hey, buddy, is that Nana and Gramps just ahead?'

Logan stopped a few moments later as a car pulled up just by the park entrance.

Relief rushed through Kat. Surely the timing couldn't be more opportune, she decided as Jamie dropped their hands and begin to career ahead of them across the grass to his grandparents.

Tentatively, Kat tried to breathe again.

Out. In.

'She didn't mean anything by it,' Logan said quietly, as she snapped her eyes open to realise he was watching her carefully. 'That woman, I mean. She couldn't have known that we aren't a family.'

And even though, logically, Kat knew that he was trying to make her feel better, it only made the pain sear all the hotter inside her.

We aren't a family.

The words echoed even louder as Jamie shouted a final goodbye and waved alongside his grandparents and Logan waved back.

The fact was that Logan, and Jamie, and the little boy's grandparents *were* a family. She was the only outsider here. The one who wasn't part of them. The one who didn't have a family—at least, not one she saw any more.

Through her own choice. And not, as she'd always pretended, because they were scattered all over the globe. They were living their lives. Having families of their own. And she hadn't been able to bear it after losing Carrie.

A fresh lance of pain stabbed through her, almost crippling her. Reminded her how utterly broken and lost and defeated she'd felt when the little girl had been taken from her.

For the little girl's sake, she'd clung to the hope that Carrie finally had her own, true family back. But for her own sanity she'd decided that she could never again go through that torture of loving a child so deeply, only to completely lose them.

But rather than protecting herself, was she really just hanging onto the pain?

Kat wasn't sure that she could tell any more. Confusion threatened to overwhelm her.

'I know that woman didn't mean anything by it.' She would have preferred it if her voice didn't sound so clipped, so distant, but it was better than giving in to the emotion she was only barely keeping at bay right now. 'Still, people should watch what they say, and not make assumptions.'

He eyed her again and she tried not to squirm under the scrutiny.

'Do you really hate the idea of kids that much?'

Her chest kicked. Hard.

How could he read her so well in one sense and yet not at all in another?

'I don't hate kids at all.' She reached tentatively for each word.

'I didn't say you hated kids,' he corrected calmly. 'I've seen you deal with plenty of children in the hospital, and you're a natural. I asked if you hated *the idea* of them.'

She wanted to answer but she couldn't. She couldn't even think straight.

'You're wonderful with Jamie, too. But there's something...*guarded* about you. I can't figure it.'

How was it that someone who had known her for barely a couple of weeks could read her better than the colleagues she'd worked alongside for months?

It was simultaneously thrilling and daunting.

It made some secret, mutinous part of her want to stop desperately trying to contain all the bubbling emotions that seemed intent on spilling out all over her, and just...*talk*.

She could feel the logical, superior part of her brain battling to smother it. To regain control. And it was succeeding.

But not before her tongue let loose for a moment.

'I don't hate the idea of kids. I...'

Can't have them.

She trailed off, horrified at the way the admission hung there, tainting the air. Casting a bleak shadow on what was meant to have been a fun day. *Ruining* it.

Only Logan didn't look like his day was ruined. He looked very much as though he was interested. Worse, he looked as though he *cared.* And she didn't think she could stand to see the compassion in his gaze.

It made something inside her shift when she needed it to stay as resolute as ever.

As she stood there, wondering what she could possibly say next, the sky darkened, there was an ominous rumble, and the rain dropped straight from the heavens down on top of them. Soaking them right through.

And still she didn't move. She didn't care.

Not until Logan grabbed her hand and ran towards the park's glass pavilion.

CHAPTER ELEVEN

LOGAN DIDN'T CARE much for what was going on deep inside his chest.

This low heat. The dark hunger that seemed to scrape away at him every time he was with this one woman. Weakening and exhilarating him all at once.

The Santa Dash was over and they should be going their separate ways, yet he couldn't tear himself from Kat even now. He could tell himself all he liked that it was merely about the sexual attraction but he knew it wasn't true.

She'd been about to tell him something out there, before the rain had started. Before she'd clamped her mouth closed and made it clear that she regretted uttering a single word. It was ridiculous how badly he wanted to know what that *something* was. That was emotional connection, rather than physical.

It was as though it was another piece to the backward puzzle that was Kat Steel. The kind of jigsaws that Jamie and his nana did together, where the picture wasn't the one you saw on the box but merely the other side of the so-called camera. A clue. A hint. But not the real person.

It should concern him that he wanted, so badly, to put that puzzle together and understand who Kat Steel really was. A wiser man would have walked away.

But he wasn't sure he'd been a wise man for the past six years or so. Ever since that last tour of duty. He felt as though he'd been lurching from one thing to another. Isola Verde, bodyguarding. Sophia.

For Jamie's sake he'd known he needed to ground himself. And since returning to Seattle he'd felt more like his old self. It would be foolish of him to pretend that the time he'd spent with Kat—ice-skating, Christmas decoration hunting, going on runs—hadn't also played a part.

She'd helped him without realising it. Now he found he wanted to help her, too.

'Kat—' he began, but she cut him off quickly.

'Don't.' Her eyes were fixed on his shoulder, staring at it intently as though she could see right through the skin and bone.

He tried to stop himself from hooking a finger under her chin and tilting her head up, but it was impossible. He needed her to look at him. To *see* him.

It made no sense.

'Please,' she choked out.

Reluctantly, he moved his hand from her chin. The questions squatted heavily in his chest. As if it didn't tear him up to bite them back.

She looked so vulnerable. So broken. She looked the way he had felt six years ago. If only he knew why, maybe he could help her.

But to what end?

Logan's mind raced, and he was helpless to stop it.

Did she really hate kids so much that she couldn't bear even a stranger to think that Jamie was her own? And, if so, what did it even matter to him?

It didn't matter to him.

Thrusting his hands into the pockets of his hoodie, Logan marched to the glass panes and stared out at the heavy grey-black sky. Clearly, somewhere along the line he'd given Kat the impression that he wanted more from her than anything they'd agreed, and she was panicking.

He didn't know why that notion should generate this… feeling in him that if he hadn't known better he might actually have mistaken it for *hurt*.

But it couldn't be. Of course it couldn't be. Because he was no more looking for more from Kat than she wanted from him—they'd agreed *no strings*, and that suited him just fine.

And if a part of him was balking at the idea, then he was determined to dismiss it as the misguided notion that it was.

Now he just needed to convince Kat of that.

'I'm not asking you to be Jamie's family,' he ground out, not sure why he was still speaking. 'He has a family. He has me.'

'I didn't think, for even a moment, that you *wanted* me to become anyone's family.'

Her voice was sharper and higher than usual. Clearly she didn't quite believe him. In hindsight, crashing her charity run only to then drag her along when he was with Jamie, as well as his parents, had been too much. Understandably, it had sent the wrong message when they'd only ever agreed to being casual.

'We agreed no strings, and that hasn't changed for me.' Gallingly, the words almost stuck in his throat. 'I presume it hasn't changed for you?'

God, how he hated those shutters across those expressive eyes of hers. And was it only his imagination that had him wondering if she hesitated just a fraction too long?

'Kat…?'

'Of course not,' she threw out abruptly. 'No-commitment fun, that's what we said.'

'So why let some random comment from a stranger get to you?'

She glared at him, her teeth worrying at her lower lip. He had to fight to drag his gaze away. But it was the misery in her eyes that seemed to reach into his chest cavity and pull.

'Forget it.'

'Happy to,' he managed breezily.

For what seemed like an eternity they stood opposite one another. Not speaking. The only sounds were of the rain pounding off the glass and their breathing.

'I should leave,' she choked out at length, spinning around to stalk to the door. Rain be damned.

She didn't just mean this pavilion. Kat was ready to walk away completely.

And a wiser man would have let her.

Instead, Logan found himself crossing the space between them, his hands reaching for her shoulders, compelling her to turn and face him.

'What the hell's going on, Kat?' She snapped her head up at his tone but didn't pull away. 'We've been having fun, haven't we?'

He waited for an answer, but when she didn't speak he carried on. Her proximity was making his blood heat. Hotter, thicker than ever.

'Nothing heavy,' he ground out, no longer sure who he was trying to convince. 'Just enjoying each other's company, like we said?'

'Yes,' she admitted reluctantly.

'So what's all this about? Some stupid comment from someone who doesn't know us from Adam?'

Her eyes scanned his, and he got the sense that a million thoughts were racing around in her head.

And he hated that he ached to know every single one of them. Without realising what he was doing, his hand encircled hers and he found himself stroking the skin on the back of her smooth hand. So much for this very conversation being about reinforcing the fact that they didn't owe each other anything like that.

'I like spending time with you, Kat. And you like spending time with me, too.'

It wasn't a question, but with a faint bob of her head she answered it anyway.

A strange sense of victory punched through him. She still wanted to be with him. She just didn't want the additional complication of Jamie.

It was the wake-up call he hadn't even realised he'd needed.

He never should have allowed her to become so entangled in his son's life. He never would have if she hadn't been the one to have found Jamie that day in the park. Or if she hadn't brought Terrence to their home that night.

But that was then.

As long as he kept things just to the physical chemistry between them now, they should be okay. And if a tiny part of him whispered that he might want more after all, he was quite prepared to crush it until it was dust.

He'd been there with Sophia—letting his heart rule his head—and look what had happened. How her abandonment could have hurt Jamie. He would never put his son through anything like that again.

Not that he would compare sweet, kind Kat to the charming but calculating Sophia.

Nevertheless, keeping Jamie's life drama-free had to be his priority. From now on he needed to keep his private life and his family life in separate and distinct compartments. Jamie was his everything. Kat was simply fleeting fun—as she'd just reminded him.

And whilst he shouldn't have needed the reminder in the first place, he wasn't prepared to risk blurring those lines again. He would take this one night together then he would let Kat go.

One more night and then he would get back to the real world.

* * *

The pavilion was cold but dry, and they'd been in there for the past five minutes, deliberately not speaking. Kat couldn't get warm.

She should have walked away when she'd been feeling strong. When the hurt from Logan's comment about not needing her in his family had still been raw. When it had reminded her of exactly how it had felt to be rejected by Kirk.

Only Kirk was the last person on her mind. It was a shock to realise that she'd barely even thought about how unwanted he'd made her feel ever since she'd met Logan.

It wasn't the same, she knew that, but being sexually desired by a man like Logan eased any number of perceived scars left by someone like Kirk. So much so that Kat had begun wondering if she had ever really loved her ex-fiancé at all.

Had she stayed with him all those years because she couldn't imagine her life without Kirk? Or because she couldn't imagine a life *with* anyone else?

'It's dying down now,' Logan said suddenly, peering out of the rain-drenched window. 'We'll be able to get out of here in a moment.'

But it wouldn't have mattered if there had been a storm going on out there, it wouldn't have come close to the one raging inside her right at that moment.

She was still painfully aware of her hand in his. The way his thumb was stroking the back of hers. And that dark, hungry look in his eyes.

Her stomach flip-flopped. He wanted to kiss her, there was no mistaking it. And she, heaven help her, was willing him to.

'The rain has stopped,' he murmured, leaning his head in that fraction closer.

Just not quite close enough.

'Right.' Her voice felt scratchy.

'We should leave,' he gritted out.

Only he wasn't moving any more than she was.

She couldn't. She didn't want to break this moment. Even though it had already been broken. A firework display was going off inside her body right now and suddenly she wanted to be bold. And daring.

'I live less than half a block away.'

The words were out before she could have second thoughts.

His blue eyes gleamed.

'Is that an invitation?'

Her heart pounded louder. Harder. This went against every bit of common sense. There was something about Logan Connors that had sneaked under Kat's skin. Letting him get closer was inviting danger.

But suddenly she wanted it—*him*—too much to care.

'It's an invitation,' she managed.

And it was all the more thrilling when Logan didn't ask a second time. He simply bowed his head, gripped her hand that little bit tighter, and led them out of the pavilion so fast that she had to walk-jog to keep up. A gurgle of excitement threatened to spill out of her, and she just about managed to swallow it back down.

No need for him to realise quite how nervous or impatient she felt.

'Where, exactly?' he demanded gruffly.

Kat fought to keep her voice low as she gave him the address. Letting him lead her as they dodged through the crowds also pouring back onto the paths now that there was a break in the weather.

She bit her tongue. Was it just her who felt as though they were swimming against the tide, the only two trying to head in a different direction from everybody else?

For fifteen minutes they weaved their way along and

then, at last, they were outside Kat's building. Her whole body trembled. And it had absolutely nothing to do with the fact that she was rain-soaked and windswept.

Wordlessly, she led him into the lobby, sent silent thanks for the vacant elevator and jabbed her floor button with her finger.

He barely even waited for the doors to close before he backed her into the wall and claimed her mouth with his.

In all her life Kat had never felt so wanton. So daring. She wrapped her arms around his neck and surged against him, pressing her body as close as humanly possible, letting the heat from his body sear into hers.

She forgot that they were both cold and wet through. He warmed her from the inside out. More than that. He scalded her, and she welcomed every single second of it.

His body was so hard. Sculpted and perfect. And she wanted to wrap her body around every single inch of it. She ran her hands up his arms, revelling in the feel of those solid biceps under her palms, exulting in the exquisite pain as her tight nipples chaffed against his chiselled body.

She wanted more. So much more that she was afraid she would never get enough.

The doors pinged open and Logan reluctantly pulled back from her, making Kat realise that she'd never even felt the lift stopping. Hadn't even realised it had been slowing. She'd been too caught up in this. In Logan.

It should have been the warning she needed. But it wasn't.

Somehow they made it out of the lift, along the corridor and to her door. She fumbled with the keys a couple of times before he slid the set out of her shaking hands and slid the correct one into the lock. The door opened and they fell inside.

Finally, they were alone. There were no more safety nets. And Kat knew there was nothing left to stop them.

He kissed her. Over and over, demanding and giving, his mouth branding her, his tongue invading her, and she welcomed every second of it. She pressed herself to him again, but this time she found the barrier of their wet clothes to be a hindrance she couldn't stand. She shivered, partly with the thrill and partly with the cold, and when she dropped to hook her fingers under the hem of his T and began to lift it, he stayed her hands.

'Logan…' she protested.

'I have a better idea.' He cut her off roughly, a certain thrilling urgency to his voice.

Then he lowered his hands to her bottom and lifted her up, wrapping her legs around his hips. The hardest, most male part of him nestled into the softest part of her, sending an unexpected jolt through her, sending everything suddenly so white hot that Kat gasped.

'The bedroom's over that way.' She had no idea how she managed to speak.

The feel of his shoulder muscles bunching under her fingers was almost too incredible. And then he began to move, carrying her as though she weighed nothing, his mouth never leaving hers.

She wasn't sure when it occurred to her that he wasn't in her bedroom but her bathroom, and he was flipping on the shower until steam rose from the all-too-inviting hot water.

'It isn't exactly built for two,' she began.

'Then it'll make it all the cosier.'

The look he shot her was nothing short of carnal, and when Kat shivered again she was sure it was for a completely different reason than the cold. He was reaching for her again, kissing her with the same hot intensity as before and stripping them both with such efficiency that she hardly noticed they were naked until he swept her up and carried her into the shower, the hot water like another kind of bliss on her cold, clammy skin.

And then he tipped a generous handful of shower gel into his hand and began to soap her body in what had to be the most incredible foreplay she'd never known to exist. He started with her neck and, moving in small, circular movements that only seemed to move a few millimetres at a time, he began to slowly work his way first down one shoulder and then the other.

As though they had all the time in the world.

He moved down one arm, worked the foam down to the elbow, and then he switched his attention to the other arm. He worked it down from the elbow to the wrist. And then he repeated it on the other side.

Then he knelt down, repeating the whole process down each of her thighs then each of her calves, his mouth so close to her sex she could practically feel his hot breath blowing on her, making her belly clench, and a fire blaze unbelievable brightly.

'Logan,' she muttered, her eyes feeling heavy as she stared down at him, the throbbing between her legs excruciating and exhilarating.

'Patience,' he ground out, and deep in the recesses of her mind it occurred to her that he was barely keeping any more control that she was.

He soaped every inch of her whilst the water sluiced it off, all the while taking his damned sweet time, like an exquisite form of torment. Feeling his big hands all over her body but never where she ached for him most.

Finally, he turned her round so that she was facing the shower wall and worked his way over every inch of her back. And at last he slid his hand around to her front and he began using his magic there.

Kat could hardly even stand. Her legs felt weak with a longing, a *yearning* so fierce it almost floored her. She swayed back into Logan, subconsciously seeking strength there, but the feel of his hard chest up against her back, and his arousal pressed into her backside, only made things all the more dizzying.

And still Logan didn't stop. With one hand he cupped her hip, whilst the other hand drew whorls and swirls over her chest, scorching her skin wherever he touched but always, always skimming tantalisingly past her nipples. Never quite touching them.

Until she ached so much she thought she might die if he didn't take her. And that she'd die if he did.

He lowered his head, letting his lips graze her neck, and Kat heard a low moan as she tilted her head to grant him better access. It took her a moment to realise that moan had been from her.

Still, *still* he raked his hand over her body, down over her ribs, her abdomen, fleetingly to the juncture of her body and her legs and then slipping back up again. Need juddered through her again and again, and Logan simply laughed that low, raspy sound of his and carried on teasing her.

Finally, he let his fingers dance over her skin to take one taut nipple in his hands…and he rolled it.

Lust rocketed through Kat—along with something else she didn't care to examine at that moment. Instead, she gave herself up to the slew of sensations that rolled through her as Logan experimented, as though he had all the time in the world to get to know her. To learn what she liked, and how. He increased the pressure, and he released it. He drew patterns and he used his palm to abrade her skin.

Every stroke, and flick, and roll stoked the fire within her until the dull throb right *there*, at the apex of her legs, had grown into a deafening roar.

When she had long since gone past the point of being able to bear it, he grazed the back of his hand over her side, her hips and right to the place where she was molten for him. Kat cried out as his skilful fingers slid into her slick folds and he began to stroke her.

Sensations walloped through her. All she could do was revel in the feel of his hand between her legs, his impossibly chiselled body at her back and his wicked mouth on her neck.

It was too much; yet not enough.

She was lost.

And she didn't think she ever wanted to find her way out.

Higher and higher, Logan stoked the fire inside her. Every flick of his finger sending shudders of pleasure right through her. As the rhythm grew, he slid a long finger inside her, making her feel hotter, and wilder, and almost mad with need. And Kat could feel herself hurtling towards the edge.

And then, suddenly, he twisted his hand and sent her over. Spinning and spiralling, like a twisting Catherine wheel, and every bit as beautiful. She braced against the tiles just to keep herself from falling, and she gave herself up to every last, perfect second.

She had no idea how long it took her to come back down, but when she did Logan was still there, holding her, kissing her.

Twisting around in his arms until she was facing him, she looped her arms around his neck and pressed her lips to his, rocking her hips into him until his hardness was pressed into her newly wet heat. He grunted. A low, wholly male sound of appreciation that made her feel the hunger all over again.

Pulling back from him, she flashed him a wicked smile that she hadn't even known she possessed, and dropped to the shower floor, right in front of him. With her hands braced against his mouth-wateringly muscular thighs, she poked out her cheeky tongue and licked him—all the way up his length.

* * *

Watching Kat run her clever tongue over him, from base to tip, was one of the sexiest things Logan had ever seen.

He'd been pleasured this way in the past, yet no woman had ever come close to having the effect on him that Kat had. Physically and emotionally. She made his legs feel as though they weren't quite there and his brain feel as though it was swimming.

He felt light-headed and greedy all at once. Not helped by that dark, almost hungry expression in her eyes as she knelt there, looking up at him. And then she suddenly tipped her head forward and took him right into her mouth, and he thought he was about to come apart there and then.

Sliding his fingers into her hair, more to anchor himself than to exert any pressure on Kat, he watched her as she used her mouth, her tongue and her hands to set a cataclysmic pace that he feared would make him lose what little control he'd thought he had left. She licked him, sucked him and even grazed her teeth on him, just the right amount to have him groaning with the sheer gluttony of it.

Then she gripped him tighter and he realised he wasn't going to keep a rein on himself at all if he didn't stop her. *Now.*

'No.' Pulling back, he cupped his hand at the back of her head and urged her to stop. 'Not like that.'

She looked up at him with an unexpectedly devilish pout.

'Spoilsport. Like what, then?'

It was possibly the most sensual response he could have dreamed of. And it was nearly his downfall.

Shutting off the water, he grabbed a towel, patting briefly and only half effectively at them both, and loving the rumble of her laughter. Then he scooped her up and carried her out to the bedroom, lowering her almost reverently on the bed.

'Like this,' he growled, moving his body to cover hers as he nudged her legs apart with his knee.

'This,' she sighed dreamily, shifting her hips and winding her legs around his waist obligingly, 'is something I can live with.'

'Wait,' he groaned, reaching over to the bedside table and retrieving a pack of condoms.

'Brand-new. Untouched,' she noted, and he rather liked what that said about them. And about what they were doing.

'Brand-new,' he confirmed, deftly sorting himself out despite his fingers feeling as though they were fumbling in his haste.

And then, done, he thrust inside her with long, steady strokes, a sense of triumph punching through him as she gripped his shoulders and arched her back in pleasure.

One thought coursed through him.

Mine.

It was misplaced, and inappropriate, and Logan didn't care. He could tell himself that it was just about the physical, the sexual, the chemistry, but there was clearly a part of him that wanted more.

That wanted *Kat* to want more.

But it was ludicrous, and this wasn't the time to think about such complications. Besides, he didn't *want* to think about them. He just wanted to concentrate on the here and the now.

She was already so wet and ready for him he had no idea how long he could last.

He pulled out and slid in again, slightly deeper this time, feeling her stretch gloriously around him, seeing her head push back into the bed as she gasped his name. When he bent his head to take one proud nipple into his mouth, she raked her hands down his back and cupped his backside, taking him even deeper.

'Careful.' He barely recognised his own voice, it sounded so feral. 'I don't think I can do this for long.'

'I'm counting on it,' she bit out, lifting her hips up to meet him, rocking into him, tightening around him.

It was too much. *She* was too much.

His whole body was going up in flames, and all he could do was thrust into her, matching her movement for movement, hearing her groan as he did, even her breath entwined with his.

Then she was urging him on, curving her back up to press her breast into his mouth, clutching at him and making the most erotic sounds. He saw precisely the moment the wave overtook her. The way her eyes closed and she moaned and bucked.

Mine. Always mine.

As she cried out his name, he finally let go and followed her into perfect oblivion. And he wondered how he'd ever thought one night would be enough.

How was he supposed to go back to the real world after this?

CHAPTER TWELVE

'YOU DON'T HAVE any Christmas decorations at all,' he noted
a couple of hours later when they'd finally stopped reaching for each other and realised they were hungry for something else altogether.

So now they were sitting in her pretty, homely kitchen-
living-room-diner, eating take-out that they'd ordered and
chatting as if they were an actual couple.

Logan realised he liked the sound of that more than he
might have thought.

It was peculiar, the way Kat seemed to have unlocked
some door inside him, and suddenly all these possibilities
that he would have balked at—even up until a few weeks
ago—no longer felt so outlandish.

It was like a light was spilling out from behind that door,
with Kat the source of it. And Logan wasn't quite sure how
to contain it all. Or even if he wanted to.

'I didn't get around to it,' she answered automatically,
and they both knew she was lying. 'Fine. I didn't want to.
Christmas isn't…well, it isn't my favourite time of year.'

She didn't offer anything more but this time he wasn't
prepared to let it go.

'Really? That surprises me.' He shot her a grin. 'You
have a ton of photos of what is clearly a great family unit.
And the way you've been getting into Christmas with
Jamie I'd have thought you loved this time of year.'

'Don't flash me your best charm-the-awkward-patient grin!' She arched her eyebrows at him, but she was laughing. 'But, yes, they *are* photos of my family.'

'One of your brothers is in the UK and one is in Oz?'

'You remembered?' She seemed surprised.

'I remembered the fondness with which you talked about them. I know you miss them.'

'I do.' She wrinkled her nose. 'I keep promising myself I'll visit them. Maybe one of them next year, and the other the year after.'

'If you don't have your own family.'

He didn't know what had made him say it but her face clouded over instantly.

'I won't have my own family.' Her teeth were gritted.

It was as though she was trying to hold the admission back but couldn't contain it.

Surely he ought to feel guilt that he was the person prying something so clearly personal out of her? But he didn't feel anything like guilt. If anything, he felt something urging him on all the more.

'Want to talk about it, Kat?'

For a moment she just stared at her almost empty plate. Abruptly, her head snapped up and she glowered at him.

'No. I don't.'

'You're sure? Because you look like you want to talk.'

She narrowed her eyes at him.

'We went through this in that pavilion. We agreed— again—that this thing between us was about sex. Nothing more.'

'It's just a question, Kat.' He feigned nonchalance.

'A very personal question. We had sex, I opened my body to you.' Her words were choppy. Unrehearsed. 'I *didn't* agree to open my personal life to you.'

The silence stretched out between them, and he could feel her fury and something else—something altogether too much like *fear*—bouncing around the room. He wanted so badly to understand, even though he knew it was none of his business. But not now. Not yet.

He needed to break this silence between them.

'Great sex.'

Her brows pulled into a frown.

'Sorry?'

'We had great sex. Not just sex,' he deadpanned.

She hesitated.

'What are you doing, Logan?'

'I'm lightening the mood.' He shrugged, his heart hammering.

'Oh. Well…' She wavered, clearly trying to pull herself together. 'I'm glad you think so.'

'You don't? It was the way you screamed my name that gave it away.'

She blushed faintly and he found it surprisingly becoming. Still, she wasn't backing down.

'I may need another demonstration just to be certain.'

'I'm sure I can oblige,' he drawled.

'You don't need to get home for Jamie?'

'Jamie is going to spend the next couple of days on a road trip with his grandparents whilst I'm on call tomorrow, and I have that hospital fundraiser on the twelfth.'

'I keep forgetting about that.' She pulled a face. 'I can't say I enjoy fundraisers either. And before you say it, yes, there are plenty of things that I enjoy.'

'I know there are. Running and ice-skating for a start…'

'Right.' She bobbed her head gratefully. 'Great sex with you, for another.'

This time there was nothing subtle about her flush. A stain of fiery red spilled over her cheeks and extended down into the soft T she was wearing. It made him want to rip it off her and explore exactly *how* far.

It was the effect she'd been having on him ever since

they'd first met. Yet having her tonight hadn't satiated that driving need. If anything, it had only deepened the thirst.

'That's one hell of a blush for someone who was so bold in that shower.'

'Maybe I felt more confident there,' she tried to quip.

'And you don't now?'

'Not when we're talking about hospital fundraisers.' She was diverting the conversation, but he let her. 'I never really know anyone and it's all about networking.'

It was on the tip of his tongue to ask her to go to the ball with him. As his date.

Logan stopped himself just in time. He might have realised that he was only lying to himself by pretending that this thing with Kat was *no strings*, that some traitorous part of him didn't want more, but that didn't mean coming out to the entire hospital as a couple.

The question still remained: *how much more did he want?* How much more did Kat want?

Up until a month ago he'd had no intention—no desire—to even date. The ground was shifting so fast beneath his feet that Logan could hardly keep his balance. Yet there was a vast distance between a one-night stand and taking a colleague on a date to a work fundraising ball.

He refused to think beyond that because anything more—never mind with a woman he'd met a scant few weeks earlier—was truly preposterous.

Of course it was.

And yet…there was no escaping the fact that Kat got under his skin a way no one else—not even Sophia—ever had.

His head felt insanely jumbled. But it wasn't the worst sensation. He watched her reaching for another spoonful of chicken with stem ginger and one of egg fried rice, already knowing just how she would fold the two together on her plate until it was mixed just the way she liked it.

She was definitely edging her way into his life and he couldn't seem to make himself object to it. If anything, he was beginning to…grow accustomed to it.

Kat looked up unexpectedly, flushing as she caught him watching her. And then, flustered, she blurted out a question he hadn't been prepared for.

'Have you visited your…employer recently?'

'Say again?'

'The whole hospital knows you visit him regularly, and it isn't in your capacity as an ER doctor. Why?'

Logan wasn't sure if he stopped breathing.

'I'm not sure…'

'It's just small-talk, Logan,' she said pointedly, apparently pulling herself together as she threw his earlier words back at her.

He could concede her point. He had asked her personal questions about herself whilst never having told her anything significant about his own personal life.

In a career of being a military trauma doctor, and then another as a bodyguard to King Roberto, he had long since perfected the art of a poker face. Yet right here, right now, sitting across the table from a woman who made him feel…*things*…he hadn't felt in years—*or ever*—he found he couldn't deceive her.

He didn't want to.

'Which question do you want me to answer first?'

Kat stared at him.

'Any. I know you visit the man you brought in, even though he's in a coma now. I wondered if…if you felt the accident was somehow your fault.'

It floored him, how well this woman seemed to read him.

'Maybe I do. In a way,' he began slowly. 'My head knows that's nonsense, but my heart and my gut sometimes think I should have done more.'

'No,' she refuted. 'I read the report. The parts that weren't redacted anyway. There was nothing more you—anybody—could have done.'

It felt better than it should, hearing her say those words.

'I know that,' he conceded slowly. 'Most of the time.'

'But you still feel guilty?'

'It's complicated.'

She bobbed her head.

'I guessed as much. But try me.'

And as he sat there, watching her, he wondered if it was time to finally let go of his past for good.

'Like you said,' he began, awkwardly at first, 'I was a military trauma doctor before I became a bodyguard, and I did multiple tours of duty.'

She waited silently when he paused. Not pushing him. Just waiting until he was ready.

Logan drew in a deep breath.

'During my last tour there was an ambush. I lost some good buddies and I ended up quitting the forces.'

'And you became a bodyguard? Why not just practise medicine in a civilian hospital?'

He fought back the images that assaulted him. Demons he had battled so many times over the past few years. He hadn't thought he'd ever get hold of them, but then Jamie had needed him and he'd had no choice. And the longer he'd pulled himself together for Jamie, the more he'd begun to believe that he *could* heal.

Bit by bit, the night-terrors that had woken him, screaming and sweating, had begun to get fewer. To the extent that he'd known it was time for him to move on from protecting Roberto Baresi and return to medicine.

Yet now, for the first time, it occurred to Logan that the nightmares had practically stopped altogether these past few weeks.

Because of Seattle, obviously. Not because of Kat. And

yet he couldn't deny that she had played a part in helping him to feel so at home, so quickly.

'I wasn't ready to return to medicine initially, so a friend recommended this role as a bodyguard.'

'Must have been some role,' she commented. 'The hospital rumour-mill is rife with speculation.'

'And your guess?' he asked, casually.

Kat looked unimpressed.

'I don't guess. If people wanted me to know, they would tell me.'

Logan didn't care to analyse what shot through him at that. He'd expected nothing less from Kat, and yet he felt vindicated all the same. She was exactly the woman that he thought she was. Compassionate, loyal, discreet.

'I was bodyguard to Roberto Baresi,' he confessed, and instantly it felt like a weight lifting from his shoulders. 'He was...*is*...the King of a place called Isola Verde.'

Kat didn't answer. He hadn't really expected her to. Yet it felt good, sharing that burden with her. The guilt and fear he'd felt ever since that car accident. The gnawing worry that he could have done something more. Something to stop the accident in the first place.

'You were a king's bodyguard?'

'I was.'

She sucked in a long breath then shook her head.

'Wow. I mean, *wow*. So that's why you said your wife married you for the glamourous lifestyle?'

And suddenly, whether it was because of what he and Kat had just done, and the fact that he suddenly felt different somehow...changed, Logan couldn't have said. Either way, he found himself talking about Sophia without the slightest bit of the resentment or anger that had threatening to colour his words in the past.

'Sophia was beautiful. Charming. Manipulative.' He shrugged. 'Only I couldn't see it.'

'Why not?' Kat asked, and there was no challenge in her tone, only interest and care.

Everything that he knew her to already be. Everything that his ex-wife had never been.

'I was fresh out of a theatre of war. A tour that had gone bad. I'd lost men—friends—and I was in pain. She was skilled in reading people, you might call her a social chameleon. And maybe I also saw what I wanted to see.'

'You had a void, and she presented herself in the perfect shape to fill it?' Kat guessed.

'That's a pretty accurate way to put it,' he conceded. 'I don't doubt that she was probably running from her own demons—maybe she still it—but she was attracted to the status I had as a royal bodyguard, accompanying the King wherever he went.'

'I remember you saying it was a glamorous lifestyle.'

Logan pulled his mouth into a self-deprecating smile.

'The King's life was glamorous. Mine was not. But I didn't realise that's what Sophia had been after until it was too late.'

'Until Jamie was born.'

Logan thought back to the first moment when he'd cradled his precious son in his arms and how, in that instant, everything had changed.

'I took one look at him—my son—and I realised that none of the baggage I'd been carrying around from my military days was worth passing on to this innocent baby. I realised what I'd been missing for the past few years. I also realised what Sophia really was.'

'Is that when you left her?'

'She left me.' He shrugged. And, for the first time, he realised it no longer scraped inside him as it once had. She no longer mattered to him. 'She realised I couldn't give her the lifestyle she craved, so she found someone better suited.'

'And Jamie?'

'He was a means to an end for her.' Logan screwed up his fists instinctively.

Sophia might no longer have any kind of hold over *him* but it still ate him up inside that Jamie would have to grow up without a mother who loved him.

'Is that why you don't, can't—*won't*—entertain a relationship with anyone else?' she demanded. 'Because Jamie has to be your sole focus?'

It was insane the way Kat seemed to read him so easily. Or perhaps that was the point, that it wasn't *insane* at all. It was all too telling. He wanted to tell her, to open up to her. But how could he tell Kat anything when he was still working it all out for himself?

'So you don't wouldn't want to meet someone? Get married?'

He opened his mouth to say *no* yet, startlingly, something stopped him.

A month ago he would have hesitated for a second, the idea of marriage having been locked behind a heavy-set door in some pitch-black, far-away corner of his mind. Oddly, he still couldn't imagine marrying again and yet, at the same time, that door was visible again. Heavy-set and locked, but no longer in such a dark, remote place.

'Maybe,' he hazarded. 'One day.'

'Someone to settle down with in Seattle perhaps?'

With anyone other woman, he might have thought that she was fishing. Putting herself up for the role. But this was Kat—not Sophia. Still, he wasn't sure how to answer that right now.

'I don't know. Perhaps.'

And he actually meant it. Still, he was conscious that the more he answered, the more edgy and uneasy Kat was becoming. He couldn't fathom it.

'One day maybe you'll have a sibling for Jamie.'

There was something too bright and too hectic in her eyes for Logan's liking. Like he was saying all the wrong things to her. And yet he'd felt that connection when they'd been in bed together before. Why was she fighting it so hard?

'It certainly isn't something I've given much thought to,' he answered after a moment. 'But I guess one day, in the future, it's possible. I was an only child and it was sometimes lonely. However, that certainly isn't something I'm considering now.'

'But, one day, it's a possibility you would want that?'

And it suddenly occurred to him that when he looked at Kat he thought that perhaps one day, he actually would. There was that damned shifting sand again.

'I won't rule it out,' was all he said.

But when she snagged his gaze, holding it and making some of the raw emotion simmer down, he thought he could read something in her expression that went deeper.

And as she snatched her eyes away and turned to look out of the window beside her, he suddenly wished he knew how to read this enigmatic woman.

Kat swallowed hard, relieved that she had disentangled her gaze from Logan's, and admitted to herself, for the first time, that she was in way too deep.

It had been creeping on so slowly—right from the start—that she hadn't noticed it. Or she had been able to pretend that she hadn't noticed it. But she couldn't keep lying to herself any longer.

Never mind the *just sex* agreement. She was beginning to fall for Logan Connors. And that absolutely couldn't happen. She had to end things now. Before she couldn't end them at all.

Misery wound itself through her.

He wanted a family. And children. Maybe not now, but

someday. Yet, no matter how many days, weeks, months passed by, she could never, ever be the one to give that to him.

She needed to get out now.

He came over as she was staring out of the window, her arms pulled tight across her chest, staring into the darkness of the night.

His arms slipped around her easily, his breath tickling the back of her neck, and she had to fight back the sudden thought that she could have happily stayed like that for the rest of the night.

For the rest of her life even.

'Forget what may or may not be in the future. Can't we just focus on the here and now?' He broke the silence. 'Come with me. Be my date to the ball.'

She felt like she was cracking open. That quickly.

That easily.

'We agreed *no dating*.' She barely recognised her own voice in that hoarse whisper.

'Fine.' She could feel him shrug against her back. Controlled. Unconcerned. The exact opposite of the way her own heart was beating so fast in her chest she feared it might beat its way out entirely. 'Don't call it a date.'

'You just did,' she forced herself to point out, whilst he lowered his head further, his mouth grazing the back of her neck and sending her thoughts spiralling.

'Then it was a poor choice of words. I apologise.' He grinned, and she could feel his teeth skimming her skin. He didn't sound remotely apologetic. 'I take it back.'

'You can't just take it back.'

'Sure I can.'

And it was terrifying how desperately she longed to accept. It sounded like such an innocent suggestion—a simple date. But the truth was that there was nothing *simple* about it.

Going to the hospital ball as Logan's date would send the entire hospital rumour mill into overdrive, and the last thing she wanted to have was her colleagues gossiping about her.

But more than that, going as Logan's date would be as good as accepting that whatever was going on between them went beyond the physical act of sex. It would mean acknowledging that she wanted more from Logan—and Jamie—especially after the comment that old woman had made as they'd been swinging Jamie through the park.

She could still feel the pain that had sliced through her in that split second. Much like the pain that had sliced through her a few moments ago.

Wanting so much *more* that it was like looking into the deepest, blackest abyss, knowing that if she fell she would never climb out again.

And she couldn't do that. She *wouldn't*. Not after Carrie. Not after all that had happened. She couldn't risk opening up her heart again, only to go through that pain again.

'Kat?' His voice broke into her thoughts, soft and concerned. 'What's wrong?'

If she told him, that would be it. Over. And she wasn't ready.

She just needed one more night, one more touch, one more taste.

She had to have that one final memory that she could cherish for ever. Long after Logan and Jamie were out of her life.

Cranking up her smile to mega-watt level, Kat shook her head.

'Nothing is wrong at all.'

He wasn't buying it for a moment.

So she did the thing she knew that would work. The only thing she knew to be the truth between them.

Twisting around in his arms and pushing him back so

that they could see each other, Kat hooked her fingers under the over-sized shirt and pulled it up and over her head, so that she was standing in front of him completely naked.

Her nipples pulled tight as the cool air caressed them. But, then, with Logan's gaze on them they would have anyway.

And he dropped to his knees, right there, and hooked one of her legs over his shoulder, until she was leaning back against the wall, her hand threading through his hair and her breathing ragged in the mere anticipation of his touch.

He waited. So infernally long that she thought she might die, then, at last, he pressed his mouth to the inside of her thigh, laying waste to her wherever he kissed. He moved up and down the thigh, lifting her foot so that he could trace his kisses, and his tongue, all the way down to the back of her knee. Over and over, until her supporting leg was shaking and she feared it might collapse beneath her.

And then he carefully unhooked her leg from his shoulder and turned his attention to her other leg.

How was she ever going to live without this? How had she ever thought that *no strings* with a man like Logan could even be possible? He made things shine brighter in her than she'd ever thought they could.

But wasn't that the problem?

Because she was coming to rely on that light too much. She was coming to need it. So when it was gone—and it would be gone, at some point or another, for the same reason that perfidious Kirk had left her—she risked being smothered by the sheer blackness of it all.

And if Kirk's rejection had left her feeling abandoned, undesirable and worthless for all these years, it would have to be a hundred, *a million* times worse to lose someone like Logan.

Unless she controlled it herself.

Unless she was the one who chose the moment to walk away.

But for now she lost herself in the feel of Logan's mouth on her skin. The softness of his lips, the wetness of his tongue, the graze of his teeth. Back and forth, up and down, almost tormenting her in how close he could get to where she *ached* for him without actually touching her.

And then, just as she thought she could stand it no longer, Logan slid his hand up to hold her in place, nudged her legs wider with his shoulders, and licked.

Straight into her core.

Kat cried out. She called his name and grabbed his shoulders for purchase, and when his low laugh rumbled through her, she thought she might splinter and come apart right there and then in a white-hot, blinding light.

Nothing would ever be this good, this *perfect*, again.

Logan used his tongue and his teeth, making her ride him and propelling her closer and closer to the edge. She was shaking apart in his hands, and still he held her there. Right up to the moment when he sucked on her. Long, and hard. And she catapulted right over the edge into oblivion.

She had no idea how long it took to come back to herself, but when she did she realised Logan had carried her across the room to lay her down on the rug in front of the fire, and he was lying next to her, watching her with a smug smile of satisfaction.

'Next time you want to shut me up, try another distraction,' he suggested. 'Just remember what I can do to you if I want to. And I always want to.'

Something clenched low in Kat's belly at the words. So accurate, so glorious, and yet so terrifying. She thrust them to the back of her mind. Her one last memory wasn't complete yet. But it would be.

Before he could react, Kat reached out to push him

onto his back, straddling him, fitting him into her heat without letting him slide inside. Then she leaned down and pressed her breasts to his chest, her mouth kissing the hollow at his throat.

'Is this supposed to be your punishment?' he demanded.

'Think of it more as a demonstration of what *I* can do if *I* want to,' she murmured, rolling her hips against him and relishing Logan's guttural moan.

So undiluted. So carnal.

He muttered her name and she moved again, like a reward, coating him in the slickness he'd just created. And then, when she was ready, she edged up and forward until he was nudging her entrance with his blunt tip.

For a moment she held herself there, her eyes locking with his as though they could somehow transmit all the things she couldn't say. Pouring herself into this moment. Wanting to bask in it yet simultaneously mourning what it signified.

Because she couldn't keep doing this with him. Not without giving away something far more precious than her body—her heart. Because it was too broken and too damaged. It couldn't take another knock.

So, instead, she leaned forward with her hands on his shoulders and kissed him as deeply and as thoroughly as he'd ever kissed her. And then she sank down, taking Logan deep, so deep inside her.

He cursed and grabbed her hips, trying to slow her down.

'Too fast,' he muttered.

'I didn't see you slowing down for me before.' She grinned, easing up him again before sliding back down.

'Is that a complaint?'

And she smiled and shook her head.

'Not at all. Definitely not.'

Then she began to move on him. She might have known he would never let her get away with it.

He grabbed her hips, his fingers biting into her skin, not roughly just *enough*. He always knew how much was enough. It occurred to her that it was one of the things she loved most about him.

The realisation made Kat freeze.

She fought the urge to lift one hand to cover her breast-bone in the hope that could stay the desperate, clawing desolation within.

She *loved* him.

How had she not seen this coming? How had she left herself so open? So vulnerable to attack? And no matter that some voice inside her argued that Logan would never do that to her—that he wasn't like Kirk—who knew if a person could really be trusted? Not when it came down to it.

She *loved* him. Logan. This maddening, clever Comic Book Hero who had crashed into her life when that car had crashed on the black ice.

He was vibrant and funny, generous and kind. Whilst she was far too broken to ever be able to offer anything to him or to Jamie. She couldn't never make their family whole. She couldn't even make her body do the one thing it was biologically designed to do.

How long before he realised that and left her for some-one who *could*? And that was why she needed to end this fling now.

Whilst she still could.

CHAPTER THIRTEEN

'I'VE GOT A burn in Room One,' Kat told her chief. 'I've left her rinsing it in running water for the next ten to fifteen. I've a woman with unspecified chest pain in Room Two, so I'm waiting for the results on her, and I've an ETOH in Room Four. He's a frequent flyer so I've done the usual vitals and blood sugar and left him with a candy bar.'

'And you've just completed discharge for Room Three?'

'Right,' Kat confirmed.

'Okay, good. You were due off duty…' the chief glanced down at her watch '…half an hour ago.'

'It's fine.' Kat shrugged, thinking of her empty apartment.

The quiet had never bothered her before. In fact, she'd always rather welcomed the peace. But not now. Not since Logan had filled it with life and fun.

And she had to stop thinking that way.

'Okay, have a good afternoon, and be glad you're going off duty. This place isn't too bad for now, but I'm betting it's going to get slammed soon.'

'I'm not betting against you.' Kat smiled. 'Although I think I'd prefer the chaos of the ER to the chaos out there.'

'You're not shopping at Christmas, are you?' Her chief looked aghast.

'Couple of last-minute errands, that's all.'

No need to mention that she'd been putting them off for

weeks, still in denial about Christmas without Carrie. But now there was no choice, they had to be done.

'We missed you at the ball last week, by the way.'

Kat froze, unprepared for the well-intentioned comment. She cranked up her smile and wished it didn't feel like a thousand needles in her face.

'Yeah, well, I took an extra shift.' It took everything she had to keep things light and airy. 'A bit of extra money never hurts at this time of year.'

She didn't need the money, but it was plausible enough. And certainly a better explanation than the fact that she hadn't been able to stand the idea of facing Logan. Of seeing him talking to other women who would surely have made a beeline for him.

'Ah, right.' The chief nodded in understanding, just as Kat had banked on. 'Anyway, have a good afternoon.'

'And you.' Kat managed one final smile as she walked away.

Then again, she couldn't seem to win, she thought as she headed for the lockers to retrieve her bag. Her head was now swimming with thoughts of Logan, despite her best intentions.

She didn't feel strong enough to face him again, and yet this last week had been horrible *without* him there.

To talk to, to share a laugh, or simply to go for a run.

He'd called her and texted her. And she still didn't know how she'd had the strength to delete each and every one of his messages.

To pretend that she didn't care when everything in her was screaming to go to him.

She hadn't been able to bring herself to attend the ball, afraid that she would crumble and fall back into Logan's arms if she saw him. Not that she knew he'd have wanted her.

Sorting her uniform out and gathering up her belongings, Kat headed for the atrium, calling out greetings on autopilot to various colleagues, even as her head swam with thoughts of one man.

She'd steeled herself for the gossip the day after the ball, of course. Telling herself that she was prepared to hear he'd left with someone else—she'd known from enough other nurses that they'd been intending to make a beeline for him that night. And Kat had told herself that her heart hadn't lifted when she'd heard instead that he'd left early. Alone.

It made no difference to her. Whatever she and Logan had had, or hadn't had, was over—and that was certainly for the best. There was only a finite number of times she could repeat that last part to herself without her brain finally realising it wasn't true.

She missed him. So badly that it made her lungs hurt to simply breathe.

So much for coming to Seattle to keep her distance from memories of Carrie. Of loss. She'd ended up meeting Logan and letting herself get attached all over again. But it could only end in hurt.

Even if he wanted more from her, too, ultimately he would want things she could never give him.

Like a family of his own.

Thrusting aside the stab of pain, Kat hauled open the door to the atrium and shot through…only to practically collide with a large, well-built, painfully familiar figure standing just off to one side.

'Logan?'

Half an exclamation, half a whisper. Her mind raced whilst her internal organs appeared to be playing a frenzied game of musical chairs.

'Kat.' He looked up, his expression lighting up for just a fraction of a second before he began to distance himself.

And she *hated* it. She hated it with a vengeance.

'You're not on duty today, what are you doing here?'

He eyed her strangely and, too late, she realised that she'd given herself away. That he would realise she'd been tracking his duties, moving her own shifts so that they didn't coincide with his.

For a split second something flashed in his eyes, chasing away the guarded expression. It told her far more than she wanted to know, that she revelled in that fact.

'I'm helping out at the grotto.'

'Oh?'

'They saw me in that tutu at the Christmas dash so I'm playing an elf,' he deadpanned.

'Oh.'

Belatedly, it occurred to Kat that he was teasing her. Her lips seemed to want to curve up at the corners of their own volition. All her carefully repositioned armour crumbled in an instant.

'You're not going to the grotto at all, are you?' she challenged, chuckling.

'I am,' he assured her. 'But I'm playing Santa Claus.'

'Oh, I didn't know. You never said.'

As if she had a right to know what went on in his life. So much for trying to keep her distance.

'They only called me up this morning.' He shrugged easily. 'Some doc from Paediatrics was due to be playing the role, but they had to drop out when a major case came in overnight. I knew they had to be desperate to call me on my day off, so I said I'd stand in. It's only for an hour or two.'

'Nice of you.'

But not a surprise. She had no trouble imagining Logan volunteering on behalf of those kids who wouldn't be able to go home for Christmas.

'Reckon I'll make a decent Santa.' He grinned. 'What do you think?'

'Sure. Though not like any that I've ever seen.'

The words were out before she could clamp them back. Kat flushed hotly, but the fact remained that Logan would be the fittest, buffest Santa that Seattle General would have ever seen.

Or *anybody* would have ever seen, for that matter.

'Is that so?' Logan asked, as if he could read her every last lustful, terrible thought.

She didn't dare look at him. The heat in his gaze was doing funny things to her body. *Again.*

Thrusting the indecent images out of her head, she plucked at the first neutral topic she could think of.

'So, Jamie's with your parents, then?'

Not exactly neutral, but enough of a distraction from X-rated thoughts of Logan as a naughty Santa.

'No, he's just over there, getting a hug and a selection box from one of the day-care assistants he saw as she headed off duty.'

Kat glanced over and recognised the young girl who she now realised was watching them a little too intently. Clearly, Jamie wasn't the only Connors man the girl was pleased to see today.

'You've brought Jamie with you?' She fought to keep her tone bright.

Not to let Logan know that she'd noticed the girl or her interest in Logan.

'Not by choice. Unfortunately this was the only day my parents couldn't look after him. I'm hoping to keep him out of the way, though. He believes in the magic of Christmas so I don't want him to recognise me dressed up as Santa and start questioning anything.'

'No, of course not.'

A memory of Carrie swirled around her. This would have been the year when the little girl would have really begun to understand the magic of this time of year. Kat could feel herself starting to fall when Logan's voice rescued her.

'So, anyway, he's going to be at the day care whilst I'm going around the wards.'

As if he'd realised where her mind had been headed.

'And when you have to play Santa for day care?' she managed thickly.

'Ah, well...' He cast her a wry smile. 'Then I was hoping to talk someone into taking him for an ice cream or something.'

'Is that your way of saying you were going to ask me?'

It was ridiculous how her heart thumped so heavily.

'I wasn't intending to,' he told her, and she couldn't tell whether he was telling the truth or not. 'But it seems fortuitous that we should bump into each other, don't you think?'

She didn't want to think. It made her confuse notions as simple as coincidence for something far more romantic. Like *fate.*

'You didn't want to ask that day-care assistant?' she couldn't help asking, and was gratified when Logan pulled a face.

'I think she might read a little too much into that, don't you think?'

No doubt about it, Kat thought. Not that she was going to say as much. But then, before she could think of anything else to say, one of the other nurses poked her head around the atrium doors, relief smoothing her taut features as soon as she saw him.

'Logan, thank goodness. Someone said they'd seen you arrive, but I wasn't sure. The rounds are done and we're just squaring the last few tasks away so now's about the perfect window for Santa to visit. I've got the suit, and the kids are so excited.'

'Fine, I'm coming now.' Logan shot her a warm smile before turning to call Jamie.

'Come on, champ, time to go.'

As the little boy turned and spotted her, Kat wasn't prepared for the way his face lit up with unadulterated happiness.

'Kat!' he cried joyously, as emotion slammed into her, stealing the breath from her lungs.

And then he was dashing across the atrium on his little legs and flinging himself at her. She scooped him up, swinging him around and hugging him tightly, breathing in that young-child scent. So like Carrie, yet so much his own person.

'Come on, champ,' Logan cut in gently. 'Let's get you to day care, I have to go and work.'

Was it just her imagination or was Logan's voice different somehow? Because of Jamie's reaction to her? It had certainly blown her away, so how had it made Logan feel?

Then again, it probably wasn't anything to do with her. It was more likely that he was concerned about keeping the kids waiting. They both knew that in hospitals like this there were only limited windows for visits from Santa in between rounds, meals, medication and handovers.

Logan needed to get going now.

'I have one quick errand to run, but if you like I can some back and pick Jamie up from day care in time for that ice cream.' she heard herself offering quietly. 'You know, when your alter ego needs to go in there.'

He cast her a sharp look and, for a brief moment, she wondered if he didn't realise she was talking about when he had to play Santa to the children. But then he spoke.

'I wasn't trying to make you feel obligated.'

'You didn't.' She toyed with a smile. 'Jamie did that all by himself.'

Logan didn't answer immediately, and when he did she heard the faint glow of pride and awe in his tone.

'Yeah, the kid will do that to you.'

It was like being invited into the privacy of their father-son relationship.

Like family, a voice whispered, before she quashed it, nodding robotically instead. Not adding that she wasn't entirely sure if it was Jamie who had sneaked past her defences or Logan.

Or, more likely, both. And if it took more effort than it should have done to turn around and walk away from the pair of them, well, that could stay her guilty secret.

Kat raced through her task list. Somehow the prospect of returning to the hospital to Jamie, and to Logan, made the long-overdue errands far more palatable. Soon she was hurrying back through the doors to the main entrance and stowing her bags under the reception desk with a grateful smile.

Threading her way through the visitors and mobile patients, Kat headed for the day care, only slowing down to soak up the sight of Jamie playing, happy and oblivious, with a little girl she recognised as the daughter of a cardiac consultant.

A single mother. The thought sneaked into Kat's brain, torturing her with images of Logan and Jamie playing happy families with the consultant and her daughter.

What was wrong with her? She'd been over this. She wasn't doing this because she wanted something more with Logan, she was just helping out a colleague who was trying to do a good Christmas deed for the kids. And the sooner she got Jamie out of there, the less chance there was that Logan would appear and his cover would be blown.

Picking up her pace, Kat knocked on the door to the day care and waited for one of the assistants to let her in.

And then, suddenly, as the door was opened to her and Kat looked inside, everything seemed to slow down.

She saw the other child sitting on Jamie's untied shoelace a fraction of a second before Jamie launched himself towards another toy. Instinct made her lunge forward, but she was too far away and he hit the floor with a thud, landing on his arm.

He went from shouts of glee to shouts of pain in a split second. His cry was heart-wrenching.

'Okay, sweetheart, you're okay. I'm here,' she said, reaching where he'd fallen and instinctively beginning to soothe him.

But she could tell something was wrong. Just the way he was crying and holding his arm. It wasn't quite right.

'Let's get him to X-Ray.' She turned to one of the daycare workers. 'And can you get Logan Connors? He's probably in Paediatrics now.'

By the time Logan reached the orthopaedic trauma unit, his heart hammering so hard in his chest that he feared it was going to punch its way right through his ribs, Kat had the situation well in hand and was just finishing up a festive cast on Jamie's right arm.

'I'm so sorry, champ.' He hugged Jamie as carefully as he could, trying to discreetly check his son in the process. 'I've only just got the message.'

'Look, Daddy, a Christmassy cast.' Jamie shoved the fractured arm under his nose, his face surprisingly wreathed in a smile.

The fear receded a little, but still he blew out a frustrated sigh as he turned to Kat.

'I was just around the corner when the girl came in with the message, but no one realised it was me under that damned suit until now.'

'It's fine. We're fine, right, Jamie?'

'Fine,' Jamie agreed easily. Kat had evidently worked her usual charm.

On both of them.

'Though I can see you surreptitiously trying to check him over,' she commented dryly. 'He has a physical stress fracture. He tripped over and used his hand to try to save himself. The wrist took the brunt of it and the cast is to help with the pain.'

He raked his hand through his hair.

'I came as soon as they told me, and I don't want to leave him, but I haven't finished the...'

'Assignment?' she supplied helpfully as he trailed off, glancing at Jamie, who was admiring the festive red colour of his cast.

It was impossible to tell whether the little boy was listening or not.

'Right.' Logan nodded, grateful to her. 'I ditched the... clothing outside.'

It seemed he was often grateful to her. As well as something else that he was rapidly becoming sick of trying to fight.

'It's no problem. I can stay with Jamie.'

'Thanks.' His gratitude was evident. 'I'll be as quick as I can.'

'Take your time,' Kat suggested. 'Better that you can't be recognised.'

'Who can't be recognised?' Jamie lifted his head curiously.

Logan told himself it was the earlier fear, and not Kat, that had fuzzed his mind and left him uncharacteristically scrabbling for a quick response.

'Your superhero daddy,' Kat improvised, when he wasn't fast enough.

'Oh.'

To his credit, Jamie looked a little confused before he

seemed to shrug to himself and carry on with his proud inspection, just as one of the ortho nurses poked her head around the corner.

'Kat, is this room free?'

'Yeah, pretty much.'

'I look like a robot.' Jamie showed her proudly.

'Yes, you do,' the nurse enthused. 'I think we've even got some special festive cast stickers at the nurses' station. If you want to see, Kat, I can stay here with your patient and start clearing up. Oh…hi, Dr Connors.'

'Afternoon,' Logan managed politely, dropping a kiss on his son's head and casting a grateful glance at Kat. 'I'll walk with you.'

The sooner he was finished playing Santa, the sooner he could get back to Jamie. And to Kat.

They were just hurrying out when he heard the nurse speak again, and they turned simultaneously, but it was too late.

'So, little man, of all days you might have had to come to the hospital, today is the best one you could have picked. Because Santa Claus is in the main children's ward right now.'

'Oh, wow.' Jamie shuffled his bottom off the bed, even as Logan felt his stomach clench in apprehension. 'I've got something I really, really, really have to ask him.'

Kat just looked horrified.

'Oh, no, Jamie… I don't think…'

She tailed off as he cast her a devastated look.

'I can't meet Santa?'

'Listen, champ…' Logan began, but when Jamie's eyes began to tear up he hesitated.

His mind raced with what might happen if Jamie recognised him. But Jamie was only four, and he truly believed in Santa Claus. Would his son even recognise him in that padded suit complete with beard and glasses?

'I don't see why not,' he relented, his heart in his mouth. 'Just wait here a little longer whilst Kat gets your stickers, then maybe she'll bring you along.'

'You're sure?' Kat whispered nervously beside him.

He wasn't. But now the nurse had put the idea—however unwittingly—into his son's head, how could he refuse? He'd just better hope that the disguise was a good as he thought it was.

'It'll be fine,' he assured Kat, turning his back so that Jamie couldn't see him. 'Just give me time to get back in there.'

How was it that this one woman made him feel like anything was possible?

And, more to the point, what was he going to do about it?

If he hadn't been so on edge about his son watching him, Logan might have enjoyed the moment as Santa a little more.

Child after child waited for their turn, telling Santa their name and their favourite things to do, and then the gift they wanted most. And despite the fact that he knew his fake accent was shockingly bad—a mixture of several accents he only half knew—Jamie didn't appear to notice anything unusual.

Even Kat, clearly tense when she'd first accompanied Jamie to the ward, was now beginning to relax. Logan took that as a good sign.

Finally, it was Jamie's turn, and he liked the way Kat followed the little boy up to where he sat, ready to help Jamie onto his knee so that he didn't damage his injured wrist.

She caught his eye as he lifted his son up, that telltale flush creeping down her cheeks. He still affected her, which meant that her cold-shoulder treatment over the past two weeks was about her vulnerability, not about the fact that she wasn't still attracted to him.

The thing was, he wanted more than just her being attracted to him. But what exactly did that mean? For himself, but also for Jamie? His son might love her company now, but that didn't mean he would feel the same if Kat was in their life more frequently.

Maybe that would be too much for a young four-year-old whose mother had never really been present, even when she'd been around.

And then Logan caught Kat's eye and something rushed him, chasing all the thoughts from his head. Right up until the moment his son started to speak.

'I'm Jamie. I'm four.'

'Hello, Jamie, who is four,' Logan drawled in a stranger's voice, quite convincingly to his mind. 'And what are your favourite things to do?'

'Hmm.' Jamie cocked his head, stroking his four-year-old chin thoughtfully in some imitation of something he'd clearly seen.

Logan smothered a snort of laughter whilst Kat, as far as he could see, was doing little to keep her shoulders from shaking. But he wasn't prepared when Jamie eyed him quite conspiratorially and started to speak.

'I like the park with Daddy. And with Kat. And I like Kat baking with me. And I like it when Daddy is happy.'

He was spinning madly. Wildly. He could feel himself, but he couldn't do anything to stop it. He would never know how he managed to make any kind of response.

'And...what would you like for Christmas?' he choked out, not that Jamie seemed to notice.

His little son was too caught up in his own thoughts.

'The only thing I want for Christmas is for Kat to be my mommy.'

Everything seemed to stand still. Logan wasn't even sure if his brain was working.

The simplicity, and impossibility, of the request rocketed through him.

When he'd wondered how Jamie would feel about Kat being a bigger part of their lives, he hadn't anticipated this. How did he even begin to answer such a wish?

'Jamie, I can't...'

And even though he'd forgotten the accent, and the fact that he was Santa and not Jamie's daddy, none of it mattered. Because Jamie was staring at him earnestly.

'Daddy loves Kat. Kat loves me. Daddy loves me. Kat loves Daddy.' He ticked them off in his little hands as though he was forty, not four.

'Jamie...'

'Nana says they do,' he continued blithely. 'I heard her tell Gramps.'

Logan felt a pang of compassion for his mother. She would be mortified if she knew Jamie had overheard her.

But that didn't make it true. He and Kat had an agreement. *No strings, no hassle.* And it had been working just fine for them so far.

Hadn't it?

Suddenly he couldn't be sure any more.

'I tell you what, ch... Jamie,' he corrected just in time. His son would realise his true identity immediately if Santa slipped up and called him *champ*. 'I can't make any guarantees, but what if I promise to see what I can do?'

Jamie swivelled his head and fixed him with a bright, trusting gaze. But Logan was even more aware of Kat's shocked, deeply unhappy expression.

'You're Santa,' Jamie declared confidently. 'You can do it.'

It took all of Logan's not inconsiderable acting skills—and he was never more relieved that he was a doctor, not an actor—to carry on after his young son clambered down from his knee and the remainder of the kids took their turns.

He barely knew what he was saying to them, his mind still locked firmly on Jamie, and on Kat.

Less than an hour ago he'd been acknowledging that Kat had changed his life. That things he'd thought impossible a few months ago were starting to feel real. Like opening up his life—and Jamie's—to someone new.

No, not just to *someone*. To *Kat*.

But it had taken his four-year-old son for him to finally acknowledge exactly what he'd meant by that. Exactly *how* much he wanted Kat in his life. In *their* lives. Making them better, fuller, happier. And how was it that even his mother had seen it before he had?

Still, his mind whirred with exactly where he was supposed to go from here.

The next hour passed in a blur. It felt like an eternity before he was able to politely excuse himself, go and change and return to Jamie, but he knew he must have done all right when the ward manager thanked him profusely afterwards.

Still, a part of him knew that once he collected Jamie from her, Kat would dart off. She would do everything she could to avoid having a conversation with him about what she'd overheard Jamie say.

And when, indeed, that was exactly what she did, it was almost like a triumph to realise that he could read Kat Steel precisely as well as he'd imagined that he could. That he could knew her better than she knew herself. That she wanted to be with him—and with Jamie—as much as he'd thought she did.

Perhaps all he needed to do was to convince her how much he wanted them to be a family? Kat and him and Jamie.

And, in time, expand their family further?

CHAPTER FOURTEEN

'WHAT ARE YOU doing here, Logan?'

Leaning one arm on the doorjamb to Kat's apartment, he cocked his head to one side and there was little use her pretending that the whole world wasn't tipping, shifting in his presence.

'Is that any way to greet Santa Claus?' he demanded. 'Aren't you going to invite me in?'

'First, you aren't dressed as Santa any more,' she pointed out, with no idea how she kept her voice even. 'And second, *no*.'

But she didn't close the door in his face, which she knew revealed to him a lot more than her words had. She wasn't surprised when he eyed her curiously.

'Are you mad because you didn't want me to answer Jamie, or are you mad because you did?'

Kat narrowed her eyes at him and tried to stand taller. To exude a confidence that she didn't really feel.

'I'm not mad,' and she wasn't entirely lying. 'If anything, I'm…confused about why you gave a four-year-old boy false hope.'

And not only Jamie. He'd given her false hope, too. Perhaps that was the part about which she was maddest.

'Is it?'

She blinked, not following his question.

'Is it what?'

'False hope?' He took a step forward and she backed up into her apartment.

Logan promptly followed her inside, as though he thought that was the closest thing he was going to get to an invitation. As though he didn't realise how close she stood to the edge. Or how that edge was crumbling with every second she spent in his company. All because she wanted him.

She'd never stopped wanting him.

'Of course it's false hope.' She dragged her mind desperately back to the conversation. 'We agreed this was just *no-commitment fun.*'

'It was.' He shrugged. 'Until it changed.'

'It didn't change for me.' She shook her head.

'Liar.' He chuckled, and that threw her as he'd known it would. 'I saw your face yesterday. I know you feel something more.'

'You're wrong.' The denial tipped out, only to fall— hollow and leaden—to the floor.

His eyes gleamed. Hot and hungry, and rolling through her like the most beautiful storm.

'Am I really wrong, Kat?' he asked softly.

And when she didn't answer him—when she *couldn't* answer him—his voice became even softer again.

'Why don't we put it to the test?'

She swayed. She didn't mean to but she felt herself doing it all the same. She shifted her gaze around the room, from one thing to another as though she couldn't find something to focus on, to keep herself upright.

'I don't need to put it to the test,' she answered at last in a thin, reedy voice. 'I don't want to commit to someone. I don't think I ever will.'

'But how will you ever know, if you never let anyone close enough to find out?'

She could feel the moment things turned. The moment

she went from cold disengagement to allowing her emotions to show. Or perhaps it was less about *allowing* her emotions out and more about no longer being *able* to contain them.

'You don't know what you're talking about,' she threw at him, wanting to bite back every word but unable to do so. 'I did let someone close. Once. And they walked away from me.'

Yet even as she said it, it occurred to Kat that she was comparing Logan to Kirk, when really there was no question which was the man and which had merely been a boy pretending to be a man.

Still, it shocked her when Logan's face twisted into a look of disdain.

'You hang everything on a four-year-old girl. But she didn't walk away from you. She didn't even have a choice in the matter.'

He thought this was about Carrie?

But, then, of course he would, because he didn't know any different.

Kat shook her head. Inside it felt as though she was breaking. Shattering into a million tiny fragments. And every single one of them shredded her like a million tiny paper cuts as they went.

'Do you really think I'm that shallow?'

'No,' he answered simply. 'I don't think that's who you are at all. Not deep down. But it's what you've told me.'

Sorrow scraped inside her, paring away at her. Keeping away from him had been the right thing to do because now, face to face with him, she could feel her resolve crumbling away. As if it was no more substantial than a badly baked gingerbread man—like the kind Jamie had said Logan had made.

She should ask him to leave. But she couldn't.

'It's part of what I've told you, Logan,' she confessed. 'But it isn't everything.'

'Then what is?'

'What does it matter?' she cried. Frustration and grief worked their way up, as though they could suddenly see an outlet and refused to be contained any longer. 'We agreed to fun, nothing more. But now *Jamie* is caught up in the middle of things, and we can't offer him what he wants. More than that, what he wants is *impossible*.'

'No one can predict the future,' he said scornfully, and she couldn't tell if he was angry or just unimpressed.

She reminded herself that she didn't care. And then Logan spoke again.

'But what is it that's so *impossible*, Kat? I can't imagine how losing Carrie must have hurt. When I think about Jamie…it just doesn't bear thinking about.'

'No.' Sadness threatened to engulf her, and she was afraid she wasn't going to be able to hold it at bay. 'It doesn't.'

'But you can't keep running away from every chance at a connection because of that one terrible experience.'

And at that moment she felt something else charge her. A little of her old fierceness. It occurred to her that Logan was deliberately provoking her. Trying to help her get past her own memories. But that didn't make sense.

'I do not *run away*,' she bit out hotly.

'You do. You veil it in self-sacrifice, but it's still *running away*.'

'My God, you're so smug. You don't know everything.'

'Is that so? Then enlighten me.'

'And say what?' she demanded.

'Tell me why you're so frightened of opening up to anyone. What is it that makes keeps this barrier between you and anybody else? I know Carrie is a part of it, but what's the rest of it?'

She was teetering. She could hear the words piling up in her head. Logan knew it, too. Perhaps he'd even understood it in her before she had. But that only made him all the more dangerous to her.

'You have to trust someone, sometime, Kat. Why not me, and why not here?'

She wavered a moment longer, memories of Carrie and of Jamie interweaving. Images of Logan that she would probably hold onto for the rest of her life. And then other, less pleasant images of Kirk.

It was all building so fast that it was inevitable that when she broke, it all spilled out so fast that she could barely keep up.

'I've always known that I couldn't have children. At least, I couldn't have biological children. I was twelve when I was diagnosed with osteosarcoma.' She lifted one hand, almost subconsciously, to the top of her left arm, just by the shoulder.

He could barely stop himself from hauling her into his arms and holding her, as though that might somehow erase all that he instinctively knew she must have been through. But her delivery was robotic, and clipped—her way of protecting herself—so he made himself keep his distance.

'Because it was caught early,' she continued, her gaze still not quite meeting his, 'I had a round of chemo, surgery to remove the affected portion of bone and a bone graft with a metal prosthetic and another round of chemo.'

'Kat,' he breathed.

'By the time I was eighteen my body had gone through menopause. Back then, although they'd already begun working with cryopreservation, it wasn't done as routinely as now. Now they can freeze a section of ovary from a baby barely a few months old, complete with all its eggs, and reimplant it during adulthood. But back then it wasn't an option for me.'

'I see,' he mused, his mind searching for the right words. The words he knew Kat—*his* Kat—would want to hear. 'So you think that I wouldn't want to be with you if you couldn't give me a child? A biological child?'

'You said it yourself.'

She shrugged. But he could see how much it cost her to do so.

'I want *you*. I want a family with *you*. And if we adopt, like you were going to adopt Carrie, that won't make that child any less *ours*.'

'Why would that be enough for you?' she cried, her palms twisting around each other like she was trying to contain a decade and a half's worth of emotions.

'Why wouldn't it be?' he countered as evenly as he could.

'Because…because…' She pulled her hands to her chest then rubbed at her face, before staring at him with something approaching despair. 'Because it *can't* be.'

Logan didn't answer straight away. Instead, he cupped her face and finally made her meet his gaze.

'Why not, Kat?'

She stared at him for what felt like an eternity. Then she shook her head.

'Please, Logan, just leave.'

A plea? Or a demand? He wasn't sure even Kat knew.

'What was his name?' Logan demanded suddenly. 'What did he do to you?'

She blinked once. Twice.

'His name was Kirk,' she managed slowly, and he got the impression she was testing every word before it came out. 'He was my fiancé.'

Logan hated the guy already.

'When?'

'When did we split up, do you mean?' Her lips pulled into a taut line. 'Seven years ago.'

His brain whirred.

'Before you started fostering?'

She nodded stiffly.

'What happened?'

He waited a beat as the silence stretched out between them. Then another beat.

'Logan, you don't want to hear all this.'

'I do,' he gritted out.

And he saw her fight one last wave of emotion...and then capitulate.

'We'd been together since we were fifteen,' she began slowly, woodenly. 'I met him in the hospital.'

There was a pounding in his chest. A roaring. A storm. But Logan held it back. He forced his voice to sound even, though he had no idea how he managed it.

'You'd both had bone cancer?'

'No.' She squeezed her eyes shut. 'But we'd been through chemo together.'

So, of all people, this Kirk should have understood Kat's circumstances. Down at his sides, out of her sight, Logan clenched his fists. How was it he had the sense that Kirk had been the one to let her down and destroy her trust? Her sense of self-worth?

'Go on,' his voice rumbled, low and commanding.

He couldn't stop himself.

'Kirk knew about the menopause, and that I couldn't have children naturally. We talked about fostering together. Even adopting.'

It was all he could to nod encouragingly. But he didn't speak. He didn't trust himself.

'When we got engaged, we started the fostering procedure. Then, about three months before we were due to get married, Kirk told me that he couldn't handle us never having biological kids together. He said that he might not have been ready for kids at that moment, but that he would be in the future. And when he did, he would need to have a child that was a *real part* of himself.'

'He left you?'

For the longest time she didn't react. And then she gave the vaguest hint of shrug.

It was enough.

Logan seethed on Kat's behalf. If he could have laid the guy out right now, in front of her, he would have. Though he doubted she would appreciate such a gesture.

It occurred to Logan that the depth of emotion he felt for Kat went far beyond anything he'd felt for anyone—bar Jamie—before. Certainly not Sophia. Even when she'd left him for her wealthy new lover, he hadn't felt a fraction of the contempt he felt for this Kirk guy.

It only served to confirm that he would walk over searing coals for Kat Steel. He just needed to make her realise it, too.

'The guy was a prize jerk, Kat.' He barely recognised his own voice. Or the man behind it. 'You have to see that?'

She pulled her mouth into a thin line but said nothing.

'He wasn't worth your love. He wasn't worth *you*, for God's sake.'

'I know.' It was the barest scrap of a voice. It certainly didn't convince Logan.

'Don't lie to me, Kat. Telling me what you think I want to hear. I need to know that you truly believe it. That you really know you deserve better than a guy like that.'

She opened her mouth to answer, but something stopped her. As though she'd been about to lie to him again but had decided better of it.

'I understand what you're saying,' she managed slowly, though he could see every word sliced her. Wounded her. 'I think you even believe it. But the fact is that he was entitled to want a family—a biological family—of his own. It's a basic human desire.'

'You can't seriously be defending him.'

She shrugged.

'I can't blame him for wanting something I couldn't give him. A child. A family. One that can't be taken away from you after years of being the only parent they'd ever known—' sadness and bitterness interweaved through her tone '—just because you didn't give birth to them.'

'You're talking about Carrie, and I can't begin to understand what you went through when you lost her. But I can tell you that just because a person gives birth to a child it doesn't make them a parent,' Logan growled, as anger seared him, white hot and so vivid it was almost blinding.

He didn't expect the sharpness in Kat's expression.

'Yes. And yet, if she came back now and wanted to play a part in Jamie's life, she could.'

'I'd like to see her try.'

'You say that now because you're angry. But take emotion out of the equation and think. You might fight it initially, and you might hate the very idea, but ultimately, once you were as satisfied as you could be that she wasn't intending to hurt Jamie again, you would let her into your lives, Logan.'

'No—'

'Yes,' she countered softly. 'Because that's the kind of man you are. And because, at the end of it all, no matter what has happened in the past, she is Jamie's mum, and she always will be. I can never have that, and so I can never give it to whoever I'm with either.'

Logan opened his mouth to argue yet suddenly, abruptly, he stopped.

As much as he hated to admit it, he could concede that Kat had a point. If Sophia came back into Jamie's life he would move heaven and earth to fight her until he was unequivocally sure that she wouldn't hurt their son again. But if she was sincere, would he really have any right to block her from Jamie's life?

Logan felt unexpectedly powerless. It was an alien sensation, and he didn't much care for it.

He might not entirely agree with everything Kat had said, but now he was forced to concede that there was a kernel of truth in her words.

Kirk and then her experience with Carrie had left her battered. Bruised. Battle-scarred. Pushing her now would only force her to close those wounds over before they'd had time to fully heal.

Telling her he cared about her, that he wanted her in his life—and in Jamie's life—was one thing. But if he truly cared for her, he should back off and let her have the space she needed so that she could heal in her own time.

It was what a good man should do. And if anyone deserved a good man, it was Kat. Without another word, Logan dipped his head and dropped a lingering kiss on Kat's cheek before straightening up. And then he simply walked away.

As if it wasn't the hardest thing he thought he'd ever had to do in his entire life.

CHAPTER FIFTEEN

CHRISTMAS DAY IN Seattle General was nothing like Kat had expected. The hospital practically crackled with energy and cheer, not least because their most celebrated VIP— the man whose life Logan had saved that dull day in late November—was making a textbook recovery.

How was it possible to feel so very different from the way she'd felt barely a month ago, Kat marvelled as she stood on the gallery and eyed the festive tree in the atrium below, telling herself that she wasn't looking out for Logan?

After their last conversation, she still felt as though a revolving door was spinning in her head. He'd walked away, exactly as she'd asked him to. He'd finally accepted what she'd been trying to tell him. Surely she deserved a sense of victory at the fact that she had been right all along? Instead, she just felt pain—more pain that she'd ever known.

She'd lost Logan, and Jamie, and impossibly it felt even worse than she'd felt when she'd lost Carrie. She felt as if she'd known them her whole life. Or perhaps it was more that she felt as if she'd been waiting her whole life for them...

But Kirk? Logan had said that he was a total jerk, and that she deserved better than that. Which was why she was standing on the gallery, pretending that she wasn't looking out for Logan.

She had to tell him that he'd been right about that much, at least.

It was odd the way she'd been spinning ever since Logan and Jamie had walked into her life. Like the fun of a fairground ride surprising and startling but ultimately giving a sense of exhilaration. Much as life with Logan and Jamie had done.

Unexpectedly, as if talking about them had actually conjured them up, Kat's eyes slid to the doors and she watched as Logan and Jamie hurried inside. They were laughing together, looking as though they were sharing a private joke, and her heart swelled at the sight.

Then, suddenly, Logan looked up and right at her, leaving her wondering if he had somehow sensed her there, watching them. His face split into the most open, inviting and frankly sexy smile, and her stomach swooped and vaulted.

It was terrifying how much he—they—meant to her. But when it was over? What then? She could hardly stand to think about it. Stuffing those fears down, Kat pulled her shoulders back and returned his smile. She would deal with that when it happened. Not before.

So, instead, she just let herself smile as he tapped his son on the shoulder and then pointed up to her. She focussed on waving and blowing a kiss as Jamie flailed his arms around at her, sending a score of kisses her way. And she exulted in the sense of belonging—however long that might last.

Then, heads bent together, they took a handful of presents out of the bag they were carrying and set them at the foot of the tree. Surprise flooded through her when Logan stepped forward to usher his son up the winding staircase to her, whilst he remained down by the base of the huge tree. Hurrying forward, she met Jamie as he reached the top of the stairs.

'What are you doing, coming up here on your own, sweetheart?'

'You have to come with me.' He slipped his tiny hand into hers and a sense of bliss filled Kat.

'Come with you where?' she asked. 'Back downstairs? Were you sent to get me?'

'To Daddy,' Jamie confirmed.

She couldn't have said why her chest tightened as it did. There was clearly some plan afoot, but there was no reason for it to make her breath catch in her lungs. Still, Jamie's cheeky, mischievous grin wound around her and she couldn't help but laugh.

'Well, we'd better not keep Daddy waiting, then, had we?'

'Nope.'

Together—with Jamie's hand still fitted snugly into hers—they made their way back down the stairs.

'You sent for me?' She grinned wryly as Logan met them at the bottom.

'I did. I knew you wouldn't be able to resist Jamie's charms.'

'No, well...' She licked her lips. 'There's something I need to...*want* to tell you.'

'Us first.' Jamie jumped up and down, unable to contain his excitement any longer. 'We have a Christmas gift for you.'

She cast Logan a pleading look, but his expression was surprisingly secretive.

'Us first,' he repeated simply.

Then he reached down to the bag and selected another present, dreadfully wrapped in the loveliest dinosaur wrapping paper. Happiness bubbled inside her.

'It's beautiful,' she told Jamie. 'Thank you.'

And there wasn't a fibre of her that didn't mean it.

'Open it,' Jamie squeaked, practically beside himself.

She slid her gaze from Jamie to Logan in surprise.

'Here?'

'Here,' Logan confirmed quietly.

She couldn't explain the gleam in his eye. Until she unfolded the wrapping paper.

A larger version of Jamie's pterodactyl toy peered out at her.

'It's a mommy Terrydac,' the little boy cried out, clearly unable to contain himself any longer. 'It's for you. You're the mummy, I'm the baby.'

Kat tried to answer but it was impossible. Her throat was too constricted and tight. Heat prickled behind her eyes. All she could was nod.

'You're crying.' He wrinkled his nose at her. 'They are the happy tears? Or the sad tears?'

'They're the happy tears.' She had no idea how she managed to speak.

'You haven't seen my gift yet.' Logan's rich voice suddenly rumbled in her ear.

She lifted her head to look at him querulously, still not able to trust herself to speak.

'But before you do, you need to know that from that first moment I spent with you, in that damned treatment room, you made me feel things. Things I'd never felt before. Things I don't even think I believed I could ever feel.'

'Logan…'

She had intended to tell him what she'd been steeling herself all morning to say, but he shook his head, needing to go on. And she found she wanted to let him.

'You've been my salvation, and my hope.' He hooked one finger under chin, his eyes holding hers. 'You've made me believe in a future I thought would never be for me. I can't predict the future in terms of family, Kat. But, then, no one can. I can only promise you that you will always have me, and you will always be the only one for me. I'll never want anyone but you.'

'I'll never want anybody but you either,' she whispered.

And he couldn't stop himself any more. He slid his hand to the back of her neck and drew her to him.

'I don't care if we have a child biologically, or if we adopt.' He dropped his forehead to rest against hers. 'I don't care if you don't want any of it. I don't care if you want ten. As long as we decide together.'

'You say that now, but…'

Her hand still hung by her sides, and it only made that thing inside claw at him all the more. He had to make her understand.

'Would you always see another child as more precious to you than Jamie?'

'What?' She tried to snatch herself back, but he wouldn't let her. He kept that contact. Her cool forehead against his. 'Of course not! That's a horrible thing to say.'

'Then why should I feel any differently about any child we might choose? Or, indeed, if we were lucky enough to have them choose us?'

'It's…it's not the same,' she managed.

But she didn't look so convinced any more, and he wanted to punch the air in triumph. Kat was beginning to understand. She was *his*. They were meant to be.

'I will never let you down, Kat. I promise you that you, and Jamie, and whoever else comes along will be part of our family. Equal in every way.'

'But—'

'No.' He silenced her. 'I came back to Seattle to try to make a home for Jamie and me. To try to find a way to connect with the son who I thought I knew, but it turned out I didn't after all. I certainly didn't know how to communicate with him. But then you appeared, and you taught me how. You made everything happen, but more than that you opened up my heart.'

'I came here to try to heal after everything that had happened,' she whispered, her eyes lifting to him even though neither of them had moved their heads.

And, at last, her arms lifted and her small palms rested lightly on his upper arms.

'And have you? His voice sounded as raw as it felt.

'So much so that I can barely even remember where the wounds were.'

It was possibly the most beautiful sentiment he'd ever heard.

When he lowered his head and kissed her, Kat forgot where they were, and who was around. She lost herself in the magic of the moment, the magic of Logan. The magic of Christmas.

It might have been an eternity before they resurfaced had Jamie—incredibly patient up until that moment—not decided to reinsert himself.

'Daddy, you still haven't given your present.'

'Right.' Logan pulled himself away, but to Kat's intense relief—and the relief of her now shaky legs—he kept his arm tightly around her.

As if he didn't want to let her go.

'Time for my gift,' he muttered, his voice thicker than usual.

She found she rather liked having that effect on him. Logan nodded back towards the dinosaur.

'Turn it over.'

Dutifully, Kat tugged her gaze back down to the toy, but there was nothing obvious. She reached out to turn it over and found that her hands were inexplicably shaking, as if they sensed something her brain hadn't yet worked out.

And then she saw it. Nestled over the back foot of the

pterodactyl. A white-gold band. Her eyes snapped to Logan then back down, as her fingers fumbled to twist it around.

A stunning pear-shaped diamond winked back at her, and tiny diamonds were set into the shoulder of the band itself.

'It's…stunning,' she breathed, once she could trust herself to speak. 'But… I didn't think…'

'How could you not have thought?' His voice was both a promise and a chastisement. 'The simple truth is that I love you, Kat Steel. You stole our hearts—mine and my son's. So what we want to know is if you'll marry me.'

'Us.' Jamie poked his head up solemnly. 'Will you be my mommy for real?'

'Will you marry *us*, and be Jamie's mommy?' Logan asked with a laugh that was a smidgen too thick with emotion. *'For real?'*

It was almost Kat's undoing.

For a long moment she let her hands rest on the toy, scarcely able to believe that what had started out as a move to Seattle to get away from the grief of losing the child she'd begun to think of her as her own had turned into her finding a family of her own.

Being the happiest she thought she'd ever felt in her entire life.

'If you want to,' Jamie added. And just for a moment his eyes clouded over with an uncertainty that Kat couldn't bear to see.

'I want to,' she choked out, dropping on jelly-like knees to put herself face to face with the boy who loved her so much that he wanted her to be his mommy. He—they— wanted her to make it *for ever*. 'How could I ever want anything more?'

When he threw his arms around her neck, squeezing so tightly that she'd thought she might die, she poured everything she could into hugging him back.

She had no idea how long they stayed like that, but eventually she felt his little hands disentangling them, his voice in her ear.

'Then I think I'd like to play with my new toy, now, Mommy.'

And as she handed him the pterodactyl, she laughed at how, just like that, everything was right in his uncomplicated world.

Finally, she stood up again, her eyes locking with Logan's, her hands moving instinctively to rest her palms on his solid, far-too-tempting chest.

'I love you, too,' she whispered. 'I think I have done since almost the first moment we met. Since I saw you, so protective and loyal to the King, even if I didn't know who he was then.'

'He was duty. My pride. You—and Jamie—are my world. And I intend to make sure you feel that—every single day.'

'I'll hold you to that,' she muttered, reaching up on her toes until her mouth was scant millimetres from his. 'And I know you always keep your promises.'

'Always,' he confirmed. 'Merry Christmas, Kat.'

'Merry Christmas,' she breathed as he lowered his mouth to claim hers.

The first kiss of the rest of their lives.

* * * * *

THE PRINCESS'S
CHRISTMAS BABY

LOUISA GEORGE

MILLS & BOON

PROLOGUE

August

IT WAS HIS idea of hell.

When Lucas Beaufort had said to his best friend Domenico that if he ever needed any help with anything, just ask, he hadn't meant he'd be free at the drop of a hat to babysit his friend's reckless younger sister who made the papers for all the wrong reasons.

But there it was. Sometimes friendships required going above and beyond. He only hoped he'd manage to get through this weekend unscathed.

Which he highly doubted. Take one wilful and wayward, spoilt Princess...with a capital P. Literally. Add her ability to make trouble for herself wherever she went. Sprinkle in a rogue weekend in Seattle during which she was expecting to be entertained, and he knew—even though his cooking was generally woeful—that he had a recipe for utter disaster on his hands.

'Hey, Captain Sensible!' She flung herself at him as he opened the door to her loud hammering. 'Long time no see.'

'About ten years, give or take.' And he'd hoped for longer, but there it was. He tried to extricate himself from her hug but she kind of held on. Captain Sensible, eh? Great. He guessed he probably deserved it. He wasn't exactly known for his witty repartee. 'Come in, Giada. Welcome back to Seattle.'

She finally let go and grinned as he took a step outside to grab her suitcase and let her into his house. As they walked through to his living room she flung her floppy sunhat onto his sofa and slipped off her over-sized sunglasses. She was wearing a strappy, white sundress and... well, hell. She'd changed since he'd seen her last.

Whereas years ago she'd gone through a typical but lengthy rebellious, pale-skinned goth phase, with ripped jeans and black clothes totally unbefitting a royal, she was now a picture of glowing health—all tanned arms and legs with long shiny black hair that cascaded in waves over her shoulders. Her dark brown eyes glittered as she smiled and made him want to take a second look. Her mouth.

God...it was very bad that he was looking at his best friend's sister's mouth.

She also smelled exactly how he imagined her home, the Mediterranean island of Isola Verde, would smell: fresh, flowery, warm. Weird that he'd even notice.

'Well, this is nice,' she said as she ran to the huge picture window and took in the expansive view over Lake Washington. Her voice was sing-song and...happy. Which made him feel immediately wistful. Happy. Yeah. Half turning, she twisted to look at him. 'No, not nice. It's gorgeous here, Lucas. Thanks for putting me up... I mean...' she laughed and made quote marks with her fingers '...*putting up with me* for the weekend.'

'It's not a problem.' Although, judging by the fact he'd noticed her perfume and was taking another look at her pretty face, it could well turn into a problem. She was so off limits it wasn't funny.

'I promise I'll be on my best behaviour, Lucas. Too bad Dom has to spend the weekend at some dull conference instead of showing his sister around the city he prefers to his beautiful island home.' She whirled round to face him fully, her dress flaring out around her thighs.

Lucas looked. So sue him. 'It's fine. Um… What would you like to do?'

'Swim first? Or a shower. But I'd prefer a swim if I can, just to have a good workout and stretch. I really need to freshen up after that flight.'

'Sure thing. Lake or pool?'

'Lake. There's nothing better than swimming in nature, right? It reminds me of home.' She let out a big sigh. A sigh he couldn't read. 'Oh, and call me Gigi. Everyone else does. You want to come for a dip?'

He couldn't remember the last time he'd swum in the lake. Just the usual fifty laps of his pool each morning. Clinical. Routine.

The thought of his feet sinking into warm sand was definitely appealing. As was seeing more of those long shapely legs. She was a lot more attractive than he remembered. Softer too…none of that spiky aggression he remembered. None of the artifice, the heavy make-up she used to hide behind.

No…she wasn't pretty, she was stunning. He was not going to think of her in a bathing suit. Or, *God*…a bikini. His body prickled in response.

So basically he needed a cold shower, not a swim with her. 'I have work to do. The lake is at the end of the garden. It's safe for swimming and the little beach is very private so you won't be disturbed. When you get back we can make a plan for the rest of the weekend.'

'Oh, come on, Lucas. It's after six. You should have clocked off by now.' She brushed against him as she breezed over to her suitcase and he felt the hairs on his arm stand to attention. 'Surely you can spare an hour for a swim? Dom tells me you work too hard.'

'You don't get to be an emergency consultant by taking

time off whenever you feel like it. Or by endless partying.'
Or getting onto the front pages by being drunk and messy
on some celebrity's yacht. Or crashing the stage at festi-
vals. He decided not to mention her past antics, though;
she'd clearly changed. Outwardly, anyway.

'Ouch.' She laughed. 'I take it that was a jab at me and
my sorry life to date?'

'No.' He wasn't going to add to the mess he was starting to make here.

'Well, I'm grateful you've taken this weekend off for
me. Really, I am.' Despite his unforgivably negative tone
her smile was warm and did something to his gut. 'But it's
fine. Stay here and do your work. Maybe we could go out
for a meal or something later. I'd like to pick your brains
about the Isola Verde hospital project I'm working on. If
you have the time.'

Where was the flake he had known? 'What hospital
project?'

'You're busy. Honestly, it can wait. But the swim can't.
I'm too hot and sticky to think straight. I'll go get changed.'
She picked up her bag, shoulders sagging just a little.
'Which room should I use?'

'I'll show you.' He was drawn back to look at her
eyes. Wide and dark and deep with an understanding, a
knowledge of difficult times. Of pride too. And now they
glittered as she smiled and he got a glimpse of the old rebellious Giada. But she was much more than the ditzy
party girl she had once been. He took her bag and walked
her through to the guest room. 'And you'll be okay at the
lake?'

She nodded. 'Absolutely. No problem. I'm quite used
to entertaining myself.'

Her smile might have been warm but she blinked too
fast and he just knew she was pretending to be fine when
she wasn't.

'You head on down. I'll just be five minutes and then I'll join you.'

The smile of gratitude she gave him made his gut do somersaults. Which should have been enough warning.

And he should have listened.

Gigi hadn't remembered Lucas being so grumpy. Or so gorgeous. Maybe she hadn't been looking too closely all those years ago when she'd met him at some dull hospital party, and she certainly hadn't been interested in any of her brother's boring friends, choosing to find her own entertainment elsewhere.

But Lucas Beaufort was next level stunning with his dark blond hair and piercing green eyes. Just wow. And just her luck he was her brother's best friend and therefore totally and utterly out of bounds.

And now she was stuck with him for three days.

The water was soothing and coolly refreshing. She thrashed through her strokes until she was breathless and her limbs sore. Exercise had become her salve instead of the partying she'd once used to escape her life.

Take that, Captain Sensible. People changed.

He hadn't directly mentioned her past, but she was familiar with the look of judgement. Hell, she'd had it every single day of her life from her papa. She hoped Lucas didn't put her in the same box everyone else did, but it was a badge she'd earned many times over.

She was different now. If only people could believe it.

Tired, but definitely less stressed, she trod water, turning in a slow circle to take in the view of the city's high rises in one direction, the endless horizon in another, Denny-Blaine Park and... *Oddio!*

Lucas wasn't just gorgeous, he was a freaking hunk on legs, wading into the water towards her, not quite deep enough for his muscular thighs to be submerged. She traced up with her eyes...then swallowed. *My, oh, my.*

What was under those aqua-blue shorts?

She dragged her gaze higher, past the hard wall of a six, no...an eight pack, past broad shoulders to his proud jaw and unsmiling mouth.

She watched as he dived through the gentle waves and swam towards her with fast, easy strokes.

He is not hot. He is not hot.

Lucas rose up in front of her, flicking water from his hair. Little droplets clung to his impossibly long eyelashes, framing searching green eyes.

'You okay, Giada? It's quite deep out here.'

She'd forgotten he was English before she'd arrived, although his accent was very definitely infused with a Pacific Northwest twang since he'd been here almost as long as Dom had. 'It's Gigi. Yes. I'm fine. Isola Verde is an island, I swim a lot.'

'All the same, maybe we should go where it's shallower.' He stretched his arms out and her gaze was drawn to the toned biceps. The sprinkling of hair on his tanned chest. The stubble on his jaw. Those serious eyes.

What would it take to make him smile? How would he look if he did? And why did she want him to? She was only here for a couple of days and then she'd be back home, overseeing the final touches to her beloved hospital. Trying to be a better person.

Admiring a man's body was all well and good but it wasn't as if she could take anything any further. Especially not with Lucas. Brother's best friend. Inhabitant of Seattle...thousands of miles away from Isola Verde where her future lay. Her papa had always told her she dated unsuitable men and that she should set her sights on someone from one of the European royal families.

Boring.

She stole another look at this unsuitable man's broad shoulders, those full, kissable lips, that little trail of dark hair arrowing down to his shorts. Her imagination caught her low in her belly.

Just how sensible would Captain Sensible be in bed?

She dived under the water and tried to use the bracing cold to wash the very inappropriate and surprisingly sexy thoughts from her brain. Which was a mistake. Because down here she could see his legs, the ripples of his belly, his shorts…

When she broke the surface again he was frowning. 'You were down there so long I thought you were drowning or something.'

She laughed. 'I like to live dangerously.'

'So I've heard.' Of course he had. Everyone knew everything about her. Or almost, at least. He shook his head, clearly unimpressed. 'Can you imagine what Dom would do to me if I allowed you to get into trouble out here?'

'Depends on the trouble.' She laughed again, mischievously, watching the double meaning sink into his brain and the shock register in his eyes. Okay, so maybe she hadn't quite mastered *all* her spontaneity. And the cold water treatment clearly hadn't worked.

He twisted in the water, sending an arc of droplets into the air. They caught the fading light, a dozen fleeting rainbows haloing him. 'It's getting late and it's going to be dark soon. We should get out.'

'Okay, Captain. Race you to the beach.' She dived deep then, not waiting around for his reaction. When she surfaced she saw him powering ahead of her.

She dug deep and swung her arms into action and they hit the shallows at the same time. She stood up and kicked a swash of water into an arc towards him. 'Wow. You're good, Lucas.'

He looked at her, eyes dark, and she thought for a moment he was going to growl but, surprisingly, he kicked and splashed water over her. She shrieked and kicked back, following him to the water's edge and drenching him again.

'Hey. Mind the food!' he shouted, the glimpse of playfulness melting away as he pointed to the little grassy bank, where he'd left a rug and a picnic basket.

She hadn't realised she was hungry, but the thought of food made her stomach rumble. 'You brought a picnic?'

He ran and grabbed a towel from a pile by the basket and started to rub himself dry. 'Thought you might be hungry.'

'You're a proper adult, Lucas Beaufort. Thank you.'

After throwing the towel back on the grass, he reached into the basket and took out a bottle of fizzy water and two glasses. 'Honestly? I was starving.'

'Typical man, always thinking about food.'

'I had my housekeeper make it up for us.' He poured water into the glasses and handed one to her. 'Wasn't sure what a princess likes to snack on so there's plenty of everything.'

'I'm just a normal woman, Lucas. I eat anything and everything. But particularly...' She peered into the basket to discover olives and cheese and sourdough bread. 'Oh, this looks perfect. Just like my favourite Isola Verde treats. Did you know we have the best olives and tomatoes in the Mediterranean?'

'I think Dom has mentioned it once or a million times.'

'And our wine's amazing.' She sat on the rug, rubbed her damp body with a towel then wrapped it around her shoulders. 'Our grapes are perfect for dessert wine, which is delicious. Although some would say I've drunk far more than my fair share over the years.'

'Don't do that, Giada.' His tone was sharp.

She whipped round to look at him. 'What?'

'Don't put yourself down. We all did stupid things when we were young.'

'Oh, Captain Sensible, I saw you at that Medics Ball ten years ago. You were the epitome of good manners and here you are now looking after a princess in the nicest, safest way possible. There isn't even wine for us to get silly on. I can't imagine you doing anything you'd regret.'

'I've done plenty.'

'Oh?' It looked like the captain was about to share.

He shook his head. Maybe not.

She turned onto her belly, brushing his arm, gooseflesh rising at that fleeting skin-to-skin contact. It was strange, but this secluded magical place felt deeply intimate. 'Come on, Lucas. What do you regret? I bet it wasn't barfing down the side of an A-list film star's yacht in front of the world's media at the Naples Film Festival?'

His eyebrows rose. 'No. But I did see those pictures.'

'Ugh.' She shuddered at the memory. 'You and everyone else. Nothing can be as bad as that, right? Come on, what do you regret?'

He shrugged, opened his mouth then closed it again. There was something, but he clearly wasn't going to bare his soul to a relative stranger. Then he said, 'Entering a chilli-eating contest. It was for charity but even so…that was definitely not a good idea. Especially when you have work the next morning.' He snagged her gaze and she had the feeling he was on the edge of a smile.

What was he holding back?

She laughed, bewitched by the different hues in his irises—amber, gold and green. 'Can't say I'm a chilli fan.'

'And you should probably stay that way. But I couldn't back down because it was being streamed live on the internet for people to watch and pay however much they thought my pain was worth. You're not allowed to drink water or anything to help cool your mouth. I had tears running down my face, lips on fire, with a couple of thousand people enjoying my pain in real time. Your brother was the worst, egging me on from the sidelines.'

He almost smiled as he talked but didn't quite manage it. Giada breathed out, realising she'd been waiting to see the glow of joy or happiness or just plain fun emanating from him. But, even though he'd lightened up, she couldn't describe him as relaxed.

'I never even heard about that.' Though it was hardly surprising given she and Dom didn't always share details of their days or even weeks sometimes.

'Trust me, it wasn't pretty. I had my one taste of fame and I hated it. Honestly, Giada, I don't know how you can live under the glare of such scrutiny.'

She shrugged. 'I'd like to say I'm never in embarrassing situations, but that wouldn't be true. You do get used to the cameras.'

'I would never get used to them.'

A cool breeze fanned over her, making her shiver, and Lucas seemed to notice because he wrapped her towel more tightly around her shoulders. The action was so tender it made her heart catch.

He turned onto his belly then too, and somehow he was closer than before. She wasn't sure he realised it but she did. She could see the little hairs on his arms, the elongated biceps as he stretched for his glass.

This was crazy. Why was she noticing these things? Sure, she knew the power of attraction, the way two people could click, the way chemicals could align into hot sex. And the way the buzz disappeared just as quickly afterwards. Hell, she'd had her fair share of casual flings but never had her awareness hormones been on such high alert as now. She was *very* aware of Lucas Beaufort.

She stretched out on the rug, letting the last of the sun's rays warm her limbs. She looked at the tiny beach area in

front of his amazing duck-egg-blue craftsman-style house.
The sky was streaked with reds and oranges as the sun
sank. And there was no one else but them. 'I like it here.
It feels as if no one is watching.'

'I thought you liked to be watched.' Again the raised
eyebrow. 'Don't you want to take some selfies and post
them on the internet to let everyone know what you're up
to? The unspoilt beach that will inevitably become spoiled
once everyone's visited it. Pictures or it hasn't happened,
right?'

'Like you don't know.'

He popped an olive into his mouth and chewed. 'I'm at
work for more hours in the day than I care to think about.
I don't have time to do social media but lots of people do.
That's okay. I believe yours is quite popular.'

'It was. *The Princess Pages.* The blog, the website and
later 'the gram'. She rolled onto her back and shuddered at
the memories of the things she'd written; although they'd
been heartfelt at the time, they'd also had a lot of shock fac-
tor. 'That was a long time ago. And a very—how should I
describe it?—successful way of expressing my anger and
frustration and teenage angst, rather than using the plat-
form for good. Papa was horrified and with good reason.
But I'm twenty-eight, Lucas. It's time to be an adult, *si*?
And that means focusing on others and not myself.' She
chose not to mention the real reason behind her sudden
forced maturity and why she'd stopped being the Party
Princess. 'I'm opening a hospital for the people of Isola
Verde.'

'You're building a hospital?' Lucas looked impressed.

'Not actually building—I have people to do that for me.
But yes. It's much needed. At the moment we have to go
to Naples for anything more than a GP can handle. That's
difficult and dangerous if it's an emergency. Our people
need something on the island and I'm making it happen. It

was a fight to find the right place, to raise the capital and get the backers. And to get Papa on board.'

It had been a fight to get her father even remotely interested in the beginning because he hadn't had any faith in her being able to achieve it, but she was proud at how much she'd done. 'It opens in a couple of months.'

Lucas held her gaze. A frown. Deep thinking. Then his gaze dipped to her mouth and slowly trailed down to her bikini top, where she just knew her nipples were cold and pebbled.

As he met her gaze again something heated in his eyes that was surprising, even though it mirrored the way her body was reacting to him. Admiration. *More.* Interest. *More.*

Sexual interest.

And still he kept on looking and she looked right back. The stark rawness of need that suffused her body and prickled her skin made her mouth suddenly wet. It had been a long time since she'd been so intensely physically attracted to someone and it felt like a visceral awakening.

He swallowed and she just knew he felt the connection too. 'You've changed, Giada.'

'I hope so.' She picked up her glass. 'I've put my…difficult past behind me but it's going to take a while to forget the things I did and the people I hurt—my father, mainly, as he was the one embarrassed by every scandal. What's the worst thing you ever did?'

'Inhaled, probably.' He winked and for the first time in the hours since she'd met him he actually smiled. 'I am not prepared to divulge anything else.'

She almost choked on her water. Not just at the lack of anything bad in his past but at the way his face completely changed with just the smallest of smiles. Relaxed, he was simply beautiful. His eyes lit up and his mouth… God, that mouth. What would it be like to kiss him?

It was going to be a very long three days if every time she looked at Lucas she felt all turned on and achy. 'Before this weekend is over I want to know all the dirt on you, Lucas Beaufort. Dom says the only thing you've ever committed to is being a bachelor.'

'I've had my share of relationships. I just haven't publicised them. Or had any that held my interest for long.'

He was definitely single. Interesting. That made two of them...

'Pick up any Isola Verde rag and you can read about every single sorry relationship I ever had. The stupidity of youth, right?'

The corner of his mouth tipped. 'You were young; people understand that.'

'It took me a long time to grow up.'

Lucas turned onto his side to face her, propped up on his elbow. 'Growing up is overrated. I've been doing it for longer than I care to remember.'

She imagined him as an earnest child, studying his books with that little frown over his eyes. Dom had said he'd met Lucas in a locker room at the hospital all screwed up in anger over some family argument. Her brother had talked him down and they'd been firm friends ever since, so he must be a good man. A sexy as hell man. But he was far too serious.

She wanted to poke him or tickle him with a blade of grass to see if he'd laugh, but thought better of it. Hell, with any other guy she fancied she'd have just gone and done it. But with Lucas she wasn't sure. She couldn't read him, and that made him even more alluring. Instead of tickling him, she looked right into those eyes that were the same colour as her beloved Isola Verde hills. 'So let's pretend we're kids again this weekend. Let's play a little.'

For the briefest of moments he looked like a child who'd been offered ice cream...and had then remembered he was allergic to dairy products. His gaze clashed with hers and she could tell he knew exactly what she was suggesting. 'No, Giada.'

'That's it? No?'

'No.' He was determined, she could see. And yet...wavering. The way he looked at her mouth made her ache to kiss him. It wouldn't take much, just breaching the gap between them. Not far at all...

'What would you do if you could do anything at all?' she asked him.

He said nothing, just reached for a stray lock of her hair and let it run through his fingers. He contemplated her for a very long time. So long she'd almost forgotten what she'd asked him. Although the closeness, the heating of her skin and his scent mingling with the fresh cool air made her playful proposal very front and centre. It was there. They could grab it.

And still they just stared at each other until she could finally read what was going through his mind just by the way his eyes reacted.

Could they?

Should they?

Somehow they'd moved towards each other until they were touching. She felt the beat of his heart against her chest. The warm, soft breeze of his breath on her shoulder. His lips parted.

He was so close. 'Right now, Gigi, I want to kiss you.'

Oh, wow. Her tummy fluttered. Her breasts ached. She put her hand to his chest, felt the soft skin under her fingertips, the hard muscle under that. Heard his sharp intake of breath at her touch. He ran his thumb over her mouth and she heard a whimper come from her throat.

Then he drew back.

What? No one ever refused her. Not like this.

'Do it,' she urged. Almost willing to beg.

'No way.'

This was one of those once-in-a-lifetime chances. Feeding a raw need that had sprung up from...from what? Serendipity? Magic? An electric charge between them so damned bright it could light up the whole of Seattle. 'Do it, Lucas.'

There was so much heat in his dark gaze. 'No. One, you're the Princess of Isola Verde and if we do anything and it gets out, we'll both be toast. Two, I am ten years older than you. And, three, you're my best friend's sister.'

'Ah, that famous bro code again. But does Dom actually need to know? Hell, he practically forced me on you this weekend.'

'No, he didn't. He had a clash in his timetable and he asked me to help. To *help*, Gigi. That's a trust thing, okay? He would kill me if you and I stepped over a line.'

'Like this?' She wound her leg between his and aligned her body along his. God, he felt good. 'How would he ever know? Would you tell him?'

His eyes darkened. 'Never.'

'And neither would I.' She leaned closer, his lips a millimetre away.

'What's the punishment for kissing the King's daughter? Beheading?' He finally laughed, and it was the best sound she'd ever heard. Deep and yet melodic. Freeing.

She wanted to hear it again, wanted to make him smile, and she knew the best way to do that. Lost in him, she cupped his jaw. She could not stop this.

She pressed her mouth to his. The electricity was off the scale. Shocking. Intense. Amazing. Dangerous.

'It's got to be worth losing your head over, right? Just once. Or...maybe twice? Just for the weekend. No one needs to know. And phooey to the age gap. Who cares?' In truth, seducing an older, in-control man was a lot sexier than a younger hook-up. 'We could just...play. *Dio*, I need that and you do too. You're always so serious. Let's have some fun.' She saw the moment he made his decision. His eyes misted with the same need she felt.

'Gigi.' The way he said her name made heat pool deep in her belly. Then his mouth was on hers and he was laying her down on his private beach, her limbs warmed from the sun and liquid from desire.

His kiss was as demanding and desperate as she felt. A kiss that stoked the deepest parts of her, making her press against him, feeling the hard ridge between them. Making her want more. All of him. Here. Now. Pure lust. Raw need.

It was liberating to just be herself, Gigi Baresi, just a normal girl with a red-hot guy, making out on a beach.

Her idea of heaven...

CHAPTER ONE

November

IF EVER THERE was a time to play the royal card, it was now…

But the need to keep everything under the radar about the accident: her father, the reason they were in the United States en route to Seattle General Hospital and about…she pressed her hand to her belly and closed her eyes…*everything* was paramount. Secrecy was key.

Which made the screeching sirens, the ambulances and code red alert all the more ironic. Gigi didn't think her heart had stopped racing since the moment their car had skidded out of control on the ice. The concrete barrier looming up too fast. The impact. Her screams. Her dad's pained moans. Then his silence.

Her papa.

No matter how difficult things had been between them or how much she'd wanted to escape her life, she had never wanted something like this to happen.

'Another patient came in just before me. My father. He was in the car accident. Roberto Baresi?' she asked the nurse who was examining the painful welt across Gigi's chest. 'Can you find out what's happening with him? Is he okay? He was bleeding a lot and he…he was unconscious.'

The nurse—'Kat' it said on her name badge—shook her

head. 'I'm sorry, I don't know, but he's in good hands. I'll find out more as soon as I can, and I promise I'll let you know. Right now I need to focus on your injuries. Are you sure you have no tightness in your chest? There's a nasty bruise blooming there. No abdominal pain?'

Gigi took a deep breath and checked the way she felt. 'No chest tightness.'

Just blind panic. Her thoughts jumped from one thing to the next. And everything looked bad.

Was now a good time to mention she was pregnant? Probably. But she had to wait. She didn't want everyone knowing, least of all her brother—the head of this freaking emergency department! And word would definitely get to him. He would read her notes. He'd find out and who knew what would happen then. Her whole life would blow up. The whole nation of Isola Verde would catch fire with gossip and innuendo. *Again.*

And it wasn't fair to Lucas that everyone knew before he did.

'Good. You had a lucky call there. That seatbelt probably saved your life.' Kat nodded. 'You said your wrist hurt. Can I have a look at that?'

Gigi held out her arm for the nurse to prod and poke. 'Ouch. *Sì*, that hurts. But it's nothing. It's fine.'

'I don't like the look of it. I'm worried it could be broken. I'll get one of the doctors to order an X-ray for you.'

'An X-ray? Oh, no. No way.' She couldn't let that happen. She knew about the danger of X-rays and foetuses. *Baby. It's a baby. My baby.*

Our baby, she checked herself. What was he going to say when she told him? She'd been avoiding it for so long. Thirteen long weeks, to be precise. Gigi pulled herself together; she'd given the nurse such an over-the-top reaction to a sensible suggestion it would only raise more questions. 'I mean… I'm sorry, but is it really necessary just for a bit of swelling? I don't want to take up any more of your time and resources.'

Kat nodded. 'It's the only way we can know for sure if it's broken.'

This was a nightmare. If she point blank refused the X-ray it'd be suspicious. Gigi tugged her hand from the nurse's gentle grip. 'I'm sorry to be a pain, but if anyone's going to examine me it has to be Dr Lucas Beaufort. Is he around?'

The nurse frowned. 'He's with another patient.'

'I need to speak to him. Can you please tell him that Giada is here?' She managed to control the wobble in her voice, but not the wobble in her lip. Hot damn. She could not cry here. 'Now, please.'

Before I self-combust.

What about the baby? She wanted to yell. She wanted to demand a scan. To scream at everyone about the unfairness of all this. She wanted to rewind the clock until before they'd got into the car, before they'd arrived in the country. Before she'd spent the weekend with Lucas.

Instead of screaming, she cloaked herself in full, royal, Isola Verdian fortitude. *Remember who you are. You're Princess Giada Francesca Vittoria Baresi.* He might have been lying on a hospital gurney, but her father's words would stay with her for ever.

'Nurse Kat, I'd appreciate it if you could find Lucas as a matter of urgency.'

'Of course.' The nurse nodded and stood back. If she was taken aback by Gigi's response then she hid it well under a mask of professionalism.

Which made Gigi feel worse. Hell, she'd spent enough time getting Isola Verde's new hospital ready to know the dedication and hard work the medics put into their jobs. 'I'm sorry, I didn't mean to snap at you. I just need to speak to him.'

The adrenalin was wearing off now and Gigi was starting to tremble. She felt tears prick at the backs of her eyes. Scenes from the accident flashed across her mind. Snapshots of fear. Pain. The sound of metal crunching. The bang. Her father being worked on, their bodyguard covered in blood and—

Oddio, how was he? How had this happened?

Her brother had only managed fleeting eye contact with her before she'd sent him to see their papa and the others who'd been in the car and so far there'd been no news about any of them.

So she was stuck here, alone. And cold. She couldn't risk anyone finding out that Domenico was her brother and the heir to the throne...a throne he may well have to step into immediately if their father didn't pull through. A throne he didn't want. On an island he didn't even call home any more.

Her father might die. She had a baby inside her and she didn't know if it was okay. She didn't know if anything was going to be okay. Everything was going to change and she wasn't ready. Suddenly she felt very frightened and very alone and her body hurt from the impact.

She gripped Kat's arm with her good hand. There was nothing else to do but find someone to help her, and the only someone she could think of was the father of her baby. Even though he had no idea what was about to hit him. 'Please. Please, find Lucas.'

'Blood pressure dropping. Systolic seventy-five. We need to get him to Theatre *now* and fix that haemorrhaging.' Lucas looked down at the old man's pale face. He was holding on, but with a serious open leg fracture and possible head injury Lucas didn't know for how long. He nodded at Emilia, the talented orthopaedic surgeon about to take care of the nasty leg break and hopefully stem the blood loss. 'Ready?'

She nodded. 'I'll take it from here. Thanks, Lucas.'

'Good luck, not that you'll need it.' He removed his hands from his patient's head and let the anaesthesiologist take over care of his airway, then watched the flurry of activity from the staff as they hurriedly raced their patient towards Theatre, managing his lifesaving adjunct fluid therapy and balancing beeping monitors on the gurney. Then he snapped off his gloves and tapped out a history on the patient file on the computer.

Once done, he left Resus and rounded the corner, almost bumping into one of the ER nurses, Kat. She smiled. 'Oh, Lucas. Glad I've found you. There's a patient here demanding to see you and only you.'

'Oh?'

'Yes. MVA. Nasty bruising from the seatbelt and a swollen, painful wrist. Refusing any care at all, unless she's seen by you.' Kat gave him a quizzical look. 'Weird, right?'

'Why me?'

'A secret admirer?' Kat winked.

'Somehow, I don't think so.' He laughed at such a preposterous thought. He didn't need this right now. 'Has she been in before?'

'No. First time. At least, there's no other notes on the system for her. She came in with the patient that's just gone to Theatre. Roberto Baresi. She's his daughter, I think. Giada Baresi, I think she said.'

The floor under Lucas's feet felt as if it was shifting. 'Giada's here? Giada was in the car? In the MVA?' How had he missed that?

Because he'd been so focused on saving that man's life he'd paid no attention either to his name or to what else was happening in the department. Hell. His gut tightened like a vice. 'Where is she? Is she hurt?'

'Room nine. Her wrist's…'

He didn't stop to hear the rest of Kat's handover. Giada was here and she was hurting, everything else was immaterial.

As he dashed down the corridor his mind filled in the blanks. If the patient going into Theatre was Giada and Dom's father he was also…the King of Isola Verde. Yet no one had mentioned it—not even Dom, who had overseen his own father's initial care. Which surely meant that no one else knew and that must be for a reason…so he would keep it that way for his friend's sake.

Lucas's heart rate doubled. Poor Dom, to be faced with the only two members of his family injured and in his hospital. Every medic's nightmare. Lucas determined that after seeing Giada he'd seek out his friend and see how he was holding up. Be there for him. For them all. The way Dom had been there for Lucas over the years, as if he were a brother.

But, then, trouble often stemmed from families too. It was always about families. The good, the bad and the estranged.

Giada.

'Lucas?' She looked up as he threw open the door to her room. Her face was pale, her dark brown eyes huge as she sat on a plastic chair next to the examination couch, looking vulnerable and strained. Completely opposite from the way she'd looked that weekend months ago—vibrant, sexy, full of fun.

'Lucas.' She stood up and he could see the angry welt slashed across her skin, from her collar bone to the edge of her pale blue sweater.

'Gigi. My God.' He didn't know a heart could feel as if it had completely stopped and yet race at double speed at the same time. Didn't know he'd feel like this when he saw her again, awash with emotions he couldn't put a name to.

And he certainly didn't know what the right thing to do was. They'd put royal protocol aside three months ago, but things were very different now. He went to her but waited for her to make a move. This was a long way from sex on the beach. A million miles from two people enjoying each other just for one weekend.

Ciao, Captain Sensible. You dark horse, you. Thanks for taking care of all my...needs!

That smile. The wink. She'd drawn out a different side of him that weekend, but the fun had stopped the minute he'd delivered her to the private airfield and ever since he'd been...

This was not the time for that. 'Gigi, the nurse said you're hurt.'

Nodding, she stood, before swaying a little and stepping into his arms, clinging to him. '*Oddio*. Lucas, I can't stop shaking. It was... Is he going to be okay? Is Papa going to die? And what about his bodyguard? He was injured too.'

'It's okay, Gigi. I'm here.' He stroked her hair, battling the whoosh of emotions besieging him as her scent wound round him, as muscle memory made his hands fit round her waist exactly...there. As his body found space for her.

She had a way of hugging that was full contact. At least, a way of hugging *him* that felt as if she was giving everything to it. And he held her close, waiting for the ragged breathing to subside, the same way he'd held her on the beach, in his kitchen, in his bed and watched her come down from the throes of ecstasy.

But this was very different.

They stood like that for a minute, maybe more. Touch was their vocabulary and comfort.

Her touch had driven him crazy with desire only months ago and he hadn't realised he'd been craving it ever since. And yet they'd both agreed it would be a single weekend in a lifetime. No more. There just couldn't be more.

Now she was here and he didn't know what to do to make her feel better.

He mentally shook himself. He was a representative of Seattle General Hospital, a senior doctor and medical professional. He could compartmentalise three days from the rest of his life. He had to be the utmost professional now, especially with her brother breathing down his neck and her father in surgery. Added to the fact she was European royalty with a destiny very different from his.

Eventually she pulled away and breathed out deeply, tugging on a mask of coping. 'Okay. Thank you. I think I was starting to fall apart. I'm okay now.'

'You don't have to pretend, Gigi. You're allowed to fall apart at times like this.' He put a little distance between them and adopted his usual professional tone. 'Your papa is in Theatre. He's had a nasty leg injury and he was unconscious when the paramedics brought him in so we're a little worried about a brain injury—especially with the complications of his tumour.'

'You know about that?' Her eyes widened.

'A few of the more senior staff are aware that a VIP is scheduled for neurosurgery on a tumour in about three weeks' time. Dom confided to me that it was your father.'

'Of course he did.' Her hands worried at the hem of her sweater that was frayed and blood spattered. 'This is so bad.'

'As soon as we've stabilised him we'll take him for a brain scan. We won't know anything for a little while, but he's in good hands. Emilia's the best orthopaedic surgeon we have.'

She pressed her lips together as blood drained from her face. He took her hands and led her back to the chair. 'Sit down. You're in shock. That seatbelt trauma looks painful. Do you need something to help with the pain?'

'No!' She shook her head sharply. 'No drugs. I'll be fine.'

'Okay, okay.' She was clearly traumatised. He tried to make his tone gentler. 'Can I have a look at that wrist now?'

She nodded again, her eyes brimming with unshed tears as she held out the swollen and bruised arm to him. 'Kat said it might need an X-ray.'

'I'd say so.' He turned her hand over to assess the damage, hating himself for hurting her even though it was necessary to ascertain the diagnosis. 'The problem with wrists is that you can't always get a good view of the injury, so even if we don't see anything today, it may be necessary to repeat an X-ray further down the track, just to be sure.'

'Can we be sure *without* an X-ray?'

'Not really. It will mean you'd have to come back here if you're still in town. Or you could arrange to have a repeat X-ray at your new hospital in Isola Verde.' She'd been so excited about her new venture, to the point that he'd felt that excitement too.

She looked up at him through curls that had fallen over her face. 'I can't have an X-ray, Lucas.'

'It won't take much time. We'll have you all strapped up before your father gets out of surgery. You can go to him then.'

'That's not what I mean. Lucas…' She ran the back of her good hand across her forehead and blew out a slow breath. 'Lucas, I…'

'What?'

She blinked. 'I wasn't supposed to be coming with Papa for this trip. It was organised very last minute because he wanted to see Domenico about…well, about what might happen if he didn't make it out of surgery—'

'I'm sure he'll be fine. I understand his neurosurgeon for the tumour surgery is already on his way from Vancouver to discuss your father's case with the surgeons here.'

'… If he's incapable of ruling Isola Verde and the implications that has for Domenico,' she continued.

'God. Yes. Of course. Dom would become King and have to leave here and…' Dom loved his job. Loved Seattle. He hadn't been home to Isola Verde for years. Although he hadn't actually said it out loud, Lucas had a feeling that Dom was a very reluctant heir to the throne. 'They need to talk.'

'Yes, very much. Now we don't know if they ever will. Papa is frail…was frail even before this accident, and he's determined to bring Domenico back home as soon as possible. He needs his son with him to pass over a lot of royal duties.' Gigi sighed. 'But that wasn't why I came. I can't be the intermediary between the King and the heir.' She sighed again, her face creasing with concern. 'I needed to see you. To talk to you, Lucas.'

She needed to talk to him and she sure as hell wasn't professing her undying love for him. In fact, she looked apprehensive, scared even.

Lucas prided himself on being logical. On working out difficult conundrums, hard-to-solve cases.

She didn't want an X-ray. Why not? What was it about X-rays?

She didn't want drugs.

He looked at her beautiful pale face, scanned down to her full breasts. Her belly that looked just as flat as when he'd been with her. But…

But…

She put her hand over his. 'This isn't how I planned to do this, Lucas. But you have to know—'

She didn't need to tell him; he'd worked it out. 'You're pregnant.'

She nodded and looked so distraught about the whole damned situation that he had to look away.

Unable to bear the raw intimacy of her touch and the

memories that brought, he pulled his hand out from under hers. Then he stepped away too, the ramifications hitting him from every angle, jabbing at him like knives.

A baby? His baby? With the Princess of Isola Verde? What the hell had they done?

CHAPTER TWO

GIADA'S HEART FRACTURED as she watched Lucas take a step back. Two steps.

In fact, if the door hadn't been closed she imagined he'd have kept on retreating right out of the hospital, across the city, through Olympic National Park, over the water and as far away as Japan.

This was not the way she'd imagined telling him. So raw and brutal.

This was also not the reaction she'd wanted. Expected, yes. Wanted? Not so much. A smile, perhaps. A claim on their child. A hug. A promise that everything would be okay.

But, then, she'd known Lucas had been serious when he'd talked about not breaking the best friend code. Plus… okay, so she was a princess. Which made everything a million times more complicated. Pregnant and single. That would certainly attract more headlines. Although, given her reputation, it probably wouldn't surprise her people. But her father would be singularly unimpressed.

Again.

She hid her head in her hands and sighed deeply.

'I didn't intend this to happen, Lucas. I'm…' She was not going to be sad about the baby. 'Actually, I'm not sorry. Sure, it's a surprise and it took a bit of getting used to, not to mention the morning sickness. But I'm having a baby and that should be cause for celebration.' And she *was* happy. Now she'd got over the shock.

When she looked up he was still standing there, rigid, looking at her as if trying to work out a very difficult and shocking puzzle. 'Lucas. Please. Say something.'

He blinked and shook his head. 'You'll need a scan. Contracting seatbelts can cause damage to the abdomen and the uterus. I'll get the radiographer to bring the portable machine in here.'

So they were going the emotionless route. Right. 'Thank you. But I'd know, surely? If something was wrong. There'd be bleeding or pain and I don't have either.'

'We need to check.'

'Yes. Yes, please.' She'd thought he'd leave then to speak to the radiographer, but he made a quick call and stayed in the room. Silent.

After a few moments and just to say something to break the hideous impasse, she said, 'You're going to stay for the scan?'

'Of course. I might be in shock but I'm not a monster, Giada.' Not Gigi. Back to Giada. 'You must be, what, twelve, thirteen weeks? Why didn't you tell me before?'

'I wanted to be sure. Risk of miscarriage is higher before twelve weeks so I figured that if I lost the baby I wouldn't need to tell you anything. And then we wouldn't have this awkward scenario going on. But this little one…' she skimmed a hand across her abdomen '…is here to stay. As soon as everything was confirmed I arranged to come with Papa.'

He captured her gaze with dark, untrusting eyes. 'You didn't know I was going to be here.'

'You're always at work, Lucas. That's what you told me. If you hadn't been here I would have called, but I wanted to tell you face to face.'

The door swung open and an older woman walked in

pushing a large trolley with a machine on it. 'Ultrasound machine as requested, Dr Beaufort. You want me to do it?'

Lucas frowned. 'Yes.'

'Oh?' So much for the privacy she'd been hoping for. 'I thought you'd do it.'

'Sure, for a heartbeat, but not the full antenatal scan you need to have, given the circumstances.' One minute he'd been holding her, the next he was back-pedalling as fast and as far as his good manners would allow. Oh, Lucas Beaufort was good at cutting off his emotions.

Very interesting, and a smack in the face to her. That weekend had been the only time she'd felt seen for who she was as a person and not as the tabloid Princess. He'd wanted to explore her and not judge her. But now? Now she wasn't sure how the man she'd spent the weekend with could be the same cold one standing here.

Sure, he was serious by nature, and he'd been bogged down with the bro code and her being a princess and everything, but once he'd got over that he'd been very hot indeed.

She looked at him now, at his darkened eyes and clenched jaw that told her he was struggling to stay in control. At his dark blond hair, remembering the way it had felt as she'd thrust her fingers into it in the throes of ecstasy. She shivered, surprised at the hot, sharp, tang of lust that rippled through her even now. Even when he was angry and confused and aloof.

He nodded towards the machine. 'Obstetric scanning is a highly skilled process and, while I know enough to get by, I don't want to miss anything.'

Or he didn't want to touch her.

Stung by his reaction, Gigi climbed onto the examination couch and lifted her now ruined cashmere sweater to bare her belly, then wriggled her trousers down to her hips.

Lucas looked away.

She tried to read him but he'd simply closed off. Was he staying for the scan because he thought he should? Or because he wanted to? For her? For the baby?

But these weren't the kinds of questions she could ask with an audience, especially in the hospital where Lucas and her brother worked.

'Bit of jelly. Here we go.' The sonographer smiled and squirted gel onto Gigi's belly, which had grown just a tiny bit over the last few weeks. She was almost breathless at the pride she had in the teeniest bit of a bump. 'What was the date of your last period, Giada?'

She didn't need to look it up. 'Tenth of August.'

She saw Lucas do the maths and nod.

'Which makes you…?' The sonographer took a cardboard wheel out and turned it, but before she could check Gigi jumped in. 'Thirteen weeks.'

She'd counted every single day from the first day her period was late, wishing it would happen, praying for her usual cramping, hoping the painful breasts were PMT symptoms, trying to ignore the queasiness and the throwing up. Slowly getting used to the idea that she was very definitely pregnant and wondering how, seeing as they'd used condoms. But maybe…had they…every time…? Or had one failed?

Either way, she was having a baby. His baby.

She tried to look at Lucas to make eye contact to say, *See, it is yours*, in case he'd been in any doubt, but he was focused on the ultrasound screen. She knew without doubt because she hadn't slept with anyone else for a very long time. Ever since the last ill-advised lover had tried to blackmail her. Just another *cretino* trying to gain celebrity from her royal status. Way to grow up pretty fast.

'And your last scan was…?'

'Last week.' There'd been no way she was going to go to her newly opened hospital and advertise her pregnancy to everyone there, so she'd sneaked out to a private clinic and made them promise not to tell a living soul her news. 'They said they couldn't accurately tell the gender, but I didn't want to know. Other than that, all was fine.'

More than fine. She'd seen their baby properly for the first time and hadn't been able to tell a single person about it. Sure, she had friends, but she'd learnt a long time ago that entrusting people with a princess's deeply personal information could backfire. Spectacularly.

Lucas's back was taut, his whole body coiled tight as he growled, 'Can we just get on with it?'

'Sorry, Dr Beaufort. I know you're busy.' The sonographer nodded as if used to Lucas's sharp manner.

Well, Gigi wasn't. 'Please, take your time. It's better to be thorough, right? Make sure everything is okay.'

Lucas looked at his feet. 'Absolutely. Yes. Take your time.'

The room was filled the with fast *whoosh-um whoosh-um-whoosh-um* of a heartbeat. Gigi turned to look at the screen and saw the grey blurry shapes the sonographer was pointing out. The four chambers of the heart. Four long limbs...like his or her father. A cute nub nose. Perfect.

She hadn't realised she'd been holding her breath, but now she exhaled on a long sigh and, just like during her last scan, her own heart made more space for this child, and her chest filled with warmth and light. Whatever Lucas thought about it, whatever he decided to do was his choice, but she would love this baby with everything she had.

'Is it okay?' he asked, his voice catching a little.

She turned her head to watch as he peered at the screen. The stiffness of his limbs was gone. There was a softening in his eyes that made her heart squeeze. He wasn't cold-hearted, he was just in shock.

'Everything's fine.' The sonographer smiled. 'You have a little wriggler here.'

'I do—? I mean, she does?' Lucas blinked. Coughed. 'That's good news. Right. Thank you.'

'I can capture a photograph for you,' the sonographer told Gigi. 'A video too, if you like.'

'That would be lovely, thank you.' She'd brought a copy of the last scan with her to show Lucas, to give to him if he wanted it. Now he could have two. 'If you email it to me, I can send it on to the father,' she said with an eye on Lucas.

He nodded, his face unreadable; if he wanted the scan he didn't indicate it in any way. But he asked in an unemotional tone as the sonographer set the printer in motion, 'Could I borrow the ultrasound machine for a few minutes? Giada has a painful, swollen arm and, given the circumstances, I'd prefer to do an ultrasound rather than an X-ray.' Lucas turned to Gigi. 'The development of the baby's central nervous system happens between ten and seventeen weeks, so being exposed to an X-ray during that time period is ill-advised. An ultrasound is not as accurate a diagnostic tool, but it can give us a good indication of whether there is a fracture. That I am more than happy to do by myself.'

Gigi nodded, trying to translate not just his words but his manner. Having been reassured that all was well with the baby, he'd snapped back from father to medic. 'Lover' had completely disappeared at the mention of pregnancy.

'Great,' the sonographer said. 'I'm due a break now anyway, so I'll collect the machine in fifteen minutes.'

Gigi's heart clenched. Because, sure, there was a lot they needed to say to each other but the thought of being alone again with a very shocked Lucas filled her with dread.

This wasn't going well.

Lucas concentrated on keeping his hand steady as he ran the probe over Gigi's right wrist. Keeping it steady, because he was damned sure his whole body was about to shake and he didn't know how he was going to stop it.

A baby. *Damn.* It was the last thing he'd ever wanted. And with a woman he'd spent only three days with, a woman who had a future all mapped out that was very different from what he'd been working towards his whole life. Family wasn't something he did well. And he hadn't ever wanted to get invested in something that could be so quickly erased from his life, the way he had been from his parents' and siblings' lives.

And with Gigi being settled in Isola Verde and his life here in Seattle, it was very likely that he would be erased. What if she fell in love and married someone else? Would he still be seen as the father then? Would he have access rights to a royal child? How would something long distance work out? Hours spent on aircraft for both him and the little one.

Perhaps marriage was the only way of tethering himself to his child.

But…marriage? To the Princess of Isola Verde? As if that would be allowed to happen.

He was getting way ahead of himself.

Trouble was, he worked hard to keep his distance from any kind of family trap but the minute he'd seen the baby on the screen he'd claimed it in his heart. It was a living thing, a part of him. He felt blindsided by panic, and hugely protective.

As for Gigi…there was so much they needed to talk about that he didn't know where to start. Luckily, emotionless, reliable scientific logic was his go-to, so he started with that.

'I can't see any fractures. There's a lot of tissue oedema…that is, swelling. I recommend rest, elevation and strapping. A sling will help remind you not to use it and give support that will help the pain. If you need pain relief then acetaminophen will be fine, under the—'

'The circumstances, right?' she snapped. 'The circumstances being that I'm carrying your child and you're not happy about it.'

Happy? It was the worst thing that could possibly happen...a Baresi baby. Their baby.

He couldn't put how he was feeling into words. 'I've only just found out, Giada. Give me a moment to adjust. We need to sit down and talk about it rationally, once you're feeling up to it. But not right now, okay? You have enough to deal with.'

'I know.' She stared down at her bruised and misshapen hand, her eyes hollowed out, and sighed sadly. 'A very sick father, a pregnancy and a damaged dominant hand. Could it get any worse?'

Try suddenly finding out you're a father.

She needed support but he wasn't sure he was the person to offer it. 'Do you know anyone in Seattle?'

'Other than Dom and you? No.'

'Where are you staying?'

'At... Wait, I can't remember.' Frowning, she plucked her phone from her bag and scrolled through. 'The Four Seasons.'

'On your own?'

'Now, yes, I suppose so. I don't know.' Her eyes wandered around the room as if the answers were here somewhere. 'Obviously Papa is here. We had rooms booked at the Four Seasons, but I don't know what to do now. The car's totalled so I'll have to get a taxi to the hotel, I suppose. I don't know.' She ran the back of her hand across her forehead and her shoulders collapsed forward. 'I don't know what to do.'

He tried not to feel anything as he looked at her because feelings only hampered good sense but it was no use—

every time his eyes met hers he was back in bed, tumbling with her in the sheets. 'You look exhausted.'

Blinking fast, she straightened and seemed to snap herself back together. 'I'm fine.'

This was the Giada who'd arrived at his house. The one who'd pretended not to be stung by his initial refusal to play with her. The one who'd become used to dealing with her problems on her own and hated being seen as weak for wanting basic human connection.

He couldn't imagine how she was feeling given the stress she was under and the pain from the car crash. He wasn't being fair by being so standoffish so he softened his tone. 'Okay. You've been travelling for hours. The flight took how long?'

'Twelve hours.'

'Then the stress and adrenalin…none of that is good for the baby. You need to rest.'

At the mention of their child she looked directly at him. 'I understand that stress isn't good for our baby, Lucas, but unfortunately I'm dealing with a lot right now. I need to know what's happening with Papa. I won't leave here until I know he's going to be okay. And someone has to run my country, work out how much, if anything, to say to the nation. I'm going to have to try to talk Dom into going back to Isola Verde. He won't want to. But that's why we came here in the first place. To talk to him about taking over some of Papa's duties. I'm repeating myself, I think. I have such a bad headache.'

'Okay.' She was still in shock and panicked. The adrenalin would be whirring through her system, sending her thoughts scattering. He had to take control. He knelt in front of her. 'Let's make a plan. We'll deal with your wrist then I'll find out about your father, and I'll take you to your hotel.'

She sat back and sighed. 'Thank you.'

'And we'll stop off and get you something to eat. You need food.' He was interrupted by his phone's shrill tone. 'It's Dom.'

Her eyes grew wide and panicked. 'Don't tell him about the baby. Please. Please don't say anything. We need to work things out, you and me, before we say anything to anyone.'

Lucas didn't know how they were even going to begin that conversation. 'Yes, but after you've had a rest.'

She touched the back of his hand as he went to answer the call. 'Please don't say—'

'Giada, stop. Of course I won't say anything. I've got to work all this out in my head before I say or do anything else.' He pressed the call answer button. 'Hey, bro. You okay?'

'Holding up. Are you with Gigi? Kat said she was asking for you.'

'Yes, Giada's here.' He stood up and walked to the window, more for space from Giada than privacy. The room was so small she'd hear everything anyway. 'Just finished examining her wrist.'

'Is there a break?'

'No.' If…no, *when*… Dom heard about the pregnancy there would be a million questions and no doubt the inevitable betrayal accusation slung at him. Lucas didn't want to think about what this baby might do to his friendship with Dom, but for now he was going to be the best mate he could be. 'I'm organising compression and support. She's going to need to rest it for a few days.'

'That's not going to go down well with my dynamo sister. Is there anything else? Is she okay?'

She's pregnant. So, no, things weren't okay, at least not in Lucas's world.

But Gigi was clearly happy about it, judging by the look of relief on her face the second they'd heard the heartbeat.

'She's holding up, a bit shocked but getting there.' He turned and met her eyes and couldn't read what was going through her head. She held his gaze and he remembered how she'd tried every which way to make him laugh.

Come on, Captain Sensible. Stop being so serious.

She'd tickled and poked him, made lame jokes, had had him playing tourist in his own city, and he had laughed, so much, for three delicious days, feeling the lightest he'd felt in years. But now the tables were turned and the only thing he wanted to see from her was a smile instead of the hollowed-out eyes and the bruises.

One weekend was all they'd wanted and expected from each other. Without question she'd accepted who he was and what he'd made of his life. In fact, she'd respected him, and had made him proud of what he'd achieved. She hadn't made any demands on him, apart from lots of damned good sex. That was all, in reality. Nothing to hang a relationship on.

The baby changed everything.

He didn't want to be a father. Didn't want his messed-up genes passed on to anyone.

Tough luck. It was in her troubled gaze now, as if she could read his thoughts. *We're in this together, so deal with it.*

Swallowing hard, he looked away. 'She's worried about your father and his bodyguard.'

'Tell her Logan only had some cuts and bruises and is being cleaned up. Look, my pager is blaring, I've got go. I've a million other phone calls to make while Papa is in Theatre. Tell Gigi I love her, will you? That I'll call the palace and let them know about the accident but to keep everything under wraps until we know what's going to happen next. There's royal protocol coming in to play, you see.'

'I understand.' He didn't really. Couldn't imagine the weight on his friend's shoulders right now. He imagined that by 'protocol' Dom meant a succession plan could be initiated at any moment. 'If there's anything you need me to do, Dom, just ask.'

'You know confidentiality is key here, I trust you on that. No one can know about the accident until we are sure about Papa's prognosis.' Dom breathed out heavily. 'It's enough to know Giada's in safe hands and it's one less thing for me to worry about—right now, anyway. Tell her I'll talk to her as soon as I get a chance.'

Guilt shimmied down Lucas's spine. Safe hands? Once upon a time maybe. Before that August weekend when his hands had been itching to touch Giada's body. 'Sure thing.'

'Thanks, Lucas. I can breathe a bit easier knowing I can rely on you. It's good she has someone she knows with her. Stay with her, if you can. Please. She needs a friend.'

Lucas grimaced internally—that was exactly how he'd got into this mess in the first place. But this was most certainly not the time to go there.

'Of course. No problem.' The trippy ultrasound heartbeat that had somehow connected with his own heart pushed, squeezed and wriggled its way uninvited into his chest.

You've got a little wriggler there.

He sure had. He swallowed. He pushed those thoughts away—well, banked them until later—because he wasn't ever going to stop thinking about his child.

That suddenly made him wonder why it had been so easy for his family to cut off contact with him, save for the paltry annual Christmas email that was probably the same one they sent to their insurance broker. What was it about him that had made them decide he wasn't good enough to stay in touch? To call once in a while?

Families. He just didn't understand them. 'Dom, listen, I hope your father's okay.'

'So do I. More than you could imagine.' There was a beeping in the background. 'Damn pager. Got to go. Sorry.'

God, it was awful enough to have your father in surgery not knowing if he was going to pull through, but also, Lucas guessed, Dom was praying for his father's recovery because he was torn between his life here and succeeding to the throne in Isola Verde. He just needed time to get his head around the fact he was going to be King.

Lucas knew all about family expectations and how not abiding by them caused huge family rifts, but this was so much more than anything he'd had to go through. The freaking King of a Mediterranean nation?

He flicked his phone away and glanced up at Giada. *Gigi.* His heart tightened to see her looking so pale. It seemed that protectiveness he felt for his baby didn't dim when he looked at its mother. Which was beyond crazy. He didn't know what the future had in store but right now he would do anything to make sure nothing bad happened to either of them.

Somehow his involvement in this family had become so much more complicated than just being friends and he wasn't sure how he felt about any of it.

He put his phone away and turned to her. 'Right. Dom says your father's still in Theatre and there's no word on how it's going, but the minute he hears anything he'll let you know. Info on the others involved in the MVA is that someone called Logan—'

Her eyes grew wider. 'Yes? His bodyguard.'

'Has just minor cuts and bruises and is being cleaned up and—'

'Actually, you should probably know that Logan isn't just a bodyguard, he's a trained army medic and he's taking up a post here next week. Or, at least, he's supposed to be, if he's not too badly injured.'

'Logan... Dr Logan Connors?' Lucas had been briefed

about the new doctor's imminent arrival but hadn't realised the guy stemming the blood flow on the King's leg wound when they'd arrived was the same Dr Connors. That explained how he'd dealt with it all so expertly. 'Dr Logan Connors is a bodyguard to the Isola Verde royal family?'

She nodded. 'A good one too and we're sad to see him go, but he has a little boy and he wants him to go to school here. Logan's family is from Seattle and he wanted to bring his son and his parents home. Caring for a child on your own is hard.'

Gigi pierced him with a sharp look, as if poking him with the future she was facing.

He chose to ignore it. They needed to talk it all through when they were calmer. And definitely not here where people could barge in and hear. But she got in first, worry biting at her features. 'Is…is Dom okay?'

'He's busy. He's got to finish his shift and, knowing him, will probably stay here far beyond that.'

She shook her pretty head, her dark hair tumbling around her shoulders. 'He works too hard.'

'He's the Head of ER, it comes with the territory. In the meantime we need to get you out of here. Hospitals are no place for people who are generally well.'

A royal eyebrow rose. 'I spend a lot of time at my hospital. It hasn't affected me.'

'Yet. There are always bugs whizzing around. I'd prefer it if we can keep you as bug free as possible for the rest of your…' He glanced at her belly. Yes. It was sinking in. 'Pregnancy.'

'Okay. But I was thinking maybe it's not such a good idea for me to go to the hotel. I don't want anything leaking out about the accident just yet, or the fact we're even here in Seattle. Not until we get the say-so from Dom.' She sat forward, cradling her swollen arm. 'I'll cancel the booking for me and Papa. And… I know this is a huge imposition, Lucas, but could I stay at your place?'

Lucas closed his eyes at that thought. Have her back in his home? Her perfume on his sheets? Torture. 'I don't think that's a good idea. I can drop you off at a different ho—'

But he broke off as he watched her try to pick up her handbag, wince and then sit back in the chair, ashen with pain. How could he be so selfish? Thinking only of how awkward it would be to have her in his home when she had so much more to deal with. 'Of course you can stay with me, Giada. You're going to need some help while you rest that arm.'

'I'm fine. I can manage. I just need to remember that I can't use it.' She gave him a wobbly smile and his world tipped. The centre of his chest tightened.

'I don't want you to just manage. You need to rest; you need someone to help you. So, first, I'm going to apply some compression to help with the swelling.' He dug through the drawers and cupboards and found a bandage. 'Hold your hand out, please.'

She watched in silence as he wove the bandage between her thumb and forefinger and back over her wrist. She was so close he could smell not just her perfume but the scent that was uniquely Gigi. The one that he wasn't sure he'd entirely erased from his bed even after numerous launderings. He felt the heat of her gaze as he wound the bandage, as gently as he could but with enough firmness to provide support. Was aware of the rise and fall of her chest, fast enough to show she was still buzzing from the adrenalin. Felt the soft whisper of her breath on his neck.

The rhythmic weaving of the bandaging gave his brain space to think and it went immediately to the way this hand and these delicate fingers had played him, teased him, touched him.

And wouldn't he know it, heat wove through him, spiking a shot of desire sharp in his belly. So damned inappropriate.

He refused to look at her, knowing she'd see the desire in his eyes, and the memories. But they were of no use: he and Giada couldn't go back or look back. They certainly couldn't rekindle any of that madness that had kept them glued to each other for seventy-odd hours of sex-fuelled bliss. They had a mess to deal with and they needed to do it with level heads.

He stepped away and rummaged for a sling. 'Now I'm going to put this arm in a sling.'

'But then I won't be able to do anything.' She looked up at him.

'That's the plan. I don't want you doing anything with this hand. Elevation helps with the swelling, which in turn helps with the pain.' He opened the sling packet and tipped out the pre-shaped triangular bandage. Stepped behind her so he could drape the sling over her head and then over her arm, trying not to step too close or to breathe in her scent again. 'Fair warning, though, I'm useless with these.'

He came back round to look at the way he'd draped it. 'Okay, so it might be upside down.'

He shifted the bandage sideways. Had another look. Twisted it another ninety degrees. 'I have two medical degrees and an advanced trauma qualification. I will not be defeated by a simple sling.'

'Something you're bad at? Surely not, Lucas Beaufort.' The corners of her mouth twitched as he stood back and inspected it again. And then he made the fatal error of looking into her eyes.

Instead of looking away, she held his gaze.

His gut tightened. How could it be that something as simple as the organs of the human visual system were so mesmerising? So beautiful and deep? Their function was

to detect light and convert it into impulses the brain interpreted as images, a purely physiological act, and yet, right
now, also reflective of something as abstract as emotion.
One look into those dark brown irises and he could see she
was in pain, probably psychologically and emotionally as
well as physically. That the joking was a cover for the fact
she was desperate for something…he didn't know what.
Connection? Something as simple as a hug?

More?

He didn't know if he could—or should—give her more.

He straightened the sling. 'The nurses usually do it. I'm
great with endotracheal tubing or complicated suturing.
Fantastic with seizures, fractures and diabetic comas, but
bandaging…? Not so much. But…ah, we got there in the
end.' He secured the ends under her elbow with a safety
pin. 'There. This will remind you not to use the arm. At
all. Doctor's orders.'

She grimaced. 'How am I going to manage with this?'

'I will help you.' It appeared he had no choice. If only
she didn't smell so good. Or wasn't—he swallowed at the
thought of the baby growing inside her—*pregnant*.

He dug deep for a different subject. 'Now I'm going to
phone for pizza.'

'I'm not sure if I'm hungry or not but you're right, I
need to eat.' Finally a smile. Funny and a little sad that
the only smile he could get from her was about food and
not about the prospect of spending time in his home again.
'From that deli on the corner of your road? Stone fired?'

From the deli that had made the takeout pizza they'd
eaten in bed after a long afternoon of lovemaking. 'The
very one.'

He picked up her bag, making sure to avoid any physical contact with her. 'I can phone ahead and it'll be ready
to collect as we pass by. Then we can relax and wait for
updates from Dom.'

She stopped walking. 'Relax? While my father is having surgery?'

'Bad choice of words.' Seemed he was good at saying the wrong thing. Too damned good. 'But I hope you'll be comfortable there at least.'

Because he wasn't sure he would be. Not when he knew she was within touching distance. Things had felt a lot calmer—albeit far, far duller—when she'd been in Isola Verde.

CHAPTER THREE

WELL, THIS WAS a mistake of epic proportions.

She was clearly a lot more shocked than she'd realised if she'd thought coming back here was a good idea. Giada walked into his house, took a deep breath of the rarefied air that was pure Lucas, and was immediately assailed by memories.

The corridor where they'd had sex because they just couldn't wait to get to a bed or a couch. The kitchen where he'd prepared breakfast wearing nothing but a towel. The pool...*oddio*, that lap pool where they'd skinny-dipped in the moonlight after champagne and oysters. Magical. And afterwards they'd talked into the night about books, favourite films, everything and nothing.

God, it had only been for a weekend but it had felt so right.

And now, after his reaction about the baby news, everything felt wrong. Even she felt wrong-footed and yet it was him who'd had the mother of surprises. Or rather, the *father*...

She allowed herself a smile. He'd tried to hide his interest but she'd seen the way he'd looked at that blurry image. She just didn't know what the next step was. Not for Lucas and herself or for her family. It felt as if she was juggling a lot of balls in the air and she wasn't sure she would be able to catch any of them when they fell.

'Guest room?' she asked, knowing the answer but wanting to be sure. Things were awkward enough without more complications.

He was behind her, carrying her bags. She was so aware of him. Of the hitch in his breathing when her arm had brushed against his in the car. And the responding hitch in hers. The long slender fingers that had turned the steering wheel...fingers that had given her a lot of pleasure. The way his shirt strained across taut pec muscles she knew were honed from morning laps in the pool. That his arms were strong enough to hold her up as he'd entered her, pressing her against the bedroom wall, and, yes, in that pool.

Did he remember? And did he now feel as self-conscious as she did? As if they just couldn't find the right words to clear the air and bring them full circle back to that wall. That pool.

She wondered how he'd have reacted to her if she hadn't been pregnant. Would he be making moves on her? Would she be doing that to him? Would they have gone straight back to being lovers, feeding a renewed sexual hunger they couldn't stop?

But...everything was different now.

As if he knew what she was thinking, he clarified, 'Yes. I called and had the housekeeper make it up for you. Just down the hall. On the right.'

'I remember.' *I remember everything, Captain Sensible.* 'I think I'll grab a quick shower and change out of these clothes.'

'Do you need help?' He meant with her sling, she knew, and was being polite, not teasing or flirtatious.

'I can manage. I'm going to run a bath, I think that would be a lot easier for me.' It broke her heart the way they were being so respectfully well mannered around each other when she knew him so intimately. Knew how he tasted, what he looked like naked and sleeping. How his face lit up when he smiled. How she'd felt so safe enclosed in his arms. *Oddio*, she hadn't realised just how much she'd missed him. And missed his smile. Damn, a smile from him would be a good start. But she didn't have the energy to go searching for one right now.

Exhaustion tugged at every muscle in her body so she flopped down on the deliciously comfortable bed unable to summon any strength to remove her clothes, open her suitcase or…anything.

He nodded and put her bags on the floor. 'Are you sure you'll be okay?'

'I think so.' But her eyes were already closing.

'Do not do anything with that arm, definitely no lifting. Call me if you need help. Pizza will be waiting for you when you're ready.' He closed the door as he left and she wondered just how much he didn't want her to be here.

Not that she'd be here for long. Like her brother, she had some calls to make. She forced her eyes to snap back open and, using her good hand, she took her phone out of her bag and hit the call button for the first of many conversations she needed to have.

Lucas checked the time again. Giada had been in her room for over an hour and he wasn't sure quite what to do next. The pizza had grown cold and he'd just reheated it, hoping the smell of freshly cooked dough would summon her downstairs. But no.

He knew she was tired but she needed to eat, not just for her strength but for the baby growing inside her. And there he was; already making space in his thoughts for this new life. How would it be when she wasn't in the next room but thousands of miles away? How would he deal with the thoughts then?

He'd give her five more minutes. He slid the pizza from the pizza stone and onto a large plate on a tray.

Then he waited. Drummed his fingers on the kitchen counter. Three minutes.

Okay. Now.

He picked up the tray of food, walked to the guest room and, juggling the tray in one hand, gently tapped on the door.

No answer.

He pushed open the door and paused as he took her in, his heart stalling as lightness filled his veins. She was curled up on her side, wrapped in a fluffy white dressing-gown, fast asleep. Her hair was damp and curling in tendrils on the pillow. Her breathing came in little gasps, not snores but almost, and the sound was so cute and funny he held in a laugh. This was the Royal Princess of Isola Verde. Softly snoring in a guest room in his Seattle home.

The robe had fallen open around her breasts, baring a nipple. Creamy brown, darker than he remembered, but he knew pregnancy could change a woman's body in many ways. She was definitely fuller, rounder. He winced as his gaze slid over the raw stripe of bruising across her chest. But his eyes didn't linger there, instead trying to glimpse her belly through the tied robe.

Hot damn. What was he doing? Ogling her?

Okay. The pizza could wait. He needed to get the hell out of here.

Reluctantly dragging his eyes away from her beautiful form, he tiptoed backwards, banged into the door, clattering the plate on the tray against the glass of sparkling water. *Damn.*

'Lucas?' She sat up and rubbed her eyes.

'Sorry, didn't mean to wake you, but I thought you might be hungry.'

'Oh, the pizza? Yes. Actually, I'm starving.'

'D'you want to eat here? Or in the kitchen?'

'Here, please. I'm too tired to get off this bed. Is that okay?' She was being so polite.

'Totally fine.' He put the tray on the bed and helped her to shuffle up and recline against the pillows, making sure to elevate her sore arm. 'I hope you're ambidextrous.'

'What?' She noticed her robe had fallen open and hurriedly tugged it across her chest and tied it more tightly, but not before she caught his gaze. She knew he'd been looking. Her eyes heated, just for a second, and his whole body responded in kind.

No matter what their problems, the physical attraction was definitely still there, front and centre, if his trouser tent was anything to go by. He tried to think of mundane things such as folding laundry and the principles of asepsis as he sat down on the bed and handed her a plate. 'I hope you can eat pizza with your left hand.'

'It's going to be a challenge,' she admitted with a grimace. 'But trust me, I'm so hungry I'll manage one way or another. Any news on Papa?'

'Nothing yet. But I can assure you, if there was any news, good or bad, Dom would call immediately. My guess is that he's still in Theatre or Recovery.'

'Okay. Well, while we wait I may as well eat.' She picked up a piece of pizza with her left hand and, twisting her palm at a very odd angle, hooked her fingers around it. The end of the slice drooped and she dipped her head quickly to catch the dripping oil and cheese with her mouth. She ate with gusto. 'Ta-da!'

'Messy, but ten out of ten for effort.' He thought about offering to feed her, but knew that was a step beyond where they were right now.

But when she'd finished eating, he did grab a napkin, take hold of her oily hand and wipe it for her. As he did so her body seemed to relax and she smiled as she watched him. 'Thank you, Lucas. You're such a gentleman.'

'I just didn't want to get pizza oil on my fancy bedding.' He winked.

She laughed. 'No. You wanted to help me. Admit it.'

'Yes. I did. But I don't want to be overbearing.' Generally happy to be in his own company, he wasn't used to blurting out his feelings, but in this case it was important for them both to know where they stood. Their child was too important for ambiguity. 'The truth is, Giada, I'm not sure where we go from here.'

'Neither am I.' Her shoulders dipped, but she looked relieved they were actually talking. 'But you could start by calling me Gigi. Like you used to.'

'But that's a family nickname. I'm not family.'

'You called me that before.'

'Yes, when we were...' How should he put it?

'Playing?' Her eyes slid up to meet his and for the first time since they'd met earlier this afternoon he felt as if the barriers were starting to shift. She breathed out and shook her head. 'This is very difficult, *si*?'

He nodded. 'Yes.'

'You don't want a baby.'

'I didn't. Now? It's sinking in.' But he didn't want to give her the wrong impression that they were going to walk off into the sunset together. That was, if he was even worthy of being accepted into the Royal family as some sort of...what? What exactly would he be to them? A complication? An error of judgement? Always on the outside. 'But it makes everything awkward between Dom and myself, too.'

'He'll get over it.'

'I don't think you understand how a man feels about protecting his little sister. I've broken unspoken vows. He'll kill me. What did you say the punishment was? Beheading?' He was only half joking but his relationship with

Dom would be irrevocably changed and strained by this and that thought was like a low blow in his gut.

He lifted the tray from the bed and put it on the dressing table then sat down next to her again. She crossed her legs, tucking her heels under her knees. 'We are both adults, Lucas. We can do what we like. Besides, my brother hasn't been home for ten years. I can't remember him ever wanting to protect me.'

'He does, of course he does. One of the reasons he stayed here was to protect you from the fallout of him arguing with your Papa.'

She spread the fingers of her good hand and ran them through her almost dry hair, teasing out the curls into gentle waves. 'Papa does a good line in arguing, *sì*. I do love him, but he can be hard to live with. He has expectations and standards that I constantly fail.'

'Never.'

'I've been in the gossip pages for half my life and rarely for a good reason. As you can imagine, he's not a big fan of that.'

'You were forced to grow up in the spotlight. At some point you were going to stuff up.'

'Thank you for understanding.' She threw him a look of gratitude. 'He hasn't forgiven me for the things I did in the past. It feels as if he's just waiting for me to drop the ball again and drag the family into yet another scandal.' She cupped her belly with her palm. 'Looks like he's right about that. But I'm having this baby and I'm proud I'm going to be a mother.'

Pride? He hadn't thought about that particular emotion yet; he was still reeling from finding out he was going to be a father. What kind of father was he going to be? Distant, like his father had been and continued to be? No. There was no way he'd have a part of him out there in the world and not want to watch it grow up, be involved somehow.

'Sounds like neither of us exactly has a blueprint for happy families,' he said, choosing not to embellish that with his own sorry familial experiences. 'Which makes getting things right so important. I'm guessing your father doesn't know about the baby?'

'What? No! Not yet. He's had enough to deal with, with a brain tumour and surgery later in the month. And now... well he's very sick. I have to wait.'

'You are going to tell him, though? And Dom? You can't just get bigger—'

She laughed. 'Don't panic, Captain Sensible. I am going to tell them, of course. But you and I need a plan first. I'm assuming you'd want parental rights?'

'Ah, you make it sound so affirming and fluffy.' He bit back irritation, still astounded that two hours ago he'd been totally oblivious that his world was about to be tipped upside down. 'Yes, Giada. I want to be involved in my child's life.' Whatever happened, he would try to be a better father than the one he'd had.

'How? How's that going to work? I mean...' She bit her lip, frowning as if this was a very hard puzzle. 'What are your...um, intentions?'

'I don't understand.' What was she asking? 'Are you expecting...? Do we need to get married, is that what you want?'

'What? Really?' She blinked and then, surprisingly, laughed. 'Lucas Beaufort, is this a proposal?'

'Yes. Um. No. Not exactly.' He wasn't at all sure how he'd feel if she said yes.

'Good, because it needs work. No. No, Lucas. I don't *need* to marry you.' She flicked her hand towards him. 'This isn't the Dark Ages. I am perfectly capable and financially secure enough to look after this baby on my own. And by the sound of it you hate the thought of it...'

He did. At least, he had. Now, he wasn't so sure. And,

hell, even though he'd had no intention of proposing or marrying her, the rejection stung.

'It's okay. We don't need make any decisions yet; we have plenty of time to figure this out. You need to sleep. We can chat more tomorrow.'

'Ah. About that...' She pressed her lips together and looked down at her good hand. 'The thing is... I'm going home tomorrow.'

'What? You've only just got here.'

'Someone from the family needs to be in Isola Verde. I've phoned my private secretary and she's arranged for a flight...scheduled, unfortunately, but it's all we can do at such short notice.'

'Wait. You've done what?' What the actual hell? He fought to keep his shock under control. Oh, she was full of surprises, Giada Baresi. 'You just went ahead and arranged that without talking to me or Dom? What about...?' He'd been going to say 'us', but there wasn't any 'us'. It was Princess Giada and Lucas Beaufort. Two separate people brought together by lust and now forced to be connected for the rest of their lives. 'Is this how it's going to be? You making all the decisions and informing me of them, and I get no say?' He couldn't live like that. 'Damn it, Giada. I don't want control, but I do deserve an equal say in things.'

'My nation needs someone from the Royal family at home. Particularly when news breaks about Papa's accident. Dom can't go, can he? He's got to be here with our father and do his job. So it has to be me. Unfortunately, you are having a child with a princess and I have duties to perform whether you—or I—like it or not.'

She sat up and he saw the regal jaw, the tilt of her chin, the resolution in her eyes. He reminded himself that this was the indomitable and independent Princess Giada Baresi who had grown up with all the trappings of wealth, privilege and responsibility despite the occasional tongue lashing from her father, not soft, sweet Gigi who'd giggled against his naked chest and had sighed his name when she'd come.

'I am leaving tomorrow, Lucas. I have duties I have to attend to at home.' She paused. Thought for a moment. There was a tease in her eyes as she said, 'Is that okay with you?'

Well, at least she was listening.

'What would have been nicer would have been a conversation that went along the lines of…"Hey, I'm thinking I should go home. There isn't anyone else available and I think I need to be there to give some stability to the nation while the King and Crown Prince are out of the country. What do you think, Lucas?"'

'To which I could have answered, "Sure thing. That sounds like a great plan. How can I help you? Remember, you only have one active hand so you'll need extra support."' He paused to check his tone had been supportive rather than critical. 'And you could have said, "I'll be okay, Lucas, because I have people to help me, but thank you for offering."'

But even though he'd hoped she'd receive his comments well, her eyebrows rose and she looked stunned. 'You want me to ask permission before I do anything? *Dio*, you're like my papa!'

'I do not want you to ask for permission, I'd just like us to have a conversation. I'd like us to work together with this…new issue.' He looked at her, saw the confusion and, yes, anger, clouding her eyes and he knew he was stepping over the line here. 'You may well be a princess but, damn, in this house we're just a man and a woman trying to make a future that will work for us both.'

'I am always a princess, Lucas. That is something I cannot change.'

'You *have* changed, Giada.'

'You said that to me once before, Lucas, remember?' She bristled, her back straightening, her mouth flattening into a tight line. 'Only last time you said it with admiration and respect and now it just sounds bitter.'

'I'm not bitter, I'm blindsided. I'm trying to work out what we do next but you're always one step ahead of me, making your own decisions. I'm always playing catch-up. I just need a moment or two where we can talk civilly to each other.' Which was laughable because he wasn't sure how civil he could be when he wanted to kiss her again and again. She was volatile and aristocratic, fiery and unbending, but, hell, she was also sexy and surprising and beautiful.

Which, if he was honest, wasn't helping him keep his head clear and logical.

She sighed. 'Then come with me. We can talk on the plane. We can talk at the palace.'

'What? Just drop everything and travel across the world? Duck out of my job at a moment's notice? It's not that easy to leave my colleagues one member of staff down. Plus, there's an important charity event in a couple of weeks that I have to attend.'

'More chilli eating?' She threw at him with a look of scorn.

'A ball to raise money to add a new wing to the children's cancer ward at Seattle General. It's important. I have a *life* here, Giada. I have things to do, roster commitments…' He wasn't sure if she even knew what that meant. 'You have your own hospital project so you must know adequate staffing levels are always an issue. Never mind leaving Dom here to cope with your family's problems on his own.'

'He has Logan and all his ER staff around him. He can visit Papa's bedside and talk to him. Wish him better. When our father wakes up they will need time together without me being there. Papa's always better if I'm not around. And, besides, Dom's been coping without us...' she blinked and Lucas just knew she meant *without me* '...for long enough. I came here to tell you about the baby and that job is done. I need to go home.'

'And what am I supposed to do?' Follow her? Step back? If he did that he wasn't sure how involved he'd be in his child's life. He needed to make a stand now, from the beginning. Wow. His life had gone from busy yet simple to crowded and complicated in the blink of an eye. 'I understand you need to go home. Is there any way I can convince you to stay just a little bit longer so we can talk things through?'

'I have to go. I'm sorry, Lucas. I am needed. I have to be the voice of the family. You could come along later. When you have time?'

As far as he'd been concerned it would never be the right time to be a father, but he was faced with an impossible choice. Leave his job here, if only for a few days, or risk losing the first chance to make plans for a good life for his child. Time was the one thing he'd been deprived of with his own family and it was his biggest regret.

He looked at Giada. Her hair was a mess of crazy waves that stuck out at odd angles from where she'd lain on it. Her eyes were bruised with exhaustion. The slash of red across her sternum from the seatbelt was changing to purple and yellow and must hurt like hell every time she moved. Her arm was damaged and no doubt causing her a lot of pain. She needed to take some time to rest and heal but she was determined to do the right thing by the people who needed her.

She'd faced so much on her own over the years, having been left in Isola Verde without her mother or brother on side, and had risen above the hurt she'd felt from her father's criticisms. Now she was facing a royal crisis and a pregnancy that was possibly not going to be well received. And still she was determined to overcome it all, on her own.

Well, he wasn't going to let that happen.

Besides, he needed to put this child first and they needed to talk more. 'Okay. I'll make some calls and pack a bag.'

When he'd woken up this morning he'd been expecting a busy day in the ER. Not a seismic shift in his world and a sudden trip across the globe.

But if Giada Baresi was going to Isola Verde then he was going too.

CHAPTER FOUR

HE WAS IN the next room.

Was he thinking about all this the same way she was? Was his head whirling with possibilities and yet roadblocks too? What was going to happen to them all?

Was he thinking about her? About their child?

From her bed she'd heard his murmured voice in the room down the corridor as he'd talked on the phone, then she'd heard bumps and thuds. Lifting down a suitcase? And then nothing. For hours. He was probably sleeping like she should have been, but ever since her head had hit the pillow her mind had been full again, reliving the accident. Recoiling from Lucas's initial reaction to her news. His face when he'd seen their baby on the monitor.

Lucas. The only man who'd intrigued her because he'd initially rebuffed her and who hadn't been blinded by her title and riches. The only man who'd ever proposed so reluctantly it had almost made her laugh—and, yes, she had a few proposals under her belt. She almost wished she could rewind it to let him hear his tone: *I'm asking you to marry me, but please don't say yes.*

She imagined him lying on his side, dressed in his usual bed wear of…nothing. And then, just as it had so many, many times before, her mind filled with images of him. The way his eyes misted as he kissed her. The way his jaw set as he cried out her name as they climaxed together. The water droplets on his eyelashes in the sea, in the shower, in the pool. His laugh.

She'd dug deep enough to uncover the man she thought was the real Lucas Beaufort. A smiling, laughing man who was generous and funny and considerate. Who hadn't treated her as if she was in a glass cage, hadn't had any agenda but to enjoy her and to give her enjoyment. She couldn't remember the last man who'd been interested in her and not just her title. Oh, and he was as sexy as hell.

Her body tingled with a keen low ache, hot and needy, to be with him again.

Was he thinking about her the way she was thinking about him? Did he want her the way her body longed for his?

Was he thinking about her naked? About that weekend when they'd taken and given so much, exploring each other, tasting.

She could taste him now.

Stupido. He'd made it clear he was coming to Isola Verde because he had to, not because he wanted to. So lying here all hot and turned on wasn't going to help her one tiny bit.

Time to get real. It was okay, she could weather this storm on her own the way she'd weathered all the others. She didn't need anyone. She could cope perfectly well on her own. And, yes, single parenting would be hard but compared to most solo mothers she was in a far better position—or she would be once she'd explained it all to her family.

There was the sticking point. Her courage wobbled.

Giada sat up, checked her phone. A text from Dom saying their father was out of surgery and being kept in a coma but responding well. Stable.

That was good. And a lot more than she felt right now.

* * *

The airport staff couldn't do enough for her...a first-class customer who'd insisted on anonymity and got it. And somehow they'd wrangled Lucas to be upgraded to first class too, so they could sit together for twelve hours. They could talk then. He still wasn't sure what he was going to say.

He'd had to help reinstate the sling this morning, if only to remind her not to use her sore wrist. The bruising across her chest had bloomed overnight and she was walking as if every step caused her pain, but she didn't ask for help and didn't complain. Not once.

The first-class lounge was next level. Sure, Lucas flew business class when he could, but this was something else with its glittering chandeliers and hushed-voice staff.

Finally, after an early start where they'd only managed rudimentary conversation in the cab that had brought them to the airport, they were alone and able to chat. Giada smiled warily as soon as the lounge waitress finished serving them a hot breakfast of scrambled eggs and salad.

'Lucas, I know this is difficult for you, but thank you for taking time off. Did Dom ask any difficult questions when you called him? I'm hoping you didn't mention our news?'

'I didn't call Dom. He's the head of the ER, sure, but I need to clear any leave with HR. I had time owing. Hell, we all have time owing. God knows what would happen if we all decided to take it together. I said I knew Dom was busy and asked them to pass on my apologies to him and told them I needed to take time off immediately for personal and family reasons.'

He laughed at the irony of that and wondered what conclusion Dom would come to. He only hoped his best friend was too distracted by work and his sick father to put two and two together about his sister and colleague going AWOL on the same day. 'I don't feel great about not keeping him in the loop.'

If this had just been about him he'd have fronted up to his friend and explained, but it wasn't just about him, and his life wouldn't just be about him ever again.

'He'll understand, eventually.'

'Somehow I doubt that.' He'd left Dom in the lurch and short-staffed, instead of being there for his friend at a very difficult and stressful time. He'd need to do a lot of grovelling when he finally saw his mate face to face again. Swallowing his guilt, Lucas watched as Giada tried to eat her breakfast one-handed, stabbing at it unenthusiastically. 'You need to eat more than that.'

'I'm really not hungry.' With her fork in her left hand she rolled a halved cherry tomato across a slick of pesto sauce. 'One thing I've learnt is that morning sickness doesn't just happen in the morning, and even though the books say it should stop around twelve weeks, it doesn't.'

God, he hadn't even thought about that. Her body was undergoing changes and she was dealing with all that plus the accident, and now shouldering responsibility for her nation's welfare. 'Let me cut it up for you.'

Her eyes met his, her tone sharp. 'I can manage.'

So they were back to awkward conversation again. Great. His morning wasn't going well.

Luckily, they were interrupted by a staff member. 'Excuse me, Your Highness, they're calling your flight now. Time to go to the gate.'

Your Highness. Too often he forgot that. To him she was Gigi, but to everyone else in the world she was on a pedestal, out of reach, to be observed and commented on. He was utterly out of his depth here.

'Okay. Thank you— Oh. My phone's ringing.' Giada stood up but paused, her eyes panic-stricken as she looked at the screen. 'It's Dom. We don't have time, but what if there's news?'

'Take it. They'll wait for their VIP passengers.' And, wow, that felt strange. Their lives were so completely different and he'd have to straddle it all.

He picked up her carry-on luggage and watched as she spoke to her brother, telling him she was going home, apologising for the abruptness of it and for not warning him of their visit in the first place. Clearly Dom was surprised at this sudden turnabout and it didn't start out as a positive conversation, but she did a fair amount of pacifying and explaining. Someone needed to be in Isola Verde and she was the only real choice, but as they chatted the initial tension across her shoulders eventually eased until she finished off with, 'I miss you, too.' She didn't mention Lucas.

Finally, she flicked her phone off as another call for their flight was issued, and sighed. 'Papa's still stable. Still in a coma. No change. Which I guess is good news.'

'Absolutely.' He took her arm.

'One thing…they had to operate on his brain overnight. What does "intracranial pressure is under control" mean?' Worry lines etched her face, making her look beautiful but vulnerable, and his heart shifted to make space for this woman who was trying to be everything to everyone.

'It means they're monitoring the pressure in his brain. Often it rises if there's an injury and the brain swells, or if there's bleeding or a tumour.'

'He has a tumour already, so a bleed could make things so much worse, right?'

'Max Granger operated as soon as he arrived yesterday to release the pressure so I'd say he's in very good hands, Giada.'

'I know, I do and I'm so, so grateful, especially to Max because he wasn't scheduled to come over for the tumour surgery until the fifteenth of December. It's just hard to leave them. I wish I could stay, I want to. I want to be there when Papa wakes up, I want to be there by my brother's side, but… I can't. One of us has to be at home.'

She smiled hesitantly, looking for reassurance, which he gave her with a nod rather than tell her all the things that could go wrong in her father's recovery from the accident and his brain tumour from now on. She needed his support and that was what he was going to give her. She looked so vulnerable he wanted to wrap her in his arms and make her feel safe, or better, or…something. Instead, he fell into step with her towards the departure gate.

'You're doing the right thing.' He actually had no idea if she was…he couldn't imagine what the right thing was in this situation, but she was following her heart and her royal instincts and he had to make sure she felt supported in that.

She nodded. 'And Dom said he misses me.'

'I told you he would. If not for the accident, this time in Seattle would have been a good chance for you to get to know each other again.'

'We've communicated more in the last couple of days than we have in months. I just wish it was under better circumstances.' She gave Lucas an uncertain smile at the use of his words from yesterday and she softened a little, her good hand on his arm. 'Once we know what our plan is we'll talk to him, okay? I don't want you to feel bad about your friendship because of me.'

'I own this, Giada. This is on me, just as much as you. It takes two. We're in this together.'

'Thank you.' She blinked up at him then, her beautiful eyes shimmering, and he realised just how much she'd been hoping for that kind of reaction to her news. He could see how desperately she wanted him to be happy about the baby while all along he'd been thinking only about how all this affected him and his life and relationships. Yeah. Great. Selfish jerk.

He swiped his ticket in the machine at the gate and started to walk towards the front of the plane, but a buzzing in his pocket made him stop. He looked at his phone. Dom. *Damn.* Normally, Lucas would be straight onto speaking with his friend, but he let it go to voicemail.

Guilt rippled through him. He was being a lousy employee and a lousy friend so he had to make sure he was a damned good father.

The flight was long and even though he tried to talk to Giada, the engine sounds, the spacing of their seats and the staff attentiveness meant it just wasn't an ideal time or place for the kind of conversation they needed. And since Giada slept, he tried to do the same.

When the aircraft started its descent, he looked out of the window for his first glimpse of Giada's home: a large island of green in the sparkling deep blue Mediterranean Sea. He knew from both Giada and Dom that it was a fertile land producing an array of fruit and vegetables bursting with flavour and freshness. From this height he could see olive groves and lemon orchards and, as they swooped low on their airport trajectory, hillsides festooned in vines.

He was also surprised to see a smattering of high-rise tower blocks bearing the names of global accounting companies, indicating a modern, vibrant kingdom with a respectable economy and, in the distance was a shimmering white building on the top of a hill surrounded by acres of greenery. Glittering marble painted orange by the sunset. The palace. Giada's home.

His heart started to race. What was in store for him here? How would he be a father to a baby who would grow up here?

He barely had time to think before they were bustled off the plane and through the private exit door at Isola Verde International Airport to be greeted by a woman who looked to be in her early forties, wearing a navy blue trouser suit and standing in front of one of the royal fleet of cars with a small purple and silver flag sticking out of the badge on the bonnet. Well, wow.

Giada greeted the woman with a warm handshake. '*Ciao*, Maria!'

The woman dipped a curtsey with Giada's hand clasped in hers and replied in Isola Verdian.

Lucas coughed. Wow again. A curtsey. He hadn't even thought about that. Giada turned to glance at him, a smile hovering on her lips, before she addressed the woman in English, he suspected for his benefit. 'This is Lucas Beaufort. He'll be staying with us for a little while.'

'Of course, ma'am.' The woman nodded to Lucas and shook his extended hand. 'Welcome to Isola Verde, Mr Beaufort.'

'*Dr* Beaufort,' Giada interjected. 'Lucas, this is Maria, my private secretary and all-round wing woman.'

Lucas nodded. 'Hello.'

'Ah. Your arm, ma'am?' Maria asked, her face creasing in concern as she looked at the sling. 'You needed a doctor to travel with you. Is it bad?'

But Giada laughed. 'It's not broken. I'm fine. Lucas is here as my guest, not as my doctor. We're keeping his visit low-key. As in let's not mention it to my brother should he call.'

'Understood, ma'am.' Maria opened the car door for Giada to get in and was about to do the same for Lucas but he shook his head and motioned for her to get into the driver's seat. He walked round to the other side of the car and settled Giada into her seat, making sure the seatbelt went over the undamaged part of her collarbone and carefully cradled her belly.

'Lucas,' she whispered, 'I'm not made of porcelain, I'm not going to break.'

But even so, he could see the gratitude in her eyes for his care.

'Let's just be careful, okay? Precious cargo.' Wanting to touch his hand to her belly right there, to feel the life inside her, to protect it from any ensuing danger, he quickly swallowed and leaned across her, snapping the seatbelt in place, telling himself it was simply because she'd struggle to do it with her sore arm. But as he stretched back across her their eyes met.

He was momentarily frozen by the intensity of her gaze. The warm dark brown that had danced with carefree joy three months ago was now filled with concern and confusion. Nevertheless, even in this state her gaze took him back to the beach, to that teasing manner and her insistence they play. To that first touch of her lips.

His eyes lingered over her mouth. She licked her bottom lip and desire shot through him like a bolt of electricity.

She felt it too, he could see. Saw the flare of desire, watched as the wall of aloofness she'd been cloaked in since they'd got up that morning start to crumble.

'Lucas.' Another whisper against his neck.

He jerked his hand from her thigh where it had rested after he'd clipped the seatbelt then took his place next to her, shaken to the core by the intensity not just of desire but of…*emotion*. Something about this woman made him want to protect her, to let down his guard. It wasn't just the fact she was having his baby, it was more than that…it was her endearing desire to do the right thing, to put on a brave face, to carry everyone's burden, all mixed up with the playful woman he'd known three months ago, the one who'd accepted him, flaws and all, the woman he wanted to find again.

But going back to that would be impossible. He clipped on his seatbelt and vowed to keep a tight hold on his self-control for the rest of the trip.

* * *

Giada concentrated on being a tour guide instead of dwelling on the desire washing through her at his touch. She'd been too aware of the press of his hand on her thigh, the way his scent filled the car, the gravity of his gaze that was at once forbidding and enticing.

He was struggling with all of this; they both were. But here in Isola Verde she was the host and the Princess, and she'd have to work out the problem that was her attraction to Lucas and the connection that sparked whenever she looked at him.

They drove first through the old town of narrow streets and cobblestones that were as familiar to her as breathing. She watched his face as he took in the ancient buildings and vibrant marketplace bustling with activity. Loved the way his eyes lit up at the pretty marina and the children playing soccer in the street, dodging traffic and laughing as if they had no cares in the world.

Ah, *bella* Isola Verde. Even with everything clashing in her head and her heart, it felt good to be home and for the millionth time in her life she wondered, with a sharp pain stabbing her chest, how Domenico could have stayed away for so long.

She busied herself pointing out places of interest, wanting Lucas to see the beauty she saw here, wanting him to fall in love with the place the way she loved it. Wanting him to fall in love with their baby, too. She wanted him to fall—

No.

Her heart hammered at the direction her mind had taken. Falling in love with Lucas was not her plan. They were too different, had too many issues to overcome— wanting anything long term was completely irrational. She'd armoured her heart against getting involved with another man. Vowed to keep everyone at an emotional arm's length, the way her father had taught her, the way he'd lived. No show of emotion, no attachment. Cool and distant.

And, okay, she couldn't do cool and distant because she liked fun too much—she had far too much of her mother's DNA not to make the best of everything—but being broken and burnt had also taught her to keep her heart out of any romantic adventure ever again.

Her people had started decorating the buildings for Christmas with heavy, colourful garlands strung between the houses and across the narrow streets. Some of the shop windows already had nativity displays with miniature statues of the baby in the manger watched over by sparkling silver angels. One thing Isola Verde did really well was Christmas. She just hoped it would be a happy one for them all, hoped her father would be recovered and well for another year of his reign. And hoped Dom would have come to terms with his destiny.

'This part of the city is almost nine hundred years old. We can trace our family right back to the birth of our nation when the first Alessandro arrived here from Rome, claiming the island as his and declaring himself Alessandro the First. He built the cathedral.' She pointed to a magnificent marble building built in the black and white style of Florence's Duomo and felt a punch of pride for her country and its history.

'Later, his grandson opened the first real school here. We have an excellent education system and the Royal family have been both benefactors and beneficiaries of it. Both Dom and I went to school here. Obviously, Papa gave Domenico permission to go to medical school in the States, but I…well, let's say I just about scraped through the Isola Verde version of the Baccalaureate. Traditionally, Royal children stay on the island for their schooling…'

She left the rest of the sentence hanging. It was expected

that Royal children go to school here but how would Lucas respond to that? He'd said they needed to talk and that she had to consult him, which was fair, but what about ancient traditions and protocol?

'I see.' His eyebrows rose. 'I went to my local school too, as did my brother and sister. Then to Downing College, Cambridge. It's expected that all Beauforts go there, too.'

'I see.' She echoed his own response. 'I know Cambridge is an excellent university. Did you all study the same thing? Are you descended from a long line of doctors the way I'm descended from a long line of royalty?'

'No.' Something crossed his face, a shadow of pain. Then it was gone with a shake of his head. 'But I'd like to think my child could choose their own path.'

'Sometimes you don't get a choice about who you are.' But there was truth in what he was saying. Dom had railed against the path that had been forced upon him from birth and look where that had got them—barely seeing him for over a decade, a dash across the world, a skid on black ice and a lot of heartache. But there was something else in Lucas's words that jarred. 'Didn't you want to study medicine?'

'On the contrary, medicine was all I ever wanted to do.'

'I don't understand what you're saying.'

'It isn't always in a child's best interests to have their future mapped out for them. Even a royal prince or princess.'

Her eyes darted to Maria and she lowered her voice. Her secretary was completely discreet, always, but there were some things she wasn't ready to share. Yet. 'You're referring to Dom?'

'I'm referring to experience.'

'Lucas, I don't understand. What happened?'

He shook his head and looked out of the window. 'It's of no consequence, Giada. Only, hypothetically speaking, if I ever *were* to have a child…' he glanced at Maria '… I would need to have an equal say in where it went to school. As would the child.'

'Okay. Right. Good to know. I'll take your opinion into account.'

'You'll do more than that.' He glared at her.

Giada bristled with frustration. Controlling her irritation and disappointment, she raised her voice. 'Maria, straight to the palace, please.'

CHAPTER FIVE

How were they going to navigate the rest of their child's life if they couldn't even agree on one simple thing?

But, then, none of this was simple. Lucas was already too aware of that. Trying to swallow the frustration emanating through him, he climbed out of the car and gaped at the huge glittering stone and marble *palace*.

The argument melted from his mind as he took in the scale of the place, the breathtaking beauty and purity of the white stone and the striking regal purple and silver flag that fluttered proudly in the unexpectedly warm breeze.

He hadn't been sure what to expect but the palace and its grounds were beyond anything he'd imagined. A grand tree-lined avenue opened to a central three-storey building with a stepped roof and ornate central green dome. Spreading out east and west from the centre dome were large angled wings, two, as far as he could see, but possibly more. He lost count of the number of windows...too many, so many, indicating a labyrinth of rooms and corridors inside.

'It's...' he ran a hand through his hair and shook his head, lost for words all over again '...magnificent.'

Giada gave him a side-eye. 'Oh, you know, it's a bit cramped but it'll do.'

'How many rooms?'

'Two hundred and thirty-two.' She laughed. 'But you

don't have to visit them all. Most of them are dull anyway, just formal state rooms and galleries. Don't worry about your bags, Paulo will carry them up for you.'

Lucas grimaced, unsure how he felt about having people to do his bidding. 'I can manage my own bag, Giada.'

'Very well. It's up to you, of course. I've asked Maria to put you in the Napoli suite. You should be comfortable there.'

He wasn't sure he'd be comfortable anywhere here. Sure, it was luxurious but…overwhelmingly huge. 'How do you ever find your way around?'

'You learn. Places you can go, places you can't. There are shortcuts, corridors, secret tunnels.' She winked, clearly more relaxed to be in familiar surroundings. Their clash about schooling was still a bruise in his memory. They would come back to it eventually, along with all the other things they'd need to discuss, including things he no doubt hadn't even thought of yet. But for now he needed to get his bearings.

As if she'd read his mind, she smiled. 'I'll give you a tour later. First, I have a couple of meetings I need to get to. I'll be back for dinner.'

'You have meetings now? You've been on the go since dawn. When are you going to rest, Giada?'

'I slept on the flight. Well, a little.' Her eyes were edged with shadows, but her smile was warm and grateful at his words as if she'd been waiting, again, for him to show he cared about the baby. 'Okay. I'll make sure I rest later, I promise. After the meetings. I need to brief the staff and we need to make a statement about the accident. It's not right to keep secrets for too long: you always get found out in the end.'

He knew that well enough.

'Ah, here's Paulo. He'll show you to your room.' She said something in Isola Verdian to the uniformed young man who gave a low bow. The man nodded and turned, clipping his heels together, and indicated for Lucas to follow him. Giada patted his arm. 'Feel free to explore. The gardens are amazing.' She was swept away by Maria, ascending the white stone steps two at a time, and then she was swallowed up by the huge building.

And, before he had a chance to look at his surroundings, he was whisked through a security system exactly like the one at the airport, complete with X-ray machine, up a set of stairs, through myriad doors and corridors to his suite.

He stood for a moment, taking it all in—a drawing room, bedroom, bathroom and modern kitchen, all beautifully decorated with a mix of period furniture and contemporary features like a huge TV, internet modem and surround speaker system.

All very nice, but where did Giada live? Was she close to here? Where was her suite? Did she need his help?

Then he smiled to himself at the memory of her playful expression when she'd mentioned secret corridors. He'd bet she'd had fun navigating them when she was younger.

Ah, Giada. *Gigi.* His heart twisted. Why was this all so damned complicated?

After showering, he dressed in casual jeans and a shirt, choosing clothes more suitable for a temperate winter than his thick Seattle coat and boots.

And waited.

No one came and no one rang, so he decided to explore. Hell, it wasn't as if he stayed in a palace every day. He ventured down a sweeping staircase and couldn't help whistling in admiration at the vast entrance hall with a painted fresco on the roof that he was pretty sure was frosted in real gold. Everywhere he turned he saw artwork from famous artists he'd actually heard of, bronzes, statues and porcelains on plinths. There was even a huge marble fountain with a statue of a Roman god in the centre that would have filled up the whole square footage, and more, of the first floor of his Denny-Blaine house.

He lost count of the number of uniformed staff who passed him and nodded their welcome; some spoke a greeting in English, some in Isola Verdian. No one questioned who he was or why he was there—it felt as if everyone had been informed of his presence.

He stopped to admire not one, not two but three real Christmas trees in the hallway that must have been ten feet tall but still reached nowhere near the height of the dome. Decadently decorated in purple and silver garlands and festooned with tiny fairy lights, they would have given the Seattle General Hospital's famous festive tree display a run for its money, never mind his scrappy and woeful plastic tree he hadn't even bothered to get out last year. The smell was divine and threw him back to happy times with his family. Before…

Once upon a time he'd exceeded their expectations. And now they didn't even know where he was. In a palace! Go figure. How would his parents react to the news they were going to be grandparents? Would he tell them? Would they care?

His head suddenly swam with images of a toddler sitting here, opening presents. Christmas was never going to be the same. Would he even get to see his child for the holidays?

Damn sure he would.

When he reached the huge wooden iron-studded front door he was stopped by a security guard. '*Mi scusi*, Dr Beaufort?'

'Yes, I'm Dr Beaufort. Is it okay for me to go out of here? And, more importantly, will I be able to get back in?'

'Of course, sir. You have security clearance. Wait,

please.' He ducked into an office and came out brandishing a card on a lanyard. 'Here's your swipe card and ID.'

ID for walking around a house? How would he ever get used to this? How would his child?

He imagined growing up here in such opulence, with such gravitas and history. With the weight of responsibility always, *always* at the forefront of your mind. Being separate from everyone, being observed and scrutinised the way Giada had been all her life. He didn't want that for his child. He wanted normality—whatever that was. He wanted the freedom he had been given...and he wanted... yes, he wanted to be a better parent than his had been.

He followed a gravel path round to the rear of the building, meandering through a walled kitchen garden stuffed with blooming winter vegetables that gave onto the colourful *parterre* complete with the fountain he could see from his suite. Then a more formal garden with neatly clipped boxwood hedges and perfectly groomed lawns. Wanting to stretch his legs after the long flight and trying to get his thoughts in order, he walked through a copse of beech trees and found a secluded lake he hadn't seen from the palace. The fading orange light dappled and danced on the water and he inhaled deeply, finally able to breathe and think. Some peace to gather his thoughts.

He bent and swished his hand in the water...nowhere near as cold or as large as his lake at home. He hadn't actually ventured back into the lake at the bottom of his Seattle garden because swimming just hadn't been the same since his Gigi weekend. He smiled. She'd been spectacular then, glistening with water, nipples erect from cold but hot to his touch. The lust from before, when he'd skimmed his hands over her thighs, hit him again and it became very clear that when it came to Giada he couldn't be objective, at least not when it came to physical attraction.

And, yeah, it seemed like his thoughts were hell-bent on turning to her over and over and over.

'I wondered if I'd find you out here. It's one of my favourite places too.'

'What the—?' He turned quickly, heart rattling, and almost lost his footing. He waved his arms about to right himself and found himself face to face with the Princess. 'God, Giada, you made me jump.'

'Sorry.' She laughed. She'd changed out of her travelling clothes and was now wearing a form-fitting deep orange buttoned-up cashmere cardigan that hugged her amazing curves and cream trousers that nipped in slightly at her ankles. Her hair was loose, curls gracing her shoulders. Her face had been scrubbed clean of make-up and she looked fresher but still tired. Her injured wrist was supported in an inexpert sling almost as badly fashioned as his original effort, but she reached out her good hand to steady him. 'You looked so peaceful I almost didn't say anything. For a minute there I thought you might take a dip.'

He pretended to shiver, even though the weather was mild. In truth, he was just trying to steady his heart as it pounded, not just from the shock of surprise but from the shock of seeing her. She made his body react every time he set eyes on her. 'I'm used to cold water, but even I won't swim in December. How did the meetings go?'

'Good.' She nodded decisively as if trying to convince herself that everything was okay, but how could it be with the uncertainty of her father's condition? 'We're working with the new PR director at Seattle Hospital, Ayanna Franklin, to keep his location a secret. The plan is to release a statement that is honest but vague, mentioning a car accident and that Papa is stable and in good hands and that we're praying for a speedy recovery. I'm preparing myself for the onslaught of questions.'

'Do you have to answer them?'

'Journalists constantly reach out to our press office, more so at times like this, and I feel I have a duty to eliminate as much ambiguity as I can. And there's social media, of course, where everyone expresses an opinion. It's hard not to see, difficult not to look. The comments sections are always…illuminating. Not always complimentary, to be honest. Not towards the office or the King, who is revered here, but most definitely not towards things I have done in the past.' She shook her head, the light in her eyes dimming a little. 'If we don't keep abreast of what people are thinking and feeling, we lose touch. Our staff bring the relevant questions and comments for us to digest and respond.'

He'd never heard Dom talk about digesting people's opinions about the kingdom; his friend had appeared to be consumed only by study and work. But who knew how closely the Prince had followed life in Isola Verde, albeit from a distance? It felt as if his friend's life had been lived half in the light and half veiled. Unless, of course, her brother had chosen not to participate in any of this. Lucas felt a sudden sting of irritation for the lack of support from anyone close to her. 'You shouldn't have to deal with this on your own, Giada.'

Her back stiffened. 'I have Maria and my father's advisors.'

'But you still look at the comments, right?'

'Sometimes, but if I don't like what everyone's saying I look through my fingers,' she admitted, putting her hands in front of her face and pulling a pretend scared expression.

But Lucas felt unfathomably protective about this. Even though she was a grown woman, he had ten years' life experience on her. He had no qualms about not even bothering with social media. It didn't matter a jot to him, plus he was a doctor and had been taught how to deal with difficult and delicate situations. Despite having been groomed to be in the public eye, Giada was vulnerable now. She shouldn't have to be anxious about reading things in the media; she shouldn't read it, full stop. 'You need a shield from all that.'

'Oh?' She gave him a wry smile. 'Are you offering?'

Why not? He could be a stand-in for her brother. Protect her from the barrage of questions she couldn't answer. He made a spur-of-the-moment decision. 'For as long as I'm here I will read the comments and will only let you read the *relevant* ones. That is, the good ones.'

She tutted. 'That's like only reading the good reviews for a book. It doesn't give you the full picture.'

'To be honest, Giada, the only thing I care about right now is keeping the baby safe and well, which means keeping you well too.' He couldn't help but glance at her belly and was swamped by a tenderness that shocked him. Yes, he would be the shield.

'Thank you. You have no idea how much that means to me. To us.' She put her good hand on her abdomen and it took all his self-control not to cover her hand with his. To feel the growing baby there. His baby. His lifeblood. He wasn't sure he was ever going to get used to that idea. 'Lucas, we have a lot to discuss and a lot to work through, so can we try to get along? I know this situation is difficult for you and you didn't ask for any of this. But we're here now and we have to make the best of it. I don't know how to navigate any of it, but I promise I'll try to take your feelings and opinions into account, if you could try to do the same.'

She was extending an olive branch, quite apt given the plethora of olive groves they'd flown over on this lush island.

Her smile turned a little wary and he hated it that their argument earlier had made her feel as if she had to tiptoe around things—he much preferred spiky, feisty Gigi. That woman made him laugh, made his heart tug, made him hot.

Which was not appropriate right now, even though his body seemed to have other ideas. He nodded. 'I'll certainly try.'

'Me too. Good.' Her smile returned. 'And I don't want to pry, but I had a feeling in the car that something had hurt you. Something to do with schooling or college. Can I ask…? Can you explain what you meant when you alluded to having had your future mapped out?'

He wasn't going there. Not today. Not ever, if he could help it. 'It's not important.'

She touched his arm. 'Lucas, it is. I can see it is. We had a fight over it. Please tell me so I can understand. What happened?'

He cursed under his breath. He wasn't going to open that wound. 'It's—'

'Look, can we be open with each other? Please? I need to know where I stand with you.'

He frowned at her words. 'What do you mean?'

'I am a princess, surely you understand that I have my "yes" people who only ever agree to my requests, no matter how crazy they are, and also people who try to wheedle their way into my favour so they can get something from me…kudos, a favour, *money*.' Her cheeks reddened and she almost spat the last word out. She softened a little. 'But you're none of these things, Lucas. I get a sense of honesty from you. I know I make mistakes, I know I'm hasty and spontaneous and I've been trying to curb that. You'll call me on my failings. In fact, you already have. Can we keep it that way?'

He liked it that she was back to being direct. 'Of course.'

'So tell me why our child's schooling is particularly important to you.'

He blew out a deep breath, hesitating as he fished around for the right words.

'I'm afraid I'm not going to be a good parent.' The admission steamed out of him before he could hold it back.

Her eyes met his and she frowned as if trying to work him out. 'Nobody knows what kind of parent they'll be. I mean, look at me. A reformed rebel princess! I have no clue about babies, but I'll learn. *We*'ll learn. You want to do the right thing and that's the most important thing. I can't tell you how relieved I am that you care.'

He cared about the baby...that was an instinctive thing. But, he realised, he cared about Giada too, cared that she was supported and looked after. Which was a revelation considering he'd tried not to care about anyone...not deeply, not with any kind of emotional entanglement that would inevitably cost him dearly.

But there was something about Gigi that nudged and pushed and coaxed the caring side of him out of the darkest recesses of his heart. It wasn't just because of the baby she was carrying, it was her. Her sense of duty, her laughter, her gratitude. The determination to make this difficult situation work between them, no matter how unconventional...and the fact she saw the good in him.

'I had no role model, Giada. My father wasn't exactly the warm, fuzzy type.' Lucas shook his head, realising she'd prised out the thing that was haunting him most. And now, judging by her concerned and interested expression, he had to explain. 'Basically, he had plans for me and I had no say in them. I come from a family of lawyers and it was assumed I'd follow suit regardless of any dreams I had of my own. Same college, same firm, same pattern for every Beaufort for the last hundred years. Except that wasn't what I wanted to do. I didn't want to be a lawyer just because someone else had decided I should be.'

'So what happened?'

'When I told him to stuff his archaic plans and chose my own course, my parents broke off all contact with me beyond the bare minimum. A Christmas card here, a brief, emotionless text there. But after medical school, when I moved over to the States from England, it seemed to be the impetus for them to just stop answering my calls. We haven't spoken in years. I tried at first. I called. I emailed but...nothing. It's as if I don't exist. They're just not interested and have cut me out of their lives.'

Her hand went to her chest as she frowned. '*Dio*, that's awful.'

'You learn to live with it.' It had taken a long time for the sting of rejection to diminish and yet talking about it rubbed the wound raw again. His heart ached anew. 'So don't ever talk to me about happy families, because I've yet to find one.'

'Well I'm hardly a poster child for that either.' Gigi sighed. 'I think my father would gladly have cut ties with me if he could have.' She laughed, but then her face fell as she looked at him. 'They really stopped answering your calls?'

'Pretty decent parenting skills, right?'

'Oh, Lucas.' Her eyes roved his face and he was fairly sure she blinked quickly to stem a tear or two.

But the last thing he needed was her pity. That wasn't why he'd exposed his past like a raw nerve. He started to follow the gravel path back towards the beech copse. 'It's fine. Their loss.'

'Absolutely. They're missing out. I wish they could see you now. Look at you.' Her eyes blazed with passion. He assumed it was about the way he'd been treated, but there was something else there too. Admiration maybe. A readiness to fight for him. 'You're a fine man. A good doctor.'

'With bad sling skills.' He stepped in front of her and straightened the white bandage that cut across her décolletage. She'd managed to twist the sling and the support wasn't enough to raise the wrist to the correct angle. The bruising on her chest was all yellows and purples and he winced at what this perfect body had endured. When he was satisfied the sling was giving the appropriate support he stepped back. 'But improving.'

'Every day.' She wiggled her bruised fingers as she smiled, and he was shaken by the thrum of need that zipped through his body, sharp and electric. As if every nerve ending fired into life, straining to touch her.

You can't improve on perfect. 'Recovery's going to take some time, so don't go rushing to do things. Remember to ask for help if you need it, especially with the sling.'

'Yes, Dr Beaufort,' she said in a playful, sing-song voice. 'Seriously, all I did was shower and dress. Maria helped me fix the sling.'

'Tomorrow I'll do it.'

'Do what? The sling…?' Her eyes glittered and she was back to the fun young woman who he'd made love to at the lake. 'Or the shower?'

Oh, God. He thought of her naked, covered only in suds and his hands.

Princess. Out of reach. Ten-year age gap. Bro code. He swallowed. One of them needed to stop these sparks flickering into life. 'I meant the sling, of course. It needs more support at the elbow.'

'Pity.' She held his gaze for a second. Two. More.

Her clear brown eyes simmered with heat that stoked a fire deep inside him. He was hit with an intense need to touch her again and without thinking he stepped closer. Her floral perfume mingled with the evening scents of sun-kissed wild thyme and eucalyptus. Her eyes misted. Her breathing quickened, as if she was also affected by the same shiver in the atmosphere that pulled them closer.

As he looked at her everything stilled, both around him

and inside him. His gaze swept over her, over the lips he ached to kiss, the swollen breasts, the changing curves. Here, in the dappled light, she was astonishingly beautiful and utterly perfect.

She blinked up at him, desire in her eyes. Her hair was so lush and shiny, and he remembered the feel of it as it had run through his fingers. Wanting to feel it again, he reached out and slid his hands into her hair.

She covered one of his hands with hers. 'Lucas…' Her voice was cracked and the way she said his name sent arrows of need through him.

She stepped closer. Tilted her face until her mouth was mere inches away. If he dipped his head…he could kiss her again. That mouth. Her taste.

His heart thumped against his ribcage as he trailed his fingers through her hair and across to her cheek. The soft skin under his fingertips was warm but her gaze burned hot and he dipped his head. Closer.

There were so many reasons to stop, but he didn't want to. In fact, desire seemed to propel him closer.

Then she went up on tiptoe and brushed her lips against his.

Oh, God. He couldn't keep away, but he had to try. Crossing this line would only confuse things further. 'Is this the point where I call you out for being spontaneous?' he ground out against her ear.

'It's not spontaneous if you discuss it first,' she whispered, laughing as her mouth grazed his jaw.

They had a chance, then, to stop it. He should have fought, should have stepped away, but all the confusion and emotion of the last few hours coalesced inside him. She was Princess Giada. Gigi, the best lover he'd ever had. She was bearing his child. She was sexy and beautiful, and she understood he was struggling with this mind-blowing craving. Understood him.

'Do it, Lucas.'

Unable to resist any longer, he crushed his mouth against hers.

'Yes.' She moaned against his lips and opened her mouth to let him in. It started as a sweet, gentle exploration. He wanted to relearn her, discover her all over again, this new Gigi who was lush and glowing and growing. She tasted the same and yet different. Fresh, sweet, addictive.

He cupped her face, relishing the feel of her soft skin under his fingertips, the sway of her body as she pressed closer to him, fitting her body against his.

Then she wound her slingless arm around his neck and deepened the kiss with heavy breaths and throaty moans, and something inside him became undone. All his self-control, all the emotions he'd been stuffing deep inside him exploded into a need he'd never experienced before. He wanted her. Wanted to be inside her again.

She spiked her fingers into his hair, dragging nails across his scalp. '*Dio*, Lucas. This is crazy, but I can't stop.'

'I... God, Gigi.' A single *no* flitted into his brain and then blurred as he propelled her backwards towards a tree and pressed her up against the bark. He slid his hand under the hem of her cardigan and up to her breast, palming her lace bra. Her breasts were fuller, bigger, even more amazing.

She shivered against him, pressing his hand hard over her nipple. '*Dio. Dio. Dio.* Lucas, don't stop.'

He started to pop open the buttons, pressing kisses down her throat, and then he saw the bruises again...she was damaged. Hurting. He imagined the pain and trauma she'd been through and pressed his mouth as gently as he could over the yellow and purple marks. 'Giada. I'm sorry—'

'I'm okay. It's okay.' She cupped his face and tugged him up to look at her, her eyes swimming with affection and desire. 'Make me feel something good instead of all this pain.'

He covered her mouth again with his, finding the one thing he hadn't realised he'd been missing for the last three months.

This.

Her.

It was almost too much. He closed his eyes. 'I didn't think this was going to happen again.'

'You think too much.' She laughed, throwing her head back, revealing the pale white of her throat.

'We should—'

'And you talk too much.' She sucked in his bottom lip. 'Kiss me instead.'

'I was actually going to say we should go somewhere more comfortable.' In truth, those words had not been in his mind. He'd been ready to stop. But looking at her, listening to her, touching her…he wanted it all.

'I like it here. Fancy some skinny dipping?' She reached for his trouser belt, playing with the buckle, a wicked glint in her eye. 'I know how much you like doing that.'

Every sensible idea was being pushed from his brain with every touch of her fingers. 'I want to taste you again.'

Her eyes widened. 'Where?'

'Everywhere.'

'Do it.'

He didn't need to be told twice. There was no need for timidity. He didn't need to relearn her, he knew what she liked, what turned her on. They were back to where they'd left off three months ago. Hungry for each other, never being sated. He pressed his mouth to her throat as he skimmed his hand around her back and undid her bra. He groaned as first his fingers then his mouth found her nipple. He sucked in the darkened, hard nub, making her writhe against him.

'*Oddio*, Lucas. Yes.' She cupped his erection.

'Gigi—' Sudden vibrations shook the ground as something thundered through the trees.

She jerked back, swiping the back of her hand across her mouth, shoulders heaving. 'What the hell?'

Sensing imminent danger, he wrapped his arm around her and pushed her behind him as the thundering got louder and louder. He felt her shiver against his back. 'It's okay, Gigi. I've got you.'

She made a funny noise as the vibrations started to lessen and the thunder died away so he turned and wrapped her close in his arms and held her tight, vowing not to let anything harm either her or her child. Ever.

But her shoulders shook and she stepped back to look up at him. He realised then that she wasn't crying in panic but laughing.

'I'm thinking the end of the world's about to happen and yet you're laughing. What's so funny?'

'It's just someone out riding, probably exercising my father's horses.' She looked down then, biting her bottom lip, sadness clouding those beautiful eyes. 'He usually rides them here or along the beach when he can. Will he ever be able to ride his horses again, Lucas?'

Reality seeped into Lucas's blurry kiss-addled brain and he stepped away, shaking himself out of the spell they'd been under with just a look. With a taste.

He shouldn't be kissing her. Not here, not again. Not ever. The physical attraction was still very much there, the chemistry too, but they were in her territory now; their lives had irrevocably changed and different rules applied. Not just that, but she was grieving about the accident, stressing about her father, worrying about Dom. Getting tangled up in all of that would just complicate everything, for them both.

He imagined her father riding proudly through these

woods and knew he couldn't promise her anything about his recovery and certainly wasn't going to lie just to make her feel better. Hell, they'd just agreed to always be honest. He tipped her chin so he could look into her eyes, wanting to kiss her again but knowing that was over now. 'I hope he will. In time.'

'And we both know he may not have enough time, *si*? I... I need to get back to the palace, Lucas. There may be more news.' Her eyes closed briefly and he could see her mentally putting the kiss into a box and closing the lid, but not before the heat hit her cheeks too. 'Is it okay if we meet in the morning at breakfast? I'll ask Paulo to set it up in the Lega room at eight.'

'Absolutely. About before...' He ran his thumb across her swollen lips, leaving her in no doubt he was referring to the kiss. 'We shouldn't have—'

'I know. I know. We got carried away. There's so much going on. Too much. Forget it happened. Please.'

He nodded, unable to agree out loud. He would try, of course. But forgetting a blazing, desperate kiss like that wasn't going to happen any time soon.

If ever.

CHAPTER SIX

SHE DIDN'T SLEEP, of course. Not for the next three days.

How could she when there was so much to think about? Her father. Domenico. The baby… Oh, she couldn't stop thinking about that as it grew inside her.

And Lucas.

Here he was, strolling down the main staircase as if he was meant to be here. Her heart rate doubled at the sight of him. He was dressed in smart-casual beige chinos and a collared pale blue polo shirt that hugged his swim-assisted muscles, freshly shaved and with a smattering of grey in his hair that she hadn't noticed before. But, then, she'd been too transfixed by his eyes and his kisses and trying to work out how they could move forward.

He'd been here three days and she'd been the perfect hostess, showing him around her country, taking him on walks through the gardens, even a trip to the theatre to see a Christmas play. They were the epitome of polite and reserved, not referring again to the kiss, but they also hadn't got anything sorted out about the baby…neither of them seemed to have the stomach to start discussing a future that was months away.

So they'd fallen into a semi-domestic routine of meeting for breakfast, making small talk, reading through social media comments.

It was killing her.

Being so close every day and not being able to touch him.

She pretended she was fine. He kept his distance. He didn't touch her. In fact, it was almost as if he went out of his way not to touch her, as if he'd switched off that part of him. But she couldn't find her off switch. And her body strained for just the brush of his hand against hers.

Three days and her sexual awareness was off the scale. But at least he'd stayed.

He nodded as he reached the bottom stair. No air kisses. Still no kiss at all. 'Good morning, Giada.'

'Hello, Lucas.'

He'd called her Gigi down at the lake that first evening here, she remembered, and then realised she was looking at him for a sign. Something, anything to let her know what was going on in his head. Was he reliving that kiss the way she did night after night? Was he mentally pushing her up against a tree?

His face was a mask of politeness and she knew he'd retreated back behind the barrier he was too fond of constructing to keep himself free from emotional entanglements. Was that because of the way his family had treated him?

And why did it matter so much to her? She just couldn't fathom how he'd worked his way under her skin, into her head.

He nodded at her arm. 'Any better today? I see you've mastered the art of the sling.'

'The throbbing's stopped and the swelling's getting better.' She raised her right arm. 'Maria did the sling. We watched a video on the internet. She's determined to get it right for...when you're not here.'

Because there would be a time, she knew, when he would have to go back to his work. Of course, his life was there while hers was here—for the foreseeable future if not for ever, and especially while her father was sick.

There was no way she could do what Dom had done and give any of this up. She had responsibilities and duties to perform for her nation and her family. But maybe Lucas could move here? Maybe they could try to be a family? It could happen. If they both wanted it.

Stupid idea.

He was going to leave and she was going to stay. She would do the lioness's share of the childcare and he would, no doubt, appear when he saw fit. She'd cope. She had more than enough help. Everything would be fine.

'I see.' His jaw twitched and then tightened but he didn't say anything else.

In many ways he was right to put up barriers. The future was too unsure and adding her heart into the mix wasn't going to help any of them. Just one touch from him and she was all but undone but they had very different paths to follow, tied only by their child…and she knew how distant a father could be even if he was in the same room, so she couldn't let her feelings for this man get any stronger. 'Let's get something to eat.'

'I do like this room. It's so unlike everywhere else in the palace,' he said as he walked into the cosy yellow breakfast room with its simple six-seater table and a huge picture window that overlooked the kitchen gardens. She'd originally chosen this room because she'd thought he'd feel more relaxed here—she always did. 'When we first came in here I thought we'd be twenty feet apart, one each end of a long table.'

It appeared they were doing small-talk today. 'It's one of my favourite rooms in the whole palace, probably because it isn't so staid or formal. Domenico and I ate breakfast in here for years before heading off to school.' She ran her fingers over the dented mahogany and smiled at the memories of her mother shushing them as they'd chattered and laughed together. Of looking up to her clever, handsome brother and not minding one bit about how he'd refuse to speak to her in front of his friends, because in private he'd tickle her and, just to stop her bothering him, had even let her put nail varnish on his toes...as long as he could wipe it off before school the next day. Life had been so much simpler for them all back then. 'I doubt he even eats breakfast these days.'

'Probably shovels in a protein bar on the way to work, like I do.' Lucas picked up a plate and sniffed the air. 'Smells great. I'm starving.'

At least one of them had an appetite then. Lack of sleep made her head hurt and her tummy roil.

She prompted him to help himself from the silver platters on the side table that held bacon, eggs, pancakes and fruit.

He piled a stack of pancakes onto his plate alongside bacon and blueberries. 'Have you heard any more news about your father?'

'Dom texted to say Papa was still stable. Nothing new. That's good, right? I mean...obviously it would be better if he was out of the coma.'

'They're keeping him in the coma to give his brain time to heal from the surgery,' he said in the kind of tone you'd use to a young child.

'I understand that, but I want to fast-forward to where he wakes up. But then we'll have to tell him about this...' She put her hand over her belly, convinced she was bigger now than yesterday, although that was likely improbable. Lucas's eyes drifted to her stomach and she could see the softening there, the undisguised interest. 'Soon enough I'll be too big to hide the fact I'm pregnant.'

He stared at her then. 'Is everything okay?'

'As far as I know. Is it stupid to want to have a scan every day just to watch the baby growing?'

He shook his head. 'Not at all. Every mother wants reassurance.'

And father too? 'Oh, I never sent you the ultrasound video. Here.' She sat at the table and opened her digital tablet, scrolled through and clicked. The *whoosh-um-whoosh-um-whoosh-um* echoed around the room. 'Shoot! Better turn the volume off in case anyone comes in.'

He sat down opposite her and shook his head, quite vehemently. 'Just email it to me. I can look later.'

His attitude stung. 'What's wrong?'

'Nothing.'

She'd had enough of this tiptoeing around; they'd been doing that for three days and it was only making things worse. 'Is it the kiss? Are you still angry about it? Or is it something else? The baby?'

'Angry?' He frowned at her words then his shoulders dropped and he exhaled heavily. 'No, Giada, not at you. But I am…frustrated that we got into this situation.'

'You have to admit it was fun, though.' She shrugged, trying to make a joke. She wanted to see him smile, for reassurance more than anything but also because he looked so good when he let his guard down. 'I think you're still sore about that kiss.'

He flinched at the memory. 'I'm just glad we pressed the stop button.'

Funny, she hadn't been thinking that at all—sure, in theory, he was right, but it hadn't stopped her wanting a rerun. 'There's a lot for us to deal with at the moment. We can't help it if emotions run high and we get…um… carried away.'

'We *can* help it.' He gaped at her. 'We can't just let our emotions run amok and do what we want. You know full well anyone could have seen us and spread gossip and you certainly don't want to have to deal with that.'

'You sound just like my father.'

'That's probably the age difference showing itself.' He speared a piece of pancake with his fork.

'Ouch, Lucas. You didn't think much about that down by the lake. Or three months ago. Not when you had your hands on me.' She put her palm near her breast where his mouth had been. Where she wanted it again. And his eyes followed, his pupils widening.

He rubbed his forehead with his fingers. 'Giada, please. This is very difficult.'

'I know and you're not helping. I'm trying to get my head around things and a bit of light relief will keep me sane. It would be great if you could loosen up a bit.'

He put down his knife and fork. 'This is who I am, Giada. I'm a doctor, not a clown.'

'You did a lot more smiling back in August.'

'Things were very different then.'

'You don't say.' She'd been able to cajole him then, seduce him. He'd been a challenge and she'd managed to push through his reserve. She'd had a glimpse of the real Lucas Beaufort, unfettered, unworried, unconstrained, but she didn't know if she had the strength or emotional wherewithal to do it again with everything else going on.

She managed a mouthful of coffee then remembered it made her queasy. Or maybe it was the realisation that he'd retreated so far he wasn't planning on coming back any time soon that made her tummy hurt. Oh, he was a challenge all right. 'Right, eat up your breakfast and then we can get on with the day.'

She put her digital tablet back onto the table and turned it on but he covered it with his palm.

'Do you want to go through the media comments?'

'Too late. I've already looked. Through my fingers, before I got up.'

He glared at her. 'Why?'

'What can I say? I'm an independent woman. I was awake half the night and it seemed like a good use of my time.' Instead of Lucas bearing witness to some of the less savoury comments about her. *Princess Party... The Giada Problem...*

Shaking his head, irritated, he leaned forward and frowned. Again. 'What did they say?'

'There are still a lot of good wishes. Many, many from all around the world. But there are questions too. Why the silence now? Three days and no more updates. Where is Domenico? Where is the King? When is he being brought back to Isola Verde?'

He nodded curtly. 'All questions that can either be ignored or pacified with non-specific statements.'

'I'm not good at being impartial and non-specific when it's about my family.'

He shrugged. 'As a doctor you learn to keep your emotions to yourself. It isn't helpful or professional to get upset in front of a patient. I can do noncommittal when necessary.'

'Yes, Captain Sensible. I'd say you've achieved expert level.'

He blinked and sat up straight as he took in her words. Maybe no one had ever spoken so forthrightly to him before? He seemed to think it through and then wrestle inwardly for a couple of moments before he answered her. 'Tomorrow I will check them first. It's not good to look at that before you even get out of bed.'

'Okay. It's a date.' She dug for a smile, trying to show him that his attitude towards her would not bring her down. 'And today I have a treat in store for you.'

'Oh?' His expression was wary.

'Don't worry, I'm not going to lose control and kiss you again.' She watched the sudden flare of heat in his eyes and smiled to herself. Oh, yes. Lucas Beaufort could say what he liked, but no matter how much he tried he couldn't always mask the way his body reacted to her. 'We are going to see my hospital.'

He'd been too hard on her, he knew that, and guilt bit.

But it was a self-preservation thing. If he was going to survive this visit he needed to keep his distance from her. Even so, the need to see her smile again wound itself inside him. She wanted funny and relaxed but he was serious and uptight. It was yet another reason why they were so mismatched. And yet...there was something between them that went deeper, so deep it felt as if there was a real physical connection.

Indeed, the physicality was so intense it spooked him. How could it be that two people turned each other on so much and yet couldn't manage more than half a dozen civil words?

It was his fault. He was trying too hard to protect them both from the fallout of another ill-advised liaison. But should he try to loosen up? Could he be the man he'd been in August when she'd smashed his barriers down? When it had been about the now and not about the consequences?

Could he be the man she wanted him to be?

Or would that mean a personality transplant?

Thing was, he wanted to try, and that shook him more than anything else.

The car pulled up outside an impressive state-of-the-art glass-fronted building. Given everything that was happening, the new Isola Verde Hospital hadn't been at the forefront of his mind but he could feel her enthusiasm rising as they stepped inside and he felt a similar prickle of excitement.

Despite protestations, she'd told Maria to wait in the car, saying, 'I'm fine. I don't need babysitting all the time.' Then she'd rolled her eyes at Lucas. 'It's suffocating to have someone in your face all the time.'

'A bodyguard is for your own safety, surely?'

'Please don't you start too. It's annoying. Papa likes an entourage, I prefer to go incognito.' She winked. 'Besides, no one's going to bother me with you by my side. One grumpy look and you'll scare them half to death.'

He didn't know what to say to that. Mainly because she was right. There was no middle ground between them; it was either all intense desire or polite and awkward. And that, he knew, was all on him.

As they walked in a young woman dashed from behind the reception desk and curtsied. 'Your Highness.' She added something else that Lucas didn't understand.

Giada smiled and replied in English. 'I am not here on an official visit. An escort from management isn't necessary, thank you. I'm just showing a doctor friend of mine around the hospital.'

'Yes, Your Highness. Have a good day.'

'We had the official opening a few weeks ago.' Giada turned back to Lucas, her high ponytail swishing and heels clicking as they walked across the tiled floor. This was only a social visit but she was dressed smartly in a vivid blue silk blouse and curve-enhancing black pencil skirt that kicked out at the knees. And stiletto heels.

Man, those heels. The stuff men's dreams were made of. Yes, he may have been grumpy but a lot of that was due to sexual frustration. More than once he'd had to stop himself from touching her. Sure, he'd made up his mind that he would put a stop to any more kissing, but that didn't mean he *wanted* to put a stop to it. He was trying hard here…but…stilettoes.

The place looked like a hotel with comfortable sofas and

friendly welcoming staff, only the fresh disinfectant smell and signs pointing the way to Emergency, Cardiac Care and specialist wards giving away the fact they were in a clinical environment. There was a tall Christmas tree right by the front door with piles of Christmas gifts underneath.

Giada smiled as she followed his gaze. 'I wanted to make it a place where people felt looked after rather than put off by a sterile cold atmosphere.'

'We try to achieve the same at Seattle General. The annual Christmas display is always eye-catching and the kids love it.' He felt a pang of homesickness then. How comforting it would be to slip back into his old routine of work, swim, work. Yeah, not much of a life, but it was steady and predictable. Unlike life with Giada so far.

'You look like you're missing your day job. I imagine being on this island is pretty boring.' She tugged on his arm. 'Come see the ER.'

They followed the sign towards the emergency department but Lucas was stopped in his tracks by a large portrait on the wall. A stunning woman with commanding brown eyes and long dark hair swept up into a loose bun, wearing a tiara, a formal gown of purple and silver and a beautiful smile looked down at him. Giada in all her regal glory. His heart stalled as he tried to read the plaque underneath, but it was in Isola Verdian. 'What does it say?'

Her cheeks turned pink as she cleared her throat and read out, '"Our nation thanks with all our hearts Giada, the People's Princess, for bestowing this wonderful facility for the benefit of everyone in Isola Verde."' She gave an embarrassed smile. 'I asked them not to put it up but they insisted.'

'The People's Princess? They obviously love you.'

'Some do. Some really don't. Well...' She held up her sling-free hand. 'That's not entirely true. I was popular as a child, but in my late teens and early twenties not so much. It hasn't always been easy. I disgraced myself more than a few times and I've worked hard on my reputation over the last couple of years.'

'This hospital is an amazing achievement.'

She huffed. 'I wanted to do something that will benefit everyone.'

'Your father must be very proud of you.'

Her throat made a funny noise—half laugh, half derision. 'You don't know Papa. As far as he's concerned, once trouble, always trouble. He was so used to hearing bad things about me he didn't trust the good stuff.'

'So why did you decide to do this instead of partying on yachts?'

She led him down the long corridor following signs to ER, her demeanour brisk. 'Let's just say I had a life lesson that made me realise that my legacy shouldn't be about the trouble I caused but about the good I could do.'

'Sounds serious. What happened?'

She shook her head and cast her gaze around, suddenly guarded and serious. 'Long story. Not for here. You don't need to know. No one does.'

'Will I need to do an internet search on it? Will our child uncover things I don't know about you? What happened to being honest?' He wasn't sure how far to push it. He was out of his depth when it came to relationships and trust.

Her eyes closed for a second. 'I'm not proud of my silly past. But, no, I hope we managed to keep that particular escapade under wraps.'

He was intrigued. 'Tell me—'

'Hey!'

They were interrupted by a young man of about twenty pushing past them, shouting something in Isola Verdian. 'What's he saying?'

Giada froze, concerned. 'He's saying, "Help. Help my friend."'

Lucas went into autopilot, his focus narrowing in on

the guy and already going through a mental checklist of possible scenarios, but assuming nothing. 'Ask him where. Where is his friend?'

Giada blinked and spoke to the man, who was white and jittery with panic, and then followed his pointed finger behind them. 'There. Whoa.' She grabbed Lucas's arm tightly. *'Oddio.'*

Lucas whirled round and saw a side entrance he hadn't noticed before, the door rattling in the wind. On the ground, curled in a foetal position, was another man. Judging by the thick trail of red behind him, he looked as if he was bleeding out.

Okay.

Running to the man, Lucas shouted over his shoulder, 'Gigi, go to the ER and get help.'

'What?' Instead of continuing along the corridor, she followed Lucas, her eyes wide and scared as she too bent and stared at the man on the floor as if she couldn't drag her eyes away.

'Don't look. Look at me.' She may have built the hospital but she wasn't used to seeing the things he had. Straightening, he took her by the shoulders and made her focus on him. 'Gigi, I need you do something for me.'

'Wh-what?'

'Go to the ER. Quickly. Get help.'

'Okay.' She nodded, and looked as if she was mentally shaking herself, but she didn't move. 'ER. Yes.'

'Are there panic buttons here? Code buttons anywhere on these walls?' He scanned the walls but there were no tell-tale red buttons anywhere. In other hospitals they had them at strategic points for staff members to get help in an emergency.

'I... I don't know.'

'The ER, Giada.' He inhaled and blew out, biting back the retort that she'd insisted on leaving Maria at the car. 'I don't have a pager to send a code to the trauma team and I can't leave him. You have to go. Now, Giada.'

'*Sì*.'

He pushed away his emotions and focused back on the emergency at hand. He couldn't get to grips with how to act with Giada, had no idea how to be a decent father, how to fit into this Royal family, was making a bad fist at being a friend. But this? This he could do.

He knelt on the floor, doing a quick visual assessment of their patient. Losing consciousness. Pale. Glasgow Coma Scale… He was trying to work it out, and hoped the team here used the same terminology as he did. 'Hey, what happened? *Damn*. I don't speak your language. Doctor.' Enunciating slowly, Lucas pointed to his chest. 'I'm a doctor.'

The teenager's eyes flickered open then closed again. The friend hovered just out of Lucas's peripheral vision.

Lucas turned his head. 'What happened? Tell me.'

'Parkour.'

'English?' Lucas demanded. 'Do you speak English?'

The man rotated his shaking hand from side to side. A little English. 'Parkour.'

Just as the man said it, Lucas peeled away his patient's hands and saw a railing spike had perforated his abdomen on the left side. He tried to prise the man's hands further away so he could see the entry point and try to stem the bleeding. The spike would need to be surgically removed to prevent further damage, although judging by the blood loss they'd be fighting an uphill battle.

The man's pulse was thin and thready and he was already sinking into unconsciousness. There was a lot of blood. And, probably, very little time to save him.

'Giada!' he called to her back as she hurried away. 'Tell them to hurry. We need a trolley. Manpower. Fluids. Large-bore IVs. Resus.'

'Okay. Got it.' She nodded again and disappeared around the corner.

'Hey, buddy. Hey.' Lowering his face to the man, Lucas checked for breathing.

Nothing.

Cursing at being knee-deep in blood with no equipment, he laid the man flat, preparing for CPR. 'Okay. You're not going to die on my watch.'

He needed to somehow stop blood loss and do chest compressions at the same time. He could jump from one to the other and it could be manageable on his own, but not realistic for long. The friend was sitting on the floor now, head in his hands, incapable of anything but sobbing into his knees. 'Hey. Friend! Come here.'

The man didn't even raise his head, just shook it.

Not good enough. Lucas knew he was scared, but this was literally a life and death situation. 'I. Need. You. *Please.*'

But no dice. Lucas clenched his jaw. It wasn't the first time he'd had to improvise. He crawled to his patient's side and placed his hands over the man's ribcage.

And then, just as he thought he was going to have to go solo on this, he heard the rattle of a gurney, raised voices and fast footsteps. In a break between compressions he glanced over and there was Giada, running in those damned high heels, leading a team with trolleys and equipment.

His belly did a sudden leap. He didn't think he'd ever been so pleased to see her.

But he wasn't sure it was because she'd brought the cavalry.

CHAPTER SEVEN

ONCE SHE'D SETTLED the frightened friend with a nursing assistant and a hot drink, Giada sidled back to the corridor to watch Lucas in action. Truth was, she couldn't take her eyes off him. He commanded the space and the staff who had come running, stopped and listened and then did as he asked.

He was gentle yet affirmative. Completely in control and yet listening to input. Decisive and yet compassionate and totally in his element.

How could she even entertain the thought he might want to come and live in the palace and play at being consort when he could work miracles like this? The man was more at home elbow deep in blood than with Da Vinci paintings and public receptions.

He directed the CPR effort. He took control of the count to lift the man onto the gurney. He slid the IV bore into a vein. He did something to help the man breathe—a tube into his throat she thought she saw—and attached him to a portable oxygen tube. He gave the briefest satisfied nod when they got a trace on the ECG.

He sent someone to get a portable X-ray, asked another to arrange a CT scan, then told yet another to page the general surgeons as they all filed into the ER department with the trolley and the equipment and a sense of being in total control. The last thing she saw as the resuscitation room door swung closed was his gaze on her. Just for a moment.

Even from here she could see the buzz in his eyes.

And something else…something that simmered when his guard was down. Something that made her hot all over. Power, control, authority, command. He was in his element and it suited him. Very much.

Then she was locked out of the room and quite right too. No one needed a silly princess messing things up in there.

And, unfortunately, everyone was very aware that she was here. She had to make polite small talk with the staff and the patients and pretend she hadn't just seen a man almost die. The hospital chief had heard she was here and came to talk to her about budgets. There was an invitation to a hospital bed push charity event in the new year. Then the one thing she'd been avoiding…a question about her father.

'He's…he's stable.' She reiterated the words her brother told her every day, twice a day, when they spoke.

'Bring him home, Your Highness,' one of the senior nurses said as Giada sat down at the nurses' station and waited for Lucas to be finished. 'We'll look after him here. Where is he?'

'In very good hands.' With his son. The future King. Across the world. Her heart twisted and she suddenly understood how it felt to be her brother, torn between duty and wanting to be somewhere else entirely.

'That is good.' The nurse exhaled. 'I am praying for him. For you all.'

'Thank you, Bianca.'

After dropping a curtsey, the nurse's eyes flicked over Giada's body and she could have sworn Bianca's gaze stopped at her breasts and then went down to her belly. 'And can I say how well you look, Your Highness.'

Oh.

Was her pregnancy so obvious? Was she showing? Giada's cheeks burned and she fisted her hands to stop herself running them across her abdomen. Smiling as sweetly as she could, she nodded to Bianca. 'Isola Verde always makes me feel better.'

She heard laughter and was grateful for the distraction, but when she turned to see where it was coming from she was surprised to see Lucas, his head tipped back, laughing at something Alberto, the head of ER, had said. *Laughing?*

She watched as the two men chatted. Alberto did an action as if he was kicking a ball, then his eyes widened and he hid his head in his hands... Missing a goal? She didn't know. Sport didn't interest her. Lucas shook his head and raised his hands at Alberto, then laughed again.

She was surprised to feel a jab of hurt. Was Lucas only a stuffed shirt with her? She noticed he'd changed into the hospital scrubs, a bag saying 'Hospital Property' in his hand, which no doubt contained his stained clothes.

At the palace, in her territory, he was out of his comfort zone and probably felt as if he needed to be polite and formal. With the baby business he was reserved and trying to do the right thing. As was she. All of which amounted to stiff conversation and frustration, because they were both trying to be things they were not.

But she'd helped him relax before... And she was going to do it again.

Yes. She decided at that moment she would find the Lucas she'd fallen for.

Wait. Fallen for?

Didn't she mean fallen pregnant with?

Yes. That was what she'd meant.

He shook hands with Alberto then made his way over to her. 'Hello, I didn't realise you'd waited for me.'

'I didn't know how long you'd be, so I thought I'd hang around. As it is, I managed to see a couple of the managers and we arranged some meetings.' She stood up. 'You look relaxed. I'm assuming everything's okay?'

'Yes, and you were great, thank you, Gigi. Um…' His eyes flickered to the nurses who were watching them and he corrected himself. 'I mean Your Highness.'

'Gigi is more than fine. How is he?'

Lucas gently took her elbow and walked her towards the ER department exit. 'He's gone to Theatre. He's actually very lucky, apart from the huge blood loss which would have killed him. The spike missed most of his internal organs. We'll have to remove his spleen and possibly fix a laceration to his kidney, but he's going to recover well.'

She looked up at him, glad he was holding her arm, glad he was steady and capable and not like the friend who hadn't been able to cope. Not like her, who had been initially too shocked to move. 'You were magnificent, Lucas.'

He raised a shoulder. 'Just doing what I've been trained to do.'

'You do it well. You're buzzing. Glowing.'

He looked thoughtful for a minute and stretched his fingers out in front of him, his eyes glittering. 'I guess I am…er, buzzy. You get such an adrenalin hit and it takes a while to wear off. I thought I'd got used to it, but here…it's a new environment. I didn't speak the language or know the staff, but we still saved him.'

'*You* did.'

'It was very definitely a group effort.' He seemed so relaxed and freed up now. It had been a genius idea to bring him here, to this familiar environment.

They made their way to the front desk and out into the glare of the early afternoon sun. He stopped and turned to her. 'You once said to me it feels good to do good, and you're right.'

'I said that?' She laughed, putting her hand to her heart. 'I am so profound.'

'Sometimes you really are surprising, Gigi.' He smiled then and she loved the way his face relaxed, his whole body leaning into her.

She couldn't help but lean into him, too. Just the simple act of his hand on her arm strengthened the connection. But she ached for more. For him to touch her face, to run her hair though his fingers, to slide his mouth over hers.

But he wasn't going to, not here anyway.

And *Gigi*. It came naturally to him now. Such a small step, but he wasn't putting up that barrier quite as high as he had been. When he laughed, when he was relaxed, when he looked at her with glittering eyes her whole body leaned towards him, wanting more, wanting him. 'You had everyone doing what you told them to do.'

He shrugged again. 'I hope I didn't step on anyone's toes.'

'Not at all. I explained who you are and told them to let you do your stuff.'

'Even so, I wouldn't like someone coming into my department and telling me what to do.'

They reached their car, which was idling in the visitors' car park out front. She paused and wondered how he was going to take her next comment. 'They were grateful. In fact, they asked if you could stay on for a few hours.'

He turned to look back at the hospital, eyes wistful. 'To work? Here? Now?'

'They're short-staffed and, yes, I know they are in Seattle too. But you're here and it would do more good. And you'd get to feel even better.' She bit her lip. 'I said yes.'

'Without discussing it with me?' But he didn't look angry, he looked energised. 'Without paperwork? I'm not registered to work in this country.'

'I have fast-tracked the paperwork with the hospital administrator. The last few days have been boring and frustrating for you, I know. I can't entertain you all the time. I'm needed at the palace for briefings and meetings.'

'I don't need to be entertained, Giada.' His eyebrows rose in mock offence but he didn't say it was the most stupid idea she'd ever had.

'Seeing as you won't engage in the kind of entertaining that will soothe both mind and body, you might as well get out from under my feet.'

Luckily, he understood what she was trying to say. 'Wait.' He glanced around, checking to see if anyone was listening. 'You're telling me to go to work so we don't...'

'Get carried away,' she whispered, doing air quotes over her words. 'Like at the lake. Like in August. It's a good plan, *si*? When we're together we either argue or can't keep our hands off each other. There's no middle ground. And I can't spend all day, every day with you either arguing or dying of sexual frustration. Personally, I think you're grumpy because you don't have enough sex.' She held up her hand at his attempts to stop her speaking. 'Your mind is too active and your body is too pent up with excess energy, or too much buzz from saving all those lives. Sex would relieve all of that and make you feel even better. Imagine that. Remember how good it felt?'

A corner of his mouth twitched and the glittering in his eyes intensified. Oh, yes, he remembered. But he shook his head. 'I never read about that remedy in any science journal. Who's the doctor here?'

'I know, I know. But I'm right? *Si*? And, seeing as you don't think sex with me is a good idea, we need to have another plan.'

'Gigi...' He looked as if he would either devour her right now or explode with frustration.

'Unless you *do* think sex with me is a good idea?'

He couldn't lie. His eyes told her that he thought sex

would be a very good idea. But he growled, 'This isn't helping. I'm trying to do the right thing.'

'Avoiding the subject won't make it go away, so maybe we should face it head on. For the record, I think sex with you would be fantastic. I'm just not sure about what happens after that.'

He frowned. 'That's exactly the problem.'

'It's not a problem.' She leaned closer, close enough for her to breathe in his freshly showered scent, close enough to look deep into his eyes, but not so close as to arouse suspicions from any onlookers. 'A conundrum, maybe. A puzzle.' She put her hand on his chest and gave a very gentle push. 'Now...go back to work.'

'Are you sure?' Just one glance at his eyes told her she had him. He was interested and he wasn't hiding it. 'You don't need me?'

'No. Go do your thing. I don't need you this afternoon.'

Funny thing was, she almost did, as much as she'd needed anyone. She liked his logical thinking. He *listened* to her and that was something new in her life when it came to the people close to her. Usually, she was told she was too young, too inexperienced or just a distraction. Or someone who could be used as a stepping stone to the monarchy's inner circle and influencers. Someone to trample all over her. But Lucas was different; he didn't want to use her. 'The minute you saw that kid your whole demeanour changed. You were born to be a doctor, Lucas, anyone could see that. I could never get in the way of you doing what you're called to do. Just...'

'Just what?'

'I'd like to see you after work and hear all about it.' She waved her hand to dismiss him, as if she didn't need him or want him, when every cell in her body strained for him. She took the paper bag from his hand. 'Now, get back to work. I'll get your clothes laundered and bring some fresh ones. I'm going to make a reservation for dinner. I'll be here at six o'clock.'

CHAPTER EIGHT

HE WAS LATE, of course, as doctors generally were, and she clearly wasn't used to being kept waiting. 'What happened to six o'clock, Lucas?' she half joked, when he arrived breathless from running the length of the ER corridor. But he could see she was irritated.

He looked at his watch and grimaced. Never a good look to keep a woman waiting, particularly not a princess. 'Twenty-three minutes late. I am so sorry. But I just couldn't leave halfway through stabilising an airway for a four-year-old girl.'

She looked horrified. 'Oh! No, of course not. What happened to her?'

'Fell off her pony. Neck injury. Too traumatised to keep still for a scan so we had to sedate her.'

'And…?'

'She's going to be sore for a few weeks, but no broken bones and no long-term damage.'

Gigi brightened, fist pumping her slingless left hand. In fact, when he looked, both wrists were sling-free and all she had on now was a bandage on her damaged arm. 'Thank goodness. So you had the parkour incident, a pony incident, what else did you do?'

He wasn't used to going over his day with anyone and he had to admit it was kind of cool to be able to debrief with someone who was actually interested. He climbed into the car and sat next to her in the back, also unused to being chauffeured. But at least here they could talk. 'One difficult shoulder dislocation. Two acute cardiac arrests. A couple of twisted ankles—'

'And a partridge in a pear tree?' She laughed, looking almost as energised as he felt by his work. 'Sounds busy. And the staff were nice to you?'

'Of course. The language is a problem, although most of the staff seem to speak some English, the patients too. At first we did a lot of gesturing and speaking very slowly, and then I found an app that translates from English into Isola Verdian, which made things a lot easier.' He brandished his phone and showed her the app. 'I speak and it translates. Clever. So we managed. We didn't have the chance not to, to be honest. There's never a quiet day in ER, but that's why I love it.'

'I can see that.'

'We did have one sad case…an elderly lady with dementia. The daughter found her on the floor at home. It's clear she needs to be in care, but she's resisting. The daughter feels guilty about not being able to cope and is angry at her brother for not helping enough, even though they're meant to split the care equally. The son wishes it would all disappear so he can get on with his life. Neither of them agreed on anything.'

Their bickering had made him realise how easy it could be to slide into selfishness and not put the most important person as a priority. As he'd watched, he'd decided he'd prioritise his baby and would work on compromising with Giada, however difficult that would be.

She rolled her pretty eyes. 'Families, eh?'

He shrugged. 'Why is it always families that make your heart hurt?'

She looked at him then for a second, two. 'I don't know, Lucas.'

Damn. He'd obviously reminded her of her own family troubles and he regretted mentioning anything, especially as they were finally getting along. For a few moments she'd been the woman from August and now he'd brought her very definitely back to being the haunted November Giada. 'How was your day?'

She sighed. 'I'm trying to get up to speed with the succession plan, just in case…well, you know, just in case Domenico becomes King soon. There are protocols we need to put in place the minute any announcement is made.'

'It may not get to that for a very long time.' Lucas smiled, trying to be positive.

But she shook her head, as sadness filled her eyes. 'Dom says he spends all his spare time at Papa's side, pretending to be a concerned friend rather than his son, just so no gossip gets out. There's no change. Dom talks to him, even though he's in a coma. Apparently, there's research that says the patient can hear even if they can't respond. At least, they are comforted by a familiar voice. I thought I might send some voice messages to the hospital for him. What do you think?'

'Great idea. Anything to help.'

'If you think it will? I'll do some when I get home.' Her stomach growled. 'Okay, I need food now. This baby is hungry and isn't wanting to wait.'

'What do you need? Pizza? Pasta? Indian?' He realised his whole body smiled in response to her nourishing his child. He was getting used to the thought of being a father, his heart making space for a daughter or a son.

Or both?

The idea of a growing family shook him. He didn't do families. And yet…

'I have the perfect place in mind.' Gigi opened the sliding hatch in the grille between the front and back seats and spoke to Maria. 'Angelo's, please.'

They drove for a few minutes through the back streets then wound down a secluded cobbled road that became narrower and narrower until they reached a small sandy cove. The only building there was a small seafront restaurant that looked more like someone's home. It had a white-painted stone facade with table and chairs outside, glorious cooking smells tinging the air, and a flat roof festooned with red flowers.

The owner greeted them as if they were long lost friends, and when Giada introduced them Lucas understood why. 'Angelo is the father of one of my closest school friends.'

There was no formal bow, just a bear hug from the chef, and it was easy to see that Angelo had a lot of affection for Gigi. The feeling was clearly mutual. 'He also makes the best risotto in the country.'

Lucas nipped into the restroom to change out of the scrubs and into the clothes she'd brought him—a collared shirt, jacket and chinos, then he was led upstairs to a roof garden that looked out to the Mediterranean. Lucas was surprised to see no other diners, no set tables apart from theirs. But Giada wasn't sitting, she was leaning against a railing and looking at the water, taking greedy deep breaths, her shoulders instantly relaxing.

He took a moment to just look at her in profile. Her lush dark hair cascaded over her shoulders, and he ached to thrust his hands into those curls and run them through the soft silkiness. From this position he could see the tiny swell of her belly and he wanted to press his hands there too, to feel the outlines of her growing body. She was stunning.

If only...

If only what? If only she wasn't a princess destined to be constrained by duty? If only there weren't so many complications?

As if she felt him looking she turned and smiled. 'There you are. More comfortable?'

He tried to find his voice but he was blown away by the sight of her silhouetted by the setting sun, and all his words were gone. So he just walked to her and settled against the railing, keeping his distance. Wishing he didn't have to.

She turned to him. 'We have the place to ourselves.'

'When you said you'd book, I didn't think you meant the whole restaurant.'

She nodded. 'All taken care of. Including the bill.'

Well, damn, she certainly wouldn't be depending on him for financial assistance for their baby—although he'd make sure she got it.

He looked out to the orange-red horizon, across syrupy blue water dotted with the occasional yacht or fishing boat. 'The view is amazing.'

'You can see the palace from almost everywhere on the island, apart from here. Here, I forget who I am supposed to be and get to be just Gigi.' Inhaling deeply, she pointed out to the right, towards a little wooded area accessed by a rickety metal gate that he could just about pick out in the dusk. 'Just beyond that gate is Angelo's private beach. When I was younger I used to sneak out to meet my friends there, until I got caught by one of the security team as I was racing through the palace gardens with a bottle of wine I'd stolen from the palace cellars. I got my marching orders from Papa and was grounded for a month. Being grounded as a princess means guards at your door... trust me, it's not fun.'

He smiled at the thought. 'I hope our baby is less trouble than you or I'm going to go prematurely grey.'

'Oops. Too late.' She reached out to the little silver strands at the side of his head and gave a little shrug, mock pity on her face.

He touched her hand, cupping her fingers in his. 'Hey! I've only had these greys for four days.'

'You're saying I've turned you into a silver fox in just four days?' She laughed. 'I don't believe you.'

'Okay, maybe they appeared a few months ago. Since... August?' The idea she'd turned his hair silver was ridiculous and yet...he had felt tangled up since August. But he laughed and it felt freeing, as if something inside him was unravelling.

'Really? These are all my fault?' She shook her head but kept looking at him with a curious expression. 'You look so good when you smile, Lucas. Even better when you laugh. You seem different tonight.'

'Today was a good day. I was useful, I saved some lives, made some friends.' He leaned back against the railing, simply because the view of her was far better than anything nature had created.

Her hand slid down his chest, taking his with it, and he thought about letting go but she held it tightly and he wondered if she needed to be held or comforted and he wasn't going to deny her that. She'd pushed him today and encouraged him to do the one thing that made him who he was: work. She'd recognised he'd needed that and he recognised she needed something too. He just wasn't sure he could give her it.

So they stood there, holding hands, chatting as if this were the most natural thing in the world. And his chest felt as if a golden light had sparked to life there. Truth was, she brought out a better side of him. Although she also brought out an extraordinary sexual need in him too.

'So, I have decided to *try* to lighten up a little and make the most of being in Isola Verde,' he confessed. 'You're right... I am grumpy. I was thrown by our news. Thrown by being here and I retreated into myself.'

'Ah.' Her eyebrows rose. 'You don't like change much?'

'I've never really thought about it. I don't suppose I do, not in my private life at least. I guess that means I've grown insular.' He shook his head. 'And it seems that the more time I spend with you, the more I learn about myself.'

'Well, I am profound, after all.' She winked at him, teasing, finally slipping her hand out of his. 'You know what? I like it that we talk about important things, even if we do get a little heated.'

By heated she definitely didn't mean angry. Her eyes met his and lingered, simmering with something that reached into his gut and tugged. She bit her bottom lip and all his resolve to be friendly and open came crashing down around him. There were ramifications to them being less guarded. The most important one was letting flirting slip in, and who knew where that would lead?

But no matter how much he tried to hold his emotional barriers in place, they crumbled when she was around and he found himself wanting to relax and not fight any more. He wasn't used to sharing his thoughts and his feelings but it looked like he was going to have to try. 'I'm always telling my patients how important communication is and yet I need to work on it too. Clearly.'

'We all do. Including me...' Gigi paused while Angelo brought them antipasti. 'He doesn't have a menu, just cooks whatever's in season. It is always delicious.'

And, my God, it was. A selection of locally made cheeses and salami. Bread that was crisp and warm from the oven. Olives grown and cured less than a hundred yards away. Wine from the vineyard down the road. Then melt-in-the-mouth risotto. Lucas had two helpings and so did Gigi. It was good to see her feeding her body with the best that nature could provide. Good to see her laugh at the lighter moments of his tales of the ER and be interested in the drama of his day.

After dinner she took him down to the water's edge and they walked along the beach, which was lit by the silvery moon and huge flaming torches Alberto had driven into the sand. Lucas lingered behind her for a moment and watched as she navigated the sand in her wedges, and, much as it pained him to do so because her legs looked stunning in them, he called to her, 'Take them off.'

She whirled round, her eyes widening with interest. 'What did you say?'

'Take your shoes off.'

'Oh. Shoes. Right. Yes.' She shook her head as if she'd been thinking of something else entirely.

He nodded. 'Come paddle with me. It's the best remedy after a hard day's work.'

'Not skinny dipping this time? Oh, come on, don't look so sour, Lucas, you can't pretend it didn't happen.' Reaching with her good hand to slip off her sandal, she lost her balance and cried out, gripping his arm and laughing. 'If I fall it'll be all your fault, Dr Beaufort.'

But he was there, catching her, holding her, lowering her to the sand. He slipped her shoes off and they put their feet in the cool water, watching as it lapped lazily at their ankles. She was right, it had all happened and keeping a stiff upper lip about it wouldn't change a thing. He needed to loosen up.

'Is it okay if I…?' She leaned her head on his shoulder. 'Can I ask you a question?'

His heart hammered as he realised he preferred the joky kind of loosening up to the answering questions kind. 'Depends what it is.'

'Why me, Lucas? You could have any woman you want—yes, you could.' She laughed as he shook his head. 'Why me? Was it just because I was there? Was I… convenient?'

'God, no.' He hadn't been sure what she was going to ask, but he sure as hell hadn't imagined this. He thought back to that weekend. First impressions. The way she'd insinuated herself under his skin. And he tried to be honest…even though he'd never said anything like this before to any woman. Mainly because he'd never thought or felt anything like this before. 'You dazzled me, Gigi. You were so fresh and vibrant and happy and fun. Everything I'm not. And that bikini…wow. You're seriously beautiful. The question you should really be asking is why did you choose me? The serious, dependable, boring older man?'

He felt her shiver against him. 'Your kisses are far from boring, Lucas. You are amazing. Gorgeous, dedicated, handsome. Your passion for your job shows the minute you walk into the hospital and lasts a long time after you've left. You're older, sure, and that has a definite appeal—I am so over men my age. You just can't trust them.'

'What does that mean? I'm pretty sure I've always been the same me.'

'I imagine you have, but some guys need to grow the hell up.'

'What happened?' His interest was piqued.

She shook head. 'I want to talk about you, Lucas. That's far more interesting. When we met you were very aloof and out of reach, which, let me say, is also very sexy. At first, I admit, I thought you were a challenge. I wanted to know if I could…well, I wanted to seduce you.' She lifted her head and turned to look at him. 'God, I sound so childish…but you turned me on the moment our eyes met.'

'And was I so easy to seduce?' He laughed as he drank in her beautiful features, her heated eyes, that perfect kissable mouth. Wanting to stay in this moment with her, he pushed back the cryptic comment that had accompanied the sudden hardness in her eyes as she'd talked about immature men. Something had happened and he was going to find out…later.

Right now, Lucas wanted to remember the seduction of that August weekend. 'I tried to do the right thing.'

'You put up a *bit* of a fight, sure.' She smiled, her eyes glittering.

He wanted a rerun of that weekend. No…he wanted this Gigi, the one who was carrying his child who could be sincere and focused and yet light-hearted. Who took her responsibilities seriously and yet saw the fun in everything. He wanted to make love to her here on the sand, in his bed back in Seattle, even in his gilt-edged suite at the palace. He wanted her.

She swallowed as she looked at him and he knew she was feeling the same tumult of emotions. This was getting deeper, their connection getting tighter, more complex. 'Oh, Lucas, I liked your loyalty to your friend, that you had standards. I liked it that you liked me too, but thought you shouldn't. That kind of…oh, chivalry, I guess, is lacking these days and is very sexy.'

His eyes roamed her face, dipping to her mouth. He could still taste her. Wanted to again. 'And now?'

She smiled. 'Nothing's changed. I still think you're sexy, but also deep and thoughtful. I know you can laugh and play, but you keep forgetting how. I think it's my job to help you remember.'

'Oh?'

She nodded, her hand creeping to his chest. 'And did I mention sexy? We could… You could kiss me again.'

He ran his thumb over her bottom lip, wishing, wanting to put his mouth there. 'You know I want to. But, like I said, you dazzle me. You make me want things I can't have.'

'You can have me.' Her eyes glittered again and she smiled, whispering the last word against his throat. 'Tonight.'

He inhaled her scent. Curled towards her throat. Imagined stripping off that dress. There was nothing he'd rather do. Nothing. So saying what he said next was damned hard. 'But that will cloud our judgement. Make decisions more difficult. If we're going to get through this with any sanity we have to just stay friends. Like today…we've got on well. We've talked; I feel as if we're making progress building a foundation for the future and for our child. We're having a good evening…at least I am.'

'We can make it even better.'

'Or a lot worse. Do you think we will be able to work things out when we're clouded by our emotions? Do you think we'll be able to decide what's best for our child when we're kissing each other senseless? And what next? We both know a relationship is unlikely. We can't go on chasing each other halfway around the world just for sex. What about when one of us decides they want to have a proper relationship with someone…more suitable?'

By that he meant she was destined to marry someone royal. Not a doctor. Not him. One day she'd tire of her sensible plaything and get real with someone out of his league, and then where would he stand?

And how would his heart recover? Because he knew… he knew that, to him, this was much more than desire. He liked her, admired her, enjoyed her. Wanted to spend more and more time with her, and that could only be to the detriment of both their futures.

'More suitable than a…stupid, silly princess, you mean? I thought you were different, Lucas, but it turns out that you're just like everyone else,' she ground out, as the tease whooshed out of her.

Then she pressed her lips together and he watched her shrug on the metaphorical royal armour, straighten her back, her eyes glazing with an emotionless film, visibly retreating behind decorum. An eerie *sangfroid* she'd been taught to wear her whole life, to cover up any emotional reactions in public.

He'd expected her to shout at him, even wanted her to, but she was so quiet, so contained, so in control that it scared him. And he'd made her like that by his safeguarding and sensible choices. Yeah, he was the stupid one, not her. Never Gigi.

How to wind the clock back? 'Giada, I—'

'No.'

It was too late. He knew he'd pushed her away one time too many.

She scrambled up, grabbed her sandals and walked up the beach, waving goodbye and blowing kisses to Angelo, pretending everything was just fine. When in reality Lucas had just made everything a million times worse.

CHAPTER NINE

'GIADA, WAIT. WAIT!'

No.

She did not, would not wait for him. This was the last straw. She wasn't going to allow this to happen again. She was going to close herself up, instead of being an open book. She should have learnt that lesson with Leandro. Thought she had. Where were her promises not to get involved again? What happened to her resolve to keep every man at an emotional arm's length? To play and not let her heart get embroiled? And yet here she was, making a fool of herself, offering herself up on a plate, just to be rejected. Again.

'Wait! Giada!'

She only stopped because she'd reached the car, so she whirled round to look at him. 'Why? So you can reject me again?'

The driver's side door blasted open and Maria was there, her hand at her hip, ready to grab her weapon, eyes darting from Lucas and then back to Giada. 'Your Highness? Is everything all right?'

'Yes, it is, Maria. We're just...' Lucas glared back at Giada's right-hand woman, breathing hard and fast. If he was shocked at Maria's readiness to intervene, he didn't show it.

'What exactly are we *just* doing, Lucas?' Giada asked him, unable to keep the anger out of her voice.

'I need to talk to you. In private.' He glowered at Maria and then back at Giada. Neither of them moved. Something flickered behind his eyes. 'Oh, hell. Okay. Giada, come. Now.'

'Where?'

He took her hand and tugged her back towards the restaurant, then swerved sharp right to the secret cove. Before they'd even managed to close the gate he pushed her gently back against a tree.

'Gigi.' His hands cupped her face. 'Come back to me. Come back.'

'Who?' she threw at him. 'The Silly Princess?'

'No. You're not. You're… God, I can't even say it. I'm so…damned tied up.' He closed his eyes and she could see the struggle in him. She knew how hard it was for him to let go of his control. How he feared rejection so much that he was always so buttoned up. How he feared what might happen tomorrow so he wouldn't take the best from today, from her.

But then he stroked her hair back from her face and looked deep into her eyes. And just like that very first time, she saw him make his decision, saw the clarity and need in his gaze.

'I want you. *My* Gigi, not the polite public face. I want you. The real Gigi. The one with heart and soul. The one who cares deeply, who fights fiercely. The one who loves fun and wants nothing more than to enjoy life, and why not?' He shook his head as if realising something for the first time. 'Why the hell not take what we can, when we have the chance? We don't know what's around the corner.' He took her bandaged arm. 'Or when something bad might happen. Grab that chance, right? With both hands.'

My Gigi. Her heart squeezed. These angry moments

were raw and ugly but each one brought them closer and closer. He just needed to stop fighting it. They both did. What they had was something she'd never experienced before, something intense and imperfect and yet beautiful and wonderfully wild. Who knew if she would ever have it again?

She pressed her palms, both the good one and the sore one, against his cheeks and laughed. 'I'm here. Your Gigi. And I'm not going anywhere until you've kissed me.'

'I can't… I can't stop this… I try to hold back but I can't. It's like there's an invisible force compelling me towards you. I thought I'd got over it after you left but you walked back into my ER and bang! Here it is again.'

Then there was no more talking because he slid his mouth over hers and her body almost exploded with desire. How could she feel this way about someone who was so utterly different from her? So wrong in so many ways? How could she want so much from him? With him?

But he saw her. Knew her. Saw beyond her title and her money, saw the real Gigi, and he wanted her.

His kisses brought her home, made her new. She wanted…oh, she wanted so much. Everything. She wanted to feel him against her, on her. In her. Wanted and wanted and wanted until she thought his kisses and his touch would never be enough.

His hands moved over her body, slipping the flimsy straps of her dress over shoulders, freeing her breasts so he could suck her nipple.

'Yes,' she moaned, arching her back at the sensation of his wet mouth on her tender skin.

Dio. She wanted his mouth everywhere.

She reached through the space between them so she could cup him, stroke him.

He groaned into her hair. 'Are you sure this is safe?'

'I'm not going to get pregnant, because I already am.' She laughed. 'Surely a doctor should know that?'

He raised his head and his gaze snagged hers, so intense, so true. Raw hunger filled his eyes. A desire so pure and bright she felt it in her soul. And then he smiled...not just his mouth but his whole face, his body, shrugging off that stern tightness. 'I need to be inside you, Gigi. I meant...is there a chance anyone can see us here?'

'It's dark. No one apart from Maria knows we're here. And Angelo, possibly, if he's seen my car is still here.' She clamped her arm around his neck as he made to step away from her. 'Don't go.'

'There's nowhere I'd rather be than with you.'

But she knew that wasn't true. Sure, for tonight he'd stay, but he'd go back to Seattle soon enough. But they had tonight. They had this.

'But...' He kissed her again, hard, then stroked her face. 'I am not going to put you at risk of being caught out here with me, doing the kind of things I want to do to you.'

'Lucas,' she moaned as her imagination ran riot. 'I don't care about being caught.'

'I do. This is not my private beach, it's someone else's. We don't know who we can trust.'

'But Angelo is...' Not wanting the magical spell to break, she nibbled Lucas's ear. And from her own bitter experience she knew well enough not to trust anyone. 'I just love it here. I'm sure—'

'We are going back to the palace.' He slipped the straps of her dress back onto her shoulders.

She grabbed his arm. 'I can't run the risk that between here and the palace you'll put your Captain Sensible head on and leave me all aching and frustrated.'

'I want you, Gigi. I will still want you at the palace. And tomorrow, and the day after. You make me want to be Captain Slightly Less Buttoned Up. Captain Sponta-

neous. Captain Devil May Care.' Laughing—such a joy-
ous melodic sound coming from his throat—he crushed
her against the bark, enslaving her mouth with deep, wet,
hungry kisses.

When she drew breath she giggled, pressing her body
against his to feel the outline of his erection against her
thigh. Wishing they were naked. Wishing he wasn't Captain Sensible trying very hard to be someone he wasn't. But
she liked him all the more for trying for her sake and she
knew she could only push him so far. She wiggled against
his erection, making him groan. 'Captain Seriously Sexy.'

'Who is taking you back to the palace. We are going
to bed. But don't worry...' he traced a fingertip down the
front of her dress, between her breasts, making her shiver
in anticipation '... I am not going to let you sleep for a very
long time. Do not argue.'

He linked his fingers in hers and walked her back to the
car. 'How fast can Maria drive this vehicle?'

'I'll ask her to step on it.'

She could barely breathe, feeling the heat of his body
next to hers, knowing he wanted to be inside her...wish-
ing he was. But when he slipped his hand out of her grip
and stroked her thigh, bunching her dress in his fist so
he could access higher and higher, she thought she was
going to die of frustration and need. They couldn't get
home fast enough.

As they walked through the front door the security
guard nodded. 'Goodnight, Your Highness.'

'Goodnight, Enrico.' She waved, upping her pace. Bedroom. Now.

Lucas fell into step behind her, following her up the
grand staircase. They passed one of the housekeepers, who
gave a little bow. 'Sleep well, Your Highness.'

'You too, Nicole.'

It wasn't until they'd turned the corner into the empty

corridor leading to the Napoli suite that Lucas caught her hand again. 'Is there ever a moment when this place isn't like Piccadilly Circus? Where have all these people come from?'

She laughed. 'They live here.'

'You have no privacy. Ever.'

She remembered how they'd made love in his bath, in his pool, in his kitchen, not having to worry about being seen, and wished they were free to roam around her house, doing the same. She sighed against him. 'It's my life.'

'I don't know how you live with so many people underfoot all the time. I value my freedom too much.' He shook his head. He didn't want this kind of life, that was obvious.

But he did want her.

They reached the door to his suite and she hesitated. He tugged her into the shadows, pressing his mouth to her throat. 'I don't suppose there's one of those secret corridors between here and your rooms?'

'Indeed there is. Why do you think I suggested you stay in this particular suite?' She giggled against his chest, breathing in his scent of something wild and male that drove her crazy with desire.

'I love how you future-proofed my stay.' He grinned.

She shrugged, her fingers playing across the neckline of her blouse. 'What can I say? I'm an eternal optimist.'

'Is it easy to find? In the dark?' The growl in his voice drove her sexual hunger up a notch.

'Oh, Captain Sensible, I'm turning you! You love this cloak and dagger life, right?'

'If it means I get to undress you again, then yes.'

'It's just there.' She pushed open the door to his suite and pointed to a panel in the wall. 'I'll come to you.'

'You'll come with me. Over and over.' He pushed her hair back and kissed behind her ear. 'You have sand on your cheek, Princess Gigi.'

'I'll shower.'

'No,' he growled. 'We can do it together.'

She was nervous. Stupid, considering they'd done this before. Even more stupid because she was carrying his child and they were connected in so many ways. But there it was. She wanted to be perfect for him, but her legs shook a little as she descended the steps between her rooms and his. What if…what if this wasn't perfect? What if she let herself fall under his spell, gave him her heart and he stamped on it?

But no, she told herself. Captain Sensible wouldn't do that.

She wouldn't let him. She'd take tonight but she'd keep her heart safe. And she would never ever trust a man. Never again.

But sex? Scratch that insatiable Lucas itch? Hell, yes.

She knocked quietly but there was no answer.

'Lucas,' she whispered as she pushed open the panel and stepped into his room. And, wow…in the few minutes she'd been upstairs he'd transformed the place into a soothing soft space lit by myriad candles. 'Lucas?'

The sound of running water drew her to the bathroom and she found him there, testing the temperature of the water in the large gilt sunken bath. More candles filled every space, every shelf, and bathed the suite in a golden magical glow.

He'd removed his shirt but his trousers were still on. Her eyes slid over the naked skin and she sighed at the sight of the corded muscles she'd committed to memory three months ago, itching to span them with her hands.

He turned. Saw her. Stilled.

It felt as if time stopped, the whole world stopped, as they looked at each other. He said nothing, but his heated eyes spoke volumes. No need to be nervous. He liked what he saw—just a barefoot woman in a simple silk sheath dress. And very expensive underwear...although he didn't know that yet.

His gaze heated her, made her feel exposed and yet desired. Adored. Craved. Her skin prickled in anticipation of his touch. She raised her chin, an act of defiance. *You want me, but I will have you.*

She was a princess, he was a successful ER consultant with more letters after his name than she could count, but in here they were equals. Lovers.

She shivered. His pupils dilated and he took a step towards her.

'I always did like this room,' she said, just to break the heavy lust-laden silence.

'Almost as fine as the bedroom.' He closed the distance between them and palmed her cheek, his fingers damp and cool. 'Hello, Gigi.'

'Hello, Lucas.' Unable to resist touching him, she brushed her fingers across the smattering of dark hair on his chest, ran her nails up to his throat, palmed the back of his neck and tugged his face down to hers.

'God,' he groaned, his mouth centimetres from hers. 'No small talk?'

'Have I ever said that you talk too much?'

'Maybe—'

'Too much talking and not enough kissing.'

She bridged the gap between them, crushing her mouth to his, giving no more space for thought. Just touch. Skin and heat and wet and hot.

Deepening the kiss, he slid his tongue into her mouth, exploring, hungry. She raked her fingers across his back, his shoulders, his arms, spanning those muscles, desperate to touch every inch of him. Wanting him inside her, filling her.

He pulled her dress over her head, consigning it to the

floor, then he unclipped her bra, letting her breasts fall free. Groaning in appreciation, he cupped them, playing his fingers over her nipples, softly at first then harder until her breasts ached and her nipples peaked at his touch. A soft hurt that she didn't ever want to stop.

He propelled her backwards to the vanity, lifted her to sit on the edge of the counter, pulled her legs either side of him, grasped the curve of her hips and rocked her against him.

Hard. So hard.

'Trousers. Please. Off,' she managed through desperate kisses, and he obliged, discarding the chinos and boxers. Then he was in front of her, solid and steady and strong. And ready.

She took him in her hand and stroked his length, watching the mist descend in his half-closed eyes.

'Gigi.' It was a growl. A warning. A sigh, as he grasped her wrist. 'I—'

She rubbed against his erection. 'I need you. Please.'

'But I had so much planned.'

'Later. After. More. I just need you now. Lucas.'

He kissed her again, greedy, rough kisses as he settled in front of her, pulling her to the very edge of the counter, pulling her to the edge of her control, holding her close, pressing his body against hers until she felt his imprint everywhere, his scent…everywhere.

This man who was a danger to her equilibrium, this man who would leave her.

This man who understood what she needed, where she wanted his touch, where her body ached to be kissed, stroked. This man.

Then he was sliding inside her, filling her, his fingers slipping into the apex of her legs, stroking her most sensitive part as he slid inside, over and over. Stroking and sliding. Fast and deep.

His thrusts slowed and he opened his eyes and captured her gaze. This man who had changed her future, changed her life in so many ways. He stroked her cheek with a tenderness that squeezed her heart and made it ache.

He kissed her long and slow, angling his hips to thrust deeper until she knew nothing more than this sensation, this kiss, this man, this pleasure mounting inside her, over her, through her.

As the sensation became almost too much she gripped his shoulders, his name on her lips over and over. Then he rocked harder and faster inside her, filling her completely, until she felt his release throb through her, taking her with him.

His eyes locked onto hers, his gaze honey and whisky, golden and hot. 'Gigi. *God*, Gigi.'

And she knew soul deep that this man was hers.

At least…for now.

She was wrapped around him, tight and hot, her mouth on his shoulder, her legs around his waist. His hip dug into the sharp edge of the vanity unit and he was getting cramp in his left leg but he couldn't think of anywhere else he'd rather be, even though he did not like this palace with its legion of staff and lack of privacy.

His breathing came in gasps and he couldn't find words. After all his efforts not to do this again, he'd done it. And he didn't care, because he'd been honest when he'd said there was nowhere he'd rather be than with her. If only they didn't have to sneak around. If only they were free to be themselves, together. A—his chest hurt at the thought— family.

But that was impossible. He'd never wanted it, and yet when he was with her he wanted everything.

He held her tight against him, stroking her back, kissing her as she came down from her orgasmic high. When she was breathing normally again he unpeeled her from his skin and kissed her softly. 'This can't be comfortable.'

'Oh, you know. It's slightly more comfortable than wearing that floss masquerading as underwear.' She grinned and nipped his earlobe between her teeth.

He peered at the scraps of lace on the floor and frowned. 'That was your underwear?'

'Very expensive underwear.'

'I'll buy you some more. Lots. Just so I can rip it off you.'

'You have the best ideas.' She laughed, a wonderful perfect sound that brightened his heart even more.

'Yes. Yes, I do. You are one of the best ideas I've had.' He untangled her legs from his and stepped away, his eyes catching the soft swell of her belly. His own gut contracted. 'Damn, Gigi. I didn't even think. Did I hurt…? Are you okay?'

She smiled, spanning her stomach with her fingers. 'Absolutely okay. Do you want to…?'

She reached for his hand and drew it towards her, then pressed it against skin that was as soft as the silk dress he'd torn off her. He couldn't find words as he stroked across her belly. Emotions bundled up inside him, hitting him hard in the chest. This tiny swell was his baby. Theirs. It was real and happening.

He lowered his head and kissed just below her belly button. Tears pricked his eyes. Hot damn. He blinked quickly, making sure to keep his head bowed so she wouldn't see this reaction. He never cried. Ever. And he wasn't going to start doing it now.

'Lucas?' She tugged him up to look at her, concerned eyes scanning his face.

The feelings inside him were strange, unfamiliar. As if his heart was growing with a swell of pride and something else he couldn't remember ever feeling. And a good dose of panic too. He would be responsible for this tiny human for the rest of his life. And responsible for Gigi too. Because they were inexorably linked, tied to each other for ever. 'I will never let anything bad happen to either of you. I promise.'

But he had no more time for thinking when her mouth sought his again. This time it was greedy, possessive, a kiss deeper and longer and better than any other. A kiss of longing and want that bruised his heart, branded him as hers.

Eventually he lifted her from the counter and walked over to the bath, lowering her gently into it. 'Now, do I get to do all those things I had planned?'

'Totally.' She splashed water at him, similar to that first day in late summer. 'Join me?'

He didn't need to be asked twice so he slid in opposite her, the warm water easing his bones, although the tension he'd been carrying since they'd arrived in Isola Verde seemed to have already disappeared. He slid under the water then came up to see her watching him with a curious expression. 'What?'

She smiled. 'If I'd known how badly you've been missing work I'd have shoved you into that hospital the minute we arrived.'

He laughed. 'I'm sorry I've been a pain to live with.'

'I have you back, that's all that matters. Captain Sensible's gone rogue. Again.' After kissing him, she turned and backed up so she was leaning against his chest.

He reached around her, hugging her closer, kissing her neck, her head. His chest almost burst with lightness as he palmed her breast. Was this for real? 'I can't get enough of you.'

'Lucas...' She turned, planting a kiss on his nose then following up with foam bubbles. 'You already have all of me, and more.'

Sure he did. Right here, in this bath, in the palace, in the country he didn't live in and in secret.

He had her, yes. The difficult question was: for how long?

CHAPTER TEN

'IT'S A BEAUTIFUL MORNING. The sun is shining; it's so pretty. I know how much you love the island in the winter. We have the trees all decorated and it feels very Christmassy. When you get better we can walk in the gardens.' Gigi slapped her hand on the breakfast table. '*Stupido!* I never say things like that. Because we never walk together. Why am I even bothering? Okay. Okay.'

She took a deep breath, deleted everything and tried again, pressing 'Record' on the audio app on her phone. *Take forty-five.* 'Oh, Papa, this is so hard. I barely talk to you face to face, never mind via a phone app.'

She stared out of the window and watched the lightning shadows of his horses galloping through the trees.

'I hate to think of you lying there with all those machines around you, and with Dom not even being able to admit he's your son. I wish I'd tried harder, Papa. I wish you'd loved me as much as I love you. I wish we could have been a proper family, instead of having so much distance between us. And I wish I could have trusted you enough to tell you about Leandro and how he was trying to blackmail me. I wish I hadn't made that mistake in the first place but, well… I was lonely and he was fun at first.'

Lucas had been the polar opposite to Leandro. He'd been serious and uninterested in her and immediately she'd thought he was different. That was what had attracted her to him. His steadiness. His honesty.

She smiled at the thought of him. How many times had they made love in the last ten days? She'd lost count. Funny, she'd thought he'd hightail it back to Seattle as soon as he could break out of here but he'd stayed. Although she had a feeling he wasn't here just to support her—the hospital work was part of the draw too.

'I wish I could tell you about Lucas too…it's actually really difficult. I don't know what to do. I like him. I mean, I like him a lot. I'm having his baby, did you know that? Of course you don't. We all keep secrets from each other. He's…he's lovely. You'd like him. Although if Dom hears about what we've been doing he might just kill him.' She shook her head at the thought of all the complications this relationship brought with it—was it a relationship? 'But, *Dio*, it's nice to have someone here to keep me company instead of rattling around the place on my own like I normally do. I don't think you realise how lonely it is here for me.'

The door opened and Lucas breezed in. 'Hey, Gigi. You got up early.'

'Lucas.' She fumbled, trying to click off the app, almost dropping the phone in the process, which made it look as if she was doing something she shouldn't. She laughed, trying to cover up her sudden awkwardness. 'Um… You heard that?'

'Just a muffled sound. Nothing really.' He brushed a kiss on her head then helped himself to pancakes and berries.

She breathed out. *Phew*. 'I'm trying to record another message for Papa, but I still feel silly talking into a machine.' She pressed the 'Delete' button and then looked at him. 'Binned that attempt too. I think I'm up to take forty-six today.'

He smiled, popping a berry into his mouth and putting

a plate of food in front of her. 'Eat. I know you won't have and you need to. You're doing great. Just say what you feel. Tell him what's going on in your life.'

'I don't think Papa wants to hear about my everlasting nausea. Or about our child. Or about us. I'm basically hiding my whole life from him at the moment.'

Lucas's eyes widened at the mention of *us*. 'Just tell him what the weather's like, that kind of thing.'

The recordings weren't supposed to be a confessional, then. It had been a weird kind of therapy, though, just saying her feelings out loud.

Lucas looked out the window. 'This place still confuses me, even after two tours. Remind me, where's King Roberto's suite?'

'In the Verde Wing at the other side of the palace.'

'And Dom's?'

She pointed towards the central dome and beyond. 'Gathering dust over in the East Wing.'

'So you generally mooch around here on your own?'

Had he heard her say she was lonely?

The last thing she wanted was him analysing that. 'I have Maria and my staff. Friends you haven't been introduced to yet. Growing up, Dom and I shared the nursery and then I moved into the Bella Vista wing. Oh, I spoke to him earlier and he mentioned something about the charity ball at your hospital on the twelfth and do I want to go?'

'Oh? Interesting.' Lucas frowned and she could see guilt slither back into his features. 'He texted me this morning, too.'

Coincidence? Giada's heart hammered. 'Do you think he's suspicious about where we are?'

'I don't think so. It was just a friendly You're missing some fun times in the ER text. Fairly sure it wasn't fishing for information…at least not in relation to you. More about when I'll be back.'

'And are you going to the ball? Back to Seattle?' She'd known he would because he'd mentioned the charity event before they'd set off to come here.

An ache crept under her ribcage. This lovely bubble would burst the minute he stepped onto his plane and then she'd lose him to his life there. She'd tried to shield herself, of course, but he'd been too all-consuming to ignore.

As she expected, he nodded. 'Of course. It's the biggest charity event of the year and duty calls. I asked him to grab me a ticket. Are you going to go?' He caught her gaze. Paused. Then, 'Do you want to come? As in...*with me*?'

Her chest bloomed with warmth and excitement. 'Lucas Beaufort, are you asking me on a date?' So far, over and above their public outings, their intimate *getting to know you* had been in the confines of each other's suites.

He grinned, scraped his chair back and came around to her side of the table. He pulled her up, twirled her round, sat down and pulled her onto his knee. His mouth found hers and his kiss was filled with promise. Interesting, after an already *busy* kind of night. He was insatiable. *Grazie Dio.* 'It'll have to be an incognito date.'

'The best kind.' She grinned. 'And I can see Papa too. That will be wonderful. I'll make arrangements for my absence. Yes, I have to make formal arrangements, I can't just flit around like you do.'

'Will we tell Domenico?' His hands circled her waist under her blouse. 'About the baby?'

She shivered at his touch and in anticipation of where his hands would go to next. 'Not yet. After Papa's operation. But he'll definitely need to know before the announcement.'

'Announcement about...the pregnancy?' His hand stilled.

She thought about the way Bianca had looked at her the other week. 'I was thinking in the New Year. I can't just hide away until the baby is born, I need to be out working and I can't risk more gossip and speculation. Women instinctively know when other women are expecting—it's a thing.' At his raised eyebrows she said, 'They do, I promise. And, yes, just being the public face of the hospital is work for me. A royal endorsement brings in sponsorship. Outside the palace I'm always working. My life isn't my own. It belongs to the nation and...' he knew already but it had to be said '...so will our child's.'

Lucas looked as if he'd swallowed a lemon at that, but he wasn't the only parent of this child; they both needed to learn how to compromise. She steeled herself against his reaction. 'I know, Lucas. I know, you have something to say about that too.'

But to her surprise he nodded. 'Okay. Yes. I understand. An announcement early in the New Year. This is real, isn't it?'

'Yes. It is.' She put his hand on her belly. 'I was thinking...'

'Oh, no.' His head shot up and he winced jokingly. 'Is that a good thing?'

'Always. You'll need to tell your parents too before the announcement is made.'

His mouth went flat and his eyes grew dark as he visibly shut down emotionally. 'No.'

'Lucas. Please. They need to know. I don't think you quite appreciate the media interest.'

'I've read the social media comments. I'm learning.'

'So you'll understand that your family will be bombarded by journalists. Their social media accounts will be scrutinised. They'll be followed, hounded. Even if you don't care what your family thinks about this child, you need to at least warn them about what's going to happen.'

'No.'

'Lucas. Please. It's not fair.' He didn't have to say that

his parents hadn't been fair to him because she knew they hadn't. She turned round and straddled his lap. 'If I could erase any of what they did to you, I would. I hope this child will be the balm you need to believe that families can be a good thing.' His lip curled. She kissed it. 'I know you don't want a family, Lucas, but I guess...in some shape or form we will be one.'

And yet, despite knowing how much he didn't want a family, she kept having this image in her head of the two of them with a baby and it looked so...perfect. So...*everything.*

Impossible.

He stilled. 'How? How will we be a family?'

'We'll work it out.'

He blinked. Looked at his food then lifted her from his lap and sat her down next to him. There was a strange awkward silence as he filled a glass with orange juice. Did he even want to work it out?

Then his voice cut through her worried thoughts. 'Who is Leandro?'

'So you did hear.' So much for this being a beautiful morning. It felt as if all the happiness she'd been feeling for the last few days was suddenly sullied.

Lucas stared at the plate of food. 'Maybe a little.'

'Leandro is in the past.'

'I want to know what happened.' After the emotionless response about his parents, this heated reply was interesting. He was all or nothing, a roller-coaster of emotions when it came to people he cared for and blankness to those who'd hurt him. Now his eyes blazed, which meant, she realised, he cared a great deal. 'Is he the one who blindsided you?'

Not wanting to remember that episode of her life, she blew out a breath. 'He was a big mistake I'd rather forget.'

'But not enough that you mention him to your father.'

She inhaled sharply. 'You heard it all?'

The lonely bit? The bit about her caring for him? Her heart hammered. He couldn't… She wouldn't… She didn't want him to know how much she liked him, and give him ammunition to hurt her in the future.

His eyebrows rose. 'I caught the tail end. Paulo stopped me in the corridor and asked about laundry. Then as he left I heard you talking. I didn't realise it was with your father. I didn't want to interrupt. Tell me about Leandro.'

'It's all been deleted anyway. Now you have to go to work.'

'Tell me, Gigi. I know every time you're thinking about him because I can see the pain and hurt in your beautiful face. Tell me. No secrets.'

'This is all a secret.' She waved her hand around the room, finishing with her palm on his chest, wishing she could scream to the world that she'd spent ten wonderful days with Lucas.

'I meant…' He took hold of her hand. 'No secrets between us.'

So there was no escape, and he was right too: he'd been honest about his parents and that had helped her understand so much about him. Maybe, this way, he'd understand why Isola Verde was so important to her and why she was determined to do some good for her people.

She sighed, wrung her hands together and began. 'Leandro…was the ultimate life lesson. I met him in Naples at a party. He introduced himself as the son of an old aristocratic family. Good breeding, of course. I liked him. By which I thought he was hot… Oh, the craziness of youth only ever attracted by good looks and witty words. Turned out he was liar and a cheat and he played me.'

'A player played you?' Lucas's eyebrows rose. 'Wow, Gigi. I'm surprised.'

'You and me both. Turned out he was just a social

climber who hadn't been honest about his background. We'd been dating a few months and then out of the blue he proposed. I was shocked, you know? We hadn't been serious; it had been fun but he wasn't special to me.'

She thought back to Lucas's proposal. Well, hell, they were two completely different scenarios. One empty question but with a backdrop of roses and champagne and a private plane to Paris, the other an off-the-cuff panicked question in a Seattle bedroom with takeaway pizza.

But even though Lucas hadn't been wanting her to say yes, his proposal had at least been made with the best intentions. She sighed. 'When I said no, we were too young, it was too sudden, he became difficult, angry, threw things. Nothing violent towards me, but *because of me.*' She shuddered at the memory. 'This was one time I was relieved to have Maria in the next room. I had him thrown out of the hotel, told him I never wanted to see him again and thought that was the end of it, but it wasn't.'

'He threatened you? Hurt you?' Lucas's hands fisted.

'Not physically. A few weeks later I started to receive calls, no message or voice but replays of our conversations, of our…intimate moments. You know, the things you say when you're unguarded, when—you know, in the throes of passion.'

'There was a sex tape?' Lucas's lip curled and his eyes darkened.

Humiliation hummed through her. 'I don't know if there was a video. I don't remember anything about a camera… ever. But there was a recording and enough to tie that voice, those…sounds to me. Pretty soon texts came thick and fast, belittling me, repeating things I'd said about my father. Then there was a request for hush money.'

'Blackmail too?' Lucas looked at her in disbelief but there wasn't judgement, just shock.

She nodded, her mouth drying. 'I paid the first amount,

but he wanted more. I refused. Then he said he'd sell the story to the local press, but that he wouldn't stop there.'

'Total jerk.' Lucas shook his head. 'Gigi, I am so sorry this happened to you. Not all men are like that.'

'I know.' She'd just allowed herself to be duped by the worst sort. 'I don't know if the sale was made. I managed to keep it quiet, well—between me, Maria and a big threat of Royal action and a court case. Plus, after a little digging into his background we had a few more things we could use against him. He eventually got the message that we were serious and I haven't heard from him since.'

Lucas stroked her cheek with the back of his hand. 'I am so sorry, Gigi.'

'Me too. I'd come so close to shaming my family, the Crown, the country. Remember, I already had a reputation as a troublemaker and party girl and Papa was at his wits' end. I was reeling from the lucky escape I'd had by managing to keep it from him, always being on tenterhooks that Leandro would somehow get the recording to him. I didn't know what to do; my head wasn't clear for a while. I was broken and felt like I was going around in a daze.

'Then, one day, I went for a drive around the city and passed the beautiful gardens that had been created in my mother's memory down in the old quarter. There were children playing, people enjoying the flowers and the sunshine, smiling, laughing in a space where she would always be remembered as someone special. She'd done so much for the community and was adored by everyone, and it got me thinking that all I'd ever created was pain and embarrassment. What was my legacy? Trouble, that's all. It hit me hard then… I didn't want to be remembered for yet another salacious gossip story; I wanted to create something I could be proud of.'

Lucas's eyes lit up as he joined the dots. 'The hospital.'

'Exactly.' She nodded. 'I dedicated a ton of time and energy to it and I'm damned proud of it. It was much needed and has already made a big difference to people's lives. And while I hate that portrait in the foyer, it reminds me how far I've come.'

'I can't even…' Lucas kicked his chair back and stalked across the floor. 'Where the hell is that scumbag now?'

'Long gone and I don't care. You shouldn't either.'

'I want to punch him. I want to… Giada, I am so angry…'

He was so passionate about defending her, so ardent in his rage *for her*, it made her blood pound. She caught him and put her hands to his face. 'Lucas, you are magnificent.'

'I can't…' He shook his head, nostrils flaring as he swayed out of her hands. 'How could anyone treat you like that?'

'Because I let him. Because…' Her heart stung with the memory of embarrassment, self-hatred and the very sharp wake-up call that she could not be the Silly Princess any longer.

She'd never told anyone about this before, apart from Maria, of course. But saying it out loud was freeing and meant she could place it firmly in the past behind her. She knew she could entrust it to Lucas. Seeing his reaction, she knew he was on her side. 'I just wanted to be important to someone.'

He stared at her, so much empathy and affection in his eyes as he pulled her into his arms, wrapping her tight.

'Hell, Giada, you're important to me,' he whispered against her throat.

'Oh, Lucas.'

No one had ever said anything like that to her before. It was an understanding of who she'd been and how far she'd come. That she was worth something. He saw her, he heard her. He accepted her.

It was everything.

Something had shifted between them, something deep and profound. More, she knew it had taken him a lifetime to be able to say those words to someone. And he'd chosen her.

Her heart stuttered as she took his kisses and his ardent, passionate words.

And wished, with all her being, she could let herself believe him.

CHAPTER ELEVEN

GIGI SMOOTHED DOWN her dress as they stepped out of the cab in front of Seattle's famous Polar Club Hotel—the venue for the charity ball—and asked, 'How do I look?'

Breathtaking. Lucas held his hand out to steady her in her silver heels. 'You look radiant and beautiful. And if we weren't in the middle of Seattle I'd peel your clothes off and make love to you right here.'

'Tempting, although I'd freeze to death.' She laughed. 'Seriously, does this dress make me look pregnant?'

She was wearing an exquisite floor-length gown in the Isola Verdian regal colours of purple and silver, with a shimmering bodice, one shoulder bare, a nipped-in waist and a full skirt. Her hair was pulled up as it was in her portrait and there were diamonds worth hundreds of thousands of dollars dangling from her ears.

His chest hurt every time he looked at her…a good hurt, an ache he wanted to never wane, whether she was wearing jewels and finery, jeans and his old T-shirt, or absolutely nothing.

He inhaled the icy night air that was a far cry from the temperate climate where he'd spent the last couple of weeks. But he didn't give a damn about the weather; his sole focus on getting through this evening when he couldn't touch her, and without betraying himself to his best friend, because… Secrets.

They started to climb the white stone steps.

'No way am I commenting because, whatever I say it will be the wrong thing.' He leaned closer to her. 'And, for the record, I prefer you wearing nothing apart from me.'

'Lucas!' she whispered, her cheeks burning. She let go of his hand. 'We have to behave.'

'What can I say? You've unleashed a beast.' He'd grown too used to having her to himself, of stripping her naked whenever they were able to slip through the secret corridor… Decorum had slipped from his vocabulary.

But underneath the joky facade his gut was a tight ball of stress. There were so many people buzzing around—people he worked with, people he worked for; there were bound to be questions about what his family crisis had been about and where he'd spent the last two weeks. And he wasn't sure how he was going to answer any of them.

Tonight was the end of the bubble they'd been living in for the last few days. Days that had been shaped by work and fun and sharing more than he'd ever shared with anyone else. Weird, really, because he'd never imagined enjoying the intimate life that smacked of family and belonging, but he had. And now reality was crashing down.

As if she could read his mind, Gigi gave his arm a squeeze. 'Relax, Lucas, you're all coiled up. It'll be fine. Dom won't suspect a thing. Plus, you're back in Seattle now. Work tomorrow.' He wondered if he imagined the flicker of sadness in her eyes, but then she smiled, putting her palm to her chest as they entered the Aurora Dome room amid the loud chatter. 'Oh, this is lovely.'

He looked upwards. 'Almost as impressive as your palace.'

She followed his gaze to the huge stained-glass domed ceiling that had been lit up in festive colours, her eyes sparkling almost as much as the chandeliers and the crystal glassware on white–linen-covered tables. 'You haven't seen us do Royal properly, Lucas. Trust me, that is something to behold. But this is simply stunning. Oh, there's Max Granger. At least, I think it's him. He looks very like the man I spoke to on video calls. I need to speak to him about Papa.'

Wishing they were still back in his house, naked, exploring each other again and again, Lucas followed her through the throng of partygoers towards the tall man loitering by the bar, and shook hands with him as Gigi introduced them.

Max smiled at Giada. 'I heard you visited your father today.'

'I went straight to the hospital from the airport. He looks so...vulnerable.' She nodded, her eyes darkening but her back straight and smile in place. To anyone else she would appear perfectly composed, but Lucas could see she was hiding her pain. 'I've been talking to him, but it's hard to know if he hears me.'

'All the research says patients respond more positively to treatment if they hear a loved one's voice,' the neurosurgeon said. 'He's doing well. We have a scan booked first thing tomorrow morning and if all is as good as we hope it is, we can proceed with the tumour surgery as planned on the fifteenth.'

'That is great news. Thank you.' Her hand fluttered at her throat and he wondered if her veneer of calm was starting to shatter. But she held it together. 'I'm so sorry to have interrupted your evening with work business, Mr Granger.'

'Not a problem.' Max smiled reassuringly, then his eye settled on a dark-haired woman in a long green dress walking towards them, and his attention to their conversation seemed to wane. He took a step away. 'Enjoy the ball, Your Highness,' he said, his voice low so no one around them could hear. 'Make sure to save room for the dessert. London Fog cake. You'll be blown away.'

'How would he know about dessert? We haven't even had the starters yet.' Gigi asked once Max had walked away.

Lucas shrugged. 'Must have insider info.'

'Who cares? It sounds amazing.' Gigi rubbed her stomach. 'I'm definitely having some.'

Lucas watched her and smiled, straddling the eternally difficult question of whether he should point out to her that when she flattened the fabric of her dress over her abdomen she did indeed look a little...rounder? But a female voice came from behind, *sotto voce*, saving him from that particular minefield. 'Excuse me, Princess Giada?'

Gigi turned, frowning. 'Yes?'

The hospital's new Head of PR—the dark-haired woman who Lucas thought may have distracted Max—stepped forward. 'I'm Ayanna Franklin. I've been dealing with your office regarding your father's accident.'

'You're Ayanna! Good to meet you.' Gigi shook Ayanna's hand. 'Thank you for working so hard to keep this all under wraps. I know you've been busy.'

'Learning the ropes, to be honest. I'm new in the role but what with having VIP guests at the hospital and organising this ball I've hit the ground running. You have no idea how difficult it is sourcing London Fog cake for this many guests.' Ayanna grinned. 'I really hope you love it.'

'I'm sure we will.' Lucas nodded. 'Sounds delicious.'

'It certainly does,' Gigi joined in. 'Max was just talking about it.'

'Max was?' Ayanna's eyes widened in what looked like panic.

Lucas clarified, 'Max Granger. Yes. Do you know him?'

'Er...we've met. Yes.' Ayanna's cheeks flamed and he was left contemplating what was going on between the neurosurgeon and the PR director. Given his own secrets, he pushed it to the back of his mind. None of his business.

Gigi replied, snapping him out of his thoughts. 'Well, Ayanna, I can't thank you enough for helping us at such a difficult time.'

It astounded him that she was able to be so animated and gracious after a twelve-hour flight followed by two hours at her father's bedside. She astounded him, full stop.

Having finished her conversation, Gigi turned to him but something, or rather someone, caught her eye. She raised her hand in a small wave and muttered out the side of her mouth, 'There's Logan, our old bodyguard. AKA your new trauma surgeon. I can't remember whether I'm supposed to know him or pretend I've never seen him before... I've got baby brain. Oh, he hasn't seen me anyway. Maybe I'll catch up with him later.'

'How is it that I work here and yet you know more people than I do?' Lucas laughed as he scanned the crowd, seeing nothing but a sea of faces, suits and sparkling jewels. The chatter was reaching epic volumes against the backdrop of an orchestra playing classical music. There was an excited buzz and he had no doubt the hospital charity was going to raise a lot of money tonight. 'Gigi?'

He waited for a response but she'd paled a little and her whole body seemed to freeze. She touched Lucas's arm. 'There's Dom. Should we...?'

No. His gut tightened and his first instinct was to run, but that was certainly not what he was going to do. That would only increase suspicion. 'Sure. We have to do it sometime.'

'Okay. Keep your distance, we're friends, that's all.' She gave him a conspiratorial wink. 'Remember, no one knows I'm Dom's sister.'

'Yes, Your Highness,' he ground out through gritted teeth, not wanting to keep his distance at all. Not wanting to be here at all. 'This is going to be awkward on so many levels.'

Luckily, Dom was standing with their colleague, orthopaedic surgeon Emilia Featherstone, and the small talk between them all was general, brief and light before they were called to dinner.

Even though they were seated at the same large circular table as Dom and Emilia, they were separated by other guests, far enough away for intimate conversation to be difficult, particularly in front of the other six diners with them. But the sharp ache under Lucas's ribcage didn't fade at all. He'd got away without interrogation this time, but it was going to happen. And either he was going to have to lie or front up to his best friend very soon.

He breathed out, grateful for a reprieve, and tucked into a particularly delicious Caprese salad reminiscent of Isola Verdian cuisine.

'Do you think he suspects anything?' Lucas asked Gigi, glancing over towards his friend.

'I think he's barely registered that we're here. He's only got eyes for Emilia.' Giada watched her brother whisper something to Emilia. 'How did he put it? Old friends? I bet there's something more going on there.'

'Do you think so?' He had to admit that they did look cosy. Had something been going on that he didn't know about? Were Emilia and Dom involved? He was starting to think he didn't know his best friend at all.

Giada swallowed. 'That dress is something else, she looks amazing. No wonder he's distracted.'

'It's red, yes. Kind of nice. But not a patch on yours.' He meant it. She was the most beautiful woman in the room.

'You really don't have to say that.'

But he could see her heart wasn't in this conversation as her eyes kept darting to her brother. Lucas realised that, unlike him, she wanted to talk to Dom. 'I'm sure he'll make an effort to talk to you properly later.'

'You think so? When he has a beautiful woman at his

side? Domenico is smitten.' There was no bitterness in her tone, although it was a little wistful and resigned to the fact that Dom had other things on his mind than his sister. Again.

Lucas's heart stung for her. All her life she'd been wanting someone in her family to notice her. He couldn't fathom how they hadn't—she was dazzling in every way. 'There's been no evidence of any kind of relationship between them, other than collegial friendship, for as long as I've known them. I'm sure it's just a coincidence they were chatting when we went over. Anyway, it's none of our business.'

'It is very much my business if she's going to become Queen of Isola Verde.'

Okay. He hadn't thought about that. 'I'm really not sure that's on her agenda. She loves being a doctor. I can't see her giving that up. I doubt Emilia even knows Dom's real identity.'

'If she does know, it's because Dom thinks she's special. Look at the way he's gazing at her.' Gigi drank her sparkling water, her gaze returning to Lucas. 'You don't have to see the ramifications but I do.'

'Oh, I see them all right. We only had a very quick chat with them and even then I stuffed up. Did you see Dom's eyes narrow when I called you Gigi? And then I said Isola Verde is beautiful and I'm not supposed to have been there.' He hit his head with the heel of his hand. 'I am so not good at lying.'

'Yes, you are. When you're on duty you mask your emotions and it's just the same for me. You learn very quickly not to let things affect you, and if they do you simply cover your reactions with a smile.'

He much preferred the animated, emotion-filled Gigi. The one he'd made love to just before she'd put on that sexy dress. The one who'd cried out his name while stealing his heart. Damn, he wished they weren't here right now, playing grown-ups when they could be at his house, playing an entirely different game.

But all this talk about Domenico and the King reminded him that this affair with her was fast coming to a conclusion. Soon the truth would be out about Roberto's operation—they certainly couldn't hide it for ever and, whatever happened to the King, Dom would have to return to Isola Verde and take his rightful place there.

Gigi's pregnancy would be obvious. There would have to be an announcement and Lucas's part in this would break up his friendship with Dom.

What then for Gigi?

A flicker of hope lit up inside him. If Dom became King and returned to Isola Verde then Gigi would be off the hook there. She wouldn't have the burden of shouldering the monarchy's responsibilities like did now. Would she consider moving here? She'd be free to—

'Hey, Lucas.' Arvi, the paediatric endocrinologist on his right, leaned over, swirling his glass of red wine. 'Are you going to the Seahawks game tomorrow?'

'Er...no. Who are they playing?'

'Vikings. Gonna be a tough one. That new quarterback...'

Not wanting to be rude, Lucas applied the mask of interest and immersed himself in football talk while his *date* chatted to the woman next to her.

Only she wasn't his date. He couldn't hold her hand, couldn't parade her onto the dance floor. He couldn't kiss her under the mistletoe someone had strung up, he couldn't cradle her belly and rock in time to the music. He couldn't announce to everyone that she was carrying his child, because that announcement had to be timed and worded carefully and sent out to the world's media, and he wasn't even sure his name would be mentioned.

Being with her these last few weeks had changed him. She'd taught him to look for the positives, to cling to hope. To make the best out of every situation. She'd made him laugh.

Simply, she'd made him happy.

He felt the brush of her leg against his and the rush of desire almost overwhelmed him. He slid his hand under the tablecloth and found hers. She turned her palm upwards and he stroked lazily over her skin, knowing where her sensitive places were and that his touch drove her wild. He heard her breathing quicken and felt her shift closer. As close as public decency would allow. They, like Domenico and Emilia, were old friends after all.

The first chance they had to get out of here he'd take it. If reality was going to be hitting them soon he wanted to live in the bubble for as long as he could, which meant tonight would probably be their last.

The main course was served. Beef. He was now involved in a conversation about new diabetes management technology. And almost dying of pure lust whenever Gigi turned to him and he got a glimpse of her smile, the waft of her perfume, the profile of her gorgeous breasts.

He was going mad. He couldn't stop thinking about her.

Somebody gave a speech about something…he wasn't focusing on anything but her.

Dessert was something fancy—a cake that tasted like Earl Grey tea with smoky grey icing, and indeed, as delicious as both Max and Ayanna had suggested it would be.

'Good?' Gigi asked as she swallowed her final piece before making a start on the rest of his.

'Amazing. More than amazing.' And he wasn't just talking about the food.

She'd twisted in her seat and was turned towards him now, her knees between his, her foot stroking his leg… all hidden by the long drape of the white linen tablecloth. Her hand crept over to his thigh.

He blinked. Swallowed. 'Gigi,' he warned, wishing he didn't have to say it. 'We're supposed to be behaving.'

'No one's here, Lucas. Look around, no one's interested in us and no one can see.'

He'd been so absorbed in her he hadn't realised that their table was empty, apart from themselves. Domenico and Emilia were on the dance floor and Gigi was watching them with a curious expression.

Judging by the way they were dancing so closely there was definitely something going on between his friend and the surgeon. And if there wasn't…there would be soon.

Lucky Domenico. No one knew his real identity here so he could wine and dine and dance and risk being the subject of hospital gossip for a little while…and then his life would change irrevocably when he was crowned King.

Lucky? Dom's life would never be his own again. Lucas was going to miss his friendship and camaraderie in the ER. Things wouldn't be the same.

A bit like his own life. Who would have thought he'd be at a charity ball with a princess rubbing his leg very close to his crotch?

God, he wanted her. Wanted more than this. Wanted everything. And the fact she'd opened up to him and started to trust him a little gave him hope that they could work this out somehow. As a family. The three of them.

Whatever that meant. Even the word made him panic, but he calmed himself. Others managed it.

He touched her hand, to stop it ascending to his trouser zip more than anything. Because he wanted to sink into her, hip deep, and he wasn't sure how tight a grip he had on his self-control. 'Do you want to dance?'

She shook her head and smiled, her fingers wriggling under his hand and tiptoeing upwards. 'Not the way I want to dance with you.'

His gut tightened in anticipation. He had the feeling

of falling and he didn't want it to stop. 'You can show me later.'

'Oh, Captain Sensible, I will.' Her eyes danced and she scraped her chair back. 'Do you think it'd be rude if we left now?'

'I think it would be the best idea you've had in a long time.'

They barely made it from the taxi to his front door without kissing at every step. Which excited and frustrated her. She wanted him inside her, to scratch the itch that had been niggling her since she'd watched him dress in his tux earlier.

Eventually, he thrust his key in the lock and they tumbled through the door. Gigi laughed as he backed her up against the wall, her heart full of only him. 'Oh, wow, Lucas. Happy to be home?'

'I'm happy to be wherever I can strip your clothes off... with my teeth.' He kissed her hard then pecked a trail across her collarbone and snagged her dress...with his teeth. 'You were driving me wild back there. All I wanted to do was sink into you.'

'That would give the bigwigs something to talk about.' She tugged his black bow-tie loose and let it fall to the floor. Shame. The man looked indecently good in formal wear, but he looked even better naked. Her fingertips slid inside his shirt and she tugged the crisp white linen out of his trouser waistband then slid her hand down to stroke his erection, enjoying the way he moaned against her hair. 'We missed the charity auction. Is that bad?'

His mouth was on her décolletage and tracking lower, his fingers unzipping her dress. 'I'm sure they'll make enough money without us.'

'Once the truth is out about Papa being here, I'll make a generous donation to Seattle General Hospital by way of a thank-you.' It *was* bad. It was selfish to want this and only this. To crave being with him, to have his skin against hers, to wrap herself in a cocoon of *us*. But it was all she could think of.

Lucas tore his mouth from her breast. 'We need to talk to Domenico. *I* need to—'

She silenced his words, her finger against his lips. 'I do not want to think about my big brother when I'm doing this.'

'Good point. I want you. Here. Then we work out our plan.' The plan they'd been avoiding because they both knew it meant the end of this.

Or the start of something. Her face lit up. Maybe...?

He growled her name against her throat and tugged her into the kitchen, lifting her to sit on the counter, her dress forgotten somewhere on the hall floor. He stepped back and looked at her, his eyes sliding over her face then to her shimmery dove-grey strapless bra and matching panties. His gaze burned hot. Then he came closer and pressed first his palm then his lips to her bump. 'God, Gigi. You are incredible.'

'Stop looking and start doing,' she commanded, even though the way he made her feel with just a look was just as much a turn-on as his touch. Well...almost.

She wound her feet around his waist and pulled him to her, her skin, her everything straining for him. Not just for his touch but for him, the essence of him, the imprint of him against her skin, his taste. His heart.

Wordlessly he stroked her face, her throat, her breasts and lower, withholding kisses. Making her want and want and want. He smiled. 'I could look at you all day.'

'You'd get very bored very quickly.' She laughed and shook her head.

All day? All year? A lifetime? The thought stilled her. This. Him. For ever. It scared her. Excited her, too.

When she couldn't bear it any longer she cupped his face and pulled him to her, snatching wet, hot hungry kisses, tearing at his shirt and his trouser zip until he was stripped bare.

His hand glided from her glittery sandal up her calf, her thigh, and then he ripped her panties and laughed. 'Another set bites the dust.'

'Plenty more where they came from.'

'I prefer you without them anyway.' He sucked a nipple into his mouth, making her shudder with pleasure. 'I prefer you exactly like this.'

'What is it about you and counter tops?' She laughed as he pulled her to the edge of the granite, remembering their first time in his bathroom at home.

Her home, not his. The thought struck a chord of pain inside her. She was getting carried away on what-ifs when they still had so much to work out.

'Now who's talking too much?' His hand was on her cheek. 'I like to have you right here, because I love to see your face, Gigi. When…'

'When…?'

'Now…' he groaned as he slid inside her, eyes locked on hers. 'Right there. That look. The mist. The joy. *Dio*, you are beautiful.'

'You spoke Isola Verdian,' she gasped, breath catching as sensation after sensation rippled through her. Hot. Dazzling. The light in her heart was swelling and growing. She clasped his shoulders. 'Lucas…'

He pulled her closer until there was nothing but skin and kisses and heat. And he moved and he moved and he moved. Long slow strokes that whipped her breath away and made her want more. Then she felt his pace change, angling differently, catching her…there.

And yes, yes. His grip tightened. She shuddered against him and he called her name into the darkness.

Dio. It was everything. *He* was everything. Her Lucas.

CHAPTER TWELVE

IT TOOK A few minutes for the world to come back into sharp focus, his heat and body still tightly holding her as if she was something precious he couldn't bear to let go.

Reluctantly she peeled herself away and laughed. 'Bedroom next time?'

'Everywhere, please. Although I'm not sure there's a room here that we haven't made love in.' He smiled, little beads of perspiration dotting his forehead, his breathing still heavy. 'We're free here, Gigi. No one to bother us, no sneaking around.'

Ah.

That was what he wanted, she knew. To be free. And she wasn't and could never be, unless she relinquished everything she knew and walked away from her royal life.

She kissed him again and slipped down from the counter, an ache settling deep in her chest. She rubbed her ribcage with the heel of her hand, but it didn't go, lingering even after they'd cleared up and slid under his cool linen sheets.

Within minutes he was asleep and she watched him for a while, stroking his back as she went over the day's events in her head. The low of seeing her father attached to those machines. Seeing Domenico looking happy. The sting of pain that they hadn't managed a proper conversation about things that really mattered. The high of Lucas in his finery, his laughter. Holding his hand, stroking his thigh in public…almost.

They never did get the chance to dance.

Thinking of her brother with a woman he clearly adored brought her own future starkly into focus. Because, for all Lucas's *I'm happy to be wherever I can strip your clothes off*, it just wasn't true, was it?

He didn't want to be tied by conventions and formalities, didn't like the palace—her home. Didn't like intrusions and distractions. Didn't like her life. Didn't, in fact, like the idea of a family. And it wasn't fair to foist all of that on him or to suggest he had to be part of it.

She was the Royal, not him. She was the one with her future fated. All he'd ever wanted was right here in Seattle. His lovely house, his amazing job, his friends. His life.

She couldn't be Mrs Sensible here in Seattle and he really, really didn't want to live in Isola Verde.

But how could they co-parent across the world?

Her head hurt with the possibilities; none of them felt right. Her heart ached with the realities. With the way she'd allowed herself to feel something for Lucas when, even from the beginning, she'd known nothing would ever be possible.

Maybe she'd just have to be honest with herself, even if it felt as if she was tearing her own heart apart. She needed to put this firmly in a box. Lucas was a temporary thing. Like the others. He was a challenge she'd conquered.

But he'd conquered her too. Broken down her defences and made her his.

She didn't want to remember how his kisses made her feel as if she was drowning and she never wanted to surface. How he understood her like no one else ever had. How he saw her for who she was, and who she wanted to be. She didn't want to remember his touch, his low, rumbling, hard-to-earn laugh.

But she did. She remembered all of it, playing slowly around her head, haunting her, torturing her. Emotions zipped through her heart. It was too complicated. Everything was crashing in on her. If one of them got their way, the other would have to give too much. More than anyone should have to give, just to be together.

So maybe it was time—and kinder to both of them and, most importantly, to their child, who did not need parents who were together and unhappy, wearing masks to hide their real feelings.

Time to walk away.

Her side of the bed was empty when Lucas woke up, but, ever aware of her, he sensed her moving around the room. Still half-asleep, he lifted his head and scanned the semi-darkness. She was over in the corner, hair neatly tied back in a sleek ponytail, a pretty grey woollen dress and knee-high boots gracing her blossoming body. Not the gorgeously crumpled, sex-addled woman he'd held all night.

He yawned, shuffling up the pillows. 'What time is it?'

'Sorry. Did I wake you? It's seven-fifteen.' She gave him a tight smile and then bent again, her hands moving backwards and forwards over something he couldn't quite make out in the dim light.

'What are you doing, all dressed up and princess-like? And early? So early. Come back to bed.' Then his heart kicked into a weird beat, unsettled and jerky. Because he'd just worked out what she was doing.

Her voice was as tight as her smile. 'Lucas. I… We…'

She was folding up clothes and putting them into her case.

She was leaving.

Her shoulders sagged a little and she held an item of clothing close to her chest. 'I'm packing.'

He didn't understand. Tried not to anyway. The jerky heartbeat sped up. 'To go where?'

'Home.'

Not this home. Clearly. He threw back the sheets and dragged on a robe because he couldn't do this naked. He felt suddenly weirdly vulnerable and off balance for the first time in decades. Since he realised his family didn't want him. It was happening all over again. He tried to stay calm. 'But you've just got here, Gigi.'

'I know and it was an amazing ball, but now I have to go to the hospital to say goodbye to my father, then I have a plane to catch. I thought… I assumed you knew I'd go home after the ball.'

'At some point, yes. But not so soon. Not today. We barely slept.'

A sigh. 'It was wonderful, *si*? Now I have a car waiting.'

'No.' He stalked over to her, closing the lid on her suitcase. 'We can't carry on like this. We have to talk about these things. I need to know where I am.'

'You are here, Lucas, where you belong. I am going back to my home, where I belong. You know how things are there. We can't leave the place for long with no Royal presence.'

Panic gripped his gut. He'd been wilfully negligent in pushing the agenda because it had suited him, but what the actual hell? He pushed his fingers through his hair. 'What happens now?'

'When Papa is better and Dom is back home, then we can talk some more. I don't think…' She sank onto a chair, suddenly looking every bit as if she'd only had a couple of hours' sleep and needed much more. 'I don't think we're in a place to start making decisions about the future.'

Panic morphed into anger. Not at her but at their singularly stupid reality. 'So you thought you'd just up and go. If I hadn't woken up would you have even said goodbye?'

'Of course, Lucas. I was just sorting my things out.'
The smile she gave him was completely devoid of any
emotion and he saw it then. Saw the way she was emotionally withdrawing, the way she'd been taught. His gut
went into freefall.

He wanted to shake her. 'For God's sake. Why are you
acting like this?'

A stiff shake of her head. 'I'm not acting.'

'Hell, Gigi, I know you.' She was erecting walls, putting the barriers back in place. Sliding on that mask he'd
seen her wear for other people but not for him. Not for
them. She'd always been open and honest, her true self,
and now that fun-loving Gigi had gone. 'Stop being that
damned automaton. Come back to me, Gigi.'

'I'm sorry, Lucas.' She shook her head, all Princess
Giada now. 'I have to go.'

She clicked the lock and then lugged the suitcase upright, wincing as she strained her damaged wrist. And,
God help him, even though every part of him hated it that
she was leaving, he gently moved her aside and grabbed
the case. 'I don't know why I'm helping you, to be honest.'

'Because you're a good man, Lucas. Don't forget that.'
She clipped downstairs and walked, straight-backed, to
the front door.

She was really going. This was the end for them.

Pain bubbled up again, closing his throat, tripping his
heart. She was actually leaving.

'Gigi…' He wanted to ask her to stay…for ever. He
wanted her to promise never to leave him because he loved
her, and if she loved him back then this could work. 'Can't
we just—?'

'No. I have too much in my head, Lucas. I can't… Look,
the taxi's here.'

He wanted to slam the door closed and wrap her in his
arms. 'No. Gigi. We talk now.'

'And what? End up in a big fight? Achieve nothing but heartache? Best to just cut our losses right now, don't you think?'

'What about last night, the last two weeks? I thought you…' Maybe he'd been kidding himself. Falling for her, believing she felt the same. When, let's face it, he was completely the wrong guy for her and they both knew that.

The ache under his ribcage intensified as he realised he hadn't just fallen for her, he loved her.

Whoa.

No.

That had not been the plan at all. Because she would not move here, he knew that. He'd seen her in her country, how much she loved the place and the people. How much she belonged there. Not here, not in this world.

And what then for their child?

The last couple of weeks they'd avoided discussing the realities, choosing instead to fall in love with the growing bump.

Falling in love. There it was again. The ever-present swell in his chest. The same for his child as for the woman carrying it.

He rubbed his forehead.

How could he have been so stupid as to allow himself to fall for her? He was on a trajectory that could only end in pain. She did not need him. Was not destined for someone like him.

In his experience, love was conditional on how you acted, whether you performed to a particular standard. Love could be cut off.

And yet he couldn't cut off this feeling now. Couldn't stop it.

He shook his head. He had to stop it. He had to draw a line in the sand. She was leaving, again. It would always be like this and he would know only hurt and dissatisfaction.

She was committed to one thing only: her country. He could see that now, could see her hands tightening on her handbag straps, the yearning of her body to get to the car.

He inhaled as she opened the door and the cold early morning air wove around them, an Arctic blast that made her blink fast.

Or was that because she was going? Was she fighting tears? But why? She was the one leaving.

Rejection was the one thing he wasn't prepared to accept again. He could walk away but he would not be pushed. He would not hear her say the words. Worse, he wouldn't wait in the silence wishing, wanting, praying to hear from her again and knowing it wouldn't happen. The way it had played out with his family. He had to have an equal say in a relationship; he couldn't be at someone's beck and call, only to be dropped when things got difficult or inconvenient.

He needed some control. 'I'll walk you to the car.'

'Thank you.' She almost looked grateful that he wasn't causing too much of a scene. 'Don't you dare think I'll cut off ties with you. This is your child and you will be part of its life.'

'Damned right I will.' He closed the car door, barely able to breathe. The pain in his chest spread outwards like a stain. 'I'll be in touch.'

She would not cry. She would hold her head up, fasten her seatbelt without letting him see how much her heart was breaking. It was the Baresi way.

Oh, God, Lucas. What am I doing?

She wanted to put her palm on the window, to open the door and run to him. Wanted to tell him how much she loved his kisses, his warmth, his laugh. How much she wanted things to work out but that she didn't know the formula to get there.

Not for the first time did she wish she wasn't a princess with duty and responsibility and a whole damn country to take into account every time she did a single thing.

Lucas Beaufort was the best thing that had happened to her and yet she was leaving. But saving herself was the only thing she could do. The car pulled away and she closed her eyes. She would not look back. Would not chase that dream. Because that was all it was—a lovely, impossible dream.

Her phone rang and she ignored it. But it rang again and again and eventually she pulled it out of her pocket. Domenico. Her heart leapt to her throat. So early?

His voice was grave and low. 'I've just spoken to Max. Gigi, it's not good news. I'm so sorry. Papa's tumour is growing.'

That was all she heard or understood. He said a few other things but everything blurred. All she knew was that she wished today wasn't happening.

A nurse met her at her father's bedside and explained that his intracranial pressure was rising. More scans were needed, more tests. Gigi sat and held her frail father's hand while chaos swam inside her. Everything was falling apart and she was being torn into a million pieces. And here again she had to wear that mask that said everything was fine. Just fine.

It wasn't.

'Do you know where Dr di Rossi is?' she asked the nurse, wanting a familiar face, someone who understood.

But the woman just shrugged and fiddled with her father's IV. 'I don't know. Probably in ER.'

Truth was, she wanted Lucas. She wanted to feel his strength and his warmth. To lean against his chest and have him stroke her hair.

Lucas would come if she asked him; he'd hold her hand

and tell her everything was going to be okay. But she couldn't do that to him. He wasn't a plaything she could pick up and throw away at a moment's notice. Emotion throbbed in the centre of her chest.

She *needed* him. She put her hand to her belly and cradled their child. They needed him, more than ever, but she couldn't go back to him and ask. Not now.

So here she was facing the stark truth: her life was changing and there was nothing she could do about it. She was utterly alone.

Which, in some ways, was a good thing because that way no one would see she was crying.

CHAPTER THIRTEEN

HER FATHER WAS AWAKE!

It was the best Christmas present ever.

The last two weeks had been exhausting as she'd twice flown back from Isola Verde to sit by her father's side. He'd initially taken a sharp turn for the worse and Max had been unsure if he could remove all the tumour, or even if her father would ever wake up again. But he'd operated anyway, because there would have been no hope if he hadn't.

So she'd clung to positivity, staying at the Four Seasons, sneaking through Seattle General Hospital, avoiding Lucas at all costs, always worrying he might see her and force a conversation where she would cry or break down. And yet secretly wishing she could glimpse him to see if he was surviving without her.

She was barely clinging on without him.

Then it was back to Isola Verde to rule the country in her family's absence. Pretending she was fine, pretending this baby wasn't sapping her energy. Pretending her heart wasn't breaking.

But today, Christmas Day, she skipped through the hospital, because her father was awake and asking for her!

Christmas carols played as she walked through the ward. The staff waved to her—one was dressed as a Christmas fairy, another had a flashing Santa hat, and everyone wore smiles—but Gigi felt discombobulated by it all. What was she going to find? Was her father going to be okay? Would he even recognise her?

She kissed his cheek, ecstatic to see his dark Baresi eyes open, direct and alert, even though he was still clearly pale and fragile. She breathed out slowly. 'You look so much better than the last time I saw you, Papa.'

'Because you're here, my daughter.' He gripped her hand as she sat next to the bed.

Wow. She scanned the area for Domenico, simply because she wanted to check their father was actually okay. He'd never said words like that to her before. She ran her palm over the back of his hand, promising to say all the things she'd wanted to say to him, starting with, 'I love you, Papa.'

'I love you, Gigi. I'm sorry... I was not the father I should have been.'

'Hush, Papa. Don't talk like that.' Tears pricked her eyes. 'I did things I shouldn't have and I'm sorry. I'm so sorry. I was angry and hurt and I embarrassed us all.'

'No. It is my fault. I struggled with you. I was lonely and sad after your mother died.' He raised his fingers. 'I've been thinking a lot.'

'You were asleep a long time, Papa.' People didn't think while they were in a coma, right?

'Dreaming. Thinking... You were by my side at the Armistice parade every year. On the balcony, waving to the crowds on Alessandro Day, in the rain, in burning sunshine.' He gave her a weak smile. 'I believed our people were there for me and they were, but they were also there for you, Gigi.'

She couldn't swallow past the lump in her throat. 'They love you, Papa. We all do. So much.'

'And now you're here after representing the family at home. Holding everything together until I return. I didn't see you before, darling girl...' He clasped her hand to his chest. 'But I see you now.'

'Oh, Papa.' It was all she'd ever wanted: to be seen, heard, respected. To be loved by her family. She blinked fast to stop the tears. 'All I want is for you to be strong enough to come home.'

'We have to talk...'

'Yes, of course. When you're stronger.'

'Now.' His voice recovered some of the regal strength she knew so well. 'Domenico doesn't want to be King, I know that. He has a life here and, from what I hear, someone he wants to share a life with. But you, *bella* Gigi... you could be Queen.'

'What? Me? No. No, I can't.' The thought was ridiculous.

'You were born for it.'

'No.' *I'm pregnant. I can't do this. Not on my own.* The hurt at leaving Lucas hadn't diminished—in fact, it had got worse. She missed him. She wanted him back. She just couldn't be Queen. Couldn't be Queen and have Lucas at the same time. It was impossible. 'Domenico is Crown Prince and will ascend the throne after you. Anyway, you have years left in you.'

Her father slowly moved his head from side to side. 'I'm tired, Gigi. My head hurts. I don't know if my decisions are right or wrong. I don't want to second-guess myself. It's a new age, I haven't embraced things... I don't know social media. I don't know the young people, but you do. You were made to be Queen. I wish it to be so. And soon.'

'Papa.' Panic gripped her belly. 'What are you saying?'

'I'm too old and sick. Isola Verde needs to be ruled by a steady hand, by a monarch who wants to be there, by someone with a future. Dom doesn't want to go home, Giada. I don't want him to do something he doesn't want to do.'

None of this made sense. Maybe he was still confused

from the operation. 'Domenico is to be king. We had a conference call with the palace earlier and the official announcement is to be made tomorrow morning.'

'No, Gigi. He does not want to be King. I know that. I saw that with my own eyes. He wants to live and work here.'

'But who will rule?'

'You will. Queen Giada.'

'I can't. I'm not—' She pressed her hand to her throat as panic bubbled inside her. Panic and…yes, some excitement too. It was contrary to the succession plan, but her father was right, she could do this. She'd been doing it for the last few months anyway. She'd held the family and the country together and it had felt…right. Her duty and her privilege.

But it would be the final nail in the coffin for her and Lucas.

Sadness choked her, mourning for what they could have had. But he hadn't reached out to her. Hadn't called. Domenico had said he'd barely spoken to him over the last couple of weeks. It was as if he'd cut himself off from the only family he'd ever had a chance to be a part of.

Her heart hurt at the loss. She missed what they'd had in those last two happy weeks in Isola Verde. But she had to be strong now and make decisions not only for herself but for her child.

'You are everything our country needs. Please.' Her father stroked her hair, a gesture so tender it brought more tears. 'Do this for me. For us all.'

She cupped his hand and brought it to her cheek. 'I don't know what to say.'

'Say yes, Gigi.'

Oh, she wanted to. So much. 'But… I can't be Queen, Papa. I have news.' This was not how she'd planned to tell him. He'd given her the greatest gift and she was going to disappoint him again. She took a ragged breath through an aching throat. 'Papa... I... I'm pregnant.'

Her father closed his eyes and she was sure he cursed in Isola Verdian. But after a moment he smiled and squeezed her hand. 'You are always full of surprises, my darling.'

Her chest was holding back a sob but she couldn't cry, not now in front of her Papa. 'And I never do things in the right order, *sì*?'

'Like I said, it's a new age. We will have an heir sooner rather than later. That is good news. And the father?'

She looked away, unable to talk about Lucas and not show her true feelings. 'He's a good man. A wonderful man.'

'And...? Do you love him?'

Did she?

She felt emotions wash through her. What had started as a challenge had grown into so much more. He had taken her heart and made it his. He was stoic and steady and funny and sexy. More importantly, he believed in her. Made her feel as if she could conquer the world, and she had no doubt he would be a very good father once they'd worked things out.

There was something deep between them. Something more than friendship, more than anything she'd ever known before. It was painful and wonderful at the same time and she didn't want to think about a future without him.

So, yes, she loved him. Very much.

And that made everything a million times worse. She'd fallen in love and then walked away and her heart had shattered into so many pieces she knew she'd never fix it again.

A rogue tear spilled down her cheek. 'He won't be coming to live in the palace, although he will visit and be a part of our child's life. But I will bring this baby up in Isola Verde.'

'As Queen?'

She could do this. For her father, her family. For her baby and her country. She could be the person she'd always wanted to be. Yes. She could do this.

Barely able to move and yet shaking all over, she pressed her lips to his forehead as his eyes drifted closed. 'If that is what you want, Papa. Then, yes, as Queen.'

Lucas was damned glad to see the back of Christmas Day.

Every time he saw the Christmas tree in the hospital foyer he thought about Gigi. When a mother brought in a sick baby he thought about Gigi and their child. The Princess was everywhere…in his head at least.

Then there'd been the stilted conversation with his parents during which he'd told them about the baby. In a gesture so typical of his family it was almost laughable, they'd sent over a formal contract for Giada to sign that guaranteed him access. That was all they'd said about the matter. No good luck wish or congratulations. No excitement or promises of knitting or babysitting.

And the ache in his chest had intensified and all the antacids in the world hadn't fixed it.

So last night he'd printed off the contract and now he was sitting in the doctors' mess, going through the legalese, feeling as if he was betraying Gigi in some way. Every way. But he had to make sure he got to watch his baby grow up. Hell, it was the only real family he'd ever have.

As he read, he had half an ear on the ever-present news channel on the TV on the wall.

Blah-blah. Blah. Isola Verde. Blah.

What? His head shot up and he stared at the TV. Isola Verde? Mentioned on the local news?

Did that mean…? Had Roberto died? But he'd thought their VIP patient was on the mend.

Backdropped by the Seattle General Hospital sign,

Giada was reading from a script she held in her very steady hand. She looked…well, hell, she looked beautiful in a blue velvet coat that hid her bump, but he knew it was there. His heart, his whole body, hurt to see her and not touch her, not hold her in his arms, not kiss her.

God, these last few weeks had been torture. Once he'd thought he'd caught the scent of her perfume and had followed it up a hospital corridor looking for her before realising he was going mad. He'd ached to phone her, to talk to Dom, but Lucas had retreated, leaving them to pull together as the family she'd always wished they'd been. They wouldn't have wanted him there, but, hell, he'd strained for any information about the VIP patient and visitors.

Lucas watched as Gigi handled herself so serenely, scanning to see if there was any hint of heartbreak in her demeanour. No. Nothing. He smiled to himself. She wore her Royal demeanour well. He zoned in on her words…

'My father, King Roberto, is regrettably stepping down as King of Isola Verde. While his health is slowly improving, the surgery was to remove a brain tumour…' She paused—he imagined to let the gravity of that sink in. 'He needs time to rest. He wishes to announce that I, Giada Francesca Vittoria Baresi, will ascend the throne…'

What the hell? Lucas's heart bumped and jolted. Not Dom? What was happening?

He jumped up and paced the room. She was going to be Queen. Their child was going to be heir to the throne? What, then, for him? For their child?

He stopped pacing. She would make sure he saw their child grow up. In that palace.

His optimism waned. Access maybe once or twice a year. He'd sit on the sidelines and watch Giada rule and marry and have more children. See another man fall in love with her, watch her eyes fill with love for another guy. Meanwhile, he'd talk to her through lawyers and they'd both wear that damned mask of indifference when inside his heart would be crumbling.

He rubbed his chest. He would not be able to bear watching her fall for someone else, or see another man touch her.

He loved her. He looked around the room. Sure, he was in Seattle and, sure, he'd spent a good part of his life securing this job he loved. But was this it? For the rest of his life? Lonely? Missing her? Traversing the globe twice a year to catch a glimpse of a family he ached to be part of?

He looked at the papers, tore them into tiny pieces and threw them in the bin. There had to be another way.

He was going to make sure there was.

A new year. A new beginning. And what a year she was going to have!

Giada opened the curtains and looked out over the gardens towards the woods and beyond, to the lake. Dappled sunshine and the beat of horse hooves reminded her that her father would soon be home. Things had healed so much between them and she couldn't wait to have him back home and to help him recuperate.

She stretched out her arms, breathing in the cooler Mediterranean air and oh! A funny little feeling in her belly. Like butterfly wings. Not nervous, more…

Oh! A smile wound through her and she closed her eyes, cupping her growing bump. He was kicking. Her little Prince…or Princess…was turning and tumbling. 'Hey, little one. Hello.'

Her throat closed over and she couldn't say much then, apart from, 'Mummy loves you. Daddy does too. I just wish… No. Daddy loves you very much.'

No more wishing. It was the first day of the year. She needed to put all that behind her as best she could. There was still a shadow on her heart that would always be Lucas-shaped but she had to concentrate on herself, this pregnancy and her coronation plans.

Her phone rang. Maria. 'Your Highness, there's a visitor for you.'

'It's New Year's Day. Can you ask them to come back tomorrow?' She had some serious baby shopping to do and a nursery to plan. 'Don't I get even one day off? I'm starting to rethink this whole Queen business.' Of course she wasn't, and Maria knew that.

'I think you might want to come down for this.'

'Why? What can possibly be more important than choosing cute baby clothes?' She'd told her assistant about her pregnancy. The only one still out of the loop was her brother.

Maria laughed. 'He says to tell you Captain Sensible's gone into retirement. But Captain Spontaneous would very much like to see you.'

Lucas!

Her heart tumbled and turned, just like their baby, and she ran to the top of the grand staircase. There he was in the hall, shimmering in the light of the dome, tall and handsome and beautiful and serious.

'Hello.' She felt nervous, just like the time she'd sneaked into his suite. Was he here to talk? To hit her with a lawsuit? To…?

He captured her gaze. 'Giada.'

Not Gigi. That was important. She descended the stairs on shaking legs. 'Lucas. Nice of you to visit.'

He fisted his hands, didn't kiss her cheek. 'I need to tell you something.'

'Go right ahead.'

'I told my parents about the baby.'

That was a step forward. 'Good.'

He shook his head. 'Not so good. They advised me to serve you with papers to ensure I was allowed access.'

That was why he was here? Her stomach felt as if it was tumbling to her feet. 'You could have emailed them. Saved yourself the journey.'

'I… I needed to see you. To talk to you. Because that's the way to do these things, right? To communicate face to face.' He reached out and stroked her cheek with his fingertips. 'I don't want sporadic access to my child. I want more than that.'

'You want full custody?' Her heart jerked and she stepped out of his reach. '*Dio*, Lucas…please…no. I don't want to fight.'

I love you.

How would he react if she just said it? Was honest with him instead of hiding behind pretence?

'Yes…' He cleared his throat and straightened. 'Joint custody. I want us to be a family, Gigi. I want my Gigi back. Not the one who walked away. I want the one who is real and honest and kisses like an angel.'

'You want… But you do know I'm going to be Queen? I can't move to Seattle.' There it was. The real problem.

But he smiled. And, God, it was beautiful. 'I know. I don't care where we live. Honestly. I'm sure I could get used to all this, given a chance. I hope. I'll try. I want to try. I spent too long fighting the idea. I blocked everything else. I didn't want to fall for you and then for you to walk away.'

Like his parents had. Love, in his experience, was conditional. 'I walked away.'

'Yes.'

'Oh, Lucas.' She'd done exactly what he'd thought she would do, the worst thing she could have done. She'd made her love conditional on him living here and when she'd thought he couldn't do that she'd walked away. 'I tried hard not to let you into my heart. I thought I could tease you and have fun but then it got serious and I got scared because the feelings I had were so intense. I didn't want to believe…'

'I know.' He held out his hand and she took it. 'I know why you did it. I understand, Gigi. You've been treated badly in the past, but you don't have to put on a brave face with me. Ever.'

He knew her better than she knew herself. And she knew him well too. 'You could work at the hospital. I think that's important. You'd be grumpy otherwise. Lucas, I—'

'I love you.'

She didn't know who said it first. Who took the first step, who leaned in first. But his lips touched hers. And then she was wrapped in his arms, the only place she wanted to be. Her home. Her Lucas.

She pulled away but kept hold of him. 'Captain Spontaneous?'

'Hmm.' He nuzzled her hair and laughed. 'Sensible has been sent into exile.'

'Good.' Now it was her turn to clear her throat. 'You know a queen should probably be married, *sì*?'

His eyebrows rose. 'Is this…? Giada Francesca Vittoria Baresi, is this a proposal?'

She laughed because, yes, it probably was. 'Papa said I always do things the wrong way round. But when you asked me you didn't mean it. So now it's my turn. And I *do* mean it. Dr Lucas Beaufort, will you marry me?'

'*Sì, bella* Gigi.' He kissed her again and again, his hand sliding round to her abdomen. His eyes widened and he jerked back. 'Is that? Did the baby just…?'

'Yes.' She put his hand back again. 'He or she is very happy.'

'So am I.' Then he got serious. 'I really think we need to tell Domenico.'

'We should call him. He'll be thrilled.'

Lucas grimaced and ran fingers through his hair. 'He'll kill me.'

She waved her hand. 'You can't kill the Queen's husband. He'll have his head chopped off. Let's call him… in a few minutes. I have Royal business to attend to first. The Queen would like to kiss her Consort.'

And then she did.

For a very long time.

EPILOGUE

One year later...

'IT'S MY TURN for cuddles.' Roberto Baresi took his grand-daughter from Gigi's aching arms and planted a big kiss on baby Chiara Alessia Giada Beaufort-Baresi's chubby cheek. 'Who's a lovely girl, then?'

'Who is he and what has he done with my father?' Dom whispered once their father was out of earshot over the other side of the room. They were all crammed into the antechamber on the second floor of the palace. The noise was reaching fever pitch inside, matching the crowds down below.

Giada made a feeble attempt to hush her inside guests. 'Thank you for coming. All of you. It's been a very special Christmas and...er...coronation...' Because why have one celebration when you can have two? 'I'm so glad we got to share it all with you. Thank you for everything. Now drink!'

Gigi laughed as she looked at the smiling faces, her heart so full of love and joy and hope. Domenico had come over from Seattle with Emilia, married now and settled together. After Gigi's announcement, the news had broken about his true identity and for a few weeks there'd been a buzz, but it had all died down. They were very happy, she could see. Still competing, still working, still very good friends.

He'd forgiven both her and Lucas for their relationship…but it had taken a few weeks for their happy equilibrium to right itself.

Dom had brought Max Granger and Ayanna Franklin over for the holidays. They'd finally admitted they were an item and Ayanna was happily planning their wedding. More fun!

Logan had come too…back to see his old boss, bringing his son, little Jamie, and his wife Kat, the nurse who'd first seen Giada after the accident. And they'd shared the happy news that they would soon be adopting. Another baby.

Gigi put down her champagne glass and smoothed her dress. 'Right, how do I look?'

'Very regal.' Emilia straightened Gigi's purple sash. 'Oh, your crown's a bit crooked.'

'Story of my life.' Gigi laughed as she put her hands onto the precious crystals and diamonds and tried to fix it.

'Wait…let me.' Lucas stepped in front of her and her heart leapt as it always did. He pressed a kiss to her cheek then did something to her crown and it felt straight and right. He slipped his hand into hers. 'I love you, Queen Gigi.'

Oh, he did, she was utterly and totally convinced of that. And he couldn't be a better father. Although the hospital work was mostly what was keeping him sane.

'Ma'am. It's time.' The footman drew back the heavy velvet drapes and the sound from the crowd intensified.

'Oh, wait… Chiara… I'd better take her. Come on, Lucas. It's showtime.'

'I prefer bedtime, but there it is,' he whispered against her throat. And she felt the thrill of anticipation shiver through her. There was so much love. She was so damned lucky.

Then they stepped out onto the balcony and a roar

erupted from the crowd. Giada waved with her baby-free hand and knew that happiness radiated from her. Her heart was full.

She had her family, her country, her baby. And her husband by her side. For ever.

* * * * *

MILLS & BOON

Coming next month

HIS BLIND DATE BRIDE
Scarlet Wilson

Ivy took another bite of her cake. It was going down well. 'What do you think would have happened if we'd actually gone on that blind date?'

She could have kept things simple and stuck to chat about work. But she didn't want to. If she wanted to work easily with Travis, they had to deal with this.

There was no one else around so they wouldn't be disturbed. It was just her and him in her cabin. It was now or never.

Travis made a little choking noise as his cake obviously stuck at the back of his throat and Ivy burst out laughing, 'Sorry, did I make that go down the wrong way?'

He laughed too and shook his head, leaning back in her chair. 'You just like to keep me on my toes, don't you?'

There it was. That teasing tone. The one that had completely drawn her in, whether it was spoken or in texts. The thing that had made Travis King something more than a potential blind date. Even if that had never been her intention.

She gave an easy shrug. 'Why not?' She held up her hands. 'It's not like there's much else to do around here.'

She was joking, and he'd know she was joking. But shipboard life was so different from being back at home where bars, cinemas, open air and long walks could easily fill her life.

Travis sat his tea on her desk and folded his arms. 'I think,' he started as he raised his eyebrows, 'if we'd gone on a blind date before meeting here, it would have been an absolute disaster.'

Really? What was it with this guy? Had none of his sisters taught him the art of talking to a woman? The words were like being hit with a tidal wave of icy water.

'Okay, then,' she said shortly, feeling like a fool, because in her head their blind date would never have been a disaster.

He held up one hand. 'No, wait, you didn't let me finish. Let me tell you why it would have been a disaster.'

She swung her legs off the bed. 'I don't need microscopic data on why we're a never-happened,' she said, pushing her 'not good enough' feelings away again.

He reached over and put his hand on her knee. His voice was low and throaty. 'Our date would have been a disaster, Ivy Ross, because one meeting would have had me hooked. Who knows what might have happened? It keeps me awake enough at night just thinking about it.'

Continue reading
HIS BLIND DATE BRIDE
Scarlet Wilson

Available next month
www.millsandboon.co.uk

COMING SOON!

We really hope you enjoyed reading this book.
If you're looking for more romance, be sure to
head to the shops when new books are
available on

Thursday 24th December

WE'RE LOOKING FOR NEW AUTHORS FOR THE MILLS & BOON MEDICAL SERIES!

Whether you're a published author or an aspiring one, our editors would love to read your story.

You can submit the synopsis and first three chapters of your novel online, and find out more about the series, at **harlequin.submittable.com/submit**

We read all submissions and you do not need to have an agent to submit.

IF YOU'RE INTERESTED, WHY NOT HAVE A GO?

Submit your story at:
harlequin.submittable.com/submit

MILLS & BOON